Distress & Determination

ALSO BY
JAMES P. WOLLAK

Insight & Suitability (2021)

Distress & Determination (2023)

Distress & Determination

-PART II-
THE FURTHER TRIALS OF FREDERICK DARCY,
YOUNG GENTLEMAN

JAMES WOLLAK

atmosphere press

DEDICATION

Again, I dedicate this novel to Miss Jane Austen in gratitude for the great pleasure she has brought generations of readers, including this author.

I hope she knows how highly she is now regarded and how beloved she and her immortal characters are all over the world.

I am very grateful for this opportunity to continue the stories of the Bennet and Darcy families. I apologize for any deficiency, lapse, or liberty on my part and hope for Miss Austen's forbearance and forgiveness for them.

ACKNOWLEDGEMENTS

I want to give my deep thanks to the following wonderful readers for their help with this manuscript; their comments and suggestions have been incredibly valuable in bringing this part of *Distress and Determination* to its present form: Jill Alcantar, Paul Bacigalupi, Joni Jones, Claudia Matlovsky, and Mary McLean.

I also want to express my appreciation for all the support, advice, and input my friend and fellow author, John Winch, has given me over the years, for this novel and my writing in general.

I especially want to give a great, appreciative shout-out to my editor, Dr. Kyle McCord at Atmosphere, whose enthusiasm, support, and incredible comprehensive feedback improved and tightened my manuscript in so many ways. I cannot thank Ronaldo Alves, Cameron Finch, and the designing and marketing teams at Atmosphere enough for all their support and help along the journey to publication.

Again, I would like to thank my wonderful parents, Erwin and Ellen Wollak, and many dear family members and friends for their encouragement, love of learning and reading, and appreciation of the arts. Thanks to all of them, my imagination has never been the same.

CAST OF CHARACTERS

The Darcys of Pemberley, Derbyshire, and the Pemberley Estate

Fitzwilliam Darcy, the Master of Pemberley
Elizabeth Darcy, the Mistress of Pemberley, his wife of 22 years
Henry Philip Darcy, their eldest son, deceased
Frederick Michael Darcy, their second son, age 18
Julia Rose Darcy, their third child and oldest daughter, age 17
Jane Elizabeth Darcy, their second daughter, age 15
Nicholas Aaron Darcy, their youngest son, age 13
Anne Veronica Darcy, their youngest child, age 10
Mrs. Reynolds, the housekeeper
Mathers and Vadney, valets and menservants
Mr. Kenilworth, the Darcy boys' tutor
Miss Kendall, the Darcy girls' governess and tutor
Mrs. Frances Winston, Jane Elizabeth's companion
Coachmen, horse trainers, and stablemen:
John Buckley, Ben Fulton, Tom Nixley, Josh Romney, and
    Luke Shotwell

Other Darcy Family members

Mr. Thomas Bennet, of Longbourn, Hertfordshire, Elizabeth's
    father
Lady Catherine de Bourgh, Darcy's aunt, of Rosings Park, Kent
Edward and Madeleine Gardiner, of Cheapside, London,
    Elizabeth Darcy's uncle and aunt

THE LINTONS:
Reverend Christopher Linton, Vicar of St. Bede's and manager
    of the Good Shepherd Orphanage, London
Mrs. Mary Linton, his wife, Elizabeth's younger sister

THE RUTLEDGES:
Edgar Rutledge, Lord Lennox, the Earl of Lennox, at Lennox
     Hall, London, a cousin of the Duke and Duchess of
     Cumberland
Lady Anne Rutledge, his wife, Lady Catherine de Bourgh's
     daughter and Darcy's cousin

THE COLERIDGES:
Sir Robert Coleridge, owner of three estates
Lady Georgiana Coleridge, his wife, and Fitzwilliam Darcy's
     sister
Mrs. Annesley, Lady Coleridge's friend and former companion

THE FITZWILLIAMS:
Colonel Edmund Fitzwilliam, Darcy and Lady Coleridge's
     cousin
Mrs. Constance Fitzwilliam, his wife

In Cambridge
Mrs. Margery Ford, Mr. Jennings' cousin
Miss Alice Fremont, her sister
Mr. Julius Haydock, headmaster at Frederick's college
Jeremiah Ridgeson, master of the Newnham residence hall
Richard Grantley, son of George Grantley, Lord Hartford,
     a student
Roderick Urquhart, another student
William Claremont, a student in the debating society
Elias Barrow, another student in the debating society
Eric Langham, Frederick's friend and fellow student
Alex Leamington, another friend and fellow student
Andrew Staunton, friend to both Henry and Frederick

In London

THE ROYAL FAMILY:

King William IV, of the House of Hanover

Queen Adelaide, his consort

Princess Victoria, their niece and Heir Presumptive to the
    throne

Duchess of Kent, the princess' mother

THE GRANTLEYS:

George Grantley, Lord Hartford, the Earl of Hartford, father
    of Richard Grantley, a student at Cambridge

Ursula Grantley, Lady Hartford, his wife

Susannah Grantley, their eldest daughter and Richard's sister

Isabelle Grantley, their youngest daughter

Louis Calvert, Lord Ravenswood, of Woodside House, London

Cecilia Calvert, his debuting sister

The Earl of Ravenswood, their father

The Earl of Chester, the Earl of Ravenswood's friend and ally

Sir Timothy Carlisle

Catherina Carlisle, his debuting sister

Sir Edward Chatterton, an eligible suitor

Belinda Compson, a debutante

Lawrence Darnley, Lord Oakland, the Earl of Oakland,
    Atherton House, West London

Helena Darnley, Lady Oakland, his wife

Emma Darnley, their daughter, a debutante

Mary Duncan, a debutante

Julian Tunney, her half-brother and escort

Sebastian Tunney, his father

Pamela Easton, a debutante
Simon Easton, her brother and escort

Sir Francis and Lady Mary Exley, Holdsworth, London
Marcella Exley, their daughter, a debutante

James Fitzrobert, the Earl of Sheffield, and the Countess
    Sheffield, of New Hampton Court, London

The Foxborough siblings: Silas, Seth, Serena, and Sylvia
Stephen Foxborough, their father

Vice-Admiral Halsey of the Royal Navy

Gregory Lawson
Letitia Lawson, his sister, a debutante

Justin Longford
Honoria Lucas, a debutante
Angelina Molyneux, a debutante
Major Alan Molyneux, her brother and escort
Marianne Morton, a debutante
Lucinda Peterbrooke, a debutante

Ansonia and Randolph Porter-Douglas
Henrietta Porter-Douglas, their daughter, a debutante

Sir Ambrose Roylston, Lady Judith, his wife, and Lady Maura,
    his sister, of Bethulia House, London
Cornelia Ruth-Davis, a wealthy widow
Eliza Ruth-Davis, her daughter, a debutante
Ben Ruth-Davis, Eliza's brother and escort

Lord Benjamin and Lady Miriam Stoddard, the Earl and
    Countess of Swindon, Wiltshire

Sophia and Hannah Stoddard, their daughters, debutantes
Samuel and Daniel Stoddard, their older brothers and escorts

Gabrielle and Christabel Tourneur, sisters and debutantes
Martin Tourneur, their older brother and escort

Rachel Urquhart, Roderick's sister, a debutante

Sir Romanus and Lady Margery Ventnor, of Dutton Ampner,
    London
Dorothea Ventnor, their daughter, a debutante

Alexandra Vinson, a predatory young lady and debutante
Lucy Robinson, another predatory young lady and debutante
Honoria Watson, another predatory young lady and debutante

Mr. Pressburg-Stilton, a dance instructor
Miss Hegedus, his assistant

Other Characters
LONDON:
Staff of the Darcys' Cavendish Square house in London:
Mrs. Jordan, the housekeeper, Jordan, her son, Peter the foot-
    man, Forrester the valet, and Emma and Margaret, maid-
    servants
Doctor Shelbourne, the Darcys' London physician
Sir Adam Wainright
Lady Rose Wainright, his wife
Mr. and Mrs. John Woodleigh
Peter, Howard, and John Woodleigh, their sons
Rosamund Woodleigh, their daughter, a debutante

CHAPTER 1

"Your name, young sir," demanded the spidery older man, bent over a desk in the main foyer of the Newnham residence hall.

Frederick Darcy blinked. He was mesmerized by the implacable dark eyes transfixing him from underneath equally dark, bushy brows and over small, rectangular spectacles. The man's dun-colored coat, waistcoat, and breeches appeared stiff and coarse, rustling as he moved. "I do not have all day," he snapped. "Must I ask again?"

Frederick swallowed. "I am Frederick Darcy, from Pemberley, Derbyshire," he managed. Thankfully John Buckley, the driver, and his young assistant, Luke Shotwell, were still outside awaiting him at the carriage and weren't witnessing his confidence evaporate.

"College of attendance?" the older man rapped. His quill started scratching the parchment-like paper in front of him.

"King's College, Sir."

The older man shot him a look and wrote for two minutes. Once he was done, he nodded and looked up at Frederick. He reached over to a rack of keys leaning against the wall, jerked a set off the hook, and rose.

"I am Jeremiah Ridgeson, the master of this hall of residence. You shall address me as Mr. Ridgeson." He transfixed Frederick with another stare. "I will now take you to your assigned lodging."

"My rooms?" Frederick sounded hopeful.

"Your room," came the curt response.

Frederick sighed and followed the hall master up two flights of steep but wide stairs. There was some light, but the building seemed dusky despite the time of day. Mr. Ridgeson stopped midway down a long hallway and unlocked a door. He gestured for Frederick to step inside.

He brightened as he looked around the room. It was spacious enough, with a wide poster bed and plenty of pillows. He noted a nightstand, washbasin, mirror, two small candelabras with a couple of holders askew and dappled with wax, and a decent-sized desk with a box of tapers and matches. A capable-looking clock on the adjacent wall stood guard over the desk. A thick-curtained window faced out onto the street, and a tall armoire braced the wall across from the bed.

"I trust you will be comfortable," Mr. Ridgeson sniffed. "Bathing and grooming needs can be performed in the room further up the hall; please take note that you will be sharing these accommodations with several other young..." He paused. "Gentlemen students." He sniffed again. "You have no valet, I presume?"

"No, Sir," Frederick mumbled.

The hall master's taut lines softened ever so slightly. "Some of our student residents do; however, that is no matter or concern to the college." He paused. "I daresay you will be comfortable and provided with enough amenities to make your term tolerable, without having some fussy valet dodging your every move and getting underfoot."

"Yes, Sir," Frederick mumbled again, forcing himself not to roll his eyes. "Thank you."

"Quite." Mr. Ridgeson transfixed him a final time. "Dinner is served in the Refectory Hall at five o'clock sharp! Do not be late, for all the courses and dishes are picked over by half past six and nothing is served after seven!" He turned and swept out of the room in an instant, with an audible surge of rustling.

Frederick sighed and went down to the front hall, where he would help Buckley and Luke bring in his trunks.

It was just past noon, and Frederick was happy to leave the dark paneling and duskiness of the hall's interior behind for the daylit street. He had not known what to expect once he arrived; the hall master had more than startled him and the day's promised evening meal seemed far off. He was grateful that he and his drivers had stopped for a quick meal of lamb pie, cheese, and bread at a decent-looking eating house just after entering Cambridge itself.

He was rapidly adjusting to his new surroundings, but didn't want his journey to end quite yet. Frederick's ride to Cambridge had been as uneventful as it was smooth; however, he would miss their traveling together, passing through towns large and small, rattling along roads in various conditions. He thought of the stretches of time he had gazed out the carriage window at trees, fields, monuments, houses, and occasional people they passed along the way.

His mind often wandered from the parade of sights and sounds he kept experiencing. Frederick had wanted to return to Cambridge and kept telling himself how eagerly he looked forward to it, but then his positivity and resolve would peter off into nothing as doubt undermined his equanimity.

He wasn't worried about returning to live in a dormitory or sharing its space and meals with other young male students; he'd done all that before he was sent down. Rather, his determination ran aground on anxieties and longings for approval and compliments on his coursework from some of the masters, as well as being able to pass all of his examinations. He hoped his participation in the debating society would help build his confidence to speak in front of others.

The return to university didn't consist solely of doubts. He reflected fondly on his conversations with Buckley and Luke as they stretched their legs, laughed, and joked over their tin cups of water, and savored the spicy scents from Buckley's pipe. He promised he would keep reminding himself of these pleasant memories, musing upon them in the late evening before he retired and in the days ahead if he could.

Buckley and Luke promised to stay with him all day, as

long as he needed them, and Frederick was grateful for their help in bringing up all the trunks and getting him moved into his room. Half the unpacking was already done when they heard footsteps approaching from down the hall. Two young men knocked on the door and entered.

"Frederick Darcy, old boy!" exclaimed the tall, angular, pale one with dark hair and eyes. "How good to have you back! I thought that we would never see you again, or that you had decided upon Oxford instead."

"Hello, Alex," Frederick grinned, pumping his hand. "You cannot still be growing taller, can you? Or is this just a Leamington family trait? For you seem taller now than when I last saw you." Which was right before he was sent down. As Alex laughed, Frederick turned to the other young man. "Eric!"

"Frederick!" They clasped hands. Eric Langham was shorter than Alex, blond-haired, green-eyed, and handsome, with a cleft chin. "How good to see you! Going to stay with us for good this time?"

Frederick laughed. "Yes, for I dare not get sent down a second time! Father threatens to lock me away in the dungeon of Pemberley if I do."

"Since when does the Great House of Pemberley have a dungeon?" countered Alex.

Frederick shrugged. "Well, come to think of it, I am not certain there isn't one, so I must be careful in any event. And if there isn't one already, Father could still have one built for me, I am sure!" Smiling, he made introductions all around. "Mr. Buckley and Luke brought me back to Cambridge," he explained.

"Is this the new Darcy manner of traveling?" teased Alex. "A full escort as you have is quite impressive."

Frederick didn't mind the joke, but gave a lopsided smile. "Well, it is one of my father's new ideas – no more hired coach drivers and carriages – because of Henry, you know." The two young men sobered and Alex apologized for his levity. "It is quite all right, Alex, so please do not worry about it. I am quite grateful to Father for all the pains he has taken for me. Mr. Buckley and Luke are excellent drivers and it has been a very smooth journey, just as Father intended it should be." The drivers thanked him, and he added, "My sister, Jane, is visiting cousins in London and was escorted by our other drivers, Tom Nixley and Ben Fulton." His friends still looked pensive, so he was determined to restore geniality to their reunion. "Well, we are all safe and sound! Now tell me what you have been doing," he added, looking as haughty as he could, "for I have heard nothing from either one of you all these months; this, from my two best friends!"

Eric laughed and lightly punched Frederick's shoulder. "How you do go on, Master Darcy! Come to think of it, we have not received any letters from *you* in quite a while; I know I certainly haven't. Alex, have you received a missive from Master Darcy here?" Alex shook his head and all three laughed. "I will be honest then, Frederick, that I am not always a trustworthy correspondent."

"Nor am I," admitted Alex.

"Nor I, so my sisters tell me," Frederick said more dryly than he intended. "Well, that makes three of us."

"No wonder, then, why we are all such good friends." Eric was still laughing. "Master Leamington," he addressed Alex, "doesn't our long-lost friend appear different to you than when we saw him last?" They studied him, and Frederick fought to keep his face straight. "Notice," Eric continued, "the cut and condition of his fine suit despite the long journey; there is hardly a crease or speck of dust to be seen, even on his gleaming boots."

"I quite see what you mean, Master Langham." Alex stared down his long nose at Frederick, who was losing the battle not to laugh. "I say, I believe our fine young Frederick is sporting slightly shorter hair – if that is even possible for him – as well as the beginnings of some fine, manly side-whiskers. Do your parents approve of them?"

Frederick tried to glare but could not hold his expression, much to the drivers' amusement; they had never seen Frederick banter like this with males his own age, for there weren't really many of his class in and around Pemberley. "How you do go on, Eric," he finally managed to say. He still tried to sound haughty but was chuckling too much. "Allow me to return your compliments; what do you call these?" he said, gesturing to their long coattails. "Tail feathers? Plumage? And I do believe your hats are twice as tall as mine. How has all of this come to be?"

Alex laughed. "You have been away at home for over half a year, my dear young sir, and I am afraid that you are not as stylishly attired as we. In fact, you are quite out of fashion for a young man, though you still make a fine appearance." Frederick thanked him but almost sniffed.

Eric laughed. "These are the latest fashions from London, and you will need to become a young gentleman of fashion again yourself."

Frederick's face relaxed. "I shall have to, it seems, especially in time for my sisters' debuts in the spring."

"We shall help you with that," Alex declared.

"I am depending upon it." Frederick pulled over a couple of chairs for them to sit down. "Now please stay a while, for I must finish unpacking and prepare for my first day of classes the day after next."

"So must we, though we are both two terms farther ahead in our curricula than you," Alex pointed out, but then brightened. "Say, Frederick, how will you dine this evening?"

He shrugged but did not remember the Refectory Hall. "I have no plans, other than to retire early. I am quite at my leisure, for Mr. Buckley and Luke will be preparing to return to Pemberley tomorrow."

Eric and Alex exchanged a glance. "Then let us dine together!" Eric exclaimed. "We can talk about what we both have been doing for so long. We can enjoy ourselves for a few hours and still get to bed at a decent time. I was about to suggest that we go to a favorite eating establishment of ours called Tudbury's for it is not very far from our college. Well, what do you say, fellows?"

Alex quickly agreed, while Frederick looked thoughtful. He had become much more careful about spending his money, whether it was really his father's or had been given to him to use. The loss of those fifty pounds a year ago still bothered him; but he also knew he had enough pocket money to afford such outings, as long as they were infrequent and he didn't stay out all night when he did. He brightened. "That sounds like a fine way to spend the evening, dear friends!"

"Excellent," Alex said. "Shall we return to collect you, say, in about an hour?"

"Certainly, and I shall be ready," Frederick promised, grinning.

He looked forward to their evening together. His friends made their farewells to all of them and left for their own rooms in another residence hall. With the drivers' help, Frederick quickly finished unpacking and laid out his copybooks and writing supplies, wound the wall clock, and put the clothes he had selected to wear off to one side in the wardrobe. There would be no Mathers or Vadney to help him now, so he would have to get up earlier than he usually did to wash, groom, dress, and have his breakfast. He would have to remember to check for towels and cakes of soap in the common washing room, but he had remembered to pack his bath robes. He carefully stacked some treasured volumes he had brought on the far left-hand corner of the desk as a final touch.

Frederick invited Buckley and Luke to join them, but they politely declined, though they appreciated the invitation. Both men desired to have their early, full dinner, a tankard or two of ale, and retire early for the trip home. Frederick shook their hands, telling them how grateful he was for all the pains they took in bringing him safely back to King's College; he would write to his parents to commend them both.

Gratified, they took their leave of him, and Frederick puttered around his room until Alex and Eric came to claim him for their dinner. As high spirits carried the three of them down the stairs to the hall's front door and out into the street, Frederick happened to glance up at his new temporary home.

Dark eyes, bushy brows, and a pointed nose drooped down upon them. Frederick sighed silently and reflected he would need to stay on the hall master's good side, if that were possible, starting with this evening. He promptly forgot the stiff, implacable man and hurried off with his friends; there was no need for him to worry. And, as enjoyable as it turned out to be, Frederick kept his promise to be in bed by ten o'clock that night.

CHAPTER 2

Fall passed into winter, and winter into spring. Frederick was so busy with his studies that he failed to notice how quickly one week ran into the next, and then beyond into yet another. It seemed that his daily hours were filled with lectures, papers, and examinations, and his evenings filled with study, either in the libraries or his room, or scratching out his expositions on ink-filled pages. Nightly he bent his head over his books, as the taper flames reached to the ceiling; more than once he fell asleep at his desk. Already one term was over and he was being pulled along through the second since his return to university. He shook his head often as he made his way to the next lecture, study hall, or professor's chambers.

Frederick knew he was being truly diligent, as expected, but at times would simply push his straight backed chair from the desk to think about nothing; or put his head down on the desk, shoving aside his books and papers to close his eyes. These minutes of weakness troubled him as much as they tempted him. He cherished any moments he quit his stuffy room for some fresh air, sitting in a park or on a bench along the Cam, though he felt guilty about them afterward. He would think about his father, a strong, proud man, and feel sudden stirrings, powerful and controlling, that he guessed he would have to act upon eventually and learn how to use. He missed going out frequently with Alex and Eric, but this he knew was something in which he could not indulge. Usually, when he was exhausted, he resented that his freedom over his own time and decisions was curtailed but had to admit he understood why. And so he kept on reading, studying, writing, dozing, and hoping.

It was now early spring, near the term's end. Frederick checked his appearance, cleared his expression, and tried to control the tension he felt as he knocked on the door of Mr. Haydock's chambers. When the headmaster replied, Frederick stepped inside and stopped in front of the great man's cluttered desk.

"Ah, Master Darcy," Julius Haydock boomed, giving him a searching look. "Please sit down." As Frederick complied, he added, "I appreciate your timeliness."

"Thank you, Mr. Haydock." Frederick tried to look composed, not wanting to relax in front of this huge, formidable gentleman.

Haydock drew some written papers towards him. "Ahem! Let me see." He shot Frederick another firm glance. "I summoned you so that we can discuss your progress over the last two terms. We do this as a matter of course, especially after your disastrous first term. I will, of course, apprise your father, Mr. Darcy, of your results." Frederick nodded, not daring to speak, and waited for him to resume. Haydock continued reviewing the pages written by his professors, then finally looked up. "Master Darcy, your instructors inform me that you are doing well – quite well – in Latin and composition. You are doing more than satisfactory work in mathematics and commercial law. However, you are performing only satisfactorily in history and ethics." Haydock pursed his lips, looked away, and then back at Frederick. "In all, not bad," he said grudgingly, "as it is an improvement over your first term."

Frederick swallowed. He had hoped for more congratulation and encouragement, so Haydock's lack of enthusiasm bothered him because he felt he had improved a great deal. "If I do well on my final examinations," he offered, "I will take a first in Latin and a second in composition."

Haydock glared at him. "As I said, Master Darcy, not bad. But this is hardly a time to flaunt one's laurels."

Frederick was stung. "Have you not summarized my performance these past two terms, Mr. Haydock? You may not be giving me much in the way of encouragement, but can I not be happy with what I have accomplished in the fall and winter terms?"

"Master Darcy," threatened Haydock, "you forget yourself! And you also forget that I am the one who ultimately decides how successfully you have completed your studies during any term, not you. Students in general tend to have exaggerated ideas not only of their own performance, but also of their own native intelligence. Do not fall into this erroneous kind of thought, I warn you, or consider me someone who is easy to please and placate, for I am neither! Do you understand?"

Frederick had to look down as he mumbled his assent. Curse him, he thought; what an intractable, disagreeable old man, but one with great power over him.

"Good," came the curt reply. "Be sure you remember what I have told you."

"Yes, Sir." Frederick let out a breath slowly so it wouldn't sound like a sigh or something disrespectful, and sat up. "Is that all you wished to tell me?"

The headmaster glared back. "Yes, I believe so." He stopped. "Well, no, on second thought, I am not yet done; there is something more I shall add." He paused. "I expect you to continue improving and excelling in your studies." He lightened his tone. "All right then, you have done well, I will allow. But this is how you should have done in your first term, as a start to your education here at university, not as a step up. You must continue to do well, because you are more than capable of it, and your future position in society requires it."

Frederick blinked; he had not expected such comments from the headmaster. May the Devil take him for catching him by surprise! "Er, thank you very much, Mr. Haydock. I understand the points you are making. I do intend to keep doing well, and I am quite motivated to do so."

"I am glad to hear it," Haydock grunted. "You are dismissed, Master Darcy."

Frederick stood. "Thank you, Sir." As he turned to go, he

could not help asking, "You will inform my father of my progress, will you not?"

Haydock gave him another strong stare. "I do not care for flippancy or insolence in my students, young man. Take care with your tongue – guard it well and employ it with the debating society you have joined." He gave a thin smile. "However, I shall write to Mr. Darcy to inform him of your progress."

"Yes, Mr. Haydock," Frederick managed. "Thank you, and good day, Sir." He did not wait for an acknowledgment and quitted the chamber as quickly as he could.

Frederick left the wing housing the King's College official offices quickly behind him. It had been a rocky, unpleasant meeting, but Frederick knew he would occasionally have to suffer through them unless another master was assigned to take Mr. Haydock's position. Since this was unlikely, Frederick sighed and tried not to let the headmaster's grudging comments upset him.

He decided to have his midday meal in a favorite eating house near Newnham Hall. As he consumed his beef and vegetable pie and mug of cider, he thought about his studies and Mr. Haydock's sharp pronouncements.

He had to admit that Haydock's skepticism concerning his resolve to continue striving for academic success bothered him – but he understood it. He supposed he must have gotten off to a very bad start with the headmaster when he performed so poorly his first term and got sent down. Well, Frederick sighed, it was a matter of record and many knew about it, so he had to prove himself now and in the future. He hated to admit Haydock was right when he said he should have done so well during his first term, not as a continuation or improvement in his second and third. Frederick tapped his fingers on the table. No, he did not like Mr. Haydock, but he would try his best to beat him at his own game – and hoped someday to earn his respect, if nothing more. Let him begrudge and minimize my success, Frederick thought, for I will show him!

Haydock was not the only master who was unimpressed with Frederick's performance, but some of the other masters were changing their opinions about him. Bennington, the Latin master, was more than pleased with his efforts, and Master Whitehull remarked favorably on several of his compositions. Master Carnaby was equally demanding in his expectations of his students learning the finer points of commercial law, but was helpful in suggesting books from the university library to aid them – and Frederick visited his chambers often to discuss complicated points of law under review. Frederick was enjoying mathematics as much as Latin and composition, though Master Crawford advised that taking more time would reduce the number of mistakes he made; but he had met his match in his final two subjects.

Master Arundell exhorted him to read and study more history. Both he and Frederick were unsure why he struggled so much with dates and events, though he wrote tolerably well when he did remember and linked them together. And Frederick's troubles with ethics, and philosophy in general, continued to plague him; Master Rodgers-Talbott sighed and shook his leonine head at the jumble Frederick made of the subject matter, and Frederick avoided him as much as he could outside of the lecture hall. The only reason he wasn't failing was because Alex was tutoring him in this subject as well as history; Alex, his fine friend who was usually at the top of all his classes and even more intelligent than Eric. Frederick wanted to do as well as both his friends at Cambridge.

Frederick pushed his empty plate and mug aside. Despite Haydock's reservations, he felt proud of himself for doing as well as he had, which still included not visiting taverns much, even with his friends. He went out only once a week, on a Friday or Saturday night, and held himself to only one pint or tankard each evening. When he scored the highest on his midterm Latin examination, though, he gave in and had two more to celebrate. However, he watched his pocket money and sobriety carefully. He wanted to tell his father, but knew doing so would lessen its importance and sound like mere boasting on his part.

Much as he liked going about with Alex and Eric, Frederick was enjoying living in Cambridge as well. His confidence grew from the positive results of his studies, and he slowly increased the time he spent outside of his room, away from his coursework. He liked spending time in the college libraries and visiting landmarks like the Bridge of Sighs. Frederick was also fortunate that his residence was not far from the home of Mrs. Margery Ford, a widow, and her sister, Miss Alice Fremont, who were cousins of Mr. Jennings, his father's steward. Frederick enjoyed visiting and going around town with them. Since the ladies were his mother's age, it was as if he had a kind of family connection at the university; they could watch over him in a circumspect way, and he helped them by running errands and fixing small things around their house. He enjoyed taking tea in their drawing room and accompanying them to church services. He thought of them as aunts, so he did not miss Pemberley as much as he thought he would, as he had done during his first term.

Finally, Frederick was fortunate to meet another close friend and classmate of Henry's, Andrew Staunton. The young man sought Frederick out and they immediately began a friendship. Taking the young Darcy heir under his wing, Andrew gave Frederick much advice about getting around the university, as well as helped him plan his coursework for the next couple of terms. Andrew missed his longtime friend, Henry, and was pleased to fill the void left by his death with Frederick's friendship. Frederick, for his part, was grateful for Andrew's influence and knowledge; he could understand why he and Henry had been so close and considered himself lucky to have become friends with him as well. Frederick could not be happier when Alex and Eric turned out to like and respect Andrew, too.

Frederick opened his compact silver watch. He needed to attend a lecture, then go to the library and study until dinner. He grinned as he gathered up his satchel of books and prepared for the long afternoon ahead. He also remembered he had several letters to finish that he had begun.

CHAPTER 3

A few days later, a trio of happy young men strolled through the college grounds during the afternoon.

"Frederick, you were superb!" Alex exclaimed, clapping him on the shoulder. "Congratulations on your well-earned victory!"

Wringing his hand, Eric was no less effusive. "You and your team did an excellent job arguing your position! I do not think I have heard a better debate at university, nor did I know you to be so clear, forthright, and passionate in your arguments. Great show!"

"Master Snowden seemed quite pleased at the results and gave you all some enviable, deserved praise," Alex added.

Frederick was still giddy and glowing from surprise and satisfaction. He and his three teammates had just won the latest debate given by the university's society, which he had joined a few months ago. For two hours, Frederick and the others had advocated and defended their position on the need to reform labor laws to improve the lot of factory workers. Their opponents, led by Frederick's former friend Richard Grantley, tried very hard to best them, but Frederick and his teammates successfully countered every point or rebuttal that Grantley and his team made. "Thank you both, fellows," was all Frederick could say, as he fingered the blue ribbon he had been awarded.

"I daresay your father, Mr. Darcy, will be very pleased as well." Alex grinned. "Forgive me for mentioning it, but no one will remember your being sent down now."

"Except Mr. Haydock," Frederick grimaced.

"That old battle-axe," dismissed Alex. "There is no man alive more begrudging than he. Did I tell you he told me there was still room for me to improve because I was not taking firsts in every course?"

Frederick made a sound in his throat but joined Eric in laughing over the obstinate headmaster to whom they were all subjected. "There can be no improvement to your academic performance, Alex," he said loyally. "You are truly excellent, and I am very grateful for all your tutoring."

"Thank you, Frederick, but I think the university has become more than aware of *your* talents." They clasped hands in mutual gratitude. Alex then noticed Eric's pensive expression. "On such a happy day as this, Eric, why is your countenance so serious?"

Eric gave a half smile. "I do not mean to dampen the pleasure of your victory, Frederick, but I must admit that I am upset and insulted on your behalf by the behavior of the other debaters – that is, the ones you and your team defeated."

Frederick shrugged. "Yes, but do not worry, for that has not ruined our victory! To be honest, though, I had not thought much about it."

"Then I am sorry to have reminded you of it."

"It is no matter, as I said." Smiling, Frederick clapped him on the shoulder.

However, they were all thinking about it now. Frederick and his teammates were astonished they had won the debate and defeated Grantley and the others, who were more seasoned orators than they. Yet, when it was time for the customary handshakes after the debate between all participants, Richard and another former friend, Rod Urquhart, had barely controlled their anger at losing. Only one of the four, William Claremont, shook hands with the victors and congratulated them, while Richard, Rod, and the remaining member, Elias Barrow, a thin young man with a pinched look and sharp voice, turned away. Master Snowden had shaken his massive head over this breach of etiquette but did not reprimand them; instead, he became even more effusive in his praise of the victors. The losing team then quitted the chamber, with Richard slamming the door shut behind them. However, before they left Barrow had shot Frederick a look with an unpleasant smile. "Perhaps you can use your fine debating skills to defend all your family's scandalous behavior." Frederick had flushed but remained silent, paralyzed into inaction by this attack; thank God his teammates had not heard it.

Remembering, Frederick sighed. "Yes, they all behaved badly, except for Claremont."

Eric looked troubled. "I am truly sorry to have mentioned it."

"Do not worry," Frederick repeated, shrugging again. "I admit I looked forward to the challenge when it turned out we would be debating Richard and Rod! Barrow and Claremont I did not know at all, though Barrow appears as unpleasant as they; but Claremont so far seems to be a decent chap. Again, it is no matter." Frederick looked at his friends. "To be honest with you, I had expected something like this to happen."

"No, Frederick, why?" Eric protested as Alex shook his head.

"Unfortunately, it is as I feared," Frederick countered soberly. "I thought that knowledge of Henry, Christina, and little Henry David could have made its way here, and so it has; Barrow's swipe at me proves it. I wonder if people here know about my sister's troubles as well. However, this has not been the first time I have been snubbed."

"What do you mean?" demanded Alex, his eyes narrowing.

Frederick sighed. "There have been many throughout this term alone. Several times students passing in the opposite direction as I have collided with me; I am certain these collisions are deliberate, and only half the time does the person mutter an apology." He looked away. "I have received several stares and frowns as well, and a couple of older students I had been introduced to are barely civil; now they will not shake hands with me. Until today, the worst I have experienced occurred last week; I was waiting for the traffic to clear so I could cross the bridge road. A young man and woman in an open carriage deliberately drove through a soft mud puddle near where I was standing and their horses splashed up mud all over my clothes, even into my face." Eric gasped. "Then the man looked at me, laughed, and said something. I cannot remember his exact words, but they were basically to the effect that I might as well wear such dirt because my family had proven itself to be dirt. The young woman laughed and they drove off, leaving me wet, dripping, and filthy."

"Knaves!" Alex snapped.

"Blackguards!" Eric growled.

"Thank you, fellows, but go easy now," Frederick cautioned. "There is really nothing I can do about all of this. My brother did sire a child out of wedlock, one whom my family acknowledges and is raising as our own. However, then the poor child's mother died suddenly, and after all that, my sister Jane did some very ill-advised things." He sighed. "It is not as if all of this is untrue. People will be horrible about it. My sister was openly insulted on the streets of Lambton, so Father and Mother sent her to our cousins in London for her own safety."

"So you accept all this?" Eric asked in disbelief. "That you and your family deserve such insults?"

"No, Eric," he answered firmly, though smiling. "Still, our family has done wrong and we know people disapprove of us as a result. We must weather this, but I do not think we must suffer such cruel insults for the rest of our lives."

"I am most relieved to hear that," Eric declared.

"As am I," Alex said, his nostrils flaring.

"Of course, I want to respond to these insults," Frederick continued, "but I must be careful. Many people will expect me to fight over them but, even if I do, or give into similar insulting behavior, my entire family will suffer for that too, not just I." He sighed again. "So, I must be careful how and when I respond, and that means that some of these insults I must bear without recourse, much as they pain, embarrass, or upset me."

"I see." Alex shook his head. "What an awful situation! I

would not want to bear such insults, even if they were because of actual mistakes."

Frederick brightened. "I am sure you and Eric will never have to experience such things! Now enough of all this sobering talk and unfortunate behavior! Let us go and have some ale in celebration of my team's victory! Then we can go to an early dinner, Tudbury's if you prefer, and it will be my pleasure to treat you both!"

His friends were immediately cheered and gratified by this, and they decided to leave their satchels of books and papers at their lodgings before they set out. The clock was striking half past four as they left through the college's colonnade toward the street. Laughing and joking, they looked forward to their evening of pleasure, rare for a Thursday evening. They did not hear anyone coming up behind them.

"Well, if it isn't the great debater."

Frederick turned around to find Richard Grantley, Rod Urquhart, and Elias Barrow standing just beyond arm's reach. Richard leered at him while the others' faces registered contempt.

Checking a sigh, Frederick replied evenly. "Hello, Richard. Congratulations to your debate team, for you gave ours quite a strong challenge."

"You didn't deserve to win because you do not have enough experience," Rod shot back, but Richard Grantley held his arm.

"I would not take much from your victory today," Richard deprecated. "You won a single debate; there will be many others. A one-day wonder is all you shall be, Darcy, as my team is much more seasoned and performed better than yours, I daresay."

Frederick shrugged while his friends bristled. "You may say so, but Master Snowden and the other judges did not agree. For now, our team has these," he said and took the blue ribbon out of his pocket.

Richard's eyes flashed. "Flaunting your undeserved ribbon,

are you? Well, we shall see who bests whom in the next debate!”

"I am sure we all will look forward to that."

"You are not such an important person here at university!" Richard's voice became angrier. "You will regret your arrogance!"

"Meaning?" Frederick's voice remained mild, but his blood was racing and it was all he could do to prevent himself from taking a swing at his antagonist. Unfortunately, he remembered promising his parents he would try to control his temper. He prayed he could provoke Richard into throwing the first punch or making some such threatening move, so Frederick could retaliate in his own defense. His friends tensed in readiness.

Richard choked on his anger as Rod broke in. "Haughty as ever, and an impostor as well! I would have never taken you for an honest defender of factory workers," he sneered. "I would have expected you to take an opposing point of view so that you could maintain your vast staff at the grand old Derbyshire estate – for you and your illustrious, unbroken, *legitimate* line ensconced at the great seat of Pemberley!"

"I believed in what I argued," Frederick shot back, "though I would have done my best no matter which side of the selected topic our team would have been assigned! Again, I point out that Master Snowden and the other judges obviously thought our speeches to be the most persuasive and best argued of the day."

"Rubbish," snapped Richard. "Master Snowden is an old fool and a failed, occasional actor who fancies he teaches oratory; anyone could impress him enough to win!" He stepped toward Frederick. "Now I repeat what I said a moment ago: you will pay for your arrogance, you and your disreputable family! I will make sure all Cambridge knows of the deeds and proclivities of your ancient and overrated house!" Some passersby overheard this exchange and stopped to see what was happening.

Gasping, Frederick's friends stepped forward. "Alex, Eric, no!" Frederick cried out. "Don't let them rile you! It is what they want! They will try to provoke us into fighting, and then blame us when it is over!"

"Such insults cannot be excused or ignored," Alex declared, his nostrils flaring even more, but he and Frederick struggled to restrain Eric. "Unfortunately, I understand your point."

Grantley and Urquhart laughed. "Of course, you only think of your own skins but aren't true men enough to defend yourselves." Frederick and Alex had to keep restraining Eric, who was making angry, choked sounds in his throat.

"These underclassmen look as if they are about to start an altercation on university grounds," came Barrow's high-pitched, smug voice, "an offense usually punished by expulsion. Would you like to be sent down again, Darcy? How distressed your family would be by such a failure." His eyes gleamed behind his spectacles.

Eric choked in frustration, but Frederick and Alex would not let go of him, and Eric's face was damp and red from struggling. "Steady, fellows!" Frederick cried.

"Such condescension you have shown us," Alex disparaged. "So who is being haughty and arrogant now?" Some bystanders laughed.

"Not even a glancing blow," taunted Richard. "Really, Leamington, I thought someone of your reputed intelligence could have come up with something better than that; but I suppose you have your hands – and brain – full dealing with this boy Langham here." Alex's face darkened and Frederick feared he could not restrain both of his friends, but Richard sneered again before they could think of doing anything. "Well, Darcy, despite your victory today, I do not think you will find many people desiring your society, now nor when I am through enlightening them about your illustrious family. And that goes for your fine adolescent friends here as well." He guffawed.

"Idle gossip and defamation!" Eric burst out, still red-faced and damp, but his friends maintained their hold on him.

"You are beneath contempt," Alex snarled.

"It's the truth about a family that thinks so highly of its own importance but is compromised and disgraced by its own ethical lapses," snapped Rod. "Thank God my family is not so suspect and disreputable."

"Nor is mine," Richard said proudly, "and our family is more ancient than Darcy's. We trace our lineage back to Guillaume Soeur de Grand-lit, who aided and fought alongside William the Conqueror. Our family has not besmirched itself with its own failings, either."

Biting back his anger, Frederick replied in a clipped tone. "There is nothing wrong in tracing oneself back to a grand wagon master, even if he did aid the conquering king." He was pleased to see Richard flush, as two young men in the small crowd around them laughed. "Our ancestors began as winemakers and merchants in the province of Champagne in France, and one of them pleased Philip the Sixth with his wines." Later, the family business expanded to Troyes, twenty-five miles to the south, and finally to Paris, one hundred miles northwest of the town where the family originated.

"A wine merchant from the town of Arcis on the Aube River," Richard flung back. "Everybody must be tired of hearing it. Well, that is not as important as someone who helped William of Normandy conquer England."

"Perhaps," came Frederick's measured reply, "but we do not make our family history and heritage a source of worship." Now Richard's nostrils were flaring and more people were laughing. "Your family name has been changed and anglicized, just as ours has." Indeed, his family name was originally 'd'Arcis,' which became 'D'Arcy' in the time of Louis XIII but was rendered as 'Darcy' in England when the family began exporting there, and finally escaped France because they were Huguenots.

"So what if our name has changed its spelling? It is still a fine, proud name!"

"It simply does not make you and yours unique, that is all," Frederick deprecated. As Richard struggled to make a reply, he added, "I am impressed that you know so much of our family origins, for I would not have thought you cared about our low beginnings. Please forgive us for them." This caused more snickers from the crowd. Eric had long ceased to struggle, and Alex turned to look at their friend.

"Winemakers and merchants, and probably drunkards as well!" Richard snapped. "At least you admit to your family's low beginnings. But I still maintain that your family's current standing has diminished. You would be fortunate to be merchants now, instead of fallen gentry."

Frederick smiled, but both his friends did not like the look in his eyes. "Unlike your own family, as you have so properly pointed out. Well, Richard, enjoy your family's exalted moral status, because you have managed to do all and more recently than my own family members have, which took them a full generation to accomplish."

"What do you mean by that?" Richard shouted, and now Rod and Elias were holding him back.

"You shouldn't worry about my reputation or my family's when you personally have one of your own," Frederick answered in an even tone. "Let me think." He began counting on his fingers. "Cheater, procurer, fornicator, and now scandalmonger – all of these can be laid upon your doorstep, and they make quite an impressive array for someone of your age, do they not?"

"You filthy bastard!" screamed Richard. He lunged at Frederick who, along with his friends, simply moved aside. Grantley made a painful landing on the cobblestones, to the delight of the crowd.

"That is why he bested you in the debate," crowed Eric, laughing at Rod and Elias' looks of pure hate.

Blinking back some pain, Richard stared up at Frederick to swear at him again. "You will pay dearly for that, Darcy! I will see you disgraced properly, as you should be." Rod helped him to his feet.

"That is not advisable," Frederick said calmly. "I know several students who have lost sums of money to you at cards. Even if I cannot prove everything, I can at least have you barred from any card games or gambling in this city."

Richard growled and lunged at him again, but Frederick stepped aside once more. Richard stumbled, but his friends prevented him from falling.

Frederick turned to his companions. "Come on, fellows, let us return to our planned schedule for the rest of the day." He strode forward and passed so close to Grantley that they bumped shoulders. "Oh, pardon me, Richard," he said carelessly over his shoulder. "If you would be so kind as to let us pass."

Richard looked murderous. "Remember my warning, Darcy."

Frederick was already several feet away when he said without looking around, "And kindly remember mine." The crowd parted to let them through, and the three friends saw some approving glances and gestures as they passed. Richard Grantley was not well-liked, and Frederick thought the details passed along by some of the bystanders would add to his lack of popularity, at least for now.

But Richard was not yet done. He strode after them and shouted, "Your sister's debut will be a total failure! You'll see!"

Without turning around, Frederick gave a dismissive wave with his hand and kept walking off. No one said anything for a few minutes.

"Frederick, do you think he can do that?" Eric worried, finally breaking the silence. He exchanged a somber glance with Alex.

"It sounds so hopeless and unfair. Do you not feel burdened and anxious?" Alex asked. "How can you bear it, and what will you do about it?"

Frederick sighed. "I do think he meant what he said. I know he despises me and would like nothing more than to insult and embarrass me and my family – if in public, the better, and spread rumors about us as he has threatened." He paused, then resumed."To answer your questions, Alex, what can I do? I face the same dilemma as I would when deciding whether to respond to the snubs and insults I experience. I do not know whom I shall meet and whether they will welcome or revile me."

He shrugged. "I may not be able to do anything, or rather I *shouldn't* do anything. I cannot go around misbehaving no matter how justified I feel to settle scores and attract attention away from my sisters. It will be their debuts, so they will be rightly the center of attention, not me. My father would be furious, and I think my mother as well. They demand that a true gentleman behave like one at all times."

His friends' troubled expressions stung his heart. "Though it is burdensome and seems hopeless, Richard tends not to think things through." He rubbed the back of his neck and looked at them. "I know his sisters Susannah and Isabelle are making their debuts in London this season, just like Julia and Jane. Richard may want to denigrate us Darcys, but I think he dare not do it so openly, so as not to ruin his own sisters' debuts."

"I mean well, but I must stay I am not yet convinced," Alex said in a heavy tone.

"I am not completely convinced myself yet, either," Frederick admitted, "but even Richard must behave himself lest he bring down notoriety and disgrace upon his own *exalted* family with his actions – much as he disapproves of us. He may try to do something vile during the season's events, but I think he will have to be careful, and hope they will not be anything more than the verbal insults and casual snubs we have already experienced."

Eric caught Frederick's emphasis, as did Alex. "I hope you

are correct," Eric spoke up, "but what do you mean by calling his family exalted?"

Frederick looked at him. "Do you not know who his family is?"

"Apparently not, Frederick, not that we cared to know," put in Alex.

Frederick laughed. "Richard's parents are George and Ursula Grantley, Earl and Countess Hartford."

"I see," Alex said, while Eric groaned.

Frederick shrugged. "I believe the Grantleys were elevated to the peerage about the time my family emigrated to England. Lord Hartford is quite wealthy; people say he claims to take no interest in politics but likes being the lord of the manor."

"And Richard has more than his fair share of haughtiness and superiority as a result," Eric remarked.

Frederick laughed again. "So it would seem, though he seems chastened for now."

Alex smiled. "Thanks to you."

Eric now thanked them both for bodily restraining him. "I really wanted to pummel Grantley, but I suppose I would have been sent down for doing so, even if it was someone as deserving as he. And perhaps you both would have gotten punished, too, because of my actions."

"I thank you for wanting to defend me," Frederick said warmly. "He was insulting not only to me but to both of you as well." Inarticulate, they clasped each other's hands.

Frederick's glance swept around the street; they had only advanced a block from the square where the confrontation had just ended. He watched the crowd quickly dispersing, though it seemed young people in groups of two or three remained and were talking among themselves.

He was about to follow Alex and Eric, who had resumed walking, when he spied someone leaving the square and heading in the same direction as they.

It was the residence hall master! What was Mr. Ridgeson

doing here so close to the university? Frederick halted, which his friends did not realize at first, and sighed; had the lanky, angular man witnessed their confrontation with Grantley and his friends?

He hoped not. Mr. Ridgeson had caught up and was now passing them. The disagreeable codger said nothing but gave Frederick a piercing stare, his dark bushy brows drawn together, as he passed by.

He sighed again, wondering why Mr. Ridgeson seemed to keep appearing in various places at unexpected times. Not for the first time, Frederick wondered: had his father employed Jeremiah Ridgeson to keep watch over him? If so, the man was doing a thorough job of it, but Frederick quickly rejected the notion for its sheer impossibility. His father was stern, with high standards and expectations, but he was not rigid, vindictive, secretive, or lacking in understanding. It must only be Frederick's poor luck.

"Still thinking about those bounders?" Eric stood in front of him as Alex gave him a thoughtful look.

"No, I just saw someone else I knew leaving the square, that is all." Frederick didn't want to think any more about Mr. Ridgeson, though he had complained about him to his friends. However, before they could reply, he went on. "Now enough about Richard, Rod, and that disagreeable fellow, Barrow! Let us go and celebrate like we agreed and not let ourselves be worried, depressed, or demeaned by such rabble as they! Tankards of ale at my expense await us!"

So, laughing again, the three young men scurried off to a favorite tavern nearby to begin their celebration.

CHAPTER 4

The following day, taking advantage of a leisurely break between classes, Frederick sat munching an apple in an eatery called Loxon's, which was only a few blocks from the university. He'd just finished his sandwich of ham, mustard, and lettuce on toasted bread, and was nursing a mug of cider as he perused that day's *Cambridge Chronicle and Journal*.

Frederick didn't spend all his time outside the lecture halls reading history, economics, ethics, or commercial law. Masters Arundell, Carnaby, and Whitehull had urged him to take up the habit of reading newspapers so he could stay abreast of important things occurring around him, even if they happened far away in London or other countries. They told him they thought this activity would help him remember and relate his coursework to current events in a practical way, as well as improve his writing skills even more and prevent him from losing awareness of the life going on around him by focusing solely on his studies.

Frederick thought this was useful, though unexpected, advice and that his father would approve of him spending his precious time this way; he had to admit he enjoyed filling his attention with actual things going on around him as a contrast to his erudite but often dry subjects. His father received *The London Gazette*, *The Morning Chronicle*, *The Morning Herald*, and *The Evening Standard* at Pemberley as often as he could and read them with selective, decided concentration; it suddenly became obvious that gentlemen of consequence like his father relied on the newspapers for important information, as Frederick would need to. And so, at least twice a week, he would purchase the newspaper and read as much of it as he could; once in a while he'd even splurge on one of the London papers available in town.

Frederick grew to enjoy reading his paper as he ate his midday meals, whether at Tudbury's or another familiar eating house like Loxon's. He normally didn't have time in the early mornings to do so, only to have his usual rather rushed breakfast in Newnham's warm, noisy refectory. Besides, then he liked just to laugh and joke with his fellow student lodgers over their eggs, pork rashers, toast, and coffee; and the rest of the day he had to focus on his classes and assignments.

Frederick again savored his impressive debate win, as well as his impromptu celebration with Alex and Eric. He turned a page of the *Cambridge Chronicle* and let his eye travel over the wide page filled with print when a title caught his eye.

"Body Found in Clearing Outside of Cambridge."

At first, Frederick was rather shocked; he hadn't heard of any violent confrontations or deaths outside of the university, and Cambridge was no small, sleepy town. He devoured the short article. It seemed the body of a young gentleman, for that is how he was dressed, had been found in a clearing in the local woods outside of town, with a bullet wound to his central upper chest, near the heart; the article inferred that the young man had died as the result of a duel, but no weapons were found near his body. The lethal challenge to satisfy honor had taken place, and the other principal actors in the event had left the scene with all the evidence. The article decried the loss of such a young life, and under such supposed circumstances, as dueling was illegal yet widespread. Anyone with information regarding the terrible event was urged to inform the local constabulary.

Frederick was about to raise his mug of cider to take a mouthful when he paused. His hand suddenly shook, so he put the mug down and shoved his crumb-filled plate aside.

So, a duel had taken place – another one. Frederick swallowed. Now he recalled hearing the Newnham fellows gossip and speculate over a former resident, one Peter Gipson.

It seemed that young Gipson, twenty years of age, had

become smitten, perhaps even obsessed, with a local young lady of fine birth and fortune; unfortunately, she already had plenty of swains vying for her attentions and more, among them a brash, intense young man named Desmond Rowner. When Gipson had interfered by paying his attention to Miss Bellford, Rowner challenged Gipson to a duel. Both antagonists were accomplished fencers and so a fierce duel had taken place with rapiers early in the previous term, when Frederick had barely returned to university. After a vicious, wounding, and exhausting duel, Rowner impaled Gipson with his blade and Miss Bellford's honor and future were secured. As both victor and prize eloped, neither had experienced personal censure in and around Cambridge; after Gretna Green, they and their thousands of pounds were rumored to now reside an ocean away in Bermuda, Jamaica, or even America.

Quite a tragic story, but now it brought home more fear and anxiety for Frederick.

Despite the noisy noon crowd around him, Frederick saw Richard Grantley's sneering face. Afraid of spilling his mug or sliding off his chair, Frederick continued to tremble. Would his enmity with Richard lead him to a death challenge? Either one of them could provoke a duel; all it would take would be a few more insults.

Frederick hung his head and weakly gestured for another mug of cider. He was thinking of his parents and how he was supposed to become the next Master of Pemberley. How such a rash act would affect them and several young women – his sisters and Richard's. If something happened to him, would Nicholas mourn his death as much as he had Henry's?

Frederick blinked away a vision of a young man's body, splayed and bloodied, like his if he lost a contest of honor.

Frederick gulped down his replenished cider while his inner shakiness continued, as he failed to control it. He knew affairs of honor settled through a duel were common yet wasteful and too easy to indulge in. If he or Richard provoked a duel, how would it occur? And what did he have to fight with? He had little hunting experience with firearms and hadn't taken up fencing yet, so he wouldn't be able to use either weapon with confidence. If there was a duel, he supposed it would have to be with pistols like the unnamed victim in the newspaper story, but Frederick didn't like the idea of using weapons someone he didn't know or trust supplied.

What if the Grantleys supplied the weapons? Frederick half suspected Richard would manage it so the pistol could somehow misfire or explode so Frederick was injured or killed without Richard even having to fire a shot.

Shaking his head, Frederick took several gulps of cider. These thoughts were pointless, unwelcome, and unnecessary. He knew he couldn't ever fight Richard that way, because too much was expected of him. Still, he trembled. He should be on the top of the world, as Fitzwilliam Darcy's son and heir, and with his university record improving! But he realized the path forward would not be smooth nor easy, and so he worried.

Despite his full stomach, he felt a curdling in his gut. Frederick suddenly felt he needed a stronger beverage to ease his disquiet but knew he couldn't. What of his afternoon ahead? He still had classes and plenty of studying to do, and two papers to write over the next two days.

He gulped down the last big swallow, almost coughing, and grabbed his satchel of books. He left the newspaper on the tabletop with a tip.

Congratulating Frederick on the day of his team's victory was not enough for his friends. Late afternoon two days after their triumph, while he sat studying at his desk in Newnham Hall, Frederick was startled by sudden sounds behind him.

"Eric! Alex!" he exclaimed. "I wasn't expecting you, though I am happy to see you."

"I am certain you weren't," Alex replied then looked at Eric.

"You almost didn't see us," Eric's cheerful face dimmed. "That spider Ridgeson almost didn't let us climb the stairs to your room. I suppose it is only permitted at the end of the school week, in his mind."

"How our university life and freedom are blighted by the likes of Haydock and Ridgeson," Frederick sighed as his friends laughed. "This is an unexpected pleasure! What brings you to Newnham this afternoon?"

"Enough of all this studying in close, smothering chambers and libraries! We all need some fresh air," Eric said eagerly. "Let us go have a couple of pints at our favorite pub, The Scholar's Dilemma, and then we can have our supper there as well."

"It is only Wednesday," Frederick reminded him. "We have just celebrated, and it will be two more days before classes end for the week on Friday." He blinked. "I've already passed the number of pints I allow myself this week."

"I told you he wouldn't be interested," Alex said to Eric. "Besides, I have to prepare for a difficult examination on Thursday morning."

Eric was undeterred. "There is a time for everything, and studying can exist alongside socializing, just as sobriety can with pleasure! I'm only suggesting a couple of pints, a light meal, and a short evening, not some kind of bacchanalian carousal."

"I still don't understand why it is necessary that we go out on a Wednesday evening," Frederick said, though he was starting to like the idea because he was tired from reading history for two hours.

"It isn't necessary, it is just sensible, and we will enjoy ourselves."

Frederick's brows registered puzzlement which increased when Alex remarked, "Perhaps someone has an ulterior motive." When Eric shot him a glance, he added, "An opportunity to meet with someone else."

"Meet with whom? Another friend, someone to whom I may have been introduced?"

Alex looked at Eric, whose cheerful expression was drooping and hardening into a glower. "I doubt you have met Sally before, but now you will."

"Sally?" Frederick looked at them in disbelief. "Eric?"

Eric flicked a glance in Alex's direction and replied, "Yes, Sally. She's a barmaid at The Scholar's Dilemma, and she – she is –"

"Captivating our fine, handsome friend here," Alex finished for him. "It appears that his two closest friends do not always provide enough companionship for him, so now there is Sally to help fill the, er, lack." He rolled his eyes.

"I see." Frederick did not, but didn't know what else to say as Eric flushed. A sudden thought chilled his anticipation of an enjoyable evening. "Is this just for Sally's sake, or does she have friends we are supposed to meet as well?"

"Frederick!" Eric chided. He had not forgotten that regrettable event during Frederick's first term at Cambridge. "I would never do what Richard did to you that night, nor would Alex! We would never solicit vulgar streetwalkers to tempt and embarrass you."

Frederick apologized, as Alex patted his arm. "Thank you, Eric; I know you would not."

Eric brightened. "Then let us make haste! Onwards, for our pleasant evening awaits!" He tried to herd them towards the door into the hallway.

"I cannot wait until I meet this special young woman," Frederick could not resist teasing him. "I expect her to be exceptional in all respects."

"Nor I, and I second that sentiment," Alex added.

Eric groaned, flushing darker. "How you both go on!" he retorted. "Perhaps someday you'll find a young woman who fascinates you enough to make you want to pursue her, so you can be close to her."

Alex rolled his eyes again as Frederick disparaged that thought. "I will not be enjoying the company of barmaids once the term ends, and my sisters make their debuts. It will be their moment, not mine, so what do I care with whom I dance? I probably won't remember most of them."

They made their way to The Scholar's Dilemma as Eric harangued his friends on the joys of female companionship. At first, Frederick could not help laughing along with Alex, but he quieted as Eric became more vehement and damper in the face. Frederick no longer worried about meeting Sally, but he did still feel some trepidation being out on a night during the middle of the week.

The Scholar's Dilemma occupied the center part of the block, flanked on either side by shuttered shops. The pub had a wide front door with large paned windows on each side. Frederick and his friends entered the somewhat dark, smoky, beery interior. Normally Frederick would welcome such a place as his spirits rose in anticipated pleasure, but his conscience still pricked him over his midweek outing, and his forehead dampened.

Eric charged forward through the loud, cheerful, teeming patrons, as Alex and Frederick trailed him. Eric soon reached some sort of counter, stopped, and called over to a young woman racing to and fro behind it.

They pushed up next to him. Sally turned out to be pretty and pert in her white, flounced blouse and wide, dark skirt, with her sandy blond hair pulled up into an untidy yet attractive bun. Frederick liked the freckles on her upturned face and nose.

"Sally, my dear!"

"Well, if it isn't Langham! Good to see you, love."

Eric grinned. "And you as well! How about a round for my good friends?"

"Of course! Now be a good one and show some coin!" She noticed his surprised face. "Sorry, love, but I'm dreadfully busy right now! Maybe we can catch a word later."

"Of course," Eric echoed, deflating. She served them, then danced off.

The three of them conversed, viewing the other patrons, and traded jokes and laughs. Eric ordered another round despite their protests, but Sally remained occupied elsewhere in the pub, laughing and chatting with other patrons, and he sagged as the publican served them.

Finally, Sally passed them by with a tray full of pints. Eric quickly reached to touch her arm, but she shook him off with a glance and swept away. He tried to catch her eye, but she seemed to avoid where the three of them were sitting. Alex and Frederick had been very warm, kind, and respectful in their responses out of silent support for Eric, but all their efforts seemed to have no effect on the barmaid.

Two hours and three pints later, Eric shoved his empty glass away, his eyes filling and his head hung low. Frederick didn't know what to say, but Alex patted Eric's arm and said, "Sorry, dear fellow, but she doesn't seem worth it; is she?"

Eric's expression and mouth drooped further. Frederick took his hand, but Alex then addressed him. "Are you not grateful that you're not lovesick over someone like our dear friend here?"

"Alex," Frederick said reprovingly. Part of him wanted to grin that the admired Sally, as pretty as she was, did not deserve Eric's passion for her, but his friend's hurt, downcast expression stabbed his heart. He didn't think he could withstand such indifference himself. That's why he didn't want to think about the young ladies he'd be dancing with at the debutante balls.

Eric finally spoke. "She seemed to like me enough before, the last two times I met her here at the pub. She let me buy her glasses of sherry once the evening crowd had left and we chatted for hours." He wiped his eyes, then his mouth with the back of his hand.

"Another tankard?" Frederick suggested. "We can go to The Lotus Eater if you like." Eric made a sound in his throat and shook his head. Alex corralled him and the trio left the pub. Eric looked back for a glimpse of Sally, but she was parrying remarks good-naturedly with whomever she was serving and didn't see them leaving. Frederick joined Alex in holding Eric's hunched shoulders as they made their way towards their respective dormitories.

The weekend following his debate victory, Frederick spent another evening out with Andrew Staunton. They had dined over braised beef, hearty potatoes with cheese, and roasted vegetables at their beloved Tudbury's, and now they were nursing mugs of equally fine ale at The Scholar's Dilemma. Thankfully, Sally didn't seem to be serving that evening, and Alex had told him he would be distracting Eric with entertainment elsewhere. Staunton was a tall, muscular fellow with long, sandy blond hair, full side-whiskers, and a handsome mustache; he reminded Frederick of Eric Langham, though Andrew was a few years older than them.

Andrew was set to complete his degree within the year, but luckily he was a local young man and Frederick could count on his friendship, as well as his family's and that of Mrs. Ford and Miss Fremont, while he attended King's unless Andrew moved away. This evening he and Frederick were pleasantly debating the advantages and pleasures of Cambridge, London, and Derbyshire.

"Darcy," Andrew said, finally pushing his tankard away, "I am most grateful for your friendship, and I know Henry would be very pleased." Frederick grinned. "But I have much studying to do for my examinations beginning this coming Monday. Please excuse me, for I must return to my texts and notes."

"Not at all," Frederick replied. "Good luck on all your

examinations, Staunton, and let us meet again when you are finished with them, perhaps next Thursday or Friday? You can tell me then how they went."

"Thursday it is, and I thank you." Andrew rose, placing some coins on the table. "Good night, young sir, and do not stay up too late."

Frederick laughed. "Do not worry, for I shall not." He wished his friend a good night. Once Andrew had left The Scholar's Dilemma, Frederick drank down the last of his ale and ordered a rare additional round, his last for the evening. He was savoring his replenished tankard when a big, loud young man and his female companion stopped by his little table. Frederick looked up, stifling a groan.

"Well, Darcy," Richard Grantley drawled, without introducing his stunning, daringly dressed companion, "how well we are met tonight!" When Frederick did not respond, Richard laughed and clapped him hard on his shoulder. "So, still in the priestly state? Why, if you can't succeed at university, then I am certain the Roman Church could use you."

Frederick flushed, as the heavily made-up woman simpered. "How you do go on, Grantley." He cleared his throat. "You know perfectly well that our family attends the Anglican Church. In addition, you must realize that I do not see any honor or maturity in taking pleasure with scores of women without some regard for the lady in question."

Richard guffawed and his companion shared his mirth. "Whatever is that supposed to mean?"

Frederick drew in a breath. "I mean that a man should care about a woman with whom he is intimate, instead of using her only for pleasure and tossing her away when the dalliance ends."

"My," Richard sneered, "are we not high-handed and moralistic tonight! Did you find all that in the Book of Common Prayer? Congratulations on taking your monastic vows." He nuzzled the woman's slender, powdered neck. "Well, my dear

Saint Frederick of Derbyshire, please continue to pray for our poor, depraved souls, and save us from our base behaviors as true men and women." The woman laughed and gave Frederick a cutting glance. "You know, Darcy, I really hope that someday you know what it means to please a woman – and act as a true man would." He laughed again, nodding to her.

"Good evening, Master Darcy," she breathed, and leaned towards him. Frederick's nostrils filled with the scent of her full, moist, perfumed bosom, inches from his face, while he fidgeted and flushed even darker. He flinched as she brushed his waistcoat and thigh, and then her hand moved towards his groin. He sucked in a breath and looked up at Richard's face, full of contempt.

"Tell me you are unaffected by such beauty and physical charms," he taunted. "You cannot be any kind of man if you are not."

"That's enough!" Frederick shouted, standing up with his fists clenched. But he had bumped the table with his knee because he had stood up so quickly, spilling some of the ale, and the publican and a few other male patrons placed themselves between him and Richard.

"Please, young gentlemen," the publican began as an easy admonishment.

Richard ignored him. "Poor Master Darcy is upset, his tight breeches in a knot," he kept taunting. "Come, Betsinda," he remarked to his companion, "let us leave this poor, confused boy to calm down, and this rather low den of iniquity, to find more appropriate venues in which to spend our time together. I shall take you to La Tricolore, and we shall have champagne!"

"Of course, your lordship," Betsinda breathed, oozing with delight. She flicked her eyes over at poor, mortified Frederick, gave his breeches another low, firm grope and, laughing, left with Richard, her arm entwined in his.

Moaning, Frederick pulled at his clothes and sank into

his chair, a look of misery and shame on his face. His head drooped as the publican exchanged a glance with his brother and assistant. "Come, young sir," the publican said heartily, "it seems you have finished your ale." Frederick could barely look up at him; instead, he glanced at his tankard, which was still almost one-third full. "Here is another, compliments of the house." Frederick tried to protest and began to get up again, but the other man gently pushed him down into his chair and quietly drew another pint in a new glass over the table to him. It was too much for him to drink in one night, even at the end of the week when there were no classes the next day, but when he finally looked up at all of them, he knew what they expected him to do.

"Thank you, Sir, I am much obliged to you all," he said, and swallowed. He drank down his ale steadily, emptying both his tankard and the complimentary pint. Several moments later, he wiped his mouth with his hand, got to his feet rather unsteadily, straightened his clothes, and grabbed his hat. He left a ridiculously large tip on the table and stumbled out of the pub in the direction of Newnham. He was too bleary-eyed to make eye contact with anyone, but he saw some of the men nodding at him, one of them taking his arm and saying something to him that sounded approving.

The cold, wet air outside in the street helped revive him a little, and the tightness and uneasiness in his midsection started to lessen. He could see his breath as he exhaled, then felt moisture speckle his face. He lurched down the street until he realized he was heading in the wrong direction, away from King's. He vigorously shook his head and righted his course.

He had barely staggered a couple of blocks before a dark-cloaked figure turned out of a black doorway directly into his path. The figure pulled back its hood and opened the cloak wide. Frederick stared at the cocotte's painted face and shiny, skimpy red dress. "How 'bout it, love?" she giggled, and pressed up against him as her arms braced his back. He gasped as she mashed his mouth with hers and he felt his body tense again.

Struggling, he broke free of her arms and pushed her away. Wiping his mouth, he almost began to run, though his quickened steps were unsteady and uneven, his breeches stretched, as he heard her curses fade into the misty air around him.

Soon a heavy rain started, and he was grateful for the drenching he suffered as he trudged and slogged along to Newnham, panting. He didn't notice if Mr. Ridgeson was watching in the darkened hall for his return. In his chamber, his head thick and heavy, he scrubbed his face with water from the basin, then peeled off his clothes and fell into bed.

CHAPTER 5

Frederick continued his disciplined study habits to carry him through the remainder of the term. He had no further debating victories or even sessions, but he continued to write papers that were generally well received and did better remembering the finer points of commercial law than the facts from his history lectures. Reading and translating Latin brought him much satisfaction, though it meant more time and study.

Finally, he plodded through a full, exhausting week of examinations. He felt that they went well but chafed at not knowing the results and mourned when he remembered instances when he could have written more specific answers or details he had forgotten to include. He hoped his parents would be pleased with the summary of results that Mr. Haydock would send them. He'd even resumed limiting his pub visits to once a week so he wouldn't encounter Richard Grantley or any other questionable, grasping people along the streets at night; he didn't, but agonized that he might.

The week following his examinations, John Buckley, sent from Pemberley, collected and brought Frederick to the town-house in Cavendish Square, London. The morning after his arrival, he joined his parents in the drawing room.

Darcy surprised Frederick by handing him a small velvet sack that clinked. "Here you are, Frederick," he said. "Your mother and I would like you to have this."

Frederick thanked him and loosened the strings. "Three double sovereigns!" he gasped as the golden coins tumbled out into his palm.

"There is no need to gape, my dear," smiled Elizabeth, "for we can see how much you like our present."

"I do, Mother, but –"

"You seem almost speechless," his father added, smiling,

"but three double sovereigns it is, six pounds, and we intend that you use them for your own pleasure and not for college expenses! Yes, all three of them – one for your first in Latin, one for your second in composition, and one for your growing success in the debating society. Congratulations on your two fine terms!"

"Thank you, Father and Mother!" Frederick relaxed. "I hope I have many more positive results in the future that please you this much."

"As do we, Frederick," Elizabeth said.

"I feel quite confident about the next term! Master Bennington has also asked me to tutor other students who are struggling in Latin."

"We are very glad to hear it. Congratulations again on your success!" Elizabeth rose from her comfortable chair. "Now, let me take a good look at you, my son, for I have not seen you these past several months."

Frederick stood at attention and fought to keep his face straight as she examined him from head to toe. Darcy remained silent and serious as usual, his eyes mild and amused.

"You are confident about your next term," she was musing, "and that is very good." She nodded. "I must also compliment you on your bearing and the obvious pains you are taking with your appearance. Not a crease or smudge can I find, and your cravat is carefully arranged. Show me your handkerchief." He provided it for her examination. She smiled her approval and continued, "However, I daresay I am not so confident as to this new arrangement in which I find your hair."

"Mother?" Darcy turned away to clear his throat. Frederick had not expected a comment like this. He wore his hair longer in the back and somehow plastered it down over the top, so that some of the mass of waves stayed in place, except on the windiest days. "You do not like it?"

Elizabeth looked doubtful. "Well, it is different."

"It's one of the latest styles." He felt himself beginning to squirm and hated the pleading in his voice. He saw his father's mouth give a rare twitch, so Frederick strengthened his tone. "You would want me to be fashionable, within reason, would you not? And I should be fashionable so that I can make the best appearance I can for Julia and Jane's debut, and be as natural and comfortable as I am able." She nodded but did not reply. He took a deep breath. "I think my hair looks less wild and unruly this way."

"Well, I must say that it does," his mother decided calmly. "All right, I may even find it becoming – in time, that is, once I am used to seeing it." She sat down again.

Darcy laughed and put his arm around Frederick, in whose voice they both heard relief. "Thank you, Mother."

"Not at all, Frederick." He quietly savored returning the gold coins into the sack and putting it in his coat pocket. Turning to his parents, he said, "I am so glad we are all together again at last, here in London! I have been looking forward to it for such a long time."

"So have we." Elizabeth and Darcy had arrived a few days ago at the comfortable townhouse on Cavendish Square, just off the end of Bond Street near Oxford Street, one of the main thoroughfares. Julia, Nicholas, and Anne had accompanied them, of course, and the whole family and their trunks had barely fit into the largest carriage driven by Tom Nixley. Later today, Jane Elizabeth and Mrs. Winston would be coming over from the Staleys' home in Berkeley Square to join their reunion.

"Frederick!" came a happy shout, and Nicholas and Anne rushed into the drawing room. They mobbed him for a hug.

"Nicholas, please," Elizabeth scolded gently. "Frederick can hear you, so there is no need to shout."

"Yes, Mother." Nicholas seemed chastened but brightened as he and Anne peppered Frederick with questions. Laughing, Frederick held up his hands. "One at a time, I beg of you! We will have a great deal of time in which to catch up."

"All right," Nicholas finally agreed, then stopped. Looking up at his brother, he examined him from three different points on the carpet.

"Would you please tell me, Nick, why you are looking at me like that?"

"Then please tell *me*, Frederick," his brother countered, frowning, "do all the other fellows at Cambridge wear their hair like yours?"

"We have not seen each other for months and this is your first comment to me?" Frederick sounded exasperated, as their mother tried not to laugh. "For your information, Master Nicholas Darcy, this happens to be the latest style in the grooming of hair for young gentlemen. Do not be so critical, for even Mother thinks it is becoming."

Anne turned to her. "Do you really think so, Mother?"

She could not help laughing then. "What I actually said was I would probably find it so when I am at last used to it. I will not be misquoted."

Frederick was still stung. "Why does everyone seem to comment on my hair?" he asked the room at large.

"It is because it's so singular, Freddie," Anne explained. "Well, you are right. There is no reason to keep commenting on this new style of yours," she offered. "Julia says all things, whether fashions, hairstyles, or furnishings, go in and out of popularity over time, so you can always change it to a different one later on." Frederick thanked her, rolling his eyes.

Elizabeth giggled and Darcy spoke to prevent himself from laughing. "Well, whether it's a new style or not, let us enjoy all being together again! Your mother and I will check on the dinner arrangements, for the Staleys will be dining with us tonight once they bring Jane and Mrs. Winston home. All of you can catch up for a while and we shall return soon." They left them in charge of the drawing room, where they spent the next couple of hours happily exchanging news too recent to have written about and shared a long, sumptuous tea.

The next morning, Frederick awoke early, excited over the family's plans for the day. He dressed so early that breakfast would not be served for another half an hour, and went to pore over some books in the comfortable library adjoining the drawing room. The townhouse library was not as grand or extensive as Pemberley's, but his father had ensured the large room was filled with interesting and enticing volumes. Frederick was perusing his way through Adam Smith's *The Wealth of Nations* when Nicholas appeared and rushed him as he had the day before.

"Got you that time, Frederick!"

"OOF!" his brother exclaimed. "Why, Nick, you seem quite strong – you must have spent a lot of time exercising."

"Yes, I have." Nicholas grinned. "I've had almost exclusive use of the exercise room Father furnished for us!"

"You are lucky that your older brother isn't there to take over all the weights first!" Frederick enjoyed needling him. "We still have almost fifteen minutes to wait until breakfast is ready, and I hear your stomach growling!"

Nicholas laughed. "What about yours? I am certain I heard an unseemly noise coming from where you are standing."

Frederick examined him; Nicholas had turned fourteen while Frederick studied at Cambridge and seemed a little taller and slimmer, less like a boy who enjoyed puzzles and games. "You are stronger and a little more serious," he complimented.

Nicholas thanked him and smiled in satisfaction. "Well, I am fourteen now."

Frederick put an arm around his shoulders. "So how has it been going, with Father teaching you to help him with estate business?"

Nicholas' face clouded over. "It is going well enough, I sup-pose."

"But?"

Nicholas didn't answer right away. "I make so many mistakes." He sighed. "I have gotten some of the ledgers mixed up, and Father has made me write just about everything I have over again! Then he jokes and says I have used up an entire ream of writing paper." He shook his head. "I don't know if I will ever get it all right, but Father is patient, and – well – rather encouraging."

Frederick smiled. "There you are! Father is patient with you – as he has been with me – and he is encouraging you. That all sounds very good! What else has he said?"

"He also says that my penmanship is improving, even if my composition skills are not – but he has said I will improve even at that over time. I still get nervous meeting Father's – that is, our – neighbors and all the gentlemen with whom he conducts business. I don't know what to say to them, so I usually say nothing."

Frederick was sympathetic. "That is a sensible thing to do, but I also think you will get accustomed to meeting all these important gentlemen in time." Then he added, "It took me a while to learn how Father had everything organized. At first, I felt overwhelmed, and even though I recorded everything I still didn't do it all correctly the first time. I wasn't sure of myself with important, distinguished gentlemen that visited, either." He smiled. "Has Father ever mentioned me when you are working together?"

"He has." Nicholas shot him a look. "He talks about how well you learned everything, but I know he means to be encouraging and uses your work as an example." He grinned. "Not that you did everything right, as you say."

Frederick returned his grin. "Such a lack of respect toward your elder brother! Watch out, for I am still bigger than you!"

Nicholas laughed again. "I suppose that you are. However, I have been exercising, while you have been studying and debating. To keep up your strength, you wrote you would be taking up fencing; when is that to happen?"

"Next term." Frederick liked his brother's improved self-confidence. "But back to estate business; just keep trying, and you will do as well as I learned to, if not better!"

"Thanks, Frederick," his brother said, trying to sound grateful, "but it is still a lot of work and much to learn; I must concentrate very hard to remember what I do. And I forgot to mention that I have made several mistakes writing out and recording the cheques. I even forgot to write the amount on one of them, and Father could not help but sigh that time."

Frederick laughed, despite his brother's glum expression. "Well, I have had some experience myself with that, too. It seems to be a shared trait among Darcy sons." He told Nicholas about the incorrect cheque amount and forgetting to make a payment so that the bill became overdue – as well as failing to cancel the feed order for some of the livestock.

By the time he finished, Nicholas' bright spirits had returned and they were laughing. However, they weren't laughing so loudly that they failed to hear the low gong announcing that breakfast was being served in the dining room. Both of them looked forward to their hearty breakfast and heaping plates, for they were about to experience a full day of activities taking place all over the great city.

After breakfast, Frederick drifted back to the library and felt proud of his more studious nature. He would be studying political economy next term and wanted to read more of Adam Smith in preparation. However, when he entered the room, he found someone already there.

"Good morning, Anne," he said, smiling. "How is the future Mistress of Pemberley faring today?"

Looking up, she returned his smile. "I am quite well this morning, thank you. And yourself?"

"I am well." He laughed. "You beat me to the library! I shouldn't be surprised."

She regarded him, but her tone remained light. "Are you teasing me, Freddie?"

"I suppose I am, a little." He laughed again. "I have been so proud of myself for studying so hard lately and reading everything I can find, but I admit this is new to me – whereas you have always liked to read and fill your mind with knowledge of all kinds."

She smiled again and thanked him. "But you are succeeding at Cambridge! Mother and Father are ecstatic and have talked of little else for an entire week."

"Thank *you*, Anne. Yes, I think they are pleased and I am so glad. I do not think I will be sent down again."

"You had better not," she said severely, then giggled.

He laughed with her. "I promise you, Mistress Anne, that the next Master of Pemberley will not stain his educational record with such a failing."

Anne dropped her book on the sofa. "Oh, Freddie, I am so excited to be here in London! It will be so interesting to be presented at Court and maybe attend assemblies and grand balls; there will be so much to see and do." She turned to him, eager. "I did not realize how big London is!"

Frederick enjoyed her burst of enthusiasm. "I think you have made a fine start already." He thought of all the places they had visited the day before, St. Paul's and the Mall, among others.

"Oh, yes! I still want very much to see the Houses of Parliament, the Temple District, and Fleet Street." Frederick was amused by her choices but not surprised, for Anne was interested in many kinds of places, and not just limited to visiting churches and museums. "And there is one more place I would really like to go. Now please don't laugh at me."

He held up his right hand. "I promise. Where is it you would you like to go?"

"I want Father to take me to the Royal Academy, where all the mathematicians and scientists meet! I would love to attend a couple of lectures, even if I have no idea what they are talking about. I could learn, though, using them as a start!" She subsided. "Well, I would love to go. Father didn't sound too promising when I mentioned it – I think he hopes I shall be satisfied with the museums – and Jane didn't help matters any by wondering out loud whether they would be talking about insects or diseases. Julia was even more depressing about it."

"What did she say?"

Anne pouted. "She sighed, rolled her eyes, and told me she didn't think I could visit the society just like a museum, as if it wouldn't be proper to do so." Frederick laughed before he could stop himself. "Freddie, you promised!"

"I am sorry, Anne," he said. "I am not laughing at you, I am simply amused by Julia's reaction, for she *would* be satisfied visiting churches and museums."

"She would," Anne agreed. "Oh, I know they would not let me attend anything truly awful, like a medical lecture where they had bones or even cadavers – yes, I have heard about that kind of thing from reading the newspaper! Mother and Father wouldn't allow me to attend either, any more than I think the academy would, for something like that. But what about a lecture on exploration, curing a disease, or studying plants? I would definitely enjoy something like that and I do so want to go! I want to learn many things, not just painting or drawing, sewing, playing an instrument, singing, and dancing, none of which I am particularly good at or much interested in doing anyway. I would even be interested in hearing about financial matters, like Father's estate business that you and Nicholas are learning."

He sat and put an arm around her. "Try to think positively, Anne. If you ask Father again and explain it to him the way you have to me, he will find lectures that would be appropriate and interesting for you to attend – even a historical one – for I am certain that visitors must be allowed to such events." Anne looked eager again. "I will mention it to Father myself," he continued, "and ask if he would consider allowing you to attend some lectures with him, or perhaps Mr. Staley, or even me. I will do my best to persuade him if he still seems doubtful."

"Oh, Freddie, thank you!" She hugged him. "I am so grateful! I cannot wait."

"Well," he cautioned, "let us be patient, for I have not spoken to him yet. But I think Father will agree and persuade Mother if she has any doubts." Frederick remembered Lady Catherine exhorting his parents to spare no expense in having Anne formally educated. He thought he would also ask his father about that as well, since Anne had the most studious nature of them all and loved learning difficult subjects – even if doing so was not considered ladylike or conventional. Since she showed such motivation at her tender age, he wanted to help satisfy her thirst for knowledge.

"All right, Freddie." She picked up her book. "I will wait to hear from you and Father. Now I would like to change the subject back to Cambridge." He nodded. "It is so wonderful to see you again. I missed you very much."

He thanked her. "I missed you as well."

"You wrote to me once a month, too," she approved, and he could not help laughing again. But she sighed. "I would also love to go to Cambridge! There would be so much to learn – there must be at university! I could read and study all day long."

He smiled. "Well, you would certainly be doing a lot of that."

"I am quite serious! Oh, I know that even if I could attend Cambridge, you would be finished long before I would be old enough to attend. That, and the fact that I do not know of any girl who does attend Cambridge – or any other university, for that matter." She turned to him. "Have you seen any young women who are students at Cambridge?"

He thought for a moment. "To be honest," he said slowly, clearing his throat, "I do not think I have. I know that many of the masters and the oldest students tutor young women privately. But I will have to ask about that, as well as at the university." He thought there must be a university that taught young women somewhere, in Europe, if not in England.

"Perhaps Mr. Haydock?" she asked helpfully.

"Not Mr. Haydock," he shuddered, "but definitely some of the other masters."

Anne opened her book. "My lessons will continue because we are staying in London for so long, and Miss Kendall is here." She looked at him. "I would certainly like to learn more about history and mathematics, among other things."

He looked into her serious eyes. "I see," he said thoughtfully. "Perhaps I could help you with some of that because I have been doing tolerably well in one of those subjects, if not both. Would you also like to begin learning a little Latin?"

"Oh, yes, Freddie, please! I would love that."

"Wonderful!" he said. "Then we shall start tomorrow, or whenever your next hours of tutoring can occur." He knew he could use his own textbook as a start.

"There will be plenty of time to learn because I will be spending much time in the schoolroom, especially if it rains. But I do not mind that, and I am eager to learn nonetheless!"

He rose. "I will go find Father right away and I will leave you to enjoy your book. I will let you know all that he says, and to what he agrees."

She jumped up and hugged him tightly. "Thank you for everything, my big brother, the next master!"

He kissed her forehead. "You are most welcome, Anne." He left her poring over her book with a determined but satisfied expression of concentration.

CHAPTER 6

Frederick had been eagerly looking forward to seeing Jane Elizabeth again. It had been several months since she had left Pemberley for London, but it seemed much longer than that. Now that they had all reunited and were busy catching up with each other, sightseeing, and enjoying themselves, spending time alone or even with only one other person was difficult. In addition, there was a bustle of activity occurring, as the date of Julia and Jane's debuts was fast approaching. It wasn't until his fourth day in Cavendish Square that Frederick got a chance to speak to Jane Elizabeth with some privacy. He was anxious to see how she was feeling about herself and life in general, after all this time in the capital.

During the early afternoon, Frederick found his sister in one of the small sitting rooms with Mrs. Winston. Jane Elizabeth brightened and rose. "Frederick!"

"Jane, if I have not said so before, how well you look!" He hugged her, then exchanged greetings with Mrs. Winston. "London must agree with you."

"I am so happy we are all together again, for it has been such a long time!" Jane exclaimed. "I only wish Henry David and his nurse could have come with us, too, but I suppose that would not have been such a good idea."

"Yes, it would be feasible but not practical," Frederick admitted, "making the little one take such a long journey. And once he was here, he would not be able to go places and enjoy the city like the rest of us can."

Jane smiled. "He will probably be walking by the time we return to Pemberley." He nodded.

Mrs. Winston rose. "I am sure you would like some time together, Master Frederick," she said, laying her embroidery aside. "I shall return in a short while."

He sounded contrite. "I do not wish to disturb both of you, but I haven't had the chance to say much to Jane since we arrived."

The lady smiled. "It is no bother, and you have not disturbed us. I would like to take a short walk around the square and look at this lovely neighborhood, for none of us has had time to do that in the last few days." He thanked her.

"Enjoy your walk," Jane said.

"Thank you, my dear, I will," she answered, and left the room.

Jane turned to him, smiled, and hugged him a second time. "It is wonderful to see you, and looking so well! How are you, Jane?"

She released him and stepped back. "I am quite well." She said nothing as he looked carefully at her for several seconds; finally, he shook himself.

"Again, I am very glad that you are," he said. "Please forgive me for staring at you just now, but I wanted to be certain."

"There is nothing to forgive." Her face was expressionless but her voice mild. "You want to be certain that I am as well as I say, do you not? I hope you are convinced because I truly feel that I am."

"That is wonderful, and I thank you for your understanding!" She gestured for him to sit and went back to her own chair. Brightening, Frederick asked, "How are you finding London after all this time?"

She smiled widely. "I like London very much, and I have been enjoying myself more than I could ever imagine. The museums, plays, concerts, even the opera! Cousins Clarissa and Henry have been incredibly generous, and so have Aunt and Uncle Gardiner, now that he is feeling better. Sir Adam and Lady Wainwright, too. I am enjoying all my new gowns." She looked content. "And I am so very grateful for Frances – that is, Mrs. Winston – and her company all this time. Even Miss Kendall likes and esteems her."

His smile grew. "Again, I am so glad to hear it."

Jane focused on a point in front of her. "I wasn't always happy having a companion, as you know. I did not want one at all, and I wasn't friendly or polite to her in the beginning; I was quite rude to her." Her calm eyes returned to him. "But Mrs. Winston is so wise and understanding! She is an amazing teacher and a friend; I can even call her Frances in private! I would feel quite lost and cast down without her."

Frederick spread his hands. "I am very glad you have become friends."

She smiled in return. "We've shared so many experiences and visited such interesting places. I think several of them Julia will enjoy – when she is not preparing for her debut." They shared a laugh. "I must prepare for my own as well, but I've had much more time to enjoy London. I am not sure what Anne will find interesting, though I have been thinking very hard about that."

He grinned. "Anne wants to attend lectures and visit the royal scientific societies, even a session of Parliament. She told me she finds listening to a lecture on plants more interesting than painting watercolors or arranging flowers and would rather attend a debate than organize an afternoon tea." They laughed together again. "But that is no matter. Since you have been here so long, and become familiar with the city, I know that you will be able to take Julia places she will enjoy and she will be most grateful for it."

She thanked him. "I am looking forward to being her guide, with Mrs. Winston's help, of course."

He gave her a sympathetic look. "How are your debut preparations going?"

She gave a short laugh, which reminded him of her former reactions back home. "I must admit to you, it is maddening!" She shook her head and played with a few strands of her hair. She gave him a contrite look. "I am sorry, but it is true. I understand how important this is for Mother, Father, Julia, and even myself. I am not complaining, nor am I being recalcitrant, but it is quite exhausting most of the time, and sometimes extremely trying." She tried to smile.

"There is no need to apologize. I cannot imagine how much work it is, nor how much time it takes, or how tiring it may be; although," he shook his head, "I think I am about to find out. I am to begin practicing my dance steps with you and Julia, starting tomorrow! Mother said something about spending at least an hour each day practicing, from now until the first ball. I do not care much for dancing, but I must be Julia's escort and partner, as well as yours! I think I would rather be lectured by Master Haydock than practice like this." He gave her a pleading look. "Should I rue my fate then?"

"Yes," she replied, blinking, "you should." When his face fell, she giggled. "Forgive me, but I do sympathize with you, for only Nicholas has been spared learning all these necessary things for the debut." She shook her head again. "I do not know how Julia stands it, but she is looking forward to it all, as everything is being done for her benefit." Another thought made her smile. "There are times when I get so tired or cross – though I try very hard to hide the fact that I do – that I beg Mother to let me go stretch my legs or catch some fresh air out in the back garden! And Anne is no better than I – she pays attention but must be made to perform the slightest step or activity. Basically, she stares at Mother and the instructors until they are quite impatient with her!" They shared yet another laugh. "Anne likes to challenge them; nothing gives her greater pleasure than spending time with her books. However, it is not all so bothersome," she continued. "There are some very nice benefits because of our debuts."

"Such as?"

She gave her widest smile yet. "Oh, Frederick, I know this is a womanly interest, but how fortunate all three of us girls are! For Father has spared no expense in having new gowns made for us to wear at Court and all the balls!" She looked quite happy. "You will see when we wear them, but how exquisite they are – such fine material, with lovely flourishes and finishing touches. Not only Julia will be dressed in the height of current fashion for young ladies, I can tell you!"

Her enthusiasm rubbed off on him. "That is truly wonderful, Jane! I know you will be so beautiful at the balls; all of you will be." She thanked him. "You are most welcome." He tried to hide a smile and failed. "And does Anne share your pleasure in her new wardrobe?"

Again, she might have retorted as she would usually have done, but realized he was teasing her. "Well, not exactly," she finally replied. "The balls do not interest her much, that is true, for she is only eleven; but her eagerness at having new dresses to wear surprised us, and she even asked for special touches to her hair when the time comes."

Frederick grinned again. "Perhaps she would like to wear them to the lectures and to Parliament." They laughed for a long time, though Jane tried to scold him for making the joke, much as she enjoyed it. She did not mind; even though he teased his siblings, like Henry he did so rarely and without cruelty.

When they had calmed down, Frederick turned to look at her again. He liked her composure, which was more reserved and confident, less prone to flashes of harsh or direct comments than before; Jane said nothing and waited for him to speak. Finally, he said, "There is something I would like to ask you."

"Please do." Her expression remained calm and unchanged.

"All right then." He leaned forward in his chair. "You seem very well, happy, and contented after all the time you have spent here in London." She nodded. "I do not mean to pry, but is there anything bothering you now, or worrying you still? Anything at all that concerns you?"

She smiled. "I thank you for your concern, and I am not upset by your question." She rose and began walking past the sitting room windows with her arms crossed. After a couple of moments she turned back to him. "Well, perhaps there is one thing that concerns me now." He kept listening, changing neither position nor expression. "I hope you do not find that alarming, for I do not intend it to be so; but you did ask me, so I will answer you. First, allow me to say again that I am quite well and untroubled. I do feel happy and content here, and I am enjoying London so very much."

"That is good, Jane. Pray tell me what concerns you."

She kept pacing back and forth. "While it concerns me, it has not spoiled my time here, or kept me awake at night; however, here it is." She stopped where she was. "I cannot help wondering if – and when – I shall return home to Pemberley." He waited, so she resumed. "I am certain I cannot remain here forever, much as I would like to. Pemberley is so beautiful, with many gorgeous open spaces that London does not have. I do miss them; it is a wonderful place to live." Sitting down, she smoothed the folds in her dress. "But how long should I remain living here? And what will it be like when I return home? Will people still be cruel about all that happened – all that I did – or will they have someone else to gossip about and disapprove of? Perhaps somebody else to judge and make miserable?" She shrugged. "Above all, I wonder if I *should* go back. I am sixteen now but it will be Father and Mother's decision as to where I live." She tried to smile. "So that, dear Brother, is what concerns me."

At first, all he could say was, "I see." Running a hand through his hair, he shrugged. "It is an important question. I would like to help you with it, but I am not sure how. Yes, it would be wonderful for you to stay here as long as possible; but not to have you home with us! We would continue to miss you very much. Then again, if people in town still try to mistreat you, perhaps it is better to stay away from them and from Pemberley for a longer time. I do not think you would be happy being a virtual prisoner at home, if people outside our lands mistreat you and you want to avoid them."

"Frederick," she said softly, "please know that I do miss our lovely home very much...as well as all of you."

He smiled. "I had not thought otherwise. But you like the hustle and bustle of London."

She smiled. "I do, in fact."

He pondered that for a while. "Well, Jane," he finally said, "thank you for telling me your concerns. I have just turned nineteen myself and I must admit, even as the next Master of Pemberley –" he broke off and they shared a smile, "I am at a loss to know how to help you with it. Would you then allow me to mention it to Mother and Father? I am certain they will think of something to help you make the decision – when it is the appropriate time."

She nodded. "Yes, please do mention it to them. I do not object, and I would be quite grateful to you, for we must discuss it at some point." She clasped and unclasped her hands. "I did not want to trouble them now, while there is so much to do preparing for our debuts, but where I live may become an issue when all the balls and presentations are over. So I think we should start thinking about it, and I would feel more at ease."

"I certainly will, as soon as I can, and thank you." He rose to leave. "Now it is time for me to go exercise so that I am ready and limber for my dancing instruction tomorrow morning." She giggled at his drooping expression as she rose from her chair. "I enjoyed our time together very much."

"As did I, Frederick."

They wished each other a good afternoon, as Jane went off to find Mrs. Winston and Frederick went to his room to stretch and study the dance diagrams. Nicholas asked if he could watch, which he did, much to his amusement, but Frederick made him exercise as well – and even stand in as his partner on some of the more difficult dances. There was much laughter shared but Frederick felt glad he had made the effort, even if he wouldn't remember much of it the next day.

True to his word, after dinner that evening Frederick sought out his parents in a small sitting room near their bedrooms. He rarely did this, even back home at Pemberley, because he did not wish to disturb his parents' time together, so he approached their room very carefully. He could hear their voices, his father's excellent baritone and his mother's warm and easy tones, though they spoke softly enough that he could not hear their actual words. He knocked on the open door.

"Yes, Frederick, come in!" Darcy gestured to him.

"Good evening, dear," Elizabeth greeted him. "It is always wonderful to see you, but I hoped just a little that it was Jordan with the hot toddies."

Frederick laughed and exchanged greetings. "Father, Mother, may I have a few minutes of your time? I do not wish to disturb your evening, but –" He trailed off.

"Not at all, of course you may!" Darcy exchanged a glance with Elizabeth. "You are not disturbing us. Is there something that troubles you?"

"No, Father, not really, but there is something I wanted to mention to you and Mother...well, two things."

"Not more requests!" Darcy groaned. "Son, you will be the next Master of Pemberley and you are acquitting yourself well in preparation for it, but please have pity on me, the current one! When you are master you can reward or withhold as you please, but if it isn't asking for new gowns for your sisters or increasing the wages of the staff, it's asking me to escort young Anne to all kinds of erudite lectures, as well as a session of Parliament!" Elizabeth stifled a giggle as his expression cleared. "Do not mind me, Frederick, or protest because of it, so now tell us what you wanted to talk about."

Frederick sat down. "Even if it is another request?"

Darcy closed his eyes. "Even so."

Elizabeth gave him another glance. "Is it really another?"

"Actually, no, it is not, I am happy to say." He sat forward in his chair. "However, there are two things I would like to mention, and they both concern Jane Elizabeth." He saw their faces grow serious, so he hastened to add, "It is nothing upsetting, I think, or a cause for concern. One point is quite positive, and the other is something to think about."

"I see," Darcy said, exchanging another glance with Elizabeth. "Pray continue."

"Yes, please do, dear son," she said, "but thank you for reassuring us."

"Certainly, Mother." Jordan the footman now arrived with his parents' warm glass mugs. He asked if Frederick desired anything, but he declined. After Jordan left, Frederick met his parents' expectant looks and resumed.

"Father, I wanted to tell you and Mother that I find Jane Elizabeth in very good spirits." He saw their expressions relax. "She told me today that she feels quite well. I find her so myself, and it seems that her time in London has helped her. She seems more composed, calmer, and happier than at home. She also expressed how grateful she is for Mrs. Winston's guidance, teaching, and friendship. I think she also likes having Miss Kendall here as well."

Elizabeth could not help a tear in her eye. "That is truly wonderful! It is definitely good news, which we all need!"

"It is," Darcy agreed, "but it is also wonderful for Jane." He paused. "Your mother and I had also remarked upon Jane's confidence and poise, as well as other positive changes. It pleases us both that she now feels so fond and appreciative of Mrs. Winston, enough to call her a friend; what a fine lady she is!" He sipped his toddy. "I am also glad you find Jane happy and well-adjusted here."

"We trust your judgment," Elizabeth added as he thanked her, warmth flooding through him.

"What else did you want to tell us?" Darcy asked, gripping his mug.

Frederick held up a hand. "I repeat it is not a cause for worry, but Jane Elizabeth mentioned something she has been thinking about. I must add that she had no objection to my mentioning it to you."

"We are both relieved to know that," Elizabeth said.

"She wonders how long she will remain living in London before returning to Pemberley," he resumed. "She did not want to burden you because of her and Julia's debuts, but she does wonder how long she will remain at Cavendish Square. She has enjoyed her time in London very much and wishes it to continue – as long as you desire it. She did admit that she has missed Pemberley and all of us very much, but also wonders how people may treat her when she returns." Elizabeth looked at Darcy, who steepled his fingers and stared into the carpet. "Father?"

"Continue, Frederick."

"Yes, Sir," he swallowed. "While she is not despondent or excessively worried about this, Jane still thinks about it and would like to know what you are considering, for where she shall live will affect her future. She does not want to be separated from us but she has not forgotten how so many people in Lambton and Kympton treated her." He looked hopefully at them both. "That is all I wanted to say." A long silence hung over the room.

"I see," Darcy finally said. "You have stated it quite well; I can see how you have excelled in the debating society at Cambridge. No, there is no need to thank me! But I am heartened that both you and Jane are already thinking about her future. As Master of Pemberley, you must always think of your family members' happiness and well-being, and I am very proud of you that you are already doing this for Jane and Anne." Frederick blushed, unable to articulate his thanks, while Elizabeth beamed at him. Darcy took another sip, then rose from the sofa to stand in front of the warm fire in the grate. "However, it is an important question, one we must consider, as you both have mentioned." He stared into the fire for a couple of minutes, then turned to Elizabeth. "What are you thinking, Lizzie?" Frederick blinked at his father's endearment, one he rarely made in front of one of their children.

"Why, I must consider this also for a while," she replied, "for I do not wish to come to a decision too quickly."

"Nor do I. But do you have ideas that can help us decide sometime soon?"

She thought for a moment. "Well, Dearest," she said slowly, "I do not like our dear daughter being separated from us for such a long time. Yet I do not want her to come home, as beautiful and vast as Pemberley is, only to be mistreated and shown such condemnation and disrespect again." She sipped her drink. "Oh, I do not like to say this, Fitzwilliam and Frederick, my current and future masters! But I think we must consider what is best for her and not for ourselves."

"Agreed," Darcy said grimly, and Frederick gave a firm nod.

Elizabeth stared ahead of her and took another sip. "I think that it is best for Jane to remain here in London with Mrs. Winston for a time after the debuts are over." She sighed. "But I do not know for how long. I do not think we should bring her back to Pemberley and Derbyshire too quickly. So, I suggest we must continue to think about how much longer she should remain away from us and decide a little later." She looked at them. "Now it's my turn to ask what both of you think."

Darcy looked at Frederick, who gestured he should speak; Darcy nodded. "I think you have stated the situation quite well, Lizzie. I am ready to agree that Jane and Mrs. Winston should reside here at Cavendish Square for a while longer; Cousins Clarissa and Henry, as well as Aunt and Uncle Gardiner and the Lintons, are close by. We can even add a couple of servants to this household so there is a full staff on hand. I trust Mrs. Winston implicitly."

"As do I," Elizabeth agreed. "Since we agree, I think that Jane will continue to be content and untroubled." She turned to Frederick. "Do you have any objections or concerns, or anything you would like to add? As your father said, when you are Master of Pemberley, you will have to consider the welfare of your siblings, and not only that of your own immediate family."

Frederick swallowed again. "Yes, Mother, I know you are correct." He took a moment to clear his thoughts. "No, I do not have any hesitation over what you have said, but I thank you for asking my opinion."

"Of course, Frederick!" Darcy affirmed.

"Father, what shall we tell Jane Elizabeth and when?"

"Ah," Darcy said, his back stiffening, "let us arrange some time over the next few days – one when our schedule of events is not so full, and you and I," he took Elizabeth's hand, "will talk to her about how long she will spend in London. Frederick," he said, "you may attend if you wish, but that is your decision to make."

He nodded. "I would like to be present with all of you."

She sighed. "I feel so relieved, and I am glad we will be having this discussion!"

"As am I." Darcy sipped his drink and glanced at Frederick. "Now that this subject is settled for the time being, how would you like to spend the rest of your evening, Son?"

Frederick rose. "I am reading *The Wealth of Nations* in preparation for my political economy lectures next term and would like to make some additional progress before I turn in for the evening." Wishing them a good night, he left.

Darcy looked at Elizabeth with emotion. "Thank God for our wonderful son!"

"Amen to that, Fitzwilliam," she said, and they held each other for a long time.

CHAPTER 7

Julia could not be happier now that her family was reunited in the capital. She was very glad to see Frederick, Jane Elizabeth, and Mrs. Winston again, but was also exhilarated by all the sights and sounds of London. It didn't matter how many hours she had to practice and prepare for her debut; she managed to make time to catch up with her siblings, as well as enjoy all the great city had to offer. She rose early and went to bed as late as she dared, but somehow managed to get some sleep and maintain a level of energy that would match her mother and Mrs. Reynolds. However, she had no time to write letters to anyone, and since everyone close to her was here in London, she couldn't count on receiving any; it made her feel strangely cut off from her previously comfortable life.

Julia thought she felt ready for the challenge ahead of her. Debuting in London, including being presented at Court, thrilled her no end. She was determined to make the most of her stay because she didn't know when she might return. That would depend on whose offers of marriage she would receive, and ultimately whose hand she would accept. She half-smiled to herself; she was not overconfident, but certain she would receive offers. She was seventeen, she'd be out in society, and she thought she would attract the attention of eligible young men; this was expected of her, and she agreed – in principle. Perhaps after an acceptable engagement she would live her married life in London, or she might become the mistress of a grand estate like Pemberley in another county.

These thoughts gave her pause. She obviously owed a great debt to her parents for all they were providing and spending on her behalf. She had to do them proud and knew that she would, to the best of her ability. Of course, she was expecting and hoping for marriage proposals – wasn't she? She bit her lip. That was the purpose of a grand debut, and no, she couldn't just enjoy the gowns and the balls and return to Pemberley. She was a young lady making a splendid entrance into society, something more important than a tour of the mountain peaks or the lake country, as enjoyable as those could be. Did she want a prospective husband along with all the enjoyments?

Julia sensed that Jane Elizabeth had been pondering her future; but, like her sister, where would Julia end up residing? She intuited that it would probably not be at Pemberley, where she had lived her entire life; as much as London thrilled her, she felt pangs of loss over Pemberley – how she was most likely going to be merely a visitor the next time she went there, and not an inhabitant. And her prospective groom would be accompanying her. Did she want a husband? Of course she did, but did it necessarily have to be decided upon and planned for now?

She shrugged, as she often did. A great deal could change in a short time, and so much depended on the course of the next few weeks. Julia would try to be patient and do all that was expected of her. She was also determined to enjoy herself in the proper manner while she waited; yes, time would tell.

And how she wished she had more of it! Julia would have rather died than admit it, but on several occasions she had felt overwhelmed, when her well-known patience and good humor grew frayed to the point where she became brittle or sharp in her behavior and comments. She tried to be patient with everyone and please her tutors, whether they were knowledgeable or not or could even be pleased; she referred to the dance master as the King of Prussia and the lady that lectured her on deportment as Lady Napoleon. Julia admitted to herself, usually at night in the privacy of her own room, that several times over as many weeks she had felt her smile pasted on, even rigid, and had had to bite her tongue rather than say disappointing or sharp things that were very unlike her – and for which she would have to apologize later. But she also knew the debutante balls and other events were starting within the next two weeks; so, if she could be patient a little while longer, she thought everything would turn out well – and be worth all the time, effort, and expense! She wanted to make the best impression she could.

How she loved all the fabulous new gowns her parents had ordered for her! She indulged herself by running her hands over the rich, soft materials and fingering their special touches and embellishments; she could not wait to wear them. Her mother begged her to be careful with them, and she was, but this did not bother her. She could also spend quarters of an hour deciding which hairstyle would be the most becoming for a chosen gown; then she could enjoy trying on hats, bonnets, and riding outfits.

When she felt calm, Julia realized she hoped to meet many young men she would like at all the upcoming events. She also daydreamed about the characteristics she thought they should have. She thought a desirable young man should make a presentable appearance, have impeccable manners, be able to converse and dance, be pleasant, and, finally, be intelligent about something. She left that open, for it was too difficult to specify just yet. She did have to admit that how handsome the young man was, and how fine his physical condition would be important to her. She would admit that to herself, but never to her mother or sisters!

Julia liked Jane Elizabeth's newly developed reserve and demeanor, which she mentioned in an aside to Frederick, and he had been eager to agree. However, Julia also enjoyed sabotaging it somewhat when she suggested that the two of them go off for a "sisterly talk." Julia fooled no one – of course, she meant they would talk about young men they hoped to meet soon, and knew she could get Jane Elizabeth to laugh over her thoughts, hopes, and plans – and later on, critiques. Though Jane Elizabeth honestly wasn't interested in finding a young man herself – because she still wanted to rehabilitate herself and stay out of trouble – she was happy to share the time with her sister. She enjoyed hearing Julia's ideas on whom to court and young men in general. Frederick and Nicholas did not deign to comment on Julia's preoccupations and, whenever she and Jane Elizabeth went off giggling for one of their conversations, Anne would roll her eyes and go back to reading the book on mathematics that Frederick had given her.

This evening Julia savored watching herself brush her hair in the oval vanity mirror. She was happy, content, and relaxed, even though she knew the next several days would be hectic and full. She loved the variety and excitement of London. There would also be more dancing instruction from the King of Prussia the next day. She bore down a little hard on the brush and pulled her hair. She put down the brush, the corners of her mouth turning down. No, she was not looking forward to that, as well as she danced. She sighed, for she would be practicing with Frederick as her partner, and that gave her pause.

Julia loved and admired her older brother as she had Henry, but wondered at his newly found confidence; she knew how successful he had been at Cambridge, especially this past term. She remembered that Frederick used to avoid dancing at balls given back home, like Nicholas; of all her siblings, only Henry had enjoyed dancing and excelled at it – even though he could not sing on key! She also remembered that Frederick often said he did not think himself a good dancer in a dim, self-deprecating way. She exhaled. Well, he was to be her escort and first partner at every ball she would attend this season. Julia recovered her cheerfulness. She knew Frederick would try very hard, for he would not want to spoil anything for her sake, nor appear gangly and uncoordinated in public, at the balls, or at Court. If he has learned to do so well at studying and debating, she reasoned, he will be able to improve his dancing! As for the prospective husbands and marriage proposals, which seemed interchangeable to her, she could wait. And, with that, she made finishing touches to her hair and nightgown and went off to get some well-deserved sleep before the grind began tomorrow, all over again.

"My foot!" Julia cried out. "For goodness' sake, Frederick, watch out! Do you wish to cripple me?"

"I – I am sorry, Julia." A rueful Frederick rubbed his neck and watched helplessly as she gently stroked her bruised foot.

"Obviously we must have a delay," sniffed Mr. Pressburg-Stilton, the dance master, looking at him. "We will wait a few precious minutes more to see if Miss Darcy is well enough to continue." He sniffed again.

"Yes, Mr. Pressburg-Stilton," Elizabeth exclaimed, relieved, "thank you!"

"Naturally, madame," he answered, bowing to her and shooting Frederick another, more baleful look.

A minute later, Julia declared, "I am well enough to continue. Frederick is proud of his new boots and they have done me no injury!" She turned and gave him a smile. "I really am fine," she said, "but what if you were to change into the slippers or shoes you will be wearing to the balls?" She gave a wider smile. "I am sure our practicing would go much more smoothly."

Frederick gave an unmanly complaint, almost a wail. "I thought these boots were what I would be wearing to the ball!" His jaw reset at an uneven angle.

The instructor gave an even bigger sniff. "Most distracting and distasteful, this waste of practicing. Really, Mrs. Darcy, Miss Darcy – and Master Darcy! Please let us resume quickly, for time is marching on and our morning session will soon be over." They all knew he would exact his full fee for the agreed-upon hour, even if Julia had broken both her legs in the first few minutes and could not move at all to fill up the rest of the allotted time.

Calm again, Julia reached for her brother's arm. "Do not worry, Frederick, it was only a brief contact we made, a little stumble just now. I am fine, so let us continue." She was not vengeful, but she wished the King of Prussia would make his odious presence shorter and less obvious; how she wished daggers to him!

Frederick had regained his composure. "All right, Julia, Mother – and Sir." He did not like the dance master either and always managed to avoid saying his name if he could. "I apologize for my clumsiness just now and I am ready to begin again."

"Lovely, Master Darcy," the dance master replied, picking up his baton as his prim assistant, Miss Hegedus, started to play on the piano. "To your places, please." And so their practicing resumed.

Frederick's face hardened in concentration as he and Julia practiced their steps. Julia felt contrite for her rare outburst, despite the momentary pain caused by his booted foot stepping on her slippered one, so she kept on smiling at him. "Relax, Brother," she said in a low voice as they moved together. "Only about fifteen minutes more for today."

He still looked unhappy. "Today! Heaven help me then." He kept dancing and concentrating. No new stumbles yet, thank goodness. He brightened a little. "Thank you, Julia, for your patience. I am really sorry I stepped on your foot."

"It's all right, Frederick, I am not hurt." They executed their turns perfectly.

"I am very glad, much as I like these new boots."

"They are quite handsome, and manly," she said. "Careful now! We are coming up to that difficult transition with the other dancers." She meant Jane Elizabeth, who was practicing her dancing with Mr. Pressburg-Stilton as her partner. It was time for them to exchange partners. She heard his low thanks, and the exchange was performed flawlessly.

"Wonderful, Miss Darcy, and Miss Jane," Pressburg-Stilton

said, more approving than Mr. Haydock ever would be. "Well done, Master Darcy," he shrugged, and Frederick struggled to keep from grimacing. No, not much better than Haydock after all; why did he fare so poorly with older men who were teachers? "Now let us rest a minute before the next dance." They all forbore to mention his earlier concern about losing time due to stumbles and possible injuries.

Julia joined Frederick on one side of the room, while the dance master consulted with the stiff, colorless Miss Hegedus about the next piece to play. They enjoyed their brief time to rest, while she thought about their progress.

The lessons had gone well enough, though not incredibly so, due to the coolness between the instructor, the musician, and the two foremost pupils, not to mention the overall pressure of the debuts and Frederick's struggles. Though she loved her brother, Julia had to admit that, while he was not always clumsy or wooden in his movements, he was not becoming an accomplished dancer like Henry had been – only a competent one. The few times their father had stopped by to watch them he had been amused by it all, but then he was a fine dancer himself. Julia at first had been very patient with Frederick's mistakes in his footing and movements, especially making turns, which almost seemed to make him dizzy; sometimes he parted from her at the wrong moment or even bumped into her. But as one practice followed another, the constant, inconsistent demands of 'the King' and Frederick's struggles tried even Julia's patience, like they had this morning.

Julia prevented an inward sigh and reached for Frederick's hand. He looked surprised as she took it and smiled when she squeezed it. She really did appreciate all his efforts, even if he made frequent mistakes. As to Jane's thoughts about their debuts, she remained inscrutable even to Julia – also quite a surprise.

"All right, everyone," Pressburg-Stilton announced, "we are ready to begin again. Places!" Dutifully, Miss Hegedus began to play, the music pleasant but somehow missing much of its liveliness and tempo. Julia and Frederick began to dance and her heart was wrung by his frown of concentration. Even though he danced precisely and correctly, she could not stop herself. "Dear Brother, please relax – and smile! It will all seem easier to you, and more pleasurable, if you do."

Frederick gave a groan low enough for her to hear, but not loud enough for the instructor to notice. "What am I to do, Julia? If I am careful, I end up being graceless. If I am graceful, I end up being careless. Heaven help me! I would rather be lectured by Mr. Haydock, since I know what I would get from him. Though come to think of it, I think he has something in common with someone else with whom we are both acquainted."

"Shhh," Julia said, giggling. "You will be overheard and censured for it!" She thought for a moment. "Try this – let the music take over and let yourself float along with it – and you will be graceful and correct at the same time."

"I will try," he said, "but I do not find this is the type of music I can let myself 'float' along with during the dance." Julia giggled again, as both their mother and the instructor gave them warning looks. At last, Miss Hegedus played her final, firm, deliberate note, and the siblings gratefully came to a halt.

"Delightful, Miss Darcy," Pressburg-Stilton said with a pinched smile. "Rather improved, I would say – Master Darcy," he added, almost in an aside.

"Thank you – Sir," he replied, as Julia coughed into her handkerchief. "I was trying to float along with the music." Miss Hegedus smiled, while the instructor rolled his eyes.

"I see." He shrugged. "Well, young sir, I congratulate you and recommend you keep applying yourself to the task at hand."

"Yes, Frederick," Elizabeth spoke up, smiling. "You did look especially fine and graceful in that final dance."

"Thank you, Mother. Julia advised me on what to do."

"Well, it seems to have had the desired effect." Elizabeth smiled at her daughter.

Pressburg-Stilton cleared his throat. "Er, yes, Mrs. Darcy." He brightened as he opened his glittering watch. "My, how time flies, for our lesson is over for today." He turned to her. "Shall we practice again tomorrow morning at the same time?"

"Of course, Mr. Pressburg-Stilton." She did not seem to notice her children's resigned expressions.

"Then I shall collect my fee and bid you all a good day." At this, Miss Hegedus rose and stacked her music sheets in a loud, firm manner.

"Of course," Elizabeth said, suppressing a sigh of her own. "Would you and Miss Hegedus please follow me out?" She did not care for anyone who discussed money so openly in front of others during simple conversation. She thought she was probably old-fashioned about this, but the dance instructor refused to be paid in advance for an entire week's worth of lessons, or even one or two if he had not yet given them, which would have made it easier and less vulgar for everyone. Elizabeth supposed his insistence was probably due to some morbid sense of duty on his part, as if he would collect a fee for an entire week but expire at some point during it, before he could finish giving all the lessons. She also felt she was correct in thinking that his insistence on being paid after each lesson was probably due to other patrons forgetting or even refusing to pay him for his services. Yet, he had been highly recommended by several people whose opinions she trusted. Much as she did not care for the fussy, stuffy man or his faded, wraithlike assistant, Elizabeth would never give any indication of it, especially to her children.

Mr. Pressburg-Stilton and Miss Hegedus were not missed. Julia was drinking a glass of water, while Frederick tried to think of a way to cool off. He was removing his coat when Elizabeth returned and sat down.

"Mother," he said, "I am sorry to say so, but I am very grateful that our lesson is over for today."

"Nonsense, my dear," she said good-naturedly. She was well aware of what Julia and Frederick thought of the dance master. "You did very well today, especially in the final dances, as I said earlier."

Julia smiled, but he pouted. "I stepped on Julia's foot," he reminded them. "I know I am not a fine dancer, only an ordinary one." He could imagine Alex and Eric teasing him about his movements on the ballroom floor. Then he thought of something that made him brighten. "These formal dances can be very complicated and difficult to remember, but I can waltz!"

Julia gave him a look. "Anyone can waltz, Frederick."

Their mother surprised them by laughing. "Now stop it, Julia, please! You have done very well as always, and Frederick did well himself today. Besides," she gave them both a look, "there is nothing wrong with being able to waltz – nowadays, that is." She thought of waltzing with Darcy, and her pulse quickened.

"What do you mean by that, Mother?"

She laughed again. "I mean, dear Jane, that I was remembering back to when your father and I first met. It was before Napoleon's defeat – actually before both of them – and the waltz had not yet been brought over to England from Austria."

"When did it arrive?" Frederick asked.

"It must have been a year or two later, after the famous Congress in Vienna. But when your father and I met, no one of quality or distinction would dare to dance a waltz, even if they knew how! Yet, once it started, people kept waltzing and eventually it became popular."

"Why was it so badly regarded at first?"

"Well, Frederick, it was considered a dangerous, inappropriate, and shocking dance – immoral even – if you can believe it. Why? Because the man and the woman touch their hands together, the man puts his hand around his partner's waist to lead her, and so they dance very close to one another." She laughed a third time. "Even Mama would have been shocked! I did not dare to waltz in public for a few years, until it became popular! But now everyone does, even at Court, and we have all those delightful melodies of Lanner and Strauss to dance to."

"Yes," Julia sighed, "waltz music can be so beautiful."

"I like the idea of holding one's partner," Frederick grinned. "I certainly prefer it to all this parading about, turning, and exchanging partners."

Julia sighed again. "You would."

"Young men generally do," Elizabeth observed. She stirred in her chair. "However, these older, formal dances have their place, and still do, especially at Court. So, whether one is to debut and be presented, like you, Julia, and Jane, or one is to be a debutante's escort and present at balls along with royal and noble guests, like you, Frederick, you should all know how to dance properly."

Frederick laughed. "You offer a fine defense just now, Mother," he said. "I think you would make a fine barrister."

"Why, thank you, Frederick."

"I keep telling you there's no need to worry about any of it," Julia said, "especially about being presented at Court. I have heard that you dress in your finest, wait a long time, and it's all over in about one minute, maybe two."

"Are you nervous about being presented at Court?" he asked her.

"Yes," she admitted, "but only a little. I know I shall enjoy the experience and remember it for the rest of my life." She turned to him. "Are you nervous about it?"

"No," he smiled, "not I."

Julia giggled. "Liar!" Jane Elizabeth could not help herself and laughed.

"Julia!" Elizabeth exclaimed. Frederick had looked surprised at first, but now he was laughing. Shaking her head,

Elizabeth could not help herself either, joining in their laughter. "Frederick," she said, "do you maintain your denials, or has Julia found you out?"

He was still grinning. "She has found me out, Mother."

"I told you so!" Julia said.

"Well, whether you are both nervous or not, the season's events do not begin until next week," Elizabeth pointed out. "And that means there is still plenty of time to practice, like tomorrow morning, for instance!"

Both her son and daughter looked dismayed, and Elizabeth laughed herself for almost a full minute.

CHAPTER 8

The long-awaited evening had arrived. Julia had been ready to leave her room for almost twenty minutes but still sat at her vanity table so that she would not cause the slightest dishevelment to her appearance. She checked her reflection in the mirror for the hundredth time as she waited for the clock to chime.

She had finished her last session with the dance master yesterday morning; there were no more practices, only the time to dance for herself, her future, and her own pleasure. She suddenly wished Henry and Christina were near so she could tell them all about the balls and other season events, but toyed with her hairbrush as she let the thought slip away. There would be no tears or sadness tonight, or on any night during the next few weeks; she owed her parents too much for that.

Her eyes drifted back to the mirror. Here she was, seventeen years old, about to go off to the first ball of her London debut. Her dark hair was curled and swept up into a tasteful, mature, Grecian style and her soft blue satin gown with a white sash and lace frills was fabulous. She wore jewelry her mother had lent her, including a luminous string of pearls and matching earrings. Without arrogance or lack of modesty, Julia knew she would appear stunning; she hoped to dazzle many people tonight, whether young or old, male or female – but she hoped most of them would be eligible young men!

The clock chimed; it was time to go downstairs, where her family awaited her. She looked at herself one last time in the mirror, picked up her elegant, colorful wrap and dainty fan, extinguished the candles, and left the room, pulling the door closed behind her. She walked carefully but not slowly, and made her way down the grand staircase of the Cavendish

Square house; it was not as grand as Pemberley's but it took her a few moments, and she counted the steps as she descended. As she approached the drawing room she heard her family discussing plans for the ball. She began to smile and glided into the room, where suddenly all conversation abruptly ended.

"Julia, my dear!" Her father came over to her and gave her a careful kiss on the forehead. As he took her free, gloved hand, he said, "How beautiful you look tonight! Everyone will seek you out at the ball." He smiled broadly. "I have taken great care not to disarrange any part of your appearance."

"Thank you, Father." She blushed at his praise.

Again, Elizabeth did not worry about compliments leading to vanity. "Yes, dear daughter, you are beautiful in every way tonight. You are stylish and elegant, everything a young lady should be, and you will be a delight to everyone who beholds you." Julia blushed further and again murmured thanks.

Frederick now spoke up, taking the same care as their father not to get too close and cause the slightest change in her careful appearance. "I know your dance card will be filled tonight," he said, his eyes shining. "Will you only allow me two dances, or may I have more?"

As Julia thanked him, giggling, Elizabeth smiled. "That was very kind and chivalrous of you, but the whole point of this is to allow Julia as many partners as the rules of etiquette deem acceptable in one evening. Of course, you must dance with Jane as well."

"Naturally, Mother! It will also be my pleasure to dance with Jane!" This made Jane Elizabeth smile widely.

Nicholas' smile was broad, and all he could think of to say was, "How pretty and grown up you are!" He had seen his sister sparkle before, but not like this, and neither had Anne. As Julia swept over and kissed his cheek, Anne stood silent, rooted to the spot. Julia smiled as she waited for her sister's reaction, if she decided to give one. Anne gave her a complete examination, then stood back with a look of approval. Julia was pretty and poised, but tonight she looked like a confident young lady who would stun just about anyone. Julia did not press her to say anything and gave her a kiss as well.

"Dear Sister," Jane Elizabeth said, moving forward. She looked very mature in her own pastel pink satin gown with garnet jewelry and her hair swept up and curled, but she would not allow any attention for herself, so as not to detract from Julia's big moment and evening ahead. "You truly look magnificent tonight! We are all quite in awe of you." Mrs. Winston added her own warm compliments.

Julia exclaimed her thanks to both of them. "I know everything will go well from your reactions to my appearance," she smiled, "but it is still I, Julia, under all this finery, and there are going to be several more balls after this one."

"So that means we will have to keep complimenting you when you continue to dazzle us," Frederick said.

"That was very sweet of you! Remember, it is Jane's night as well, and see how fine and lovely she looks," Julia said, as her sister blushed at her compliments and those of the others, especially Mrs. Winston. "Now, let me see." She looked at them all.

It had been over six months since Christina's death, so her parents no longer wore their mourning black. Her father looked very handsome in a dark gray suit, white cravat, and a waistcoat the color of antiqued gold, with green accents; his graying hair complimented the darker shade of his suit. Her mother wore a dark blue dress with puffed sleeves and a full skirt, and a beautiful ruby necklace and earrings that matched the warm blush in her cheeks. Frederick looked quite handsome in a light brown suit with lapels and a velvet waistcoat of a darker shade of brown, and an emerald green silk cravat; his new boots shone and even his long, rather wavy hair seemed tamed for the evening, neither wild nor unkempt looking. Nicholas and Anne were too young to attend the ball and would remain home with Mrs. Winston, Miss Kendall, and the servants. Julia would be quite occupied during the ball, but knew Jane Elizabeth was anxious about attending without her companion, so she and Frederick would try to keep an eye on her.

Now Julia stepped back, nodding and smiling. "How fine you all look!" she exclaimed. "I think *all* of us will dazzle London society tonight."

"Oh, Julia," Elizabeth laughed, shaking her head.

Darcy glanced at the clock on the mantel, and Julia started. "Is it time to leave yet, Father?"

He turned to smile at her. "Surely you are not nervous about tonight?"

With everyone's eyes upon her, Julia faltered for the first time. "Well," she gave a shaky smile, "I suppose I am – just a little! Once the introductions are over and the orchestra begins to play the first dance, I shall be fine and give myself over to enjoyment – the proper kind, of course," she added, catching her mother's eye. "Now what about the rest of you?" She tried to sound prim. "Certainly not any of you can be nervous about such an evening, can you?" She did not need to ask Jane. This time she gave a confident smile, with just a trace of coquettishness.

Smiling, Elizabeth did not scold her. "Come now, you know everything will be just lovely. I cannot speak for everyone, but I am looking forward to this ball for many reasons." She anticipated dancing with her husband, who had always been known to be an excellent dancer – when he could be pressured, burdened, or outmaneuvered into doing so these days. And for so long there had been few moments or reasons to dance.

Darcy laughed. "I do not enjoy balls as much as our fair ladies do, I must admit, but I do look forward to your enjoyment and your successes tonight, Julia and Jane." He took Elizabeth's hand. "And, if she will consent to dance with me, I may be prevailed upon to dance with a most desirable and enchanting partner."

As their children exchanged glances, Elizabeth almost blushed herself. "Fitzwilliam, if she would consent!" She turned and gave him a special look their children could not see. "I believe she will consent most readily."

Julia smiled at their mutual warmth and turned to her brother. "Frederick?"

He did not answer right away and now wore a serious expression. Understanding what that meant, she said, "Do not worry, for we are ready to leave, and the evening's pleasures will begin, so there will be no time to be anxious." He started to smile and, satisfied, she turned to their parents. "Are we not ready to leave, Father?"

"We are," he agreed, "for it is time." They gathered their wraps and headed out into the main hallway toward the front door. Julia gave Jane a warm smile, almost skipping in anticipation; she didn't, though, to save her elegant slippers and avoid reminders from her mother.

The carriage ride to their destination was gentle and uneventful. Julia managed to keep her spirits under control and successfully resisted any temptation to fidget, even though every cobblestone they rolled over made her swallow. Frederick seemed lost in his thoughts, content to look out at all they were passing. Their parents chatted in low voices but soon lapsed into pleased silence. Darcy held Elizabeth's hand and they gave their children encouraging smiles, just as Julia tried to give Jane Elizabeth. Her sister acknowledged them with one of her own, but like their brother seemed more interested in looking out the carriage windows and listening to the gentle clattering of the wheels.

Their carriage joined the queue, a long line of vehicles that took up the entire drive and courtyard in front of Atherton House in Kensington, West London. Atherton House was a large, rambling Georgian-style mansion with several pairs of white columns supporting a wide covered porch over its entrance. Curved paved walkways gently rose from the court-yard to the tiled floor of the porch and massive front door. Now, carefully alighting from the carriage, giving her gloved hand to the coachman, Julia saw a long line of couples walk-ing up the eastern walkway to the porch, as empty carriages went past, quitting the courtyard. She exchanged interested glances with her siblings, taking in the fabulous house and all the queuing guests in their finery, as they joined the line mov-ing up to the mansion's entry.

Atherton House was the home of their hosts, Lawrence and Helena Darnley, Lord and Lady Oakland. The Earl of Oakland was a big, stocky man about fifty, with an imposing voice and florid face. He was active in politics and rumored to be one of the Prime Minister's confidants. Lady Oakland was a tall, proper woman of similar years, matronly and haughty only when she sensed breaches of propriety. The receiving line moved quickly, and Julia soon found herself being presented by her father to their hosts, whom she knew were giving this ball in honor of their daughter Emma's debut.

"Mr. Darcy!" The Earl extended his big hand as Lady Oakland gave a polite, welcoming smile. "How excellent it is to meet you at last, for I have heard much praise of the Master of Pemberley."

Darcy thanked them as he made his bows. "It is truly an honor for me and my family to be invited to your ball. May we offer you our congratulations on Miss Darnley's debut?"

"You may," the earl laughed, "and Lady Oakland and I are most gratified to receive them."

"You are most welcome," Darcy resumed, "and now may I present my wife, Elizabeth?"

Their hosts seemed quite impressed with Mrs. Darcy as they exchanged bows and curtsies. Lady Oakland expressed her pleasure at finally meeting the exquisite and vivacious

Mrs. Darcy, about whom she had heard so much. Elizabeth could still be incredulous that people of consequence could find her so interesting, for she visited London only occasionally; but sometimes she forgot the visibility of her position as Mistress of Pemberley.

Darcy now brought Julia forward, as Frederick and Jane deliberately held back. "I would like to present our daughter, Julia, to you." Julia smiled prettily, greeted them, and dropped into a deep, elegant curtsey. Their hosts could not contain their delight.

"How lovely you are, Miss Darcy!" Lord Oakland's smile reached to his ears as he helped her to her feet.

"Indeed," Lady Oakland exclaimed, "your daughter is so charming and beautiful, Mr. and Mrs. Darcy! I am certain you are quite proud of her, and rightly so!" She smiled at Julia's blush and gave her hand an affectionate pat. "We are quite overcome, Miss Darcy! We do hope you enjoy the ball."

"Thank you, Lord and Lady Oakland, for your warm compliments," Julia managed to say. "I hope I shall deserve them, for I am sure there are many accomplished and beautiful young ladies here this evening, including Miss Darnley. I am also certain your ball will be most enjoyable."

Everyone seemed pleased with her comments. Lady Oakland nodded to her husband, who now brought forth Emma. Miss Darnley was eighteen, tall with a classically beautiful face, perfect cheekbones, and a patrician nose that could make her look haughty. However, her green eyes, though veiled for propriety's sake, were friendly, and a small smile played about her thin but pleasing lips. She could not help liking and admiring Julia, not after that young lady's compliment to herself. Julia admired Emma in return, liking the simple but elegant dressing of her curled blond hair, as well as the soft lavender shade of her gown. The remaining Darcys expressed their delight at meeting Miss Darnley and were no less complimentary.

Emma Darnley had perfect manners, correct and cool but

pleasing, to complement her beauty. In a low alto voice, she thanked them for their sentiments. "I look forward to speaking more with Miss Darcy this evening about all kinds of subjects."

Julia was grateful that Miss Darnley had taken such a quick liking to her. "As do I, Miss Darnley," she said eagerly, "for nothing would please me more." Smiling, the two young ladies curtsied to each other and moved away so that Darcy and Elizabeth could present Frederick and Jane Elizabeth.

Frederick appeared to be at his best, in his perfect outfit and displaying his pleasing, good-natured demeanor. As he shook Frederick's hand, Lord Oakland was no less complimentary.

"What a fine, strapping young man your son is, Mr. Darcy!" he exclaimed as he kept pumping Frederick's hand. "And only nineteen! I am sure your dance card will be full this evening, young sir."

Frederick blushed but held his host's gaze. "Thank you very much, Lord Oakland, for your compliments! I may not be the most competent of dancers..." He glanced at Julia, who smiled at him. "But I will be dancing with my accomplished sisters." He brightened. "We all look forward to a most delightful evening." He felt warm and damp all over, and they had only just arrived!

The earl laughed, and Lady Helena complimented him on his sentiments. However, even she could not resist making her next remark, for she found him very handsome and agreeable. "Lord Oakland is correct," she said, "for I am certain you will be sought after tonight as many a young lady's partner." As Frederick blushed again and thanked her, she added, "Now I bid you to satisfy me in this – please save one dance for Emma, will you not, Master Darcy?"

Frederick smiled, his heart soaring in his damp chest. "Of course, I should be most pleased to dance with Miss Darnley." His parents' smiles could not be happier. Now if he could only go somewhere to cool off, but he knew he had duties to perform all night long, sweaty or dry.

Finally, it was Jane Elizabeth's turn to be presented. If Lord and Lady Oakland had heard anything connected with her mistakes, they gave no sign, and their greetings to her were as warm and welcoming as they had been to her parents and siblings. They congratulated her on making her debut and praised her most elegant appearance.

Jane Elizabeth was on her most sterling behavior in her greetings, curtsey, and replies and saw that their hosts' approval was not only given to Julia. She was grateful for the compliments she received, and Lord and Lady Oakland were not alone in observing that the younger Miss Darcy behaved similarly to their daughter Emma. Jane Elizabeth was determined to acquit herself well so that nothing she did or said would spoil Julia's debut or her own, and that her parents would be pleased with her. Now, as she rose and stepped back, smiling, she was relieved that it was time for them to move off into the assembly rooms, already loud and full of people, to start experiencing and enjoying the ball. The Darcy party moved forward, and Lord and Lady Oakland turned to greet their next guests, a young man named Simon Easton and his debuting sister, Pamela.

Lord and Lady Oakland's predictions proved correct, for both Julia and Frederick's dance cards filled up. As expected, Frederick led Julia out as his partner for the first dance, as all the escorts did their debutante partners; he could not help smiling broadly when he heard the opening notes of a familiar waltz. He reprimanded himself for thinking so much of his own pleasure instead of his sisters', but Julia just giggled and touched his arm – so he knew she was just as pleased. Anyone can waltz, he remembered her saying; so he enjoyed their first dance together, then danced with Jane Elizabeth.

Darcy had danced the first waltz with Jane Elizabeth, and then asked Julia for the next one; and, except for the final dance of the evening again with Frederick, Julia's dance card was open to all. After Jane, Darcy danced another waltz with Elizabeth, which they both enjoyed. By now, Julia had met so many people that she had trouble remembering them all, though she did much better at remembering her partners' names once she had danced with them.

Now came the first pause in the music, after several dances. Julia was not hungry, even though she knew dinner would not be served until much later in the evening. She looked over the trays of enticing appetizers but did not sample any. Still, she was quite warm and thirsty from all the dancing, so she drifted over to a refreshment table, with Frederick following close behind. So many people and so many scents – perfumes, pomades, colognes, and whatever else – filled the air, and made the rooms warm and stuffy. Julia wanted to swallow her punch as soon as Frederick handed it to her, but forced herself to take the dainty sips she was expected to. Frederick's gloved hand patted hers, and he quickly refilled her glass. She whispered, almost gasped, her thanks. Smiling, he excused himself to go check on Jane Elizabeth, who was sitting close by.

Julia went to refill her punch glass yet again, when a young man who had had his back to her suddenly turned towards her. He gasped but stopped himself in time, and Julia was able to prevent spilling the punch either on him or herself.

"I am so dreadfully sorry!" the young man exclaimed. "How clumsy of me, Miss – Miss –" He looked so sorrowful and helpless that she smiled.

"There is no need to apologize, Sir." She noticed the rich sheen of his suit, silk shirt, and cravat, the large, sparkling rings on both hands and his dark, curly hair and side-whiskers. "Nothing unfortunate has happened." She looked into his clear blue eyes.

"Thank you for your patience and understanding," he said,

sounding relieved. "There are so many people about that it is hard not to go barreling and bumping into people in this crush at the tables." His face became calmer and more pleasant. "I could not forgive myself for injuring a young lady or causing any damage to her beautiful appearance."

Julia felt her cheeks pinking. "Thank you, Sir."

"Not at all! But you must be wary of me all the same, for I am quite clumsy."

She smiled. "I cannot agree, for I have not seen such behavior from you."

He gave a pleasant laugh. "Thank you, again, Miss – er, Miss –"

She took pity on him. "I am Julia Darcy." She curtsied, and Frederick returned. "May I now present my brother to you?" The young man nodded, looking expectantly at Frederick. "Sir, this is my brother, Frederick." She giggled. "However, I do not yet know your name, so I do not know how to introduce you properly."

"No need to worry, Miss Darcy," he laughed, bowing to them, which Frederick returned. "I am Sir Timothy Carlisle, of London and Rochester."

"We are most pleased to meet you, Sir Timothy," Frederick replied, liking him. "Julia is making her debut, as well as our younger sister Jane, and I am trying to keep up with them on the ballroom floor."

"You danced very well," Sir Timothy said in reply, then realized he had admitted watching them – her? Somewhat flustered, he added, "One could not help noticing how beautifully you danced that first waltz."

Frederick thanked him as she smiled. "Julia is the accomplished dancer. It most definitely helps to have the appropriate partner."

"Indeed, it does." Young Sir Timothy sounded relieved that they took no offense at his slip. He gave a crooked smile. "May I prevail upon you then, Miss Darcy, to allow me a dance this evening? That is, if your card is not completely full already."

Julia felt a pang and gazed at him with regret. "I am sorry, Sir Timothy, but I am afraid that it is quite full." She noticed his expression change slightly. "However, I shall promise you that if for any reason one of my partners is unable to perform his duty, I would be happy to dance with you – that is, if *you* are not otherwise engaged at the time." Her smile was rueful, for she suddenly wanted to dance with this handsome young man and feel the fabulous material in his coat brush against her dress. Frederick's eyes moved back and forth between them.

"I understand completely," Sir Timothy replied, bowing to her again. "I appreciate your delicacy and consideration, and hope we will have the opportunity to dance very soon." He smiled and turned to go. "Let me leave you both to your recreation before the orchestra begins playing again. I am most grateful to have met you both." Smiling again, he moved off after they expressed a similar sentiment.

Her eyes dropped only an instant. "You would really like to dance with him, wouldn't you?" Frederick asked. She could only smile. "Why don't I sit out the last dance," he said eagerly, "and you can dance with Sir Timothy? And, if you do end up having an opening earlier, I can dance with you then – or not, if there's someone else you rather would."

"No, Fred," she said firmly. "Thank you very much for trying to indulge me in this pleasure. I would like to dance with Sir Timothy Carlisle, but my card is full and Mother and Father will want you to dance the final one tonight with me as they intended, since it is the first ball of the season." She gave a brave smile. "Perhaps I will have the opportunity to dance with Sir Timothy at the next ball."

"Perhaps," Frederick shrugged. "I am sorry about Sir Timothy, for he seems quite likable." He looked around. "Please allow me to spend another few moments with Jane."

"Yes, of course! Let me come with you." They went to where their sister sat, serene and content. As Julia did, though, her eyes traveled the room for the tall young man with the dark curly hair, wearing the silky rich, rust-colored suit.

Julia could hear the orchestra tuning up, and she was about to be claimed by her next partner. She was now regretting her promise, but there was no way she could extricate herself from the two dances promised, to try and claim Sir Timothy in her partner's place. Her spirits were starting to return to normal when she heard her name.

"Miss Darcy, may I have the pleasure of claiming your hand for the next two dances, as promised?"

Sir Timothy was tall, handsome, pleasant, and elegant in his shiny clothes, but this young man took her breath clean away. In front of her stood Louis Calvert, Lord Ravenswood. Her partner turned out to be equally tall, blond, with hazel eyes and a heroic, cleft chin. His dark clothes fit him perfectly, tailored to display his well-muscled, athletic body. His side-whiskers were full, his voice deeper than Sir Timothy's, and she felt a thrill when he smiled at her.

They chatted amiably as they danced. He held her perfectly, and she liked the gentleness of the gloved hand that held hers. She could not feel his touch as he guided her, it was so light. She found Lord Ravenswood to be outgoing, witty, and an excellent dancer – and as charming as Sir Timothy. When their second dance ended, he bowed to her and left her weak in the knees.

Feeling shaky inside, she sat down next to Jane to contemplate those she had met so far. She found Lord Ravenswood attractive, but so were Sir Timothy and several other young men she had met and danced with. Still, she rather forgot Sir Timothy and his fancy clothes in favor of the handsome, polished, charming lord. She began to wonder what it would be like to touch his side-whiskers, then scolded herself for giving in to such thoughts! No, she would not, and could not, do such a thing. However, she couldn't help thinking about him during the rest of the evening. Whom would she sit between at dinner, and would she be able to maintain her composure, depending on who that was?

Still, as wonderful as this first ball was turning out to be, not everything went perfectly. Julia saw Sir Timothy laughing with a young woman she was later introduced to, a Miss Honoria Lucas. She also had a few partners with whom she did not enjoy dancing at all for one reason or another, but she behaved perfectly and hid her disappointment well. Her full dance card helped her avoid many older or less attractive men, like the one with over-oiled hair and garlic on his breath, and another young man who had obviously drunk too much wine. After her polite refusal, he suddenly turned green and lurched out of the room so he could empty his stomach into something in time, she supposed. Shaking her head, Julia tried to smile again, hoping she wouldn't overhear any of the other guests condemning the poor young fellow for his vulgar behavior.

She did have a few obligatory dances with older men that were pleasant but she expected nothing from, though they all professed to be quite taken with her – Lord Oakland himself; the Earl of Chester; the Earl of Ravenswood, Louis Calvert's father; and a very nice gentleman who turned out to be Vice Admiral Halsey, of the Royal Navy. Still, she was very grateful when her brother claimed her hand for the final dance of the evening. She smiled at him, which he returned with a pleased but peaked one.

"I'm so glad this last dance is a slower one," she said, "for I am quite exhausted."

"Poor sister!" Frederick commiserated, then lightened his tone. "If only Mr. Pressburg-Stilton and Miss Hegedus could see us now…" He drifted off to concentrate on his footwork. He still felt damp all over, but his boots maintained their shine. He was trying to watch out for her feet, but fatigue made him careless, and his foot bumped hers. He made a slight frustrated sound as his head drooped. "Sorry about that."

"Forgiven." Julia smiled but could not help giving a slight

roll of her eyes. "Yes, if only! Of course, I know he would compliment my dancing, and criticize yours."

Frederick delighted her by giving her a graceful turn. "That was very adroitly done," she complimented him. "Are you sure you don't like to dance?"

They came to a graceful halt as the music ended. "I don't really," he said, giving her a weak smile. "Are you happy, Julia," he asked, taking her gloved hand in his, "and are you enjoying the ball?"

"Oh, ever so much!"

His smile grew. "Hungry?"

She blinked. "Why, yes, I am quite famished." She smiled back. "And what about yourself? You must be starving!"

"Oh, I am," he admitted, "but then I am always happy to eat something." Laughing together, they joined their parents and Jane Elizabeth as they entered one of the queues snaking into the dining rooms.

As she approached her place at the table, she noticed people whispering and looking in her direction, but this time the glances were more open, less friendly, and certainly not all positive or approving. One young man and woman gave her cool, condescending looks and two older women's expressions were dour. The first dark-haired lady was whispering to the second one, older with wispy blond hair, but as careful as they tried to be, Julia heard them both quite clearly across the table, despite the loud level of noise resulting from so many conversations going on at once in the dining hall.

"Is that not the girl who tried to drown herself, Miss Darcy, isn't it? How dreadful! And daring to come out here!" The lady made an indignant sound.

"No, Ansonia, that was her younger sister, who is also making her debut and is somewhere about now. This one, the elder Miss Darcy, has done nothing I know of."

"Cornelia, you know as much as I do how improper this is!" hissed the first lady. "Bringing along a little bundle of trouble to her debut, even if they are sisters. It cannot be borne!"

"It is indeed unfortunate. Miss Darcy seems like such a beautiful creature, but she is hopelessly tainted by her sister's behavior which, I am sure you have heard, has been *quite* forward –"

At this point, Julia had to move ahead towards her place, and so passed out of earshot of the two gossipers. She felt her face burning but forced herself to keep her smile pleasant, and her eyes from falling. She quickly looked around, at the risk of appearing inquisitive, ill-mannered, or impolite, to see if she could find Jane Elizabeth. Ah, there she was, further down on the other side of the table, with Frederick by her side, but on the same side as the two women, though they were not close to them. Her siblings saw and smiled at her, and she returned theirs. Julia began to relax; she realized it was unlikely either one of them had heard the women's comments, considering where they stood in line; Julia had only heard them as she passed directly across from them.

She finally reached her assigned place and was very gratified to be seated between Lord Ravenswood on her left and the friendly, laughing Simon Easton on her right. Mr. Easton had already settled his sister, Pamela, at his right, then held out Julia's chair for her – anticipating Lord Ravenswood by mere seconds. The young lord's eyes darkened and his fine jaw tightened ever so slightly, but he smiled and held out the chair on his left for Miss Lucinda Peterbrooke, a close friend of Miss Darnley. With Lord Oakland seated at the head of the long table, and Lady Oakland a mile away at the foot, Julia found Miss Darnley seated near her father and next to Sir Timothy Carlisle.

Julia was pleased to see Frederick and Jane Elizabeth take their places and knew her parents were quite favored in their own seats on the same side, as she struggled to hear their host at the head of the table. However, Julia was startled to see the two gossipers sitting across from her! The dark-haired lady turned out to be Mrs. Ansonia Porter-Douglas, who with her debuting daughter, Henrietta, flanked her husband, while she learned the other woman was Mrs. Cornelia Ruth-Davis, a widow, who was attending with her daughter, Eliza, another debutante, and her brother, Ben. She smiled at them, hoping for something positive; both women nodded to her without any friendliness whatsoever. Julia was shaken enough to bump her fine crystal water glass, but it stayed upright. She smiled again at the two ladies, who looked away; but Miss Porter-Douglas and Miss Ruth-Davis continued to regard her with interest, as did young Mr. Benjamin!

And so it begins, she thought dully; she should have expected this. Indeed, she had expected it – but up until now the evening had gone so well that she thought that all of them, and she in particular might be spared gossip and censure in public. This was not to be. No, news of what had occurred made it to the capital in time for her debut, and Julia wondered who the individuals were that had done the spreading. She had hoped to cause whispers only in response and admiration of her own sparkling qualities. Well, that did not matter now.

Suppressing a sigh, she remembered her declaration of strength and purpose to her sisters back home months ago. She would simply have to prepare for battle like she knew she would – battle of the most polite and appropriate kind, of course. She thought about it some more and decided she appreciated the fact that she had overheard those gossiping women who continued to give her cold glances. She was now certain of what she had to face, and how she would fight it. She would tell Frederick at some point, probably soon; she didn't want to upset him, for she knew he could become justifiably angry over the injustice of it, but realized he would need to know.

She smiled at the wide, low bowl of thick, green watercress soup being placed in front of her. Thank God for something to eat at last! As she lifted her spoon, she widened her smile and turned to acknowledge Mr. Easton's entertaining comments about his latest fishing trip in the lake country.

"Have you ever gone fishing, Miss Darcy?"

She laughed. "No, I cannot say that I ever have, though Pemberley's streams are full of fish, but it is obviously something that you enjoy."

"Come, Simon," laughed Miss Easton. "Of course, proper young ladies like Miss Darcy do not go fishing, any more than I would! Such boring, dirty work, the kind that only men could like. Surely Miss Darcy cannot be interested in such a pastime!"

The jocular Mr. Easton looked abashed, so Julia spoke up. "Well, I may know nothing about the sport of fishing, that is true, but please tell us more about the lake country! I have not been fortunate to visit it yet, and I hear it is quite beautiful."

"Oh, it certainly is that, Miss Darcy!" Brother and sister looked relieved and pleased, and he was happy to oblige her in a much more interesting topic of conversation.

Later, Lord Ravenswood reclaimed her attention and fascinated her with descriptions of his long visit to America the previous year. As she listened to his fine, cultured voice, not the least pedantic or condescending, her eyes briefly traveled to the head of the table where Sir Timothy Carlisle sat in that fine silky suit of his. Never had she seen a man, young or otherwise, wear such rich, light-reflecting material. She thought how wonderful it would be to touch and admire its sheen and softness; it was so unlike the heavier solid or patterned wool of a man's normal attire. Her thoughts surprised her.

Sir Timothy caught her glance and quickly raised his glass to her with a smile. She acknowledged his with her own, then almost laughed as both Lord Ravenswood and Simon Easton addressed remarks to her at the same time. The young lord won this time, and Mr. Easton subsided for the moment.

Julia was careful to sip her wine, but heavily relied on her water glass; to her delight, it was constantly being refilled. Really, how warm it was in this vast dining room! But she continued to enjoy her dinner and those seated around her, except for the two haughty mothers across the table.

She politely consigned them both to the Devil, with the proper decorum that required, and took another sip of water. Oh, that Mr. Ben Ruth-Davis, a pleasant but ordinary-looking young man with long, thick dark hair, was looking at her again. She gave a small smile, then carefully looked for her parents and siblings. Luckily, she caught her parents in a rare moment when they were not engaged in conversation, and they exchanged smiles. Julia was pleased to see Frederick being quite sociable, and she noticed he was very attentive to their sister on his right, and a Miss Marianne Morton on his left. Miss Morton obviously liked her brother, based on the way she gazed upon his face, but apparently she wasn't the only one. Julia espied another young lady, this one much more attractive than Miss Morton, a raven-haired beauty with deep green eyes and full red lips, looking in Frederick's direction. Julia marveled at her tasteful elegance; who was she? Julia tried to remember, for she had met so many people tonight, debutantes, all their relatives and escorts, and so many more. Suddenly, she had it – Rosamund Woodleigh was her name, though Julia could not remember anything at all about her family. Well, no matter. However, she saw Miss Woodleigh give her brother several glances that strained the bounds of propriety, though she kept her manner and expression discreet. Julia suspected the young lady did not care, but could not criticize her for it, for hadn't she let her own eyes go searching more than once for Sir Timothy? Julia smiled to herself. She had something she considered teasing Frederick about, for he seemed oblivious to Miss Woodleigh's interest in him. She wanted to shake her head; well, that was Fred. Julia was happy to notice that Jane Elizabeth looked happy and pleasant herself, engaged in a discussion with the young man on her right, a Mr. Martin Tourneur, who sported a fine, thick mustache, and long, wavy dark hair.

Now she exclaimed with delight at the dessert being placed in front of her, a soufflé dressed in cream and fresh fruit.

"After such a fine feast, Miss Darcy, you are still able to enjoy your dessert?" Lord Ravenswood asked. They both knew his question was improper, but she laughed and gave a good-natured answer.

"Well, my lord, this banquet has been nothing short of fabulous, and I am determined to enjoy every moment and morsel of it." She dropped her glance. "I will admit to you, however, that such a lovely ball can be quite taxing for a young lady. I was so wonderfully engaged in dancing that I had no time to sample the enticing appetizers I saw all around me, so I was quite dizzy – and famished – by the time the dancing ended."

Overhearing this exchange, Simon and Pamela Easton both laughed. "In fact," Julia declared, "I do not think I could have danced one more time without fainting." She smiled then to let them know she was not serious.

"I quite understand, Miss Darcy." Lord Ravenswood was laughing. "Forgive me for my impertinent question! But I do like to see a young lady enjoying her dinner."

"As do both my parents, I can assure you, my lord," was her rejoinder, and she joined Lord Ravenswood and the Eastons in their laughter.

Lord Oakland reclined in his great armchair among the wreckage of their dining hall. The clock was chiming three o'clock as Lady Helena swept over and sat down with him. Servants still scurried about, cleaning up and clearing away. Lord Oakland watched them with a benevolent air as he nursed a liqueur and shook off sleepiness.

"Well, my dear," he addressed his lady, "I believe our fine staff will have the house put back to rights in a matter of hours." He patted her hand with his big, fleshy one.

"Of course they will," she replied, though she was very tired. "Have no fear of that. Still, I do believe the ball was quite successful."

A deep, satisfied sound came from his broad chest. "It most certainly was! I could have not hoped for more! My dear Helena, you outdid yourself. Thank you for organizing such a successful evening!"

She smiled, thanking him. "It was my pleasure to give everyone else pleasure."

"Though the cost is ruinous!" He gave a booming laugh. "But I do not care. I know how special an evening you wanted it to be for Emma, and it was." He patted her hand again.

Smiling, Lady Helena repeated her thanks. "Yes, Lawrence, I too am very satisfied with the evening, especially for Emma's sake." They reflected on their daughter's obvious enjoyment of the ball, though there would be more of them to come. "Well, Emma is now out and on her way," she remarked, blinking the tiredness from her eyes. "I know our daughter will be successful in attracting offers from eligible young men, and I believe this will make her happy."

He nodded. "Our dear Emma will not be the only young lady who will be so happy, for we had a house full of pretty young ladies making their debuts, did we not?" She assented. "So many, and where do they all come from?"

Lady Helena laughed. "You know where they all come from, for we are acquainted with many of their families." Lord Oakland enjoyed young people, especially young ladies; he enjoyed dancing with them and teasing them in a fatherly or avuncular way. Lady Helena didn't mind, for her husband was kind, outgoing, and pleasure-loving, but always decent and proper.

"Were they not a wonderful group of young ladies to open the season?" He was smiling over his glass. "I hope Emma will become friends with some of them. Miss Peterbrooke, delightful! Miss Morton, very sweet and friendly! And Miss Cecilia Calvert, Lord Ravenswood's sister – what a lovely little thing she has turned out to be! Shyness can be quite attractive, I find."

"Then, my dear husband, do not leave out the confident, interesting Miss Easton, and the Porter-Douglas and Ruth-Davis girls seemed quite nice, to name a few more."

He laughed. "Well, I can think of one lovely young lady that outshined them all, except for our dear Emma, of course."

She nodded. "You refer to Miss Julia Darcy."

He sat up straight in his chair. "I do. What a beautiful, exquisite creature she is! Why, if she is not engaged before the season is over, I shall never believe it."

Lady Helena smiled again. "Yes, she is stunning; there is no other word for it. She dazzles without any kind of exaggeration, condescension, or premeditation. It must come naturally to her, for her charms are so artless and yet so pleasing. Her manners cannot be improved upon; she is friendly but not flirtatious, and she dances beautifully." She sighed with pleasure. "I am certain she can sing like an angel! Yes, Miss Darcy's star is clearly high up in the social firmament. She is worthy of only the best of men."

He regarded her from beneath his bushy brows. "Did not Miss Darcy also have a sister who attended our ball?" he asked carefully. "Do you remember meeting her, and what were your impressions? Does the younger Miss Darcy resemble her sister?"

"Yes, the younger Miss Darcy – I believe her name is Jane – was making her debut tonight as well." She looked at her husband. "I do remember meeting her." She shrugged. "Miss Jane is not stunning like Miss Darcy, but she is pretty enough, with much intelligence and fine manners of her own. She is not as outgoing as her older sister, but I am sure she will make a fine match of her own in good time."

He had finished his liqueur and indicated a servant to bring his wife something. "Is she not the young lady who tried to drown herself back home in Derbyshire?" He saw his wife's expression and was contrite. "I am so sorry to mention it, after such a wonderful evening, but am I not correct?"

"You are." She gave a flustered sigh. "I had heard about it through the Woodvilles and the Coleridges, not that any of them were being unpleasant about it. Quite the contrary, in fact – they were very supportive of the Darcys because they are related through marriage." She sipped her small drink. "Well, it is all very sad and depressing, but, yes, apparently this Miss Jane Darcy got herself mixed up with a boy near the estate, and when people treated her so horribly for it, she tried to," she paused, "end her life. Her brother rescued her from her chosen fate." Her face showed distaste. "People can be so awful! She should not have behaved as she did, but to hound and insult her so as I was told she was! It was quite cruel, I tell you."

"The poor creature," her husband said, quieted by her strong reaction. "The girl was not ruined, was she?"

She did not flinch. "No, thank God, they were prevented from *that*, in time. The boy was punished, too. However, I sometimes forget how cruel people can be, especially over something like this." She put her glass down and lightened her tone. "Well, Miss Jane has been living here in London for months with her cousins, and she seems pleasant and well-behaved enough, I daresay. I cannot find any fault with her. I can detect no sadness or indifference in her, either; and if any wildness or instability of temperament remains, I did not see any evidence of it tonight."

He reached over and squeezed her plump hand. "I am very glad of that, Helena. It must mean she is well again and has learned her lesson."

"I should hope so, but I believe she has."

They sat in silence for a moment, then he roused himself. "Did not Master Darcy, their brother, make a fine appearance as well?"

Lady Helena had noticed her husband's liking and approval of the young man. Her husband was a good man and father, very proud of their only child, Emma. He enjoyed meeting the young men as well as the young ladies. "Yes, Master Frederick Darcy is a young man anyone could be proud of; he looks just like his father."

"Just as Miss Julia strongly resembles her mother."

"That is true. But as handsome as he is, Master Frederick I have been told is not as good-looking as his late older brother was."

"Ah, yes, the young man that was killed, was it last year?" He shook his head. "Such a dreadful thing. How much the Darcy family seems to have suffered recently." He brightened. "Well, Fitzwilliam Darcy is fortunate to have been blessed with many sons and daughters!"

"I know you were quite impressed with the young man."

"I was," Lord Oakland said with satisfaction. "What a fine, intelligent, strong fellow he is! I would not be surprised if *he* attracted as much attention tonight as his sister did. He seemed quite sociable, but do you think he noticed all the attention the young ladies were giving him?"

"He was sociable enough, with pleasing manners and a splendid appearance overall," Lady Helena agreed warmly, "but I do not think he noticed many of the young ladies. I think he was just concentrating on being the perfect escort for his sisters."

He laughed. "Of course, you are right, my dear!" He gave her a teasing look. "So, you think that Master Frederick made a splendid appearance overall? What about all that hair?" he joked. "I also do not think I have ever seen a young man perspire so much in such a short time."

"Oh, Lawrence!" she scolded, but laughed herself. "Yes, his hair is – everywhere. But how could he not be flushed and in such a state, after we both flattered him so outrageously? What will Mr. and Mrs. Darcy think of us?"

"I think they will be very grateful to us for hosting tonight's ball," he answered. "Now, my dear wife, let us get some well-deserved rest after your most successful evening."

"Our successful evening," she gently corrected him. They rose from the table and retired upstairs to their private quarters.

However, Lord and Lady Oakland were wrong about one thing. Frederick had returned to Cavendish Square along with his parents and sisters. It was very late, and all of them were tired, though quite happy and sated with the evening's pleasures. Julia had warm kisses for everyone as she glided upstairs to take her well-deserved rest. Jane Elizabeth followed her with contented strides, and Frederick turned away when he saw his mother place her head briefly on his father's shoulder.

Frederick trudged upstairs, his fine clothes wilted and rumpled, and his boots heavy on his feet. Once inside his room, he stripped off his finery and, with his shirt open to his waist, clad only in his trousers and stockinged feet, he sat down weakly.

It had been a wonderful evening, and he had enjoyed it much more than he had expected to. But his vision was starting to swim from fatigue, as he recalled the long evening, the ball, and the banquet. The explosion of light from so many candles. The army of footmen and serving women, and the dozens upon dozens of guests in their glittering finery. The roar of the crowds, the loudness of the orchestra (though the musicians had played well), and the warmth and heaviness of the air. All the dancing – how his feet ached – not to mention all the food and drink. He forgot how many glasses of wine he'd quaffed, but it was at least three.

He shook his head to clear it and looked down at himself. He was still hot and sweaty from the long night. He had wanted to take a bath when he got home to the square, but it was too late for that and he needed to sleep first. Still, he was so uncomfortable that he took a towel, dipped it in some cold water from the pitcher on the nightstand, and swabbed it over his damp chest, neck, and face. That refreshed him some.

He had noticed several young ladies ogling him all night long. He had expected some of it because this was London during the debutante season, where his family wasn't well known, and because it was Julia's debut. However, he had completely failed to realize people – especially young ladies – might be interested in him as well.

He had never been surrounded by so many beautiful women before, and he was unused to such attention directed at him. Those experiences in Cambridge with the loud, tactless streetwalkers still bothered him, and he was completely unprepared for a night like this one. No one did or said anything that shocked him, but he felt on display the whole time. He kept thinking how pretty and lively each young lady was that he met but, in truth, it excited and frightened him in ways he was only beginning to understand. Yes, their smiles, pleasantries, and touches – tasteful ones, while dancing – disturbed him in a new and different way, and he was unable to forget them. Would he see these young lovelies again at the next ball? He hoped he would; then he sighed and wiped himself down with more cold water.

He felt giddy and restless, but now exhaustion was conquering his body and senses. He struggled into his nightshirt and collapsed into bed. He just wanted to sleep and forget about all the young ladies with their hair up, covered in jewelry, and parading about in their fine gowns and form-fitting bodices. But, as tired as he was, it took a while. He kept seeing them, one after another, even after he closed his eyes. God, he was tired! He moaned and stretched in bed. If he could only sleep – what was happening to him? A sudden fear shot through him.

What if all this attention caused him to lose his composure? Julia and their parents were counting on him to do his best! This debut was for her sake and Jane's, wasn't it? He turned on his side in frustration; would sleep ever come? No, he decided, half awake; he would not lose his composure over all these silly girls and ruin Julia's debut. He was her brother and escort; Henry would have done the same if he were alive. Then he thought of Marianne Morton laughing at one of his jokes – where had his wit come from, and why did she think it was amusing? He also remembered enjoying his dances with Emma Darnley and Pamela Easton, in particular. Maybe with the right partners he could learn to enjoy dancing, like his father did. Then he thought of all their lowered glances, shy giggles, and perfect maidenly responses, their dainty hands and swelling bosoms.

He moaned louder and cried out for sleep. Now he understood – he was becoming moonstruck like his friend Eric when he'd fallen for the pert, pretty barmaid Sally. He knew Eric and Alex would tease him mercilessly over all the attention a crop of pretty young ladies had paid him tonight. "God save me from such a fate," he breathed, though he didn't specify whether he meant deliverance from his friends' teasing or the young women's attentions. Maybe it was time for him to have a talk with his father about such feelings? He closed his eyes again and pulled up the covers. He decided he liked the idea of pretty girls admiring him.

And with that, his body relaxed and he fell asleep.

CHAPTER 9

The second ball of the season was underway. Louis, Lord Ravenswood, was hosting it at Woodside, the family's London mansion, in honor of his sister, Miss Cecilia Calvert, who was making her debut. Julia was excited to be invited to his home and looked forward to dancing with him more than once if she could manage it. She also hoped to see Sir Timothy Carlisle in whatever fabulous clothing he would choose to wear, as well as the Eastons and many others she had met at Atherton House. Her spirits were high, and Frederick resumed his responsibilities with good-natured amusement.

The evening had begun well, but during the extended introductions and renewing acquaintances, something finally occurred that Frederick had dreaded but almost forgotten about during the feverish preparations for the debut. He and Julia were just concluding a pleasant conversation with another debutante, Angelina Molyneux, and her brother, Alan, a major dressed in a fine red coat and shimmering tall black boots, when he heard someone come up behind him, and exhale.

"Well, if it isn't Frederick Darcy!"

Frederick slowly turned around to find Richard Grantley standing there with an unpleasant sneer on his face, and two young women, probably his sisters. Richard would appear much more handsome if he kept his expression more pleasing, Frederick thought. His spirits sank further when he also saw Rod Urquhart there with his sister. Thankfully, Jane Elizabeth was off somewhere else at that moment.

"My pleasure, ladies," Frederick said, bowing to them. "Grantley and Urquhart. May I present my sister, Julia?"

The older of the two young women standing near Richard was pretty, with a mass of tight blond ringlets all over her head, and appeared to be about eighteen. She looked Julia up and down and gave a brief curtsey. Julia gave her a proper one in return and looked at Richard.

"My sister, Susannah," Grantley said carelessly. "She is making her debut this season, and this is my other sister, Isabelle." He indicated the younger girl who appeared to be only a little older than Jane Elizabeth, also golden-haired and somewhat pretty, but looking rather haughty and cross.

Julia curtsied and greeted her with warmth, but the younger girl said nothing as she returned the curtsey. "I am very pleased to meet you, Miss Grantley and Miss Isabelle," Julia tried again, but they just stared at her. She blinked in confusion, not knowing what to do.

Good God, this was awkward! Frederick turned and bowed to Rod's sister.

At least Rod had better manners than Richard; he returned Frederick's bow. "How nice to see you again, Darcy," he said politely. "Allow me to present my sister, Rachel, who is making her debut."

Rachel Urquhart was a pleasant-looking young lady with dark hair swept back into an elegant bun. She was not as attractive as the Grantley sisters, but she had a full face and friendly air about her. "I am very happy to meet you, Miss Darcy," Rachel said, and they exchanged curtsies; she seemed the only one to be sincere in her greetings.

Julia hoped the worst was over; she was unused to such ill manners and obvious disdain aimed at her. Rod Urquhart bowed to her in greeting, but Richard Grantley just inclined his head to her, as if she were barely worth noticing. Like her brother, Julia was glad Jane Elizabeth seemed to be elsewhere and prayed she would not join them until they had managed to find more congenial companions with which to socialize.

"Did you miss Cambridge, Darcy?" With a glint in his eye, Richard turned to his sisters. "Darcy was sent down, you know, for gambling and other bad behavior."

Julia gasped, and Rachel took her arm as she gave her

brother a look. Rod sighed and managed to exclaim, "Richard!" at the same time as Susannah.

Blinking, Frederick kept his tone mild. "Well, Miss Grantley, Miss Isabelle, and Miss Urquhart, I must certainly own up to my mistakes, of which I have made several." He kept his voice light, while Rachel smiled nervously and Richard's sisters nodded. "I did miss Cambridge after I was sent down, but I have been back for two successful terms, as you know, Richard, and I will continue my studies after the debut season is over. There is too much to do and see here in London to miss Cambridge now." He gave a crooked smile. Julia was about to say something, but he gave her a quick look and she remained silent. Goodness, how badly all of this was going!

"Well, I suppose Haydock and all the regents can be prevailed upon to take anyone back – especially if the Master of Pemberley is doing the persuading. It would not surprise me if even Haydock can be bought."

Julia gasped again and hated herself for losing her composure. Rod shook his head at Richard, but Susannah smiled at this insulting remark, and her sister laughed. How odious these young people were!

Rachel's comments were firm. "My brother, Mr. Grantley, tells me that Mr. Haydock is so relentless and unyielding, that it would be quite impossible for him to be bribed into doing such a thing, much less anything else." She remained unsmiling until she turned to Frederick. "Well, Mr. Darcy, I am sure that you were welcomed back at Cambridge, and that you are well established there now." Julia gave her a grateful look.

"Thank you, Miss Urquhart." He bowed to her again. "I do agree with your assessment of our headmaster, and I assure you that I have improved in my behavior, as well as my studies." She seemed pleased with his answer.

Susannah tried to make up for her smile at his expense earlier. "How conscientious of you to admit your prior difficulties." She gave a more pleasant smile. "I am glad to hear how much you desired to return to Cambridge and your friends." Frederick thanked her.

Richard did not like any thawing between his sisters and what he considered to be a whelp of a Darcy. "Welcome back, then," he said carelessly, "not that anyone really noticed that you were gone; it's not as if your grades were very high, in any event."

Frederick blinked in dismay; he felt his sides stiffen with cold anger but couldn't lose his composure for Julia's sake. She remained mortified and he could not tell if she were about to cry or make a retort. He was desperate to end the conversation as civilly as he could and get her away before Jane Elizabeth could join them.

"No, they were not, that is true." He tried to smile. Rachel and Susannah nodded, but Isabelle disdainfully tossed her head. "However, since my return, I have been studying very hard. I have done very well these past two terms and am eager to continue in my new courses next term. Besides," he tried to joke, "you must have had an examination on which you did poorly, eh, Richard? For you consumed as much ale as I did – oh, I am sorry, ladies, for making that admission. And you too, Rod?" Silence. "Er, didn't you?"

Rod crossed his arms over his blue silk waistcoat. "I took firsts in all my classes."

"And I took seconds!" snorted Richard. "What were you doing all the time at Pemberley, after you were sent down?" he attacked, as Frederick's face flushed with a sickly expression.

"I was studying and learning how to run the estate." His reply was even enough, but it was an impertinent question and certainly none of his business.

"Well, hopefully you were more successful at that than your studies." Richard shrugged. "Did your father grant you pleasures, or have you been forbidden them at Pemberley?" He shared an unpleasant smile with Rod, while Miss Grantley and Miss Urquhart each gave their brothers an elbow. Isabelle

Grantley giggled, and the color drained from Julia's face.

Frederick tried a new tack. "We have a fine family of sheep dogs. Do you like dogs, Miss Grantley?" Susannah and Rachel exclaimed over this, and even Isabelle seemed interested.

"They're good for hunting, I will admit, but I am not overly fond of small animals, whether dogs, cats, or something else." Richard laughed. "I would rather kick one as well as pet it, I think."

"*Richard!*" Susannah frowned at him, and he seemed to realize he'd gone too far. Frederick and Julia had recoiled; Isabelle lowered her eyes but said nothing. However, Rachel was furious, and even Rod seemed upset.

"I am very sorry for that remark, ladies," Richard said, trying to sound sincere. "I was making a joke, and it was one in poor taste." He said nothing to Rod or Frederick.

"It certainly was," Rachel shot back, but her brother shook his head at her.

"We enjoy the dogs very much, don't we, Frederick?" Julia was surprised to hear her own voice. She had been horrified and shocked into silence by the malicious insults they had been subjected to. "There are Rex and Regina, and their litter of puppies." She didn't know if it was really proper to talk about this at a debutante ball, but she was trying not to collapse in the face of such dislike and disrespect. If only the dancing started, she could salvage something of the evening, but now it was all as good as ruined.

"Yes, we do enjoy their antics, Julia," Frederick managed.

Rachel appeared about to say something, but Richard spoke first. "Well, that sounds very nice for all of you," he said, "but especially you, Frederick, for it is no surprise that you would be comfortable among all those puppies."

Frederick gave an even more miserable flush and could not even make a reply. Rod snickered, only to be elbowed again by his sister.

Julia had had enough. She would not tolerate any more

insults or ill manners toward Frederick or herself. Frederick looked defeated and unsure of himself. She did not understand what Richard Grantley's remark had meant, but she knew it was nothing good; it had found its mark in poor Frederick, who looked as if he had been run through with a sword.

"Oh, you must please excuse us!" she exclaimed gaily. "Why, there are Pamela and Simon Easton, and I am so anxious to ask her about her stunning gown! Come along, Frederick." She pushed him towards other people, and away from this group. "I am so sorry to end our conversation, but you do understand, don't you?" The Grantley sisters had the grace to nod at least, along with Rachel Urquhart. "Thank you, and it was so very – *stimulating* – to meet all of you."

"Ladies," Frederick managed to say before she led him away. Looking sad and exhausted, he didn't even acknowledge Richard or Rod. He was certain they wouldn't care but didn't want to appear ill-mannered to anyone; it was too late, however, for Julia was making determined progress, leading him into the next room full of people.

They moved through the crowd as quickly as they could. Julia stopped by a table of refreshments, and the footman asked what she desired. "A glass of wine for my brother, please," she nodded, "and I would like a glass of the fruit punch."

"Of course, Miss! Right away."

She thanked the footman who immediately returned with their glasses; Julia took the wine first, for Frederick still seemed subdued. "Drink that, Fred," she said, as she turned back to accept her own glass.

She decided he looked better when he was nearly finished with it, but debated whether she should fetch him another so early in the evening, for they had all the dancing ahead of them. She decided to wait and see if Frederick regained his composure and affability. She wanted to ask who those awful people were, and why they were so hateful to them both, but especially him – except for Miss Urquhart. She sighed, knowing they would not be able to discuss it until much later, maybe even the next day.

"Frederick?" His eyes seemed calmer and his color and expression improved.

He swallowed. "I must say, that didn't go very well, did it?"

"No, it did not. Are you feeling better, or should I get you more wine?"

He gave a crooked smile. "No, thank you, but I assure you I am feeling fine."

"I am so glad to hear it!"

He looked at her. "Are you feeling all right yourself? It was quite brutal back there, and not all of it was directed at me."

At first, she did not answer and drank some punch. "It was just horrible!" she finally said, her voice shaky; she swallowed and composed herself. Concerned, he took her arm, but she tried to smile. "I am all right now. I will be fine, and able to enjoy the rest of the ball." She tried to sound hopeful. "The dancing will start soon."

"I am glad to hear that." He sighed and took her hand. "I am so sorry, Julia! I had no idea that they would be that unpleasant! I was quite afraid they had spoiled the entire evening for you."

They almost had, but she was determined not to let him know that. "They are just awful people," she said. "Do not worry about it, and there is no need to apologize. I would like to ask you for something, though."

"What is that?"

She pressed her advantage. "I would like to ask that later on you tell me how you know all of them, and why they dislike you so much." She gave him a sad smile. "I have never met such ill-mannered, hateful people! How can they mistreat you so?"

"I hope you will not meet such people again," came his fervent response, avoiding her question. "I also hope we will not have to sit next to them at the banquet, but we won't know that for hours." If they were assigned such seats, he thought, and Richard misbehaved, Frederick would think nothing of grabbing his antagonist's hair and shoving his head into his plate of food. However, Frederick dared not even joke about doing so, for it would distress Julia, not to mention all the other guests.

"I hope we do not either," Julia said frankly, "but I do not intend to worry about it all night long."

"That's the spirit!"

She laughed. "Now please answer my question, Brother."

"I do not want to distress you –"

"I will not be distressed," she said quickly, "but I would like to know and understand – for your sake, not mine."

He sighed. "All right, I promise I will tell you later. Satisfied?" She nodded and he almost smiled.

"One more thing," she added. He didn't groan but closed his eyes and bowed his head. "What is it now?" He almost sounded petulant.

"Frederick," she said, and he looked at her. "That's better! All I wanted to say is that both of us should try to keep the Grantleys and the Urquharts – well, except for Miss Rachel – away from Jane Elizabeth, for they will surely make her miserable if they realize who she is."

"And what she has done!" Frederick looked alarmed. "By Jove, Julia, you are right! I was so upset over their insults to you and spoiling your evening that I quite forgot about our poor sister!" He tried to calm his breathing. "Yes, I will try very hard not to leave her side all through the dancing, if I must."

"Sir?" The footman had returned, noticing their earnest and impassioned conversation. He did not like the look on the young man's face – either he was ill or very upset about something, and the young lady, his sister, did not seem much better. "May I fetch you some more wine?"

"Yes, Sir," Frederick replied, thanking him, "for it is quite warm here, is it not?"

"Absolutely, it is very close in here." The footman quickly returned with the wine and another glass of punch, for which Julia gratefully thanked him.

"Maybe we had better try to eat something as well," she said, "for it shall be a long time until dinner." She thought of how famished they had been at the first ball, so they shared a few appetizers, protecting their white gloves with thick cloth napkins. Then she spotted Jane Elizabeth. "There she is," she said happily, touching the sleeve of his coat. "Thank goodness, she is chatting with the Eastons! Let us go over and join her."

"Of course," Frederick agreed, and they went over to meet them.

Frederick and Julia carefully warned Jane Elizabeth about the Grantleys and Rod Urquhart. In hushed tones and with cautious glances, they indicated whom they wanted her to avoid. At first, Jane Elizabeth looked as if she might resent their advice, but she remembered where she was and what she was supposed to be doing. She could see how concerned they were for her; they were not being overbearing, just protective. She controlled her feelings and made her expression calm and pleasing again. She thanked them for their consideration but, like Julia, quietly insisted that she be told the reasons for their advice at a later, safer time. Her siblings agreed, and they continued to socialize without incident until the dancing began. However, they did not tell her how close a watch they intended to keep on her.

Oh, where were their parents? Frederick was afraid he would have to inform them of what had occurred at some point and dreaded having to do so. He wanted to fight his own battles, yet behave himself so that he didn't let them down or expose them to criticism. Still, the taunts and insults hurt and angered him. Richard's cutting reference to his familiarity with puppies was a deep wound to his manhood, but he was trying to keep his head for all their sakes. He suddenly felt like having more wine, but helped himself to two glasses of punch, after getting Julia's refilled. He was also disconcerted by the gazes of the friendly, attentive footman, who seemed to have engaged a colleague in keeping an eye on them. It seemed that every quarter of an hour or so, he saw one of the two footmen glancing discreetly in their direction. Frederick remained nervous but kept trying to smile and make decent conversation with those around him, with some success.

Julia recovered her balance from their bruising experience as well. She became her usual lively self and enjoyed everyone she met for the rest of the evening. She was very happy to see the Eastons and Emma Darnley, and was quite attracted and friendly to Angelina Molyneux and Cecilia Calvert. Again, she found herself the center of much attention, which she welcomed and basked in but was careful not to claim too much, for she did not wish to eclipse anyone, and certainly not Miss Calvert in her own home. Throughout the evening she was pleased to reconnect with Lucinda Peterbrooke, Eliza Ruth-Davis, Marianne Morton, and even Henrietta Porter-Douglas. She also met Martin Tourneur's sisters Gabrielle and Christabel, and Sir Timothy's sister Catharina, yet another debutante. She suddenly remembered to look for Rosamund Woodleigh, but never caught sight of her.

She began to forget about the three awful Grantleys and gave herself over to pleasure in dancing. First with Frederick, then with Lord Ravenswood, then her father, and, most joyfully, a dance with Sir Timothy! Originally, she only had one opening on her dance card, but her partner could not be found and she was very glad for the opportunity to dance with him. After a few more partners, she was very pleased and gratified to find Lord Ravenswood asking for yet another dance, but

Mr. Tourneur was already there to claim her. He tried again when her next partner – the disdainful Rod Urquhart – came to claim her. She felt a mean pleasure at declining her dance partner; she claimed she had a headache, and the young Mr. Urquhart wished her well and took his leave with a bow. That opened up two dances. She was undecided what she should do, for Lord Ravenswood had gone off to find something to comfort her in her supposed distress when Sir Timothy reappeared and swept her into another waltz. What a pleasure!

"I am supposed to be in the throes of a headache." She could not help giggling, and he laughed.

"Perhaps some graceful waltzing will cure you of that!" And so they whirled about until she was quite giddy.

Once their dance was over, a very solicitous Lord Ravenswood reappeared to take her gloved hand in his. Sir Timothy smiled at them, bowed, and moved off to his next partner, his sister Catharina. Lord Ravenswood watched him go with a neutral expression but was otherwise all smiles, charm, and concern when he turned back to her.

"Are you feeling recovered from your headache, Miss Darcy?"

"Oh, yes, my lord, I feel much better." They joined hands and began to dance. Julia felt a sudden need to explain her behavior. "I do not know what you will think of my conduct in your beautiful home, but I must admit to having committed some subterfuge just now."

"Really, Miss Darcy?" He gave a fine, manly laugh. "I must say I cannot believe you guilty of any such impropriety! To what conduct are you referring, if I may be so bold as to ask?"

"Well, my lord –" She could not continue at first. He caught her hesitation, and a slight frown appeared in his wonderful eyes. Goodness, the man was handsome! "I must admit that I feigned my headache so I would not have to dance with a particular young man." She sighed but kept enjoying their dance. "I am sorry to have behaved so badly and willfully at your ball, but there it is."

"Not at all, Miss Darcy! You have no need to apologize, and I know that Cecilia is most desirous to further your acquaintance," he said with more than politeness. "Please forgive me, however, for asking another impertinent question, for I seem to ask nothing but impertinent, ill-mannered questions in your presence! You refer to Mr. Roderick Urquhart, do you not?"

Blushing, she favored him with a glance. "I do." He only nodded as they danced.

Julia felt the need to say something positive. "I must say that I find Miss Urquhart, his sister, quite friendly and pleasing in her manners and opinions."

The young lord holding her could not have smiled more warmly. "I am very glad to hear it." She could not look at his side-whiskers anymore, because she always wanted to reach up and touch them; she supposed Frederick would grow some of his own soon.

The music ended and they bowed to each other; they had had two dances together and should not dance together again this evening; for three dances could indicate a serious understanding between a young man and woman, and it was only the second ball of the season. That also meant she should not dance again with Sir Timothy, either. While she stood disconcerted by her thoughts, a cheerful Simon Easton stepped forward to claim her for the next dance.

While Julia was preoccupied with her dance partners, Frederick found his attention challenged by his own, as well as his desire to keep an eye on Jane Elizabeth. For the first hour, all appeared well – Jane had many dances herself, though her dance card was not completely full, and there was no sign of the obnoxious Grantleys or Rod Urquhart. But too many conversations captured Frederick's attention; both Lord Ravenswood and his father the Earl chatted him up, along with Sir Timothy Carlisle,

Martin Tourneur, and Simon Easton. Despite his fierce concentration, he nearly stepped on a couple of his partners' feet. And so, for a while, he forgot to keep watch on Jane Elizabeth.

Jane herself was watching in admiration as Julia waltzed by with Sir Timothy. Smiling, she excused herself from her parents, who were sitting this one out, and carefully made her way to the nearest refreshment table. She had just received her glass of punch when a pretty but haughty young lady about her own age jostled her arm. Jane Elizabeth was startled to realize this person was none other than Isabelle Grantley.

"Sorry," Miss Grantley said, sounding anything but, "I do apologize, for I did not see you there just now." She remembered to look at her. "I hope I did not cause you to spill anything on your gown?"

Jane Elizabeth managed a smile. "No, not at all. Please do not worry about it."

"All right, then, I shan't!" Isabelle gave a giddy laugh.

Jane Elizabeth was taken aback. She had automatically extended her hand to introduce herself, but then quickly withdrew it. Isabelle Grantley was making no effort to make introductions, and, though Jane Elizabeth was trying very hard to keep her manners sterling, she thought she might be forgiven for such a breach this time. She remembered her siblings' warning so she dropped her hand to smooth her skirt.

"Your gown is a beautiful shade of periwinkle blue," Isabelle offered. "I am so glad I did not ruin it. So clumsy of me."

"Not at all," Jane Elizabeth repeated, then complimented her own, a bold creation of yellow and white stripes with brown buttons and accents. Isabelle's blond hair was curled and piled high up on her head. Jane Elizabeth was grateful for her own simple, tasteful coif, modeled on her mother's, with floral accents.

"Thank you." Isabelle smiled, then flicked open her fan and began to beat the air with it. "My word, but it is very sultry in here! I may feel faint very soon, for I absolutely *wilt* in the heat!"

"Oh, please do not," Jane Elizabeth exclaimed, "we cannot have that. Why do you not sit down over here and rest for a moment?" She indicated a couch nearby. "Or we could try to make our way toward the windows on the other side of the room."

Isabelle acknowledged this and sat down without a word. She kept fanning herself and made no indication for Jane Elizabeth to join her. However, Jane did, taking a seat next to her. She smiled at the dowager lady who was surrendering it as her respectable, elderly husband led her toward the dancing couples.

After a moment, Jane Elizabeth said, "What a lovely ball! Are you enjoying it?"

Isabelle gave a bored shrug. "It is all right, as balls go; but I have attended better ones – oh, I should not have said that! The Earl of Ravenswood and Lord Hartford, my father, are such good friends."

"I would not say a word," Jane Elizabeth remarked, only to keep the conversation going. She should be trying to get away from Isabelle but could not think of a polite way to do so. "What could be preventing you from enjoying yourself this evening?"

"Well," her companion replied in a petulant tone, "there is a dearth of dancers my age. Most are my brother's age, or even my father's, but I prefer to dance with a young man my own age. All these elderly men positively frighten me, no matter who they are!"

Jane Elizabeth almost chuckled in spite of herself. "I must agree with you. I would like to dance with a partner close to my own age too, but I am afraid there aren't many men so young here tonight." And, even if there were, she thought, few would like to dance; Henry had, but Frederick did not. She nodded to Isabelle, who barely smiled back. "I share your reservations about dancing with a man who is old enough to be my grandfather!" She laughed, but Isabelle just pursed her lips and kept fanning herself, looking around with a bored air.

Isabelle suddenly realized she had better improve her behavior, for she did not know who her companion was, though she was not interested in asking at this point. It would be awkward after so long a time, she rationalized. There were dozens of young ladies everywhere one looked; who cared about that one, or even this one sitting next to her, especially when she herself was prettier and more fashionable? Isabelle didn't mind Jane Elizabeth's presence all that much, but she wasn't going to encourage an acquaintance with her either. "You are very nice to tolerate my comments and forward behavior," she complimented Jane Elizabeth. "Please do not contradict me! However, I will admit to you that I find the caliber of some guests to be less than desirable for such an important event during the season. Lord Ravenswood is giving a lovely ball for Miss Calvert and all of us debutantes, but I fear we have been invaded by the masses tonight!"

"How shocking," Jane Elizabeth managed, but Isabelle did not notice.

"Of the most dreadful kind, I say! Again, I should not be so critical of the Earl of Ravenswood, but I do think people should socialize with others of their own class. Mixing them together is neither appropriate nor desirable, and the riffraff should be kept out at all costs." Isabelle gave a firm nod, proud of her opinions. "For instance, the Tourneurs; who ever heard of them? And what pretensions to higher society do Simon and Pamela Easton have? They have only been invited because their father is rich from coal mining, or some such awful, dirty commercial enterprise! The Eastons are definitely of no account to us or anyone of consequence." She took a swallow of her punch. She did not wait for Jane Elizabeth to reply, not that she appeared to even want to, so Isabelle kept talking. "There are also others here tonight who are far worse than the Eastons, and less worthy: those Darcys, for example."

Color draining from her face, Jane Elizabeth stiffened and

almost gasped. It was turning out worse than she could have feared! Hadn't Frederick and Julia warned her? Oh, why did she try to be friendly and patient with such a spoiled, mean, ill-mannered girl? Thankfully, Isabelle put a different interpretation on her visible distress.

"You poor thing," Isabelle said, touching her arm; Jane Elizabeth forced herself not to recoil. "I can see how upsetting that name is to you. Yes, there is a large group of them here in attendance tonight. I do not care how old their family is, for ours is older and more deserving of respect, and so are many of the other guests. But I tell you that they are absolutely *ridden* with scandal! Therefore, they do not belong here and shouldn't be allowed to move within our society."

Jane Elizabeth was mortified at this condemnation of her family and struggled to maintain her self-control. "How awful," she managed to say, "but what have these people done? Surely it cannot be so very bad, for they are invited guests this evening."

"Well, as I said, the earl can be quite free with whom he associates." Isabelle touched her arm again and leaned forth eagerly. Jane Elizabeth wanted to pull away, but she also wanted to hear all of it – for how much worse could it get? She thought she knew, and Isabelle was happy to tell her.

"Pray tell me these Darcys' offenses." She steeled herself as her heart sank.

Isabelle looked about her, and a nearby footman quietly moved a distance away. "Well," she whispered, "Mr. Darcy is the Master of Pemberley Estate in Derbyshire, and he had a son who was killed in some accident – obviously not the one who is present tonight as his sister's escort. She is a pretty thing," here Isabelle wrinkled her nose, "and very pleasant, but she seems shallow and unfortunately she's a Darcy; she will never live that down." She chatted on, oblivious to the furious look in Jane Elizabeth's eyes. "The late, young Mr. Darcy sired a child out of wedlock, can you believe it?" Somehow she kept her voice low, as excited as she was. "Disgusting! The child's mother is also dead, I understand, and the Darcys have formally adopted this child to save face, of course!" She shook her head. "The young Mr. Darcy present tonight is of no account either, for he behaved so badly that he was sent down from Cambridge. My brother Richard cannot stand the sight of him – he says he has little intelligence and absolutely no spine at all!" Isabelle laughed, and Jane Elizabeth felt her face burning. She had never heard any of her siblings so poorly regarded and disparaged. Poor Julia and Frederick! She so talented, and he the one who rescued her from the river. "However, that is not all!"

"What could there be, after all of that?" Jane Elizabeth asked in a dead voice. She braced herself, for it *was* going to get worse.

"Another sister – why, I believe she is also present this evening for her debut – got herself into trouble." Jane Elizabeth's mouth was so dry she could not say anything; Isabelle looked at her but chatted on. "What did this Miss Darcy do? Well!" Isabelle fanned herself furiously. "This Darcy girl almost ruined herself by carrying on shamelessly with a farm boy on the estate, then tried to drown herself when she was caught! Shocking behavior from a member of such a disreputable family!"

Jane Elizabeth swallowed. "She was almost ruined?"

Isabelle shrugged and almost dropped her fan in Jane's lap. "I do not know. Maybe she was ruined, maybe she was not! What difference does it make? At least she had the sense to try to drown herself, although apparently, she wasn't successful! I would never do such an irresponsible, wicked thing myself, but if I had behaved so disgracefully, I hope I would do the honorable thing and do myself in successfully!"

"And end your own life?" Jane Elizabeth was aghast at her vehemence. "No, that is all too horrible! Surely you do not mean that!"

Isabelle was staring at her. "I am sorry, for I seem to have upset you with what I said. I know I am much too forward in my opinions at times! And, no, I did not truly mean what I said, though I would not behave so myself. There, there," she said, patting Jane Elizabeth's arm, while Jane tried to keep her lips from trembling. "But why should you become so upset over what this Miss Darcy has done? For she has behaved very badly and can be of no use to anyone now." Isabelle gave her a puzzled look.

Jane Elizabeth counted to ten and calmed herself by taking some deep breaths. "It is just that her behavior has been so unfortunate," she said. "As you say, she has behaved very badly; but is it worth discussing among the *ton*? After all, she is only a girl our own age, a very young lady, and from Derbyshire at that."

"I suppose you are right, yet you know how people like to gossip," Isabelle said with an unconcerned expression.

"Yes, they do, don't they?" Jane Elizabeth had the grace not to look at her.

"So, what do you think of this Miss Darcy?" Isabelle asked, now interested.

Jane Elizabeth cleared her throat. "My thoughts are these. I think this Miss Darcy is most unfortunate, as all the trouble is clearly her fault. However, it seems to me that she is an immature girl who let herself treat loneliness with much too familiarity, and could not accept the consequences of what she had done," she said, censuring herself. Tears pricked her eyes, and Isabelle gave her a curious look.

"What strange remarks you have made!" she said. "Does that mean that you approve of what she did, making love to a farm boy and trying to end her own life?"

"I do not approve of any of it," Jane Elizabeth said calmly, "but I would try to understand why she did such willful things, and not condemn her, for so many other people will. Hopefully, she has learned from everything she has done." Before Isabelle could reply, Jane Elizabeth rose; she could not bear this conversation any longer. "If you will please excuse me, I must join my partner for the next dance. Good evening." She walked away, without waiting for a reply. She did not see Isabelle flush and continue fanning herself.

CHAPTER 10

At dinner Julia found herself seated between Lord Ravenswood and Sir Edward Chatterton, a lively, articulate young man with curled blond, pomaded hair. She noticed Sir Timothy was seated so far away that she could not see him. As it was, she sat among very august company, a great honor to her and her family, as Emma Darnley, Cecilia Calvert, and the Earl of Ravenswood himself were all nearby. She noticed that her parents were seated close by, but across from Lord and Lady Hartford – Richard Grantley's parents – who were seated on the same side of the table as she. Unfortunately, that left her in the direct view of Richard and Susannah Grantley, and they of her.

Richard gave her direct, hostile stares at times, with his mouth tightened. Julia dropped her gaze to her plate and tried to pay attention to whatever Sir Edward was saying to her. A few minutes later she looked over at her parents and caught Susannah Grantley looking at her. Miss Grantley's expression was not as hostile as her brother's, but her face held no friendliness in it and her eyes were cold. They nodded to each other, and Susannah gave her a tight, dismissive smile.

Julia sighed inwardly. The evening had been going badly and she wasn't even yet aware of her sister's encounter with Isabelle Grantley. As for Miss Susannah, Julia was correct in thinking that Richard's sister resented her because of her seat of importance at the table – one she should have been given because Julia did not deserve it herself. Julia shook herself a little, despite where she was. What an awful family the Grantleys must be; no wonder Frederick did not like them!

"Are you feeling a chill, Miss Darcy?" Lord Ravenswood's pleasing baritone addressed her. "Surely not, in a room as full and close as this one!"

She laughed and blushed. "Well, in fact, I did," she fibbed. What else could she think of to say? "I believe my wrap must have slipped down."

"Then allow me to assist you, I beg of you." Lord Ravenswood quickly reached over and gently raised her wrap higher around her shoulders.

"Why, thank you very much, my lord!" She blushed more. How kind he was!

"It was my pleasure, Miss Darcy."

She spent the next quarter of an hour listening to him tell more stories about his trip to America. And when she again made eye contact with Susannah Grantley, that young lady's look of hate was unmistakable.

As the banquet courses progressed, Elizabeth took advantage of a lull in the conversation around them to speak to her husband.

"Fitzwilliam," she began in a low tone, keeping her eyes looking forward, "what can be wrong with the children tonight? They seemed to have anticipated coming to the ball earlier, but now...why, only Julia seems herself. Frederick looks agitated and uncertain, and Jane Elizabeth is much too quiet, even at a gathering like this! They both appear upset about something. Whatever can be the matter?"

Darcy's eyes traveled to each one of their children, then returned to her. "Dearest," he said carefully, reaching for his glass, "I honestly do not know, and it will be a while before we can discover what is bothering them." He drew in a resigned breath. "However, I can hazard an educated guess as to what the cause might be."

She thought for a moment, and anxiety showed in her eyes, which she tried to blink away. "No, Fitzwilliam, surely not that!"

"I am very much afraid it is," came his soft reply. Mortified, Elizabeth's eyes dropped to her plate. He stirred in his chair. "I am sorry to say, it would be no surprise to me that word of all our troubles has preceded us here to London." He exhaled. "I do not wish to alarm or sadden you, and would like to be wrong, but I don't think that I am."

"I do not think you are, either. Oh, Dearest!" Elizabeth sounded as if she were close to tears, but she was a strong woman who didn't lose her composure. Fitzwilliam was right – hadn't they expected word of the scandals to be passed along? Well, it seemed they had been, she thought savagely, but she was determined that nothing would ruin their daughters' debuts – or threaten any of their children. Ever.

He patted her hand. "We Darcys are all strong, and we will weather this storm."

"Agreed," she said firmly, "and Heaven help those who try to harm our children." She looked at him and lightened her expression. He nodded, his eyes warm and loving. They turned to the people on either side of them to rejoin the conversation. As for their children, they would sit down for a long talk that night, despite the lateness of the hour.

The long evening was finally over and they were being driven back to Cavendish Square. The carriage interior was quiet. Darcy and Elizabeth were watching their children, who made few attempts at conversation. Julia still seemed in the best of spirits, but even she looked exhausted, her usual pleasant face slack and devoid of expression. Frederick's eyes looked wounded for some reason, and he kept rubbing his hands over his fine lawn trousers. Jane Elizabeth did not want to look at anyone and kept her face set but composed. Elizabeth gave Darcy a look of pained concern and his face softened, but even he could not think of anything positive to say.

Until they stopped at the townhouse, that is. "Here we are, safely home again," he declared in a cheerful voice. He received a smile from Elizabeth and two smaller, tired ones from their daughters, while Frederick just looked at him and nodded. He helped his sisters down from the carriage and languidly followed them into the house.

They gravitated to the drawing room where they all sat down in their finery. Darcy went over to the sideboard and poured them all some liqueur, as he had after the first ball. He handed each one of them a glass of cut crystal, then sat down next to Elizabeth. He exchanged a glance with her, and, sitting back, sipped and waited with an open expression.

It didn't take long. Julia appeared deep in thought and made polite, uninspired responses to her parents' questions about how much she had enjoyed the ball, to their disquiet. She wanted to talk to Frederick about the Grantleys before they told their parents anything, but curiosity got the better of her and fatigue made her careless. After a brief silence, she suddenly asked, "Frederick, what was that all about?" Then she remembered everyone else in the room, but it was too late.

"Julia!" Frederick gave her a fearful look, and mouthed the words, "Not now."

"What was what all about?" their father said, leaning forward and setting his glass down. When he received no answer, his face tightened and they all quailed. "Frederick, Julia, and Jane! Your mother and I have been watching you all evening and it is very clear to us that something is wrong, something that seems to have upset all three of you." He kept his voice firm but relaxed his glance and expression. "We will not tolerate any evasions or distractions from you. For goodness' sake, dear children, please tell us what happened to you tonight!"

Frederick and Julia both sighed, and Jane Elizabeth closed her eyes, but his sisters turned their gazes upon him; so now, as the oldest, Frederick was expected to take the lead in explaining everything. He didn't want to, but realized it would be better just to get it over with. He knew they couldn't hide the unpleasantness from their parents and thought maybe they would be able to help them deal with it. So he cleared his throat and told their parents what had transpired with the Grantleys. With Julia adding confirmations, he also mentioned how they had cautioned Jane Elizabeth and tried to keep an eye on her – and away from them. He had paced as he spoke; now he sat down wearily, awaiting their reactions. Julia looked calm, but Jane Elizabeth kept looking away and dabbing her eyes. Frederick closed his own and saw a disturbing vision, that of a splayed, bloodied body; was it Richard's or was it his? No, their enmity mustn't come to this, but would it? He almost writhed in his chair and made a weak sound but managed to remain seated; he hung his head, his exhaling nearly audible.

At first, their father and mother said nothing, and the siblings watched as a series of emotions – shock, anger, sadness, and disgust – passed across their faces. Darcy paced the floor and, resting her head against the sofa, Elizabeth made a sound.

"Monstrous," their father finally burst out, "and vicious as well!"

"Insupportable and improper – and most cruel and insensitive!" Elizabeth exclaimed. "Oh, you poor, dear children! I am so sorry you suffered through this!" She rose and went over to encircle each of them with her arms.

"I am sorry too, Mother," Frederick said, spent. "I wanted to get us away from Richard, his sisters, and Rod, but I didn't want to cause a scene, because I thought it would reflect badly upon all of us, but especially Julia and Jane." His father clapped him on the shoulder.

"Oh," was all Elizabeth could say.

Now Julia made another ill-timed remark. "Frederick," she asked, "what did Richard Grantley mean by all those things he said about puppies?" She instantly regretted her question when her brother uttered a weak sound, flushed, and turned away.

Darcy saw his reaction and became angry. "Frederick," he said, putting his arm around his hunched shoulders. Frederick looked at him, then hung his head. "Did he taunt you again? He was referring to Cambridge, was he not?" Unable to speak, Frederick nodded and rubbed his eyes. Darcy put an arm around him and made a wrathful sound in his throat; he also saw that Elizabeth understood what they were discussing. "Frederick," he said, "you are a fine young man. Richard Grantley is a cruel, insensitive, ill-mannered brute and a bully, despite his years, and you are nothing like him at all, nor are you weak and unmanly in any way. He is wrong to denigrate you so, the blackguard that he is."

"Fitzwilliam, your language!"

"I apologize, Dearest, and to you too, Julia and Jane, but I have heard plenty about Lord Hartford's son!" He released Frederick and they both sat down.

"Thank you, Father." Frederick sounded grateful and looked a little better.

Almost sobbing, Julia leaned into his shoulder. "Oh, Fred, I am so sorry to have mentioned that! I had no idea what it meant. If only I weren't so tired tonight, I would have been more careful and less curious! If it makes you feel any better, I must say that I think Susannah Grantley dislikes me as much as her brother dislikes you! I would have been slain by the looks she gave me tonight."

He hugged her. "It is all right, Julia, really. But please do not say such a thing, for Miss Grantley has no justification in disliking you. It is all because Richard hates me! As for the rest, Mother and Father now know, and you understand why we don't like each other." She nodded and dried her tears. "And you as well, Jane."

Their sister started, her eyes filling, but before she could reply, Elizabeth said, "I am very glad you tried to keep the Grantleys away from her. Aren't you, Jane?"

"Yes, Mother, except –" Her lip quavered.

"Except what, dear?" Elizabeth was puzzled.

"Except that it wasn't successful!" Jane Elizabeth cried and sobbed. Darcy and Elizabeth saw Frederick and Julia look at each other in dismay. "Isabelle Grantley bumped into me at one of the refreshment tables during the dancing, and she – she –"

Elizabeth closed her eyes and steeled herself. "What happened, Jane? What did Miss Isabelle do?"

Jane Elizabeth's face crumpled as she tried to answer their mother. Eventually, she got the entire awful episode out as both Frederick and Julia sat on either side of her, and she cried so much she needed both their handkerchiefs. Their father kept his expression set, though he alternated between anger and extreme distress over her condition.

"It was horrible!" Jane Elizabeth finally cried out. "I know I shouldn't say such things, but Isabelle Grantley is as vicious and spiteful and cruel as her older brother and sister!" Her outburst shocked them all, but neither parent could scold her at this moment. Frederick and Julia kept hugging her and apologizing for not having kept a closer watch over her, to keep her safe and apart from others who meant her harm, but she told them to stop. "It is not your fault, either one of you!" She tried to stop crying but couldn't, and finally Elizabeth waved them away so she could comfort her in her arms. She called in one of the female servants, Margaret, to fetch Mrs. Winston, despite the late hour.

"My poor, brave girl," she said into her hair, as Jane Elizabeth sobbed. "As awful as it was for you, you handled Isabelle Grantley very well – you maintained your composure and did not give in to any mean or disgraceful behavior yourself, much as you were provoked beyond endurance."

"Oh, Mother, what am I to do? She cannot be the only one who feels that way! How can I face other people? For she will learn it was I she was so blithely gossiping about and condemning! Send me away at once, please, I beg you!" She cried harder than ever.

"Jane, Jane –"

She lifted her splotchy face. "How wicked and foolish I have been! How could I have behaved so? I got poor Ned thrashed without mercy, and now I will spoil everything for Julia! I have never felt so sorry for all I have done as I do now!" She took a few shuddering breaths and wiped her face. "Father, Mother, *please* – send me away! Please don't make me go to any more of these balls, for people despise me, even here."

Elizabeth hugged her, and Darcy followed suit. "Jane," she said tenderly, "we cannot send you away, nor do we even want to. Your place is with us, your family." Jane Elizabeth shook her head violently, but Elizabeth held it in her hands to make her stop. "No, Daughter, listen to me – you will remain here with us." She looked at Darcy. "And we will continue to attend the balls together as planned."

"We cannot let you run away, Jane," Darcy added in his softest, kindest voice. "Remember that your sister and brother and all of us – including Henry, Christina, and little Henry David – have been judged and disparaged, too. The young Grantleys, whose behavior has been so objectionable and insulting, are only a few people in this entire city. I can tell you that most people we have met here in London this season have been friendly and pleased to make our acquaintance, including Lord and Lady Oakland, the Earl of Ravenswood and his family, the Calverts, and the Earl of Chester. Yes, there have been several people who have been haughty and judgmental, even rude, but not many."

"Father," Jane moaned.

"No, Jane," Elizabeth said, "your father is right; we cannot let you run away. We will face all of this together – *with* you. Your father, brother, sister, and I will do our best to protect you. That is the most that we can do. True, it may not always turn out for the best, but your father and I will do everything in our power to make sure that nothing ever happens to any one of you." She looked into her daughter's eyes, which seemed calmer. "Do you understand, my lovely daughter?"

Jane Elizabeth snuffled, nodded, and looked down. "Yes – I will try to be brave."

"That's our beloved, intelligent, and courageous daughter," Darcy said, taking her into his arms. When he finally released her, Elizabeth asked Julia to take her upstairs with Mrs. Winston, who had arrived quickly and heard enough of what happened.

"Yes, Mother. I will stay with her tonight."

Elizabeth thanked her. "You must all be so tired."

"It is no matter, Mother. Come, Jane, let us get out of these gowns and get some sleep; Margaret will help us." She put an arm around her trembling sister and they left, with Mrs. Winston supporting Jane on the other side.

Frederick suddenly stood up and wavered on his feet. He recovered his balance and said, "I am so sorry about Jane. I thought I could prevent such a thing from happening, but I failed because I did not watch her closely enough."

"No, Frederick, you did fine," his father complimented him. "I do not think it is truly possible to prevent everything. Again, I must say the concern that you and your sister showed Jane is admirable and heartening."

"Thank you, Father." A huge yawn escaped him and he blinked. "I am so tired," he complained, and tried to smile.

"Go to bed, Son," his father told him kindly. They exchanged wishes for a good night and he trudged off in his heavy boots.

Now alone, they both sagged. Dispirited, Darcy looked at Elizabeth as if all were hopeless, and rubbed his eyes.

"Dearest, would you like some more of the liqueur?" she asked him.

"No, thank you, Lizzie, for I am too tired to even taste it. Besides, I have had more than enough to please me this evening, and having more to drink would not ease my mind or relieve my distress over this most disastrous of evenings."

"I see." After a pause, she asked, "Do you think the season

can be salvaged for Julia's sake, and Jane's? I have never seen our children look so sad and defeated as they did tonight. I am sure that most of their enjoyment and excitement has been tainted by the illustrious Grantley family."

That was a rare, pointed comment from her. With raised eyebrows, Darcy replied, "Yes, but they are only one highborn family, as I said. Master Richard Grantley has quite an unsavory reputation himself for such a young man; he is only twenty years of age, just a year older than Frederick. Many people here have welcomed us, but I do not think the Grantleys' condemnation of us is shared by everyone."

Elizabeth sighed. "I agree with you, Dearest, but there is definite enmity between Frederick and this Richard Grantley; that cannot be good for either, or anyone else." She snuggled up against him and he pulled her close.

"I repeat that Grantley is a bully and a brute, and he delights in tormenting and insulting Frederick. He knows just how to hurt him by wounding his manhood – because he hesitated to bed down with a prostitute when he was neither ready nor willing."

"How awful for our son!"

"Yes," he mused. "I remember several fellows like young Grantley when I was at university. They were all about satisfying their own pleasures, heedless of the rules, and contemptuous of anyone they didn't like, or who did not want to engage in any activity they were doing themselves. Bah," he snorted, a rare reaction from him, which made her start. "I do not want Frederick to become wild, selfish, brutal, and dissipated himself, but I swear that *our* young man has been provoked many times – and that young Grantley deserves to be taught a lesson, even if it means he should be knocked down!"

"Dearest!" she scolded. She disliked any talk of violence.

"I am sorry for that, Lizzie, but sometimes it is necessary to fight, and that is how I feel." He sighed. "I must admit that I am a little worried all the same."

"Why is that, Fitzwilliam?" She didn't think she could take on any more worries.

"I worry," he replied, "because Frederick has a temper. I can only hope they somehow settle this animosity between them before it goes too far," he sighed, "for I am afraid it could even end in a duel."

"*No!*" she cried out. "Not our wonderful son! He could not be so foolish, so careless with his own life, nor desire to kill another man, no matter how vile he is!" She gave him a horrified look. "Our fine son would not do such a wicked thing! Fitzwilliam, have pity on me and do not worry me so! Even you did not kill Wickham, and God knows you had cause to challenge him!"

He returned her look. "No, I did not, but there were several times when I wanted to, or figure out a way to have him cast into prison." She sank into his chest, troubled. "Well," he sighed, blinking, "it may only come to blows with their fists, for all I know. However, I think we must encourage Frederick to keep his head and resist violence at all costs. I do not think young Grantley will make it easy for him."

"No, I suppose he won't," he heard her say to his chest. She stirred in his arms. "Oh, Fitzwilliam, I am afraid for Frederick. I am afraid for all of them!"

He kissed the top of her head. "As am I. But we must be brave and not lose hope. We must trust that our son will behave responsibly, as he has been doing for a while. Frederick will be all right – and safe – you'll see." He tried to sound hopeful.

"I hope so." Sighing, she pressed further into his chest. "Now just hold me please."

He did, and they did not move for a very long time, despite the hour.

CHAPTER 11

The third ball of the season took place at Holdsworth, the home of Sir Francis and Lady Mary Exley, whose daughter Marcella was making her debut. Julia dressed as carefully as she had for the previous balls; now she was moving up along with her family in the close, hot receiving line. She kept her smile and manners sparkling, but her feelings did not match her demeanor.

Truthfully, some of the excitement of her debut had been diminished. She could not forget the treatment they had all received, the worst of which had come from the Grantleys and been inflicted upon her siblings. She was growing tired of the stares, whispers, and lesser snubs, too. However, her practical nature reasserted itself enough to remind her of all her parents were doing and spending on her behalf, and she would see it through to the end, whether bitter or not. She also needed to be realistic; there would be more snubs to suffer, deflect, debate, and discount.

It seemed no better for Frederick, as their parents warned him to keep his head and temper in check and wear his manners like a shield. Julia sensed his tension to behave perfectly, even in the face of the snubs. Yet now, in another fabulous new gown, her hair up, she was moving up in the slow-moving receiving line with all her family.

The dancing had not yet begun, nor had they had any refreshments, but Julia's head was spinning from the sheer number of people she was meeting – many she had met at the previous balls, like the Tourneurs, Angelina Molyneux, and Lucinda Peterbrooke, but now several new ones. Miss Exley, of course, but also Miss Mary Duncan, escorted by her handsome half-brother Julian Tunney, Miss Belinda Compson, and the Foxborough sisters, Serena and Sylvia, escorted by their brothers, Silas and Seth. There were also Lord Benjamin and Lady Miriam Stoddard, and their daughters Sophia and Hannah, escorted by their brothers Samuel and Daniel. Julia liked the strong resemblance between the Foxborough siblings, all blond, good-looking, good-natured, and appearing as if they enjoyed outdoor activities; it would be pleasurable to talk with all of them, but especially the athletic and friendly young men!

On the downside, Mrs. Porter-Douglas and Mrs. Ruth-Davis were also in attendance, along with their pleasant offspring. The women looked at her as she passed by; Julia nodded to them and gave a polite smile but did not feel they deserved much more notice unless they tried to speak with her. Worst of all, the entire Grantley family was also present. Julia had heard Richard's loud, obnoxious voice first, and then his sister Isabelle's petulant remarks. Beside her, Frederick stiffened in his fine new suit and gleaming boots but turned to give her and Jane Elizabeth an encouraging smile.

"We are Darcys, and we will prevail," he said softly, and some of Jane Elizabeth's anxiety left her eyes. Somehow they returned his smile, and Julia squeezed her sister's hand. Well, if the Grantleys were here, then the Urquharts must be as well.

Julia was now pleased to notice that Sir Timothy Carlisle stood close by with his sister Catharina. After exchanging greetings, Frederick and Jane Elizabeth moved away to speak with the Eastons, with whom they were becoming fast friends, and allow Julia some time with Sir Timothy; Julia was very grateful for this.

"Oh, Miss Darcy, your gown is such a beautiful shade of green with all its gold threads as accents!" exclaimed Miss Carlisle, a doll-like beauty with soft brown ringlets and full, rosy cheeks.

"Thank you very much, Miss Carlisle!" she replied. "I must say that your rose-colored satin gown with its white lace flourishes is quite stunning, and perfectly complements your lovely complexion."

Her cheeks pinking, Miss Carlisle thanked her. Julia liked her sweet nature, and being Sir Timothy's sister was also an advantage. "Tim," Miss Carlisle said, turning to him, "I have many topics I would like to discuss with Miss Darcy, and I admit that most of them relate to fashion and accessories! They cannot be very interesting to a man of consequence such as you, I am afraid. We shall not bore you with our conversation, I hope."

"Not at all, Catharina," her brother laughed. Julia thought he must be several years older than his sister. She noticed he was wearing a suit of rich brown velvet that looked so soft she wanted to touch it. Goodness, the man knew how to dress! "However," he was saying, "I appreciate your consideration, and would not dream of dampening your pleasure by talking about manly pursuits such as hunting or fencing, or some such thing." He laughed again, and Julia decided she liked the timbre of his tenor voice. He turned to her. "I would like to secure *at least one* dance with you, Miss Darcy, if that is agreeable, for I should allow you the opportunity to dance with other young gentlemen tonight, and not just with me." Now it was Catharina's turn to laugh – a high, almost girlish one, but still pleasant.

Julia gave him a warm smile. "I am most agreeable to your request, Sir Timothy, and I do accept."

"And to what are you being agreeable, Miss Darcy, if I may ask?"

Julia was surprised, as Lord Ravenswood appeared with his sister Cecilia. He was smiling and pleasant as usual, but she realized how closely he was standing next to her, and how Sir Timothy had backed up a couple of steps to make room for them. "Well, my lord, I was just agreeing to be Sir Timothy's partner for one dance."

"I am certain your dance card fills up quite fast, Miss Darcy."

"You give me too much credit, Lord Ravenswood." She

lowered her eyes. "With so many fascinating young gentlemen here this evening, it is simply not possible for a young lady to dance with all of them."

Lord Ravenswood laughed, then Sir Timothy spoke up. "Please forgive me for saying so, Miss Darcy, and I do apologize, but did you not agree to dance at least one dance with me this evening?" He gave her a winning smile.

He had her on that one. "Why, yes, Sir Timothy, I believe that you are correct; I did agree to at least one dance." She began to feel a little nervous.

"That is quite fortunate for you, Carlisle," Lord Ravenswood said, giving the other young man, who was almost as tall as he, a steady gaze, "for I am afraid that I may be too late in requesting even one from Miss Darcy."

Sir Timothy met his gaze. "How could I possibly know that?" Smiling, he turned to her. "Why do you not ask Miss Darcy yourself, milord?"

Lord Ravenswood nodded to him and now looked at her. "Well, Miss Darcy, am I to become very happy or disappointed?" His eyes softened as he smiled.

Her heart fluttering, she thought quickly. Goodness, this man was handsome, and when the young lord looked at her like that...She wanted to fan herself, but she had to make a decision. She had had so many requests that, after her sole dance with Frederick, the final one of the evening, she had only been able to grant single dances to Simon Easton, each of the Foxborough brothers, Ben Ruth-Davis, and Julian Tunney. Since she had recklessly granted Sir Timothy in effect two dances, that only left three openings; if she reserved two for Lord Ravenswood, that would leave only one opening for another partner. She wouldn't have minded dancing with Alan Molyneux, or Martin Tourneur.

Julia did fan herself now; the other young ladies lowered their eyes at her discomfiture, and Sir Timothy was looking at Lord Ravenswood. "My, how warm it is this evening," she stalled, fooling no one. She made up her mind – it would not be fair to allow Sir Timothy two dances and not more than one for Lord Ravenswood. Thank goodness Frederick had said it was fine with him to dance only once together tonight, and their parents had supported this. "I would be happy to give you two dances, my lord."

His smile was wide and bright. "Thank you very much, Miss Darcy!"

"It will be my pleasure."

"Satisfied, milord?" challenged Sir Timothy with a smile.

Lord Ravenswood was magnanimous in his victory. "Quite, Sir Timothy." The two gentlemen shuffled their feet and went on to discuss common manly pursuits, hands clasped behind their long-coated backs, while the young ladies delighted each other in comparing notes on their favorite gowns and accessories.

A little while later, after the Ravenswoods and Carlisles moved off to chat with other guests, Julia found herself wandering over to a refreshment table for some punch. There she found a young man with wavy brown hair and thick side-whiskers, a firm chin, and a plain but not unpleasing face; he stood holding two glasses of punch and looking perplexed.

"Is something the matter, Sir?" she asked politely.

"Well, Miss, I was supposed to bring my partner some punch, but I do believe she just whirled by in the arms of Mr. Julian Tunney, so I am quite at a loss to know what to do."

"I am sorry to hear that," she commiserated, then brightened. "Well, Sir, if you do not desire two glasses of punch for yourself at the moment, I would be more than happy to relieve you of one of them."

"Well put." Laughing, the young man handed her a glass, and they introduced themselves. "Gregory Lawson," he said, bowing to her.

"Julia Darcy," she answered with a curtsey. "Again, I am most sorry you lost your dance partner."

He smiled, which lit up his face. "It is really quite all right, Miss Darcy. It is not as if I was heartlessly abandoned by a determined debutante." She laughed. "I was only deserted by my own sister Letitia, who took advantage of my absence to procure a dance with Mr. Tunney, with whom she desired to speak since she first beheld him."

Julia laughed again. "Well, then I am glad to hear it."

"I thank you for your consideration." Now he looked at her. "Forgive me for asking, Miss, but is not your father Fitzwilliam Darcy, the Master of Pemberley?"

She was pleased he mentioned him. "Why, yes, that is he. I am here tonight with both my parents, as well as my older brother, Frederick, who is my escort, and my younger sister, Jane, who is also making her debut."

Mr. Lawson went on speaking, repeating all he had heard about her father and their illustrious family. Though he spoke very highly about all of them, she was not completely comfortable with so many compliments – not after all the snubs – so she directed the conversation back towards himself and his family. It turned out that Mr. Lawson's father was a landowner whose wealth came from growing rice in the lowlands here in England, and from sugar cane grown on a plantation in the West Indies. He was quite happy to talk about his family, and she was especially interested to hear about the Caribbean Islands, which he had already visited three times. After a while, though, she heard the orchestra tuning up again, and she looked for Simon Easton, with whom she was to share the next dance.

He noticed her divided attention. "Ah, forgive me for talking so long! I am afraid I have quite worn out my welcome – in fact, that I have bored you with my long exposition."

It wasn't entirely true, so she was sincere in her denial. "Not at all, Mr. Lawson. There is nothing to forgive." Like Nicholas, she liked hearing about faraway places.

He brightened. "Er, Miss Darcy, would you happen to have

any openings left on your card to dance with me? I may not look it, but I am more than a competent dancer."

Julia was not completely convinced of that, but young Mr. Lawson was pleasant and trim enough and his clothes fit him well, so she gave him the benefit of the doubt. "Of course, Mr. Lawson, you may have the next to last dance of the evening, that is, if it is still open for you."

"Oh, my card is quite open," he gushed, then realized he had said too much. "Thank you, Miss Darcy! I look forward very much to dancing with you."

"As do I with you, Mr. Lawson." Well, that was it. Her dance card was now completely full, and she hoped Gregory Lawson was as good a dancer as he claimed.

"Well, hello, Miss Darcy!"

She turned to find an eager Simon Easton ready to dance with her, and she gave him a wide smile.

After chatting with the Eastons, Jane Elizabeth wanted to speak more with the Carlisles, but her mother reclaimed her, and Frederick wandered over to a refreshment table. He waited patiently behind a group of three excited young ladies who were gaily chatting and laughing while they blocked access to the table for anyone else. He tried not to eavesdrop on their babbling, but it was difficult not to, and he thought some of their high-spirited remarks were rather amusing; he ended up clamping his mouth shut so he wouldn't start laughing.

Suddenly, the three young women became aware of his presence behind them. Maybe it was the sandalwood cologne he had splashed all over himself, or maybe he cast a shadow over their shoulders onto the table – but then he was sur-rounded, even entrapped, by them. Frederick gulped. All three wore fashionable gowns in bright, somewhat gaudy, colors. All were bejeweled and wore their hair up in piles of curls and ringlets on the tops of their heads. They rushed up to him so fast they had to jostle for position because of the contact from each other's puffed sleeves and full skirts. A blond, a brunette, and a redhead – he had to smile at that, although he was already perspiring.

"May we be introduced, young sir?" the brunette asked.

He found his manners and tried to look pleasant. "Of course! My name is Frederick Darcy." He bowed to each one of them. "I am very pleased to meet all of you. And you are...?" He trailed off as they giggled.

"Alexandra Vinson." The blond curtsied. Her white gown complemented her golden hair, but it was hard to decide what she had more of – flounces, curls, or jewels.

"Lucy Robinson." The brunette curtsied. The shoulders of her sky-blue gown were the puffiest and, along with her dome of skirts, nearly knocked Frederick off balance when she hurried to stand next to him. Her billowing skirts covered most of his boots.

"Honoria Watson." The redhead curtsied. Her mass of curls was the most tasteful, her bright purple gown the most restrained, and her actions mincing and maidenly, until she gave him a sly glance, tapped his arm with her garish fan, and rose, smiling widely.

"Ladies," he acknowledged, and bowed again. He desperately wanted something cool to drink, but it seemed he would never get past these lively, formidable young ladies. They said nothing more at first but made no secret of taking in every detail of his appearance: his well-cut dark suit, blue and gold waistcoat, immaculate white cravat, and gleaming boots, not to mention his full, thick hair, and serious face. He really didn't have side-whiskers yet, but his longish hair made up for that.

"Your father is the Master of Pemberley in Derbyshire," Lucy remarked.

"Yes."

"Your sister is Julia Darcy, who is very beautiful in her

emerald green and gold gown," Honoria said.

"Yes, and thank you for the compliment to my sister. I will be sure to relay it to her."

"You are most welcome, Mr. Darcy," she cooed, and he gulped again.

"Forgive me for asking, Sir," Alexandra Vinson spoke up, "but is that not sandalwood cologne you are wearing?" The other young ladies laughed as he felt his face burning and his fine clothes sticking to his damp body.

"Er, yes, it is." Where the devil was one of his sisters to get him out of this? How was he supposed to answer such impertinent questions? Even he knew this wasn't an appropriate topic of conversation!

"I just love it when a man wears sandalwood cologne," Alexandra declared, rolling her eyes in a seductive manner. "I find it incredibly masculine. Don't you, Lucy and Honoria?"

"Oh, we do," they chorused. All three laughed, while Frederick choked and struggled to find something polite and correct to say.

"Why, er, thank you, ladies," he managed, as he felt sweat trickle down the back and sides of his neck.

"How tall you are!" giggled Lucy Robinson.

"Oh," he nearly groaned, "I must beg to disagree with you, Miss Robinson, as charming as I must be about it, for I am not nearly that tall for a young man! I stand at five feet eight inches, but my father, Fitzwilliam Darcy, stands six feet one inch." Henry had been as tall as their father, but giggling, impertinent young ladies or not, he wasn't going to mention that fact now.

"Well, *I* must disagree with you as charmingly as I can, Mr. Darcy," Honoria declared, "for you seem quite tall to me." Poor Frederick noticed her pile of curls made her taller than he.

"Thank you, Miss Watson." Oh, wouldn't they just stop all this nonsense and leave him alone? They seemed to delight in making him uncomfortable.

"And quite pleasing in your manners and features," she added, as he flushed.

"Yes," Alexandra said. "You are like my brother, Arthur – quite handsome, and even rugged!"

"I like a young man with a steady gaze and a fine head of hair," dimpled Lucy. "My poor brother Linus is losing his already, and he is not yet twenty-five years of age. So sad."

"Thank you very much, ladies; I am most grateful for your compliments," he said in a strangled voice. He had to get away from them! "And I have not given any of you nearly so many." That was a foolish thing to say, for now they might very well expect him to flatter them when in truth he could not stand any of them.

"There is no need to flatter us, Mr. Darcy," smiled Alexandra, "for we are quite taken with you, aren't we, ladies?" As the other two giggled, she resumed. "It is extremely complimentary enough that you have taken notice of us."

"Again, I am very much in your debt," he almost gasped out. And in such agony, he thought silently. He prayed one of his family members would appear soon to rescue him. He forgot himself and quickly looked around, but no help seemed forthcoming.

"We are so fortunate to have met you, Mr. Darcy," Alexandra was saying, "so now we must know something of your character and interests."

Well, his interests formed a more acceptable topic of conversation at least. Frederick told them about his attendance at Cambridge and the courses he was taking, which obviously bored them, then switched to talking about how much he loved to read and take long walks, which pleased them even less.

"As wonderful, manly, and sensible pursuits as I am sure these are," Honoria cooed, taking his arm, which made him flinch, "surely you must have one interesting pursuit – I mean, one that is interesting to pleasant and energetic young ladies such as ourselves." Frederick was too mortified at this to reply.

Where did these three come from? Certainly, they must have barely made it through finishing school, to be displaying such a lack of manners and decorum! His mother would never stand for such behavior. Later, he was embarrassed to admit that he had wondered how rich their fathers were – and for how long. When he didn't answer, Honoria rushed on. "Oh, forgive me for not being interested in old books and walks and stuffy old masters, for that is all I ever hear about from my brother, Magnus, who attends Oxford."

"You are forgiven, Miss Watson." Good God, could this encounter get any worse?

"Thank you, Mr. Darcy." Her eyes lit up. "In spite of all your manly pursuits, you must have some interest that is softer, gentler." She gave him a knowing smile. "You live at the grand estate of Pemberley, do you not? I know! Then you must like animals of all kinds because you live in the country!" Before he could say anything, she held his arm again. "Young ladies do not gamble, but I will wager, Mr. Darcy, that you even like small animals, and that your fine home is full of wonderful pets, cats and dogs alike!" She did not wait for him to confirm this or not. "Do you not find kittens and puppies to be such wonderful, delightful creatures?"

She couldn't have possibly known that specific word would wound him, and now he really wanted to gag. "I adore them," he gasped, and all three laughed. He was going to turn and walk away, even if it was as rude as it appeared to be, but now Lucy Robinson took his other arm, and Alexandra Vinson blocked his path.

"We are just about done tormenting you, Mr. Darcy," she said, "but there is one more thing we would like to know about you."

"And what is that?" He could not help smiling at this small burst of truth.

"We would like to know if your dance card is full!" All three of them laughed.

Frederick silently cursed the fact that he did indeed have openings, but dared not lie, for it would be obvious any time he stood out a dance and he did not want to offend anyone, even these three predators. He also remembered he was an honored guest and escort and, as a healthy young man from a fine family, he was expected to be sociable and dance – and not retreat to the sides of the room. He reminded himself that any sacrifice he made would be for Julia's sake, though he thought he'd rather chop wood or clean out a stable than dance with any of these three young women. Still, he replied, "It so happens that I have three such openings," to their exclamations of delight; so, he gallantly – if not very willingly – asked each young lady for a single dance, to which they were all most agreeable. Excited about being claimed by their current partners, they thanked him and rushed off to pleasure. And now that he had access to the refreshments, he could still hear them giggling about "a tender morsel," as they hurried off.

Frederick did not care if anyone saw or heard him. He gave an audible sigh of relief and mopped his face and neck with his handkerchief. He saw a kindly-looking matron giving him a sympathetic look as he drew his shattered, flustered decency about him, and staggered over to the table. The footman took one look at him and handed him the largest glass of wine Frederick had ever seen. "There is plenty more where that came from, Sir," he said, and waited.

Frederick thanked him profusely and drank quickly. "I believe, good sir, that I shall take you up on your generous offer." While the footman refilled his glass, Frederick passed a shaky hand over his eyes and threw caution to the wind. "I did not know there were wolves in London, and female ones at that," he said, and drank down some more wine. He was starting to feel a little better.

"Yes," the footman replied. "It seems some young ladies can be quite eager. Too eager."

"They can, Sir," Frederick agreed, "and now I have invited

each one to dance with me, and they have all accepted." His eyes were tragic.

"It is only one dance with each, is it not?" Frederick nodded. "Then it will all be over soon enough."

"I suppose so." Then he thought of something and grinned at the composed, reticent man in silken livery. "I must take care that I do not tread on their feet, for I can be quite clumsy."

A smile played at the footman's mouth. "There you have it. Now brace yourself, Sir, and I recommend that you finish your wine, for I do believe your first partner of the three is approaching." Indeed, the current dance had just ended, and Frederick saw Miss Vinson advancing towards him.

"God help me, Sir," Frederick remarked to the footman. "I shall probably desire more wine when this series of dances is ended."

"'Once more unto the breach,' and all that, Sir! I promise I shall keep your glass here until you require it again."

Frederick thanked him, took his final swallow, and turned to meet his fate in the person of the determined but smiling Alexandra Vinson.

After listening to her parents' discussion with Sir Francis and Lady Mary, and conversing with the cheerful Miss Exley, Jane Elizabeth excused herself and went over to sit on one of the couches along the wall. She desired only to rest, not even having something cool to drink, while she could be free to think and smile at the people strolling or dancing by.

Engaged in conversation, Elizabeth wasn't able to react to Jane's polite defection at first. A few minutes later, when the Exleys greeted the Carlisles, Elizabeth's gaze traveled over the large room until she found where Jane was sitting. She made polite excuses as she made her way over to her. Jane looked up when Elizabeth stopped in front of her.

"Jane."

"Mother?"

Her mother gave a tentative smile. "You are not dancing."

"No, I am not." Elizabeth waited for Jane to continue, but she remained silent, looking at her and then at others close by.

Noting Jane's hesitance, Elizabeth asked "Don't you want to dance? It is your debut, as well as Julia's, and I thought you loved this new lavender silk gown of yours." When Jane didn't reply, she added, "You will show it off better to everyone if you are out on the ballroom floor instead of sitting here."

"Yes, Mother, thank you." Jane paused. "I do love this gown." She touched the white lace embellishments on the cuff of her sleeve.

"Then why –"

"I would just like to rest for now." She smiled at Elizabeth. "I intend to dance some more, a little later."

Elizabeth appeared unconvinced. "All right, my dear, but do not wait too long. There are only a certain number of dances left, and then it will be time to be seated for the banquet. You will not be able to dance again until the next ball in a few days."

Jane nodded, and with a slight shrug and a doubtful look, Elizabeth left to go join Darcy, who had moved on to speak to the Peterbrookes. Jane went back to watching the dancing couples with tremulous relief.

Her quiet reverie was broken by an indignant noise. "There she is!" she heard and looked up. Isabelle Grantley, her hair and gown overdone again, was heading straight for her, wearing an angry, superior expression. Jane Elizabeth saw Isabelle's older sister Susannah trying to hold her back and whisper something into her ear, but Isabelle shook her off and advanced.

Jane Elizabeth looked around. Again, circumstances had played against her; she saw both Julia and Frederick dancing – she with a Foxborough and he with Angelina Molyneux – and her parents a very long distance off in conversation with the Peterbrookes. She knew she would have to face this confrontation alone. Silently she prayed for strength and tact, and then Isabelle descended upon her.

"Miss Grantley," she said coolly, "what a pleasant surprise to see you again." Not that they had ever been properly introduced to each other, but there would be no pretense this time.

"Spare me your ridiculous false manners, Miss Darcy," Isabelle attacked, "for yes, I now know who you are!" She looked her up and down and wrinkled her nose. "Well, Miss *Jane* Darcy, I must say what a sly, deceptive, arrogant little minx I find you to be! How dare you lecture me and criticize my opinions in public, yet fail to reveal yourself! Your behavior here as well as back at Pemberley has been contemptible! If I were not a proper young lady myself, no one knows what I might do, and you would deserve all of it! You are not fit to be among such august company as this."

Isabelle had managed to keep her voice down, but it was still loud enough for it to travel and earn shocked, disapproving glances from two well-dressed women her mother's age who were sitting on the couch nearest to theirs.

Jane Elizabeth shrugged and replied in a controlled voice, but with some heat. "Well, you will think what you must, Miss Grantley, but I am neither deceptive nor sly, and as for being arrogant, I suggest you look into your own mirror for that sin." As Isabelle choked with rage, Jane Elizabeth continued. "I meant all that I said to you during our meeting at the previous ball. I do despise my mistakes and all I have done! If you can believe it, I do agree with you that my behavior in the past has been contemptible. I am most sorry and ashamed for all of it. I only ask now that people give me another chance and let me live the rest of my life as I should." As Isabelle rolled her eyes, Jane Elizabeth's voice grew firmer. "I care not for your approval or forgiveness, for I know neither would be forthcoming from you and those who think as you do."

She saw Isabelle restraining herself with difficulty, her hand rising as if she were going to slap her, but Jane Elizabeth was not yet finished. Despite the horrified looks from the two ladies, she stood up and faced her enemy. "Miss Grantley, you are quite welcome to criticize me and my behavior all you like, as you have already done. I neither deserve your good opinion nor would I ever desire or accept it." Isabelle's nostrils flared dangerously, her prettiness having disappeared altogether, and Jane Elizabeth charged with her final verbal thrust. "I can forgive you your judgment of me and my behavior; but I cannot – and will not – forgive you for the harsh treatment you and your family have inflicted upon my brother and sister, both of whom are blameless in all of this." She thought of Frederick and Tom Nixley pulling her from the cold river waters. "I trust that you understand what I have said."

Isabelle tossed her head. "I care not for your low society, of you or your family. Your brother is nothing but a big, gangly boy, and your sister, as pretty as she is, will have no chance in higher society like ours as a result. No Darcy belongs in the *ton*."

"That was quite generous of you, Miss Grantley," Jane Elizabeth shot back, "but I must repeat, my sister, brother, and the rest of my family are blameless as far as my own misdeeds are concerned."

"Pooh! It makes no difference to me or mine," Isabelle retorted.

"Have it your way then." Jane Elizabeth shrugged and turned to go. Over her shoulder she flung, "As for the society you keep, I hope you will find people whose moral standards and personal perfection are as high as your own." She left, only to nod and smile apologetically at the two older ladies, whose looks were alternating between mortification and indignation – which seemed to be directed at Isabelle Grantley.

Isabelle now gave a frustrated sound, and Susannah swept over to her. "Isabelle!" she scolded. "Did I not tell you to watch what you said? For you have made a scene at Sir Francis' ball!"

"I do not care! It was that Darcy minx who provoked me to it." At that, the two older women had had enough and rose to leave. Susannah's heart sank when she saw the dark looks they shot in their direction, as they spoke to each other in tones too low to be heard.

"Oh, will you ever learn to be careful what you say, or even keep your voice down? Sister, we are guests at this ball, just as the Darcys are!"

"Richard says I can say anything I like because I am a Grantley; and, like he, I cannot stand any of these Darcys. They are beneath contempt!"

"Hush!" Susannah grimaced. "And yes, Richard would say something like that." Then she noticed a man and a woman giving them frosty stares. Susannah had had enough. "Come, Isabelle," she said, grabbing her surprised sister's arm, "let us go get something cool to drink – in the next room!"

"But I am to dance now with Mr. Tourneur!"

"No, Isabelle," her sister replied grimly, as she pulled her along. "This dance you are definitely going to sit out, for I am taking you straight to Mama until you regain some manners." If they were not at the Exleys' ball, surrounded by so many people, Isabelle would have wailed.

CHAPTER 12

Frederick danced with the three predatory young ladies, then several more partners. He was not so confident that he felt perfectly accomplished on the dance floor and could do anything, but he did resort to putting the footman's suggestion into action. He supposed he liked Miss Vinson the best – or disliked her the least – so he was very careful not to step on her feet; however, he was not so considerate of the other two young ladies. Miss Robinson seemed surprised at his misstep but didn't criticize him for it, while his trodding on Miss Watson's foot earned him another knowing, saucy glance from her.

After escaping from the brash trio, he drank a final large glass of wine, which dulled his remaining embarrassment and slightly damaged his precise footwork while dancing. Luckily, though, he was able to avoid stepping on any of his later partners' dainty, slippered feet. Still, he was glad when it came time to claim Julia for the ball's final dance. He was so tired from dancing and flirting that he almost trudged over to her. Hang the debut; all he wanted to do was sit down, eat his dinner, and go home to bed.

Julia had just danced her final dance with Sir Timothy, and her single dance with Gregory Lawson. Frederick noticed Lord Ravenswood watching them both, as well as the rather ordinary-looking young man with the wavy brown hair. My, Julia was attracting attention – two suitors, perhaps even three. Well, he was content to think that was what mattered; finding Julia eligible suitors was the entire point of her debut season, wasn't it? As his spirits began to rise, he noticed his sister's pensive expression. "Julia?"

"Oh, Fred, I am so glad to see you." She took his arm.

"Are you all right? Is something bothering you?"

She began telling him as they stood, waiting for the final waltz to begin. She told him about the exchange between Lord Ravenswood and Sir Timothy, and how she had met more young men tonight, including Gregory Lawson. Frederick thought a moment before replying, as they began to glide along with the music. He finally spoke.

"Well, dear Sister, I do not wish to distress you, but it seems Lord Ravenswood and Sir Timothy Carlisle are competing for your attentions." He tried to smile. "In addition, perhaps they do not like each other because of that, or some other reason."

"Yes," she said in a tired voice. "I am sure you are right." Her expression did not lighten.

"Is there something else?" He sounded concerned.

She looked up at him and he saw how weary she looked. "Oh, Fred," she said with a catch in her voice, "I saw Isabelle Grantley make a direct attack on Jane while I was dancing."

He choked back an oath. With a haggard look, he exclaimed, "Good God, we have failed her again! Where is she now, and how is she?"

"She told me about it during the musicians' last break. She is holding up remarkably well, for she stood up to Miss Grantley and pinned her ears back. But I can see how upset she is. Well, she is with Mother and Father now, and they are comforting her."

"Poor Jane Elizabeth," he mourned, "not dancing at her own debut. Again, I have failed to protect her." He wanted to put his head in his hands, but suddenly remembered where he was and what he was doing.

"Don't, Frederick, please," Julia begged him. "You didn't fail Jane. One could say that we all failed her, Mother and Father, too, but I do not think any one of us is truly at fault. Despite our concern for our sister, I do not believe we could have prevented it unless she did not attend the ball tonight; and you know that Mother and Father want her to attend with us. Since this is Jane's debut as well as mine, it would cause more comments if she were to suddenly stop appearing at the season's events."

"I realize that."

"Besides, Jane Elizabeth stood up to Miss Grantley, the horrible thing that she is. I am so proud of her." That was a strong statement coming from Julia. She looked at him. "I am so tired that I just want to go home! I am not even looking forward to the banquet, or between whom I will be sitting. Will this evening ever end?"

He continued to look concerned and almost hugged her during the dance. "Julia, if you feel unwell, all you have to do is say so, and I will get Father to –"

"No, Frederick," she interrupted. "I am not truly ill, only very tired and, well, dispirited." She rested her head on his shoulder for a moment. "This feeling will pass – it always does." She had decided not to tell him about the other stares and whispers she had noticed around them just yet.

"Then I am very glad to hear it." He felt like hugging her again but kept dancing.

After a long moment, she looked up at him again. "Forgive me for saying so, but *you* look rather tired."

"Well," he tried to smile, "I am. I feel I am completely worn out."

"But why?"

He almost told her then, but he did not want to worry her about anything. Instead, he kept trying to smile and repeated over and over how tired he was. "Too much dancing," he joked. He saw her skeptical glance but she kept her peace. At long last, the dance ended, and they went searching for their parents and sister so they could join the queue into the banquet rooms. Meanwhile, Frederick heartily wished he would never meet the Misses Vinson, Robinson, or Watson ever again. He hoped his poor footwork had taken care of that.

The hour was late and the Darcys spent another mostly silent ride back to Cavendish Square. Frederick looked out the carriage window at all the passersby along the way, the only one who didn't make a single comment about the entire evening. The others could not help noticing his distraction, even Jane Elizabeth who hardly said anything herself. Tears seemed to prick at her eyes, but she blinked them away and made a few rather firm, though complimentary, comments about the evening. Darcy and Elizabeth noticed their daughters' hesitant remarks, but this was the second time Frederick was behaving in a pensive, withdrawn mood after a ball, and they were not encouraged by Julia and Jane Elizabeth's behavior either. Finally, with a glance at their mother, Julia spoke in a quiet voice. "Are you feeling all right, Frederick?"

"Yes, Julia, I am quite well, thank you," came his distracted reply, barely glancing at her.

Elizabeth frowned, and Darcy leaned forward. "Is there something about this evening that bothered you, Son?" he asked kindly. He sincerely hoped that, if there were, it was not like what had occurred during and after the previous ball.

Frederick favored him with a full glance. He did not want to lie to his father, so he tried to lighten his voice. "I was just thinking about things, Father," he said. It was a vague answer, but truthful enough.

Elizabeth frowned again, for they usually did not accept such vague replies from their children, but Darcy just shook his head slightly and patted her knee. She saw the concern and patience in his eyes and relaxed. Frederick returned to looking out the window; he did not utter another word, and no one made any further remarks. Julia exchanged a glance with Jane Elizabeth; they looked at their parents but lowered their eyes. They complied with their silent wishes and began talking about some of the other young ladies' gowns that they had admired, and new acquaintances they particularly liked. Jane Elizabeth was determined not to talk about her second meeting with Isabelle Grantley but seemed more in control of herself than she had been the first time. And so the momentary lull within the carriage came to an end.

In front of the house, Frederick again helped his sisters out of the carriage, then followed them inside. Smiling, Darcy suggested they relax in the drawing room, where once more he poured them all a little liqueur to celebrate the ending of yet another evening's ball. Darcy and Elizabeth were unconvinced as they compared notes; it seemed this evening had gone better than the last, but they remained unsure. If it had not, then they wanted to find out the reasons why.

They kept making small conversation – that is, all of them except Frederick, who had gone over and sat in an armchair close to the fireplace, appearing as quiet and distracted as ever. Elizabeth touched Darcy's arm but otherwise made no sign that she had noticed. Julia looked over at her brother, but before anyone could stop her, she went over to him and duplicated her mother's gesture.

"Did you not enjoy this evening, Frederick?" she asked softly.

He blinked, almost painfully, then turned to her. He could not hide the sudden look of confusion in his eyes, and she could not help exclaiming "Frederick, what is it? Why do you look so upset?"

Their parents quickly put down their glasses. "Frederick?" Elizabeth asked quietly, while Darcy waited.

Frederick looked at them, uncertain and unhappy. Finally, he looked away and swallowed hard. "Father," he said, turning to face him, "I know it is very late, but there is something on which I would like to ask your advice. May we go off and talk privately for a while?" he asked in a plaintive tone.

With a glance at Elizabeth, Darcy nodded. "Of course." It had not been long since the Ravenswoods' ball, the last time Frederick looked so pained or confused. This time, however, he seemed to be troubled in another way, so Darcy wanted to ask him about it. That their son seemed troubled in different ways upset him more than he could say. What could be bothering him now? He gestured for Frederick to follow him, saying, "If you would please excuse us."

Jane Elizabeth nodded, but now Julia looked upset. "Frederick?" she asked as he walked past her.

"Hush, Julia," Elizabeth said quietly, "leave him be." She led her daughter over to sit beside her on the couch. Jane Elizabeth turned and patted her brother's arm as he passed by. She tried to smile, but swallowed as he followed his father out to the study.

Darcy closed the door behind him, and keeping an arm around Frederick's shoulders, gently moved him over to a chair. Darcy sat him down and, still noticing his troubled expression, went over to the decanter on the sideboard, where he poured them each a glass of brandy. He handed one glass to Frederick, who gulped it down in a few swallows, without much coughing. Saying nothing, Darcy refilled his glass. This time, Frederick sipped the fine brandy, and his father saw some uncertainty leave his eyes.

A couple of sips later, Darcy sat down and folded his arms across his chest. "Are you ready to begin now, Frederick?"

He blinked to clear his expression. "Yes, Father."

Darcy paused. "Richard Grantley did not insult your manhood again, did he?"

"No, Father. He did snub us, but not as badly as during the previous ball."

"I see." Darcy took a sip himself. He let out a relieved breath; thank God for that, he thought. "Then please tell me what is troubling you."

So, Frederick swallowed more brandy and did.

Elizabeth had long bid her daughters good night and was anxiously awaiting her husband's return to the drawing room.

She wasn't sure if she would see her son again this late night, but tried to stay alert and remain patient. A little over an hour after they had returned home, Elizabeth heard footsteps approaching and rose as her husband entered.

Darcy looked tired and a little disheveled, for his fine clothes were rumpled, his cravat loosened, and the top button of his shirt undone. A few locks of hair spilled over his forehead. Elizabeth was surprised, because her Fitzwilliam always looked fastidious, even when he was tired, wet, muddy, or dusty from traveling.

She went over to him. "Dearest, what is the matter? You look all in! And how is Frederick?" She led him over to the couch, where they sat down together.

Blinking, Darcy looked at her. "I *am* all in – but surely you must be very tired yourself, Dearest, are you not?" She nodded but waited for him to continue. "Do not worry, for I think all will be well. Frederick has told me what made him so pensive tonight, and I'm very happy to tell you it has nothing to do with the Grantleys."

"Thank goodness for that! But what is the matter?"

"Well, Lizzie, our fine, talented, scrupulous son is confused – and excited – by a host of new experiences here in London, including the novelty of receiving the special attentions of several young ladies making their debuts."

Elizabeth sagged. "Oh, dear!" For so long she had been focused on the debut for Julia's benefit that she hadn't thought much about Frederick's part in all of it...or Jane Elizabeth's for that matter, and what it might mean for both of them.

"Yes, Lizzie. Frederick has finally discovered his interest in pretty young women and the strength of their allurements. He also told me he is carried away by the apparent mutual interest he has noticed from some of them." He shook his head, laughing without mirth. "The poor young fellow wasn't ready for all of this when it was almost forced upon him at university, but he is definitely ready *now*. He finds himself the center of attention as much as his sister, and he likes this attention as much as he is bothered by it."

Elizabeth sagged further. "Oh, *no!*" How could her fine, innocent son be growing into a man who was interested in that?

Darcy smiled and took her hand. "I am afraid so. I have just spent the better part of an hour hearing about the charms and defects – physical and otherwise – of all the young ladies he can remember meeting since the first ball." She noticed his eyes glazing over and laughed in spite of herself.

"Poor Frederick! How is he feeling now?"

Darcy exhaled. "He is calm but exhausted, so I sent him to bed. He will probably be thickheaded tomorrow from all the brandy I plied him with." She giggled. "But he is otherwise all right for the moment, and I promise not to require much of him for the entire day."

Now it was his turn to laugh. "Yes, Frederick drank a fair amount as he told me about his newfound feelings and interests. He also asked for a great deal of advice on how to enjoy, control, and express these feelings. I tell you, Lizzie, I feel I could use another drink!" He noticed her disapproving expression. "I am sorry, Dearest; I know I should be more abstemious in my habits, but tonight I am just –" he trailed off. He took a deep breath and sat up straighter. "That was weak and unworthy of me. I am not complaining, and I am very grateful that, despite his fears and unease – and exhilaration – Frederick desperately wanted to talk to me about it, after all the insults he has suffered. And I gave him as much advice as I thought he'd remember."

She kissed his cheek. "It's all right, Fitzwilliam. I too am glad he sought you out."

He kissed her in return. "I really do believe Frederick will come through this just fine. I do not think he will act rashly toward any young woman, but it may be a while before he feels he is on more solid footing. He is struggling with his feelings, desires, and confidence, and wants to do what is right and proper. He still feels ashamed over what happened in Cambridge, though he should not." He shrugged. "I can only hope that all this female attention will not turn his head."

"I hope it will not, either," she replied, "but I trust in your judgment. Besides, on a more positive note, the debut season will not last forever."

He leaned back and looked at her. "No, it will not, as you say, but then he will return to Cambridge, a city where he will be surrounded by women of all kinds and ages – without us to guide him if he wants or needs advice."

She looked away. "Point taken."

They lapsed into silence as the mantel clock kept ticking. Darcy had closed his eyes but felt her stirring beside him.

"Henry was not so confused, was he?" she asked quietly.

Darcy started. "No, he was not." He stared in front of him, remembering. "As he grew, Henry always wanted to play with his little cousins and the other children, whether visitors or from families on the estate. I think he became focused and interested in meeting young ladies by the time he was fifteen. He was that confident."

"Yes, that is how I remember him, too," she said. She was too tired to think about Henry without sadness, so she changed the direction of the conversation. "What about our Nicholas? Do you think he will suffer like Frederick?"

He considered that. "I think Nicholas might turn out to be more like Henry because he has a playful, even mischievous, nature and looks to enjoy himself more – perhaps something we may have to temper later? But our Frederick is so much like how I was at his age – quiet, brooding, shy, and hiding behind a veneer of manners."

"Ah, but that was so long ago, and now you are quite the polished, accomplished, confident, and sociable man!" She laughed and gave him a little hug.

As tired as he was, he cocked an eyebrow at her and gave her a roguish look. "Yes, I do believe that my appearance improves upon further acquaintance."

"Oh, Fitzwilliam, stop!" She was laughing, though, and he kissed her hand. "How you vex and distract me, Mr. Darcy!" she exclaimed, thinking of her mother.

"I thought you liked being vexed and distracted this way." He gave her an even naughtier look, and they both burst out laughing. When they were calmer, she leaned forward. "So, were you nineteen years of age when you first became interested in young women? Or did it occur earlier than that?"

He laughed again, but began blushing; and the more he remembered, the darker he blushed. Elizabeth felt her heart overcome with love that she could not tease him any further, at least not right this instant.

"Well, Lizzie," he tried, "since you asked, I do remember that when I was eleven or twelve, I was quite taken with Miss Perdita Daltrey."

"Who was Miss Daltrey?"

"She was my tutor's daughter, and all of eight years old, but very pretty and well-mannered enough. Still, as much as I respected him and his memory, my father told me I needed to grow up and consider young women closer in age, intelligence, and social standing, not the daughter of a mere teacher." He looked away, embarrassed.

"Dearest." She put her head on his shoulder, and he clasped her to him. "How difficult it must have been for you to be told that! So, what became of Miss Daltrey?"

He shrugged. "She moved away from Pemberley with her family when Master Daltrey returned to London so he could tutor privately there." Now he tried to smile. "And so, my heart was broken at the age of twelve."

"With all due respect to your late father," Elizabeth countered, "I do not believe that at all! So your heart was broken over an eight-year-old girl? Do boys of twelve even *like* little girls?" Darcy laughed helplessly. "No, I do not believe a word of it!" she declared. "Now tell me, when did you really become interested in young women like Frederick has?"

He was still smiling as he shook his head. "How insistent you are, Mrs. Darcy! And now, to oblige you, I must dredge up memories that I am sure will vex and upset you!"

"Fitzwilliam Darcy!" She sat straight up. "How can you dare to say such things to me, your beloved wife? In all the time I have known you, no, since I first met you, I have never heard you utter such silly, outrageous, absolute nonsense! That I would be vexed or distressed by such admissions! And to charge that *I* would be jealous or upset over some poor young woman who fell for that profile and those eyes of yours before I ever met you! Oh, this is not to be borne! And I shall not." She gave him a cold glance, and he made the mistake of laughing. "For that, and all of these offenses, I shall punish you." He began to laugh harder, and she grabbed the nearest sofa cushion. She swatted him with it several times as he clumsily tried to defend himself.

"No, Lizzie," he pleaded, helpless, "not the sofa cushions again, and certainly not tonight because it is so late! Please be careful of my ribs!" But he kept on laughing as she kept battering him and slid down on his side of the sofa.

"Do you think you can vex and upset me any more than you already have? Answer me!" She clouted him again.

"Of course I can vex you more!"

"*Oh*, that is insupportable, you proud, haughty, insufferable man!" She peppered his squirming body with more blows.

"What happened to my being polished, accomplished, and so on?" he protested in a shaky voice, only to be battered anew. "OOF!" he gasped out but kept on laughing.

"I do not know, but I do hope that, whether accomplished or insufferable, a certain gentleman of my acquaintance has been properly chastened." He held up his hands in surrender, even waving his white handkerchief between them, so she gave him a final, resounding buffet with the cushion and carefully put it back in its place. "Then kindly tell me what I wish to know, for if you do not, I will think of punishments more intense and delicious."

"Intense and delicious for whom?" he retorted but sat up straight when he saw her expression. "All right! I promise I will tell you everything – just please, no more violence tonight!"

"We shall see about that." Patting the cushion, she stared at him. "Pray continue, Sir."

He held her gaze but stretched out a protective arm across the nearest cushions. "My dear Lizzie," he said with weakened formality and some apprehension, "I admit to you now that I first became interested in young women when *I* first went off to university." He saw that he held her attention, and therefore was physically safe for the moment.

"How old were you, Dearest?"

"I was not yet eighteen years of age," he replied. "I was close friends with a fellow named Jacob Cantwell; I met Bingley a while later." He paused. "Cantwell had a sixteen-year-old sister named Rebecca."

He was going to continue, but she held up her hand. "That is all right, Fitzwilliam, I do not need to ask much more, nor will I beat you for the information." He could not help giving a snort of laughter, but then sobered quickly enough.

"All right, but what would you like to know?"

She ticked off her fingers. "Pretty?" He nodded. "Sweet?" Another nod. "Well-mannered?" Yet another. Then she asked slowly, "Did your father express any reservations about her, or you being friendly with her?" A final, firm nod. "Oh, Fitzwilliam, I am so sorry, and I am also sorry that I insisted you tell me so."

He reached over and took both her hands. "Do not be upset, for I am not." He sighed. "Yes, my father did compliment Becky Cantwell on her manners and appearance, but still declared she was beneath my consideration befitting my status as the next Master of Pemberley." He swallowed. "I loved and respected my father, Lizzie, but on some things he could be quite unyielding. No matter, for it turned out to be a mixed blessing, but a blessing nonetheless."

She gave him an appraising look. "How can you say that?"

He gave her a smile that melted her heart. "Well, my father's firm ideas about what kind of young lady was appropriate to court did separate me from Becky Cantwell, and I accepted that. I think that many of my own thoughts on whom it is appropriate for our children to marry are probably more like his than I would like to admit, but I am digressing.

"After my father died, I discovered how 'eligible' I was as the young, new Master of Pemberley, and so I became aware of young women whom I felt were – I am sorry to say so – predatory, who seemed to desire my wealth and position in society, but not so much me personally, or so I thought." He gave a small laugh. "I resented finding myself in such a position and, well, you remember how I remained aloof from people, especially young ladies, and made absolutely wretched first impressions to just about everyone." She smiled at that. "I thought and acted that way for a very long time...until I met and was bewitched by one particular Miss Bennet!" And he peppered her cheek and neck with gentle kisses.

"Well said, Fitzwilliam," she almost purred as she wrapped her arms around him. "But how right you were about the others, I am sure; wealth and position arc normal conditions for marriage, but not necessarily the feelings of those involved, whether woman or man. I am also glad that *I* was the one who finally appreciated your fine manner of address, among other things." Again they collapsed into laughter, and she suddenly took his hand. "Now, thanks to your lovely comments, I have decided there is no need to beat you – for quite some time!"

He laughed helplessly and kissed her again. "Thank you, Lizzie. I, and my poor body included, am most relieved to hear you say so." He also decided that he would develop a secret plan to ban loose cushions from all the couches in the Great House of Pemberley and here in the Cavendish Square house if he could.

She smiled sweetly at him. "Do you really think Frederick

will be all right and keep his head – and desires – under control?"

He thought for a moment and nodded with a smile. "I think he will be able to do so. We know how well developed his conscience is and how hard he tries to behave properly. He knows what is expected of him." He patted her knee. "I also gave him several pieces of advice on how to temper his, er, well, impulses – if I have your indulgence *not* to be any more specific on those."

Smiling, she shook her head. "Of course, Dearest, I trust you implicitly, but you can spare me such revelations, as useful as I am sure they are."

Darcy gave a contented sound. "I am most grateful for our playful banter and laughter tonight, Lizzie. How much we needed it, after the upsetting events that occurred during and after the Ravenswoods' ball. I was afraid our children's spirits would not rally after all they experienced, but it seems they are improving. Yet I think we have not yet heard what might have transpired this evening, except for poor Frederick's hazing."

She smiled again. "Yes, our poor son, who was so shocked by the brazen behavior of those young women! I am as grateful as you are about our children's spirits improving. We must maintain our vigilance, however. We could find out later today if anything occurred that might be a concern for us about their welfare."

"Yes, we certainly will."

They held hands for some time, as weariness overcame their contentment. Then the mantel clock chimed three o'clock, and Darcy could not help giving a splitting yawn.

"Ah, forgive me," he moaned, "but I am so tired and my body battered, but I think you must be exhausted as well." He stretched his limbs. "Also, I am getting too old for all of this! Frederick had better finish growing up, and soon!"

Laughing, she rose. "Nonsense, Dearest! Frederick is growing up quite as he should, with you and me to help him. And do not forget that Nicholas is coming along right behind him, so we can go through all of this again when it is his turn!" She pulled him, laughing ruefully, off the couch and led him into the hallway. "Now, Mr. Darcy, come follow me, for there is something I can give you to heal your well-deserved bruises." She gave him a deep kiss, and he dutifully followed her upstairs into her bedroom.

Mrs. Winston and Emma had helped Jane Elizabeth out of her finery and dress for bed. Emma offered but Jane Elizabeth gently said she'd brush her hair herself. After the maid left with a curtsey, Mrs. Winston made a few hopeful remarks about the evening and their plans for the morrow, but Jane Elizabeth only smiled, speaking few words. Mrs. Winston plumped the pillows and pulled the covers up over her; she gave Jane a searching glance and parting wish, then closed the bedroom door quietly behind her.

Sleep did not overtake her despite her weariness; Frederick was not the only one kept awake by relentless thoughts. Jane sat up, her back cushioned against the pillows as she reflected on the long evening.

As soon as she closed her eyes, Isabelle Grantley's snobbery filled her eyelids, and she could hear their cutting exchanges. Jane felt tears welling, so she squeezed her eyes tighter until she stopped trembling and her breathing slowed. Jane savored remembering her repartees, pinning the hateful girl's ears back and defending her family members while maintaining her composure. Jane was certain she could not have done so in even the recent past. She did not relish encountering Isabelle ever again, but realized she only needed to behave herself, and let the other girl display her atrocious behavior and vicious tongue.

Opening her eyes, Jane Elizabeth grew pensive, even agitated. Why did people here in London have to know what happened back at Pemberley? Hadn't she suffered enough? Hadn't she regretted what she did and apologized enough for it? She gave a frisson of futile self-reproach. Wiping her eyes, she supposed she was still too naïve, thinking she might be forgiven and accepted again at some point, but that was probably a vain hope. Jane realized she still worried about and needed to concentrate on her behavior! She must be perfect in all she said and did, especially when people knew about her misdeeds.

Perhaps more pleasant thoughts could coax her to sleep. She had snuggled back under the covers, but now she opened one eye. This was her debut, too, not only Julia's; what did she think about all the young gentlemen she was meeting?

Surprisingly, Jane Elizabeth felt no pang from this thought, perhaps because she didn't feel attracted to any of them – yet. Another reason why her mother's hints about dancing instead of sitting it out didn't bother her much. She pursed her lips. No, she wasn't attracted to any of the gentlemen – period. Sometimes she wished she didn't have to pay attention to them at all. But what did she think of them?

Well, of course they were all handsome, exquisitely attired, and courtly and proper in their manners. Jane had never seen so many young men gathered together that glittered, preened, and expelled good humor and manly vigor to whomever they met. Jane realized they were as much on display as she and her fellow debutantes.

Jane Elizabeth first thought of Simon Easton; she enjoyed his colorful stories and lively, cheerful demeanor. He reminded her very much of Nicholas.

She also found herself thinking favorably of Sir Edward Chatterton. He was too old for her, of course; he must be close to thirty years of age, but she was fascinated by his perfectly curled, short, golden hair, bluish-green eyes, and the creamy, soft silkiness of his fine trousers and waistcoat. She had shared a short conversation with him over refreshments, and now savored him recounting the most recent play he had attended.

Her eyes remained closed as her mind kept working. Truthfully, she had trouble distinguishing between Silas and Seth Foxborough, even though they were not twins; she did better at keeping Samuel and Daniel Stoddard separate in her thoughts. Jane found Julian Tunney dazzlingly handsome, but off-putting in some of his remarks; he had disparaged the Eastons, as well as the Ravenswoods, for some reason – was it the church at which they worshipped? She could not recall.

Jane Elizabeth found Lord Ravenswood very handsome, too, but hard to read or connect with; though he remained reserved and slightly aloof, he was not rudely standoffish. Yet Julia seemed to like him very much, and this made Jane Elizabeth consider him in a more favorable light.

She thought Martin Tourneur quite dashing with his long, wavy, dark hair and full mustache, and interesting, though she hadn't spoken to him much, while she couldn't remember meeting Gregory Lawson or even his features. Of course, she must have at some point during the three balls so far.

Jane Elizabeth felt her thoughts slowing, her lids remaining closed longer. Now her mind rested on Sir Timothy Carlisle. She inhaled. Julia liked him as much as she did Lord Ravenswood. Jane also liked Sir Timothy, and knew she'd need to proceed with caution – not out of competition, but to avoid difficulties for the three of them. A wave of fatigue swept over her. Her memories shifted from Sir Timothy's shiny clothes to a bejeweled golden band around his right wrist.

Her thoughts dulled as she warmed under the covers. Who would be her partners at the next ball? She didn't want to engage and drifted off to sleep.

CHAPTER 13

The next ball came quickly enough, but Darcy and Elizabeth were wrong about their children's spirits improving. Frederick seemed better, more in control of himself, and ready for further baptism by fire from eager young ladies; perhaps he might try flirting with a couple of them if he liked them. Jane Elizabeth looked resigned, but what she lacked in animation she made up for in patience and pleasantness, neither of which came easily to her. Her parents considered Isabelle Grantley's direct attack upon her and Jane Elizabeth's measured, dignified response, which had amazed and impressed them.

But now it was Julia's turn to be downcast and troubled. She still kept her expression and manners perfect, but her green eyes betrayed her while the carriage kept moving. She was dreading more snubs, and knowing the Grantleys and Urquharts would be present this evening did not cheer her. As she sat in her most fabulous gown yet – a dress of garnet-colored satin with a full skirt and accents of gold thread and white lace about her bosom and shoulders – with gold at her throat and ruby earrings her mother had lent her, Julia kept fussing with her dark hair swept back into a perfect, elegant bun. Tasteful ringlets framed her cheeks. Elizabeth exchanged a glance with Darcy.

"Julia, you look perfectly stunning," she said. "Please stop fussing with your hair, for it cannot be improved upon." She smiled to take some of the sting out of her reproof.

"Yes, Mother," Julia replied meekly, and kept her hands in her lap. Jane Elizabeth smiled at her and took one of her gloved hands while their parents continued to watch.

They soon arrived at Dutton Ampner, the home of their hosts Sir Romanus and Lady Margery Ventnor. The house on the outskirts of London was a sprawling mansion, most of which was Georgian in style, but the main section of the house had been added on to a much older timbered one from the late sixteenth century. They made their way through the receiving line, and Julia made her usual perfect greetings and curtsies to everyone, including their hosts.

Sir Romanus was a tall, handsome man with an ascetic face and slow, precise, but not haughty speech, while Lady Margery was a plump, outgoing woman with dark hair and eyes, whom Julia thought would be at ease supervising an army of maidservants, cooks, young ladies in finishing school, or even factory girls. Sir Romanus and Lady Margery were proud of their debuting daughter, Dorothea, who resembled her father very much in appearance and manner. Their hosts exclaimed over Julia, who knew she had caught the eyes of many guests as well, in her shimmering deep red satin gown; she was so dazzled by her own dazzling that she did not worry about upstaging Miss Ventnor in her home, as she might have.

Many of Julia's acquaintances and fellow debutantes were already in attendance, and her spirits lifted when the first two she encountered after leaving the receiving line were Pamela Easton and Sophia Stoddard. They were chatting gaily together when Sophia mentioned she regretted that Sir Timothy Carlisle and his sister Catharina were not present this evening.

Julia's spirits began to deflate again. "I am so sorry to hear it! Pray what is the reason for their absence? I do hope Miss Carlisle is not ill." How foolish of her not to have considered the idea that maybe she was not the only young woman interested in the handsome young man. Pamela Easton was blond, pretty, and could get anyone to like her, and Sophia Stoddard had curly red hair, the fairest of complexions, and the palest eyes she had ever seen; in her sleek gown of pale blue silk, she looked exotic, elfin, and magical, as did her brothers with their heads of curly dark hair, dark eyes, and faint olive complexions. Her younger sister Hannah in plum-colored satin appeared shy and reserved, but pleasant enough, and Sophia was as much her escort as were their brothers; Julia liked her simple dark woven braids curled up and around her dainty ears.

"It seems that is precisely the case, Miss Darcy," Sophia nodded to her. "Poor Catharina has been fighting off a cold for the past few days, I am told, and Sir Timothy was so concerned that he insisted she stay home and rest until she is out of danger. I think it is wonderful how he dotes on his younger sister!"

"Yes, Miss Stoddard," Pamela agreed. "Miss Carlisle is so sweet and pleasing to the eye, and I wish that nothing unpleasant would ever befall her! But I would not be surprised if she had resisted her brother's efforts to keep her at home." Indeed, one had to have serious or compelling reasons to miss a debutante ball, since it was the reason all of them were here with their families.

Julia laughed in spite of herself. "Yes, Miss Easton, I am certain you are correct. I know that I would wish to appear at the ball even if I were at death's door, but I am also certain that my father and brother, Frederick, would prevail and keep me home as well, under a doctor's watchful eye!" They all laughed. Still, that meant that none of them would be dancing with Sir Timothy, or examining more of his elegant, light-reflecting apparel tonight. Yes, most definitely a pity.

"Well, my dear young ladies," Pamela said, "the loss of Sir Timothy need not be ours, for I am sure we will have many other fine, dashing partners with which to dance!"

Julia laughed with them. "Miss Stoddard," she addressed her, "would you happen to know if each of your brothers has at least one dance unclaimed so far? For I would very much like to dance with them."

Taking her arm, Sophia gave her a warm smile. "How sweet of you, Miss Darcy! I know Samuel and Daniel will both be delighted to dance with you, and I am equally certain their dance cards are not yet full!" Her eyes sparkled.

Pamela pretended to be cross. "And what about saving *me* at least one dance with each of them? Really, Miss Darcy, you are being quite forward!" She suddenly giggled, and Julia and Sophia joined in.

"Do not be concerned, Miss Easton, for my brothers can accommodate you, too."

"I am very glad to hear it." However, none of them could keep their faces straight, and Julia's spirits rallied again. They did not hear Gregory Lawson approach their lively little group.

"Good evening, ladies!"

If they were startled, none of them showed it, and bows and curtsies were exchanged. Mr. Lawson immediately turned his attention to Julia, which made her blush. She felt badly for her friends, and still wanted to continue chatting with them, but they smiled good-naturedly and moved away a few steps.

He had just asked her for two dances, and she was about to agree, when Lord Ravenswood appeared.

"Greetings, Miss Darcy!" He bowed deeply to her, and she almost knelt on the floor in her curtsey. "Forgive me, but if you have favored Mr. Lawson here with two dances, I hope there is still room for one dance – no, two – with me." He looked at the other young man.

Julia felt wonderful and nervous at the same time. She looked at Gregory Lawson, but he seemed not to mind, since he had already been promised his two dances. "Well, as a matter of fact, my lord," she smiled, batting her lashes momentarily, "it appears that you are in luck as well, and your timing is perfect, as I am able to grant you one – no, two – dances." She smiled a little too widely at him, as she forgot Mr. Lawson, who was smiling himself but blinking.

"Capital! Thank you so much, Miss Darcy!" The young lord had almost reached for her gloved hand with his own, then remembered himself. "I shall return at that time."

"Thank you, Lord Ravenswood. I shall look forward to it."

"As do I." The tall, imposing young man nodded to her,

bowed deeply, and left.

Embarrassed, Julia now turned to face Gregory Lawson. She tried to speak, but he smiled and took pity on her.

"I am so sorry, Mr. Lawson, I forgot myself just now, and you, and I –"

"There is no need to apologize, Miss Darcy, indeed there is not." He could not be more magnanimous in his decency and fairness. "Of course, you must dance with all of us young gentlemen, including Lord Ravenswood and myself! Why else do we hold debut seasons for young ladies as lovely, pleasing, beautiful, and delightful as you?"

"Oh, Mr. Lawson, you are complimenting me far more than I deserve, much as I am pleased by your sentiments! And you are being most understanding of my less than sterling behavior." Should she ask if his sister Letitia were somewhere close by this evening? Of course, she must be, but Julia could not remember meeting her.

"Not at all, Miss Darcy," he countered. "You should be declared Queen of the ball based on your lovely, shimmering gown alone; the color cannot become you more!"

"Thank you, Mr. Lawson," she fluttered. This was much more than the usual compliments she received, and she was starting to feel guilty about Miss Ventnor, wherever she was now. She should have been fanning herself, except she had forgotten what she had done with her fan.

"It was my pleasure, Miss Darcy." He gave her a bow as deep and perfect as Lord Ravenswood's. He promised to return for the second dance of the evening, after she had danced the first one with Frederick, for which she was very grateful.

Lord Ravenswood claimed her for the third dance of the evening, before she danced with either Samuel or Daniel Stoddard. Now his smile was wide, warm, and full, as he beheld her in her stunning finery. She enjoyed waltzing with him very much and asked polite questions about his sister Cecilia. He looked happily into her eyes but seemed diminished or reticent whenever she mentioned other guests, particularly male ones who were probably some of her other dance partners this evening! She began to realize that the young nobleman was jealous of the other gentlemen and was having difficulty concealing it. Please, dear Lord, she prayed in her head as they danced, I do not need this to happen now! Please let everything turn out all right...but she was a Darcy, after all, so she decided to challenge him.

"It seems to me you are distracted, my lord," she said, smiling and dimpling. "Pray tell me what will make you smile, for you have quite a dazzling one!"

He thanked her with a very gallant response, then added, "What will make me smile? I should not say so, but since you have asked me...What will make me smile," he declared, "is when we dance again as we are doing now! I wish I could dare ask you for a third."

She laughed, blushing. "Well said, my lord, but you must not take such risks, for dance cards fill up very quickly as you know." She did not let on but could not understand why her card remained empty from now on after the Stoddards, except for one more dance with Mr. Lawson and her current partner, unless she granted Lord Ravenswood a controversial third dance, which she really wanted to do; otherwise, there was only the one with Julian Tunney, and the final dance of the evening again with Frederick. But there were at least six open spaces for which she could not think of a reason, and sudden thoughts of why made her want to shudder with dread.

"Yes, Miss Darcy, and I thank you!" Lord Ravenswood looked properly checked, but also grateful and relieved.

She was not through challenging him yet, so she smiled and changed the subject. "I must say I am quite disappointed that Sir Timothy Carlisle and his wonderful sister were unable to attend this evening. I understand that Miss Carlisle is ill."

"Yes, how unfortunate." His expression clouded over.

"Do you know Sir Timothy well, milord?" she pressed.

His eyes registered something dark. "Well, I am acquainted with the gentleman, but I cannot say that I know him well."

"I see." After a pause, she said, "Is not his sister a lovely creature?"

"Oh, yes," he started, "Miss Carlisle is a lovely young lady, sweet and pleasing in everything she says or does."

Julia laughed. "I should be jealous of such a statement, but in truth I share your opinion of Miss Carlisle."

"How glad I am to hear that!" He gave a shaky laugh.

"You and Sir Timothy are not friends then?"

He gave her a level glance. "No, Miss Darcy, we are not."

She swallowed, but tried to smile. "Is there a reason for that? Surely, I hope not, but please do forgive me for my curiosity!"

She had him right where she wanted him – caught between saying something unfavorable about Sir Timothy while trying to behave appropriately with her, since both young men had been paying her much attention. He almost rolled his eyes. "Well, one can know many people here in London, Miss Darcy, but honestly I must say that I limit my exposure to Sir Timothy to acquaintance only." He sighed. "I admit that I do not care for the man."

"But why, Lord Ravenswood? What could he possibly have done to earn your lack of regard?" Shocked, she almost stumbled in asking her question.

Responding to the surprise in her voice, he quickly smiled. "Forgive me, Miss Darcy, for being so harsh and ill-mannered; in these things he is admirable enough, as well as the pains he takes in the care of his sister." He looked away. "However, I find his personal style too ostentatious, almost unmanly, and I think he presents himself as another Lord Byron, that is, in the sense that he is a patron of artists and actors!" He gave her a pleading look. "Please, Miss Darcy! I am neither so superior nor perfect to think that I have no defects in my character or behavior! Yet, I am still uncomfortable with Sir

Timothy, as wealthy, handsome, intelligent, and charming as he is. I hear he has a fine singing voice, as well as a flair for the dramatic. And that he spends more time caring for his sister, and associating with artist and politicians, than managing his own affairs." He sighed. "Now you have heard all that I think about him, and I await your censure for my lack of tolerance and civility."

Julia remained silent, grateful for the length of this waltz. "Lord Ravenswood, with all due respect, I shall neither censure nor criticize you for your feelings or your answers, since I was impertinent enough to ask you about them in the first place!" He bowed his head and thanked her. "Not at all, my lord," she countered. "In fact, I must beg your forgiveness for asking such questions! Please forgive me, and I shall try not to be so inquisitive again."

His eyes gave her a look that melted her heart. "You have no reason to ask me for forgiveness, but if it matters to you, then I most certainly do forgive you! Now, please, I beg of you to forgive *me* for my dislike of this young man, and my poor manners."

How could she resist such a plea? "Of course I forgive you, Lord Ravenswood." He grinned in relief, but sobered, and they danced the rest of the waltz in muted, happy silence. He again bowed deeply to her and promised to return for their later dance. He left her with a smile and a blush.

After she had danced with the Stoddard brothers and before her second dance with Gregory Lawson, she anticipated dancing with her next partner, the incredibly handsome, gregarious Julian Tunney. This young gentleman sported well-oiled, curly dark hair and a tanned complexion, with an impressive, dimpled chin and a physique as impressive as the Foxborough brothers. His blue eyes were intense and disarming, and young ladies kept straining the bounds of propriety to inspire a response from him; it was difficult to decide who was more beautiful, he or his sparkling, golden-haired sister Mary

Duncan. Lord Ravenswood had left her with much to think about, but that did not prevent her from looking forward to dancing with the much sought-after Mr. Tunney. Once they began dancing, he paid her a strange compliment.

"I am most grateful for our dance tonight, Miss Darcy, to which I have been looking forward since the last ball," Julian Tunney said, his smile displaying his almost perfect teeth. "But I must confess that I am in awe of you! I admire your fortitude and your condescension in facing such social obstacles."

What could he mean by that? Carefully she said, "Oh, Mr. Tunney, I cannot accept such compliments from you, for you are giving me far too much credit. I cannot imagine what I have done to deserve such regard."

He smiled. "Ah, do not deprecate yourself so! If I must explain myself to you, then I shall." He laughed. "I am most impressed by your willingness to associate with such people as the Stoddards, though they have been invited to every ball."

Nonplussed, she replied, "Why should it be impressive that I socialize with the Stoddards? For I find Miss Sophia and her siblings quite agreeable and attractive, and their parents, Lord Benjamin and Lady Miriam, quite refreshing and interesting to know."

He laughed harder as they danced. "As I said, how kind and accepting you are of so many denizens of the capital."

She did not like that remark, and her expression showed it. "Pray, Mr. Tunney, do not keep me in suspense, for I am but a silly young woman out for her own pleasures tonight, and I simply do not know what you are talking about." He missed her glare and laughed again.

"My dear young lady, how sweet and unassuming you are! Why, I am complimenting you on your bravery in dancing with the Stoddard brothers, for it is quite obvious that they are Jews – not to mention their sisters and parents."

It was as if he had slapped her. "So, they are Jews," she remarked. "I was not aware, but how does that affect me?"

She was surprised at how angry she felt, and how biting her tone had become.

"Why, Miss Darcy!" He grinned at her. "Surely, your naiveté is quite becoming and welcome! But, if you had known, why would you want to dance with such men? Probably their family has made its fortune from trade Lord knows how many generations ago, and as Jews they can hardly be considered acceptable members of society."

"I still do not understand," she said stiffly. "I cannot think of a reason why the Stoddards' society is neither welcome nor desirable. However, I do notice that the young men's parents are *Lord* Benjamin and *Lady* Miriam," she added in a cold voice. "I believe Lord Benjamin is the Earl of Swindon, in Wiltshire."

"Oh, he is," Mr. Tunney deprecated, "and rich as Croesus, too, or so they say. His father was Judah or Joseph ben something, and then there is Lady Miriam and her daughters, Miss Sophia and Miss Hannah – you only must look at them to see they are typical Jewesses! Even all their names give them away." He shrugged. "As for their sons, they are quite the men about town, seen everywhere and swimming in pounds! They style themselves as great patrons of the arts; so, I am sure that new opera *La Juive* must be their personal favorite." He gave an unpleasant guffaw.

Flushing, Julia could not have been angrier. She had never heard such unforgiveable insults, not even to Frederick, and displeasure filled her face. She decided that she had had enough, and would dance no longer with Mr. Tunney, even though the music had not ended. She glared at him. "Was not the Lord Jesus himself a Jew, who taught in synagogues, and all his family and followers? Good evening, Mr. Tunney," she declared, and turned to walk away through the dancing couples.

Though she moved carefully through the dancers, she had only advanced perhaps ten feet when she gave into weakness and looked back over her shoulder. It appeared that Julian

Tunney was trying to follow her; perhaps to persuade her to reconsider, or mollify her? The nerve of him to follow her after she had dismissed him! She felt both rage and fear coursing through her, and worried her face registered an unbecoming flush. She wanted to hurry and get away, but didn't want to block, bump, or inconvenience any of the other dancers. He managed to catch up to her and lightly touched her red satin sleeve.

She shook his hand away, as some eyebrows rose among the guests around them. She had passed through the last of the dancers to the sidelines of the ballroom, so she exhaled in relief instead of making angry or frustrated noises. She looked back again. Julian had halted several feet away, still among the dancers; he opened his mouth and looked foolish, as others in the ballroom realized she had abandoned him. He saw people making asides and pointing surreptitiously as he tried to slink away towards one of the walls of the ballroom.

Julia strode outside to the balcony. Quivering with anger, she felt dirty and shamed in her finery. No, she would never dance with – or even acknowledge – Julian Tunney ever again. She was equally determined that she would always be kind and welcoming to Sophia and her family, for she really liked all of them. She still had openings on her dance card, such as this moment, so she took advantage of it. She walked up and down the balcony, found her fan, and tried to calm herself. She wasn't noticing the clear evening skies, or the beautiful gardens laid out in front of her. She was still lost in outraged thought when Pamela Easton and Sophia Stoddard, with Cecilia Calvert in tow, hurried out to her.

"Thank goodness we have found you, and that you are alone!" Pamela exclaimed.

"Yes, I am quite at my leisure for the moment, for I have no dance partners for at least the next several dances." She looked at them. "My goodness, dear friends, how anxious you look! What is troubling you, and why were you looking for me?"

"Oh, Miss Darcy!" Sophia cried. "It is all too horrible to speak aloud, but we simply must tell you! I do believe there is a reason why your card is not full tonight."

Color drained from Julia's face, and she stepped backward against the railing. "A reason?" she said faintly. "Pray tell me then..." Pamela and Cecilia rushed over to support her on each side.

Pamela exchanged a glance with Sophia. "Yes, there is a reason. You have been popular and sought after at every ball, with all your dances claimed – until tonight!" She sighed. "We believe someone has started rumors about you and your behavior, and they are circulating throughout Dutton Ampner right now. We felt we simply had to warn you, as awful, cruel, and undeserved these rumors are."

Julia reached for an arm from each of her companions. "What is being said about my behavior?" She sagged.

"Oh, dear," Sophia worried, "you are looking quite ill! But we shall tell you all of it." The other young ladies nodded at her to continue, and she cleared her throat. "You see, Miss Darcy, the rumor is that, back at your Pemberley home, you were supposed to have granted your favors," here Sophia blushed and began to cry. "Oh, I can barely repeat such despicable things, especially to *you*! But it is being said that you behaved shamelessly with a farmer's son on the estate, and that he is neither the first nor the last!"

Julia was horrified. "No, this cannot be!" she cried, as the awful implications dawned on her. "It is not true!" She burst into tears. As she trembled and sobbed, she tried to explain. "It was my sister Jane who did so, but she did not 'grant her favors,' and she only misbehaved the one time! She was so remorseful, and people treated her so badly that she...she tried to drown herself!" The other young ladies could not help recoiling at this. "Our brother saved her life. But how awful this is!" She stumbled a few steps. "Poor Jane is to be mistreated all over again, and I am to be branded as loose and wanton, a harlot!" She cried harder. "Oh, what can be done?

Who started these rumors?" As distraught as she was, she knew the answer before she heard it. She had not realized how hard it would be to be brave and keep her composure in the face of such dislike and mistreatment.

Pamela looked grim as they led her weeping to a stone bench. "We do not know for certain who was the first to say these vile things about you," she said, "but I do know that Mr. Richard Grantley and his sister Miss Isabelle are both enjoying themselves by repeating them as often as they can, to anyone who will listen."

"Isabelle Grantley herself told Miss Stoddard and me," Cecilia said, white with indignation, "and so we came looking for you straight away."

Julia was already using a second handkerchief, Sophia's. "We are all ruined, utterly ruined! And this will devastate my sister, after she has healed so well!" Her face twisted with anger, despite her tears. "How dreadfully perfect a rumor it is – they criticize and exaggerate my sister's mistake, then attribute it to me! Later, they can claim they somehow got it wrong from whoever it is they say told them first – but it keeps the rumor alive and hurts her all over again! Poor Jane! How despicable this is!" She kept sobbing.

"What can we do to help you?" Cecilia asked softly.

Julia stirred. "I do not...No, wait. I must find my father and Frederick! We must get Jane away from here before she learns of this, before it gets any worse!"

"Yes, but the evening will be a very long one, and the dancing is barely half over," Sophia pointed out.

"It doesn't matter, Miss Stoddard! We must get our sister safely home to Cavendish Square immediately! I – I shall claim I have become ill; it is not so very far from the truth." She broke down into fresh sobs, and Pamela let her rest her head on her shoulder. "I do not care what happens to me, but my poor sister has suffered so much already for what she has done." She could not say much more, feel any lower, or more wretched. "All this because of some secret, stolen kisses…"

"Miss Stoddard," Pamela said, stroking Julia's hair, "please go and fetch Mr. Darcy and young Mr. Frederick! Be as insistent as you can and tell them Miss Darcy has become ill. Miss Calvert, you are well acquainted with Miss Jane Darcy, are you not?" Cecilia nodded. "Then please bring her back with you quickly – tell her that her sister needs her."

However, they were delayed, for Frederick bounded out onto the balcony, with Lord Ravenswood right behind him.

"Julia!" Frederick cried when he saw her. "For God's sake, what is wrong?" He stood helplessly in front of her as she kept sobbing into Pamela Easton's shoulder. "I have never seen her like this before," he remarked, bewildered, to all of them. He knelt in front of her and took her free hand.

"She cannot hear you, Mr. Darcy," Lord Ravenswood said calmly. "However, my dear young ladies, we hope that you can enlighten us as to how Miss Darcy came to such distress."

"Yes, my lord," Sophia replied, and between her, Cecilia, and Pamela they related the dreadful news.

Frederick flushed. "I have had enough of the Grantleys! I shall teach Richard a lesson he will never forget! He has harmed my family for the last time!" He jumped up, ready to dash back inside the house, his face murderous. All the young women shrank from him.

"No!" Lord Ravenswood grabbed him by the shoulders. "You must not!"

"Let me go!" Frederick struggled against the taller, slightly older young man, but could not free himself. "I will kill him!"

"No, you must not, I say!" Lord Ravenswood exclaimed as he struggled to hold onto Frederick. "That is precisely why I will not let you go, until you are calmer!" Though he was bigger, it took all his strength to check the enraged fellow in his arms.

Hot tears stung Frederick's eyes as he kept struggling. "Have you not heard what they are doing tonight, how much harm they are causing? Do you not know of all the insults they have inflicted upon my sisters? Let me go, my lord, I demand it! I will settle this once and for all! The Grantleys have injured us all enough, and I demand some kind of satisfaction!" The young ladies shrank further from the grappling young men.

"NO." Lord Ravenswood strengthened his grip, shook him hard, then even slapped his cheek. Frederick was so shocked he stopped struggling. They stared at each other, breathing in gasps. Finally, Lord Ravenswood spoke. "No more talk of killing," he puffed. "You cannot help your sisters that way, and you are the future Master of Pemberley." Frederick looked away. "I grant you that Richard Grantley is a callow, surly brute, but he is not worth killing or getting into trouble over, so I urge you to keep your head, young sir!" Frederick went on gasping as some of his anger and energy were now spent. They stepped back from each other and began straightening their clothes. "Good, Mr. Darcy," Lord Ravenswood wiped sweat from his face, "you seem calmer now."

"Y–yes, my lord," Frederick managed to say. "I am so sorry I –"

Lord Ravenswood held up his hand. "There is no need to apologize, for no harm has been done. I am as outraged as you for your sisters' sake. I would feel the same if anyone ever attacked and insulted Cecilia in such a manner." They slowly turned and apologized to the young ladies, who just stared at them, though Pamela's gaze seemed to contain some admiration, and Cecilia looked away, blushing.

Frederick turned back to him. "Thank you for preventing me from doing something rash just now," he mumbled and took a deep breath. Smiling in relief, Lord Ravenswood briefly clapped him on the shoulder.

"Frederick." They all started at the sound of Julia's voice, thick from crying.

He knelt again in front of her. "Yes, Julia?"

She tried to smile. "Frederick," she said weakly, "go find

Jane and Mother and Father as quickly as you can. We must get Jane away from here *immediately.*"

He stood up, focused and eager for action. "I swear that I will. You are quite correct that is what we need to do now. And I promise not to do anything else to hurt or distress you any more than you have been already."

"Do not promise me that," she moaned, "just don't do anything rash! I do not want either Jane Elizabeth or you to get hurt, for I could not bear it! I cannot take any more tonight." She had quite forgotten her long-ago professed courage.

He hugged her tightly. "My dear sister, I promise to be careful and not distress you or Jane Elizabeth any further, if that is possible." He kissed her quivering cheek. "I am so sorry for all that has happened."

"Frederick," she sighed, "stop promising! None of this is your fault, or any of ours! But do find our parents and Jane quickly, so that we can all leave this house!"

He kissed her cheek again. "Of course, we shall." He paused and turned to the others. "Again, I apologize for my wild and ungentlemanly behavior in front of all of you." They all excused him, to his embarrassment. He did not relish hearing what their parents would have to say about it once they knew.

Pamela, Sophia, and Cecilia helped Julia repair her ravaged face and regain some composure. She took several deep breaths, and managed to look calm and serious, though not her usual self. Several minutes later, their entire group, six strong, entered the ballroom through the French doors. Pamela Easton walked in on Lord Ravenswood's arm, while Sophia went to collect Darcy and Elizabeth, and Cecilia hurried off to find Jane Elizabeth. Frederick clasped Julia's arm, and she his.

They had agreed to regroup in the grand foyer of Dutton Ampner, so they took the shortest route to the ballroom doors opening out onto the main hallway. Pamela and Lord

Ravenswood made quick progress, while Frederick took deliberate care leading Julia through the throng. He handled the pleasantries as they passed Angelina Molyneux, Mary Duncan and the chastened, diminished Julian Tunney, Miss Exley, Mr. Lawson, whom Julia could barely look at, and all the Foxboroughs. Julia began to fear they would never be free of all these people and exit the ballroom, so anxious was she to go home and get Jane Elizabeth to safety. But their progress was slow, and Frederick didn't want to slight anyone, nor attract any more attention than he could. He did seem flustered when momentarily stopped by a trio of laughing young ladies – the Misses Vinson, Robinson, and Watson, no less – but he claimed Julia was ill and quickly swept past their gloved talons. They even passed a familiar-looking dark-haired beauty whom Frederick recognized but whose name he could not recall, while Julia did – Rosamund Woodleigh. She managed to say something to her as they moved forward. The entrance to the hallway seemed only about twenty feet away, when a group of people stepped into their path.

It was the three Grantley siblings, and the Urquharts. Julia halted in dismay and gave her brother a fearful look. Frederick had also stopped, and she saw his eyes harden and jaw tighten. Dear God, not this, on top of everything else! But there was no avoiding them. She heard Frederick clear his throat.

"Well, if it isn't Miss Darcy and her brother, the man and scholar," Richard Grantley deprecated, then tried to smile. "Why are you leaving the ball so early, Miss Darcy? Do you not have a partner for the next dance?"

"No, Mr. Grantley, I do not." Julia tried to sound dignified, though she thought her reply cold. "It is just as well, however, for I do feel ill, and we are leaving the ball."

"How sorry we are to hear it." Richard shrugged. "I was afraid you weren't able to find enough partners here of the rank and class appropriate for you." He gave an unpleasant laugh, while his sister Susannah tried to shush him, even though she was looking daggers at Julia. "We have learned more about your behavior, Miss Darcy, and it does not sound as if it has been appropriate."

"Miss Darcy seems to be a sly little creature, just like her younger sister," Isabelle flung at them, her head held high. Rod Urquhart laughed, while his sister Rachel tried to pull him away. "I am sure Miss Jane models her own behavior on Miss Darcy's."

"Well, it does not matter," Richard replied, "for I would not ask Miss Darcy or her sister to dance anyway."

Frederick made a sound in his throat and stepped forward to a spot only inches from him. "Frederick, don't!" Julia cried and tried to pull him back, but he shook off her arm. At first, shocked into silence by such insulting remarks, Frederick felt his anger returning and mounting. She tried not to burst into tears, but failed.

"Grantley, I demand that you apologize to my sister!"

Richard kept chuckling. "No, I do not think I shall." He shook off his own sister's warning touch.

"You have insulted a young lady, my sister, in public, and I demand that you apologize!" The thought of a dead young man suddenly stabbed his consciousness. Now people around them were quieting, backing away from them, and staring. Ladies covered their mouths with gloved hands as the gentlemen took their arms and looked grave.

"No," Richard simpered, throwing out his hand. "All right, Darcy, I give you credit for defending your sister, despite what we've heard about her behavior; all that *would* need defending." He looked around, smiling. "But you and yours have so little worthiness to begin with that it is no wonder you insist. However, I will not apologize for expressing my opinion of your low relations, even if they include your sisters."

Frederick choked and clenched his fists. "Frederick, no! Your promise!" Julia cried out. She began turning to and fro in her distress.

"One last time," Frederick said through clenched teeth,

"I demand you apologize to my sister, Miss Darcy, for your insulting and inappropriate comments, or else I shall have to take steps." He tugged at his left glove with his right, but Julia snatched his hand away.

Richard snorted. "What could *you* do?" He turned to his sisters and the Urquharts. "Do you think I am afraid of Darcy here, who didn't have the courage to act like a man when he could have? This poor boy was afraid of a couple of tawdry streetwalkers." He and Rod shared a laugh, while a horrified Rachel covered her mouth with a gloved hand. She slapped her brother's arm and went over to comfort Julia, who had lost her ability to maintain any composure. A couple of older ladies moved in to assist Rachel and glared at the Grantleys. Fear finally showed in Susannah's face, as she tried to pull Richard away again, but he resisted her. Richard addressed another remark to the empurpled Frederick. "Some Master of Pemberley you shall make. At least your late older brother was man enough to sire a male child, a bastard though it is."

Rod cried, "Richard! No!" But it was too late.

"YOU *BLACKGUARD*!" Frederick snarled and shot his fist into Richard's face. He leaped onto him and knocked him down. Both young men rolled all over the floor, pummeling each other. People around them scattered, the women screaming and the men pushing them out of harm's way. In the end, the combatants managed to knock over two tables full of glasses, bottles, and picked-over trays of appetizers. And, a few minutes after it had begun, it ended.

Frederick felt himself being pulled off the groaning Richard and hauled to his feet by two stern, older men – the elder Mr. Foxborough, and Julian Tunney's father. "Right, Mr. Darcy, that is more than enough," they snapped as they dragged him away. "Come away now." Frederick's breathing came in sweaty, hulking gasps. Somehow, he realized no music was playing.

Richard was helped to his feet by Martin Tourneur and Belinda Compson's father. Richard's left eye was turning black and, like Frederick, his nose and mouth were bleeding, but it was clear Frederick's blows had been more accurate to Richard's body than Richard's blows had been to Frederick's. "Let me finish off the little puppy!" Richard screamed and lunged at Frederick, who tensed. The men holding Richard were unprepared for his charge and watched with horror as he drove himself at Frederick. However, Frederick poised himself for the attack, and landed one last direct punch to Richard's jaw, which knocked out two teeth that landed on the parquet floor with little ticking noises. Richard cried out and fell back. As Tourneur and Compson hauled him to his feet again, censuring him and showing no mercy for the loss of his teeth, a copious number of playing cards fell from his ruined coat pocket. There were several duplicated aces and kings among the spilled cards, and Frederick heard some-one laugh and exclaim, "So Grantley does cheat at cards, and there is the proof." Then there was the sound of much harsh laughter and backslapping, and it was Susannah Grantley's turn to burst into tears. Someone shoved a handkerchief into Richard's bleeding mouth.

"Julia?" Frederick gasped out and looked for her. The image of the prone young man remained in his consciousness. He saw Julia crumpled into the arms of Rachel Urquhart and some other ladies, as Mr. Foxborough and Mr. Tunney hustled him over to a chair, into which they slammed him down, hard. He gasped again, his shoulders aching, and looked into a sea of angry, disapproving faces. His courage deserted him, and he looked down at himself.

His fine suit was ruined. His coat lapels were torn loose, his linen shirt pulled from his trousers and wide open, with his cravat hanging at an odd angle around his neck. His shirt was stained with perspiration, and his chest bare for all to see. He became aware of his face, dripping sweat and blood, which stained his clothes. His boots were scuffed and stained with food, like his coat and trousers. He looked down at the bruises on his right hand. He could only guess how his hair looked now, and how badly bruised was his face? He looked up, desperate, at those closest to him, but Stephen Foxborough and Sebastian Tunney turned away, like so many others. He gave a sorrowful moan and hung his head. Silence reigned for some moments.

"Frederick." He looked up at the sound of Julia's soft voice. Her face red and swollen, she had pushed her way through everyone to him. Somehow, she had a clean handkerchief in her hand, which she wetted and began to gently clean his face. Snuffling, she spoke soothing words to him and shot disapproving glances of her own at some of the outraged bystanders.

"Julia," he sobbed, "I am so sorry! I lost my head, I forgot myself, and my promise..." He hung his head again.

"Hush, Frederick." She continued to tend to him, not wiping away her own tears.

"It is all very well to be remorseful now!" snapped Sebastian Tunney. "Just look at what you two ruffians have done!"

"Tunney," Stephen Foxborough said in a warning tone.

Frederick regretted the fight and the damage but didn't shed any tears; he felt strangely calm. His anger was truly spent, and he realized he wasn't sorry for fighting Richard. He kept swallowing but began trying to rebuild his courage so he could face whatever punishments he would suffer.

"It was all Darcy's fault," snapped Rod Urquhart. "Darcy expected Richard to dance with Miss Darcy, and when Richard didn't comply, Darcy took offense. He demanded an apology from Richard, who refused. Then Darcy hit him; *he* started the fight!"

"That is a lie, young man!" snapped an older gentleman.

"Dare you contradict me, Sir?"

"I do," came the angry reply, "for we overheard the entire exchange. Mr. Grantley did nothing but insult Miss Darcy and her sister, then their entire family, and even Mr. Darcy himself!" He glared at the groaning but still malevolent Richard. Others around him were agreeing with the gentleman. "He was even rude enough to insult Mr. Darcy's late brother. It was insupportable!" He went over to Richard, whose handkerchief pressed into his gums, was starting to drip blood on the floor. "Mr. Darcy should have knocked out all your teeth." He turned on his heel, letting Richard writhe and choke. The man glared at Rod as he passed by.

Rod tried to laugh. "What does that gentleman know? It all occurred as I said it did!"

"I am certain it has!" Mary Duncan exclaimed, as she and her stepbrother Julian had appeared. She nodded and clutched his arm; he appeared composed but affronted. "We are well informed as to Miss Darcy's behavior, and believe her brother was trying to defend her," she paused, "from the truth." She stepped back in high-chinned triumph. "It is no wonder that this disgraceful altercation took place."

"You have Miss Duncan's confirmation. Darcy started the fight." Rod turned to his sister. "Did he not, Rachel?"

"Haven't you both done enough?" she accused him, furious. "I will tell Mama and Papa that you are *not* to be my escort any longer – that is, if any of the houses hosting more balls this season will even receive me, thanks to you and your friend!" She patted Julia's shoulder, then flounced off as her brother flushed. Other gentlemen began to debate what had occurred, while ignoring the ladies trying to get their attention.

"Yes, I started the fight," Frederick spoke slowly, "but we were leaving the ball. My sister was not searching for a dance partner because she felt ill. Then Grantley and the others blocked our way, and he kept insulting her."

He heard sounds of agreement around him, while some other older gentlemen corralled Richard and Rod. Messieurs Compson and Tunney kept Frederick sitting where he was as Julia kept ministering to him; she was now trying to clean some of the smears on his suit. A shadow fell over them and they looked up into the faces of their hosts, Sir Romanus and Lady Margery. Frederick gulped, but slowly stood up, his legs a little unsteady beneath him. His cravat started slipping, so he pulled it off completely. He was ready to face more censure.

"Well, Mr. Darcy," Sir Romanus said in an amiable but clipped tone, "would you care to enlighten us as to the reasons for your extraordinary behavior this evening? For your little battle has quite spoiled the ball and outraged the guests. I must tell you that our daughter is quite distressed, as her mother and I are giving the ball in honor of her debut into society." He stood and waited while Lady Margery stared at Frederick.

He swallowed again. "Sir Romanus and Lady Margery, I – I am very sorry for my behavior in your home, as well as the damage I – that is, we – have caused." His head was hurting. "I am most abjectly sorry for ruining the ball for Miss Ventnor." He straightened up. "I do not know whether you have heard, but Mr. Grantley insulted my sister Julia, and I demanded that he apologize to her. He refused. Then he insulted our family, my sister Jane, and me, and our late brother Henry, and so I – I –" Now he saw his parents approaching, with Lord Ravenswood, Cecilia Calvert, and Jane Elizabeth, and he looked down. He had never seen his parents so angry and seething.

They came right over to him, as Jane Elizabeth rushed over to Julia, her eyes wide at Frederick's appearance. "Go on, Frederick, and finish what you were going to say to Sir Romanus," his father rapped.

"My goodness, Frederick, what have you done?" Elizabeth cried. "Look at this wreckage, and just look at yourself!"

So, he obliged them all by repeating what had happened. He saw that Richard's parents, George and Ursula Grantley, Lord and Lady Hartford, had joined them, stern and tight-lipped, but silent. "And so, I hit him," Frederick finished, "several times." He heard Richard moan.

"I see, though some of our distinguished guests contradict

your account," Sir Romanus said, exchanging a glance with his wife. "And these," he indicated the two teeth on the floor, "used to be Mr. Grantley's?"

Frederick gulped. "Yes, Sir Romanus." Why wouldn't everyone believe him?

"I need a surgeon!" Richard cried out in a strangled voice. "Look at what that lying whelp has done to me! Help, I beg you, for I am bleeding profusely!"

"Silence, Richard!" his father commanded. He peered into his son's mouth and handed him yet another handkerchief. To Lady Hartford he remarked, "He'll live." Someone gave him a shot of bourbon, which he made his son drink; Richard almost screamed in agony. Then Lord Hartford and the others looked at Frederick again, who blanched but met their stares. Darcy and Elizabeth looked as if they were going to remonstrate with him again when Julia stood up. She was done with crying.

"Frederick did throw the first punch," she said, "but he was only defending my honor. As my brother told you, he was demanding Mr. Grantley apologize for insulting me, which he did quite openly." She looked at Lord and Lady Hartford, who made no reaction. "Mr. Grantley also insulted our sister Jane and the rest of our family, then he insulted my brother's manhood and the memory of our late older brother. It was all vile, disgusting, and inappropriate, entirely insupportable!"

Lady Hartford stepped forward. "Richard did no such thing, you impudent girl! Why –" But her husband restrained her with a furious glance.

"Your son most certainly did all those things, and in front of many witnesses." Julia gave her a cold glance. "I will not be contradicted when I speak the truth."

"Julia," Elizabeth cried, "that is enough! You cannot speak so to such people, and in public!" She gave Darcy a shocked look.

"No, Mother," Julia said calmly, "punish me if you wish for being willful and impolite, but I stand with Frederick. His actions were justified." Lady Hartford sniffed, and turned to comfort Susannah, who was still sobbing, while Isabelle looked nervous.

Elizabeth choked and Darcy sighed. He took Frederick's chin in his hand and examined his bruises. "Well, Son, it must have been quite a fight." His eyes were hard and narrow. "Are you in pain?"

"No, Sir," Frederick lied.

Darcy crossed his arms over his chest. "Then," he said in his angriest voice, "is there anything else you would like to say to Sir Romanus and Lady Margery for your extraordinary behavior?"

Frederick closed his eyes, then pulled the remains of his shirt and waistcoat about him to cover his bare chest. He approached their hosts, grimacing as his boot crunched on shards from a broken glass. "Again, I apologize to you, Sir Romanus and Lady Margery, for ruining your most delightful ball and upsetting everyone. I agree that my behavior has been unacceptable and ungentlemanly." He gestured to the wreckage. "I only cared about defending my sisters' honor. I did not intend to destroy your property in the process." He sighed. "My father shall not make restitution on this, for I shall." His parents exchanged a surprised glance. "I will find some way to pay for all the damage we have caused tonight. I feel it is my responsibility to do so since I started the fight, even though I was well provoked. I beg of you to allow me to make amends this way." Lady Margery was still tightlipped, but her eyes began to soften, and a smile played around Sir Romanus' mouth.

He turned to Lord and Lady Hartford. "I am sorry to have hurt your son, whether I think I was justified in fighting him, or not. However, I will not apologize for defending my sisters and my family from the vicious slander he uttered here in public."

"*Frederick,*" Darcy warned, and Elizabeth gave a horrified gasp.

Lord Hartford was just as stern. "And what of your own personal animosity towards our son, young man? For Miss Darcy accused Richard of insulting you as well."

Frederick blinked. "Respectfully, my lord, I ask that you – and my father – leave that between your son and me. You are well justified in reprimanding me for being angry enough with Richard to beat him because of a personal matter between us, but I will not yield on the point that I was justified, because I would not let your son blacken my sisters' characters and the rest of my family."

"Frederick!" Elizabeth gasped again. "These are your elders and betters you are addressing! What has gotten into both you and Julia I cannot imagine!"

Frederick said nothing, but stood very straight with his arms at his sides. His waistcoat and shirt fell open again, and he gave them a defiant stare.

Lady Hartford's expression changed, and she looked at her husband. Lord Hartford touched her arm, then addressed Frederick. "Well said, young man." He turned to Darcy and said, "Lady Hartford and I accept your son's apology and his explanations for his conduct." Richard made a choking noise.

Darcy swallowed, but still glared at Frederick. "Thank you, my lord."

Lord Hartford addressed their hosts. "Sir Romanus and Lady Margery, I apologize for our son's behavior, which helped spoil your splendid ball. Please extend our deep regrets to Miss Ventnor." Now he gave his own son a withering glance. "Come, Richard, it is time for us to leave." He herded his family out toward Dutton Ampner's great front door, as Richard kept moaning. Without another glance, the Ventnors turned and walked away towards other guests.

Darcy turned to Frederick. "Would you mind covering yourself?" he hissed. Frederick started and tried to comply, but Jane Elizabeth took a light-colored ribbon from her hair and looped it around the buttons on his shirt to pull it shut, tying it with a simple bow. He gave her a grateful look, even as his parted waistcoat dangled under his outer coat. Now Darcy gave him an icy stare, as the crowd of guests finally began to drift away. "It is time for us to leave as well." He turned to Lord Ravenswood. "I thank you and your sister, my lord, for helping our daughter and son."

"It was nothing, I assure you; I only wish we could have done more."

"Again, we are most grateful."

"Lord Ravenswood." Frederick stepped forward. "Thank you for restraining me earlier on the balcony, for I did not give you proper thanks then. I hope I did not cause you any injury or damage to your fine appearance." He looked down at himself. "I must also apologize for not remembering your advice to keep my head."

Lord Ravenswood nodded to him. "There is no need to apologize, as I have said, and as you can see, I am quite unharmed." He turned to Darcy. "Young Mr. Darcy here is as strong as a bull. He wished to challenge young Grantley as soon as he learned of his sister's distress; I restrained him, but I could not have restrained him much longer." Darcy nodded, and Lord Ravenswood turned back to Frederick. "I am certain Grantley will not trouble you again about anything, for he is a braggart and a cheat, and now well aware of your strength and courage. His faults have been exposed to many."

"I hope you are right, my lord," Frederick said listlessly.

Lord Ravenswood surprised them by putting his arm around Frederick's shoulders. "Let me say something more. As for not taking my advice on keeping your head, you *were* heeding it – you were trying to collect your family and protect your sisters, which he prevented you from doing. Then he said all those unforgiveable things to provoke you." He lowered his voice. "I tell you, Mr. Darcy, that in your place, and Cecilia in Miss Darcy's, I would have throttled the offender."

"Oh, Lord Ravenswood!" Elizabeth dabbed her eyes. "Please

do not say such things! We appreciate you defending our son's actions, but surely you cannot mean that!"

He gave her a level stare. "But I do, Mrs. Darcy." She looked away, nonplussed, but her daughters did not try to comfort her and they remained at Frederick's side. Lord Ravenswood saw Darcy still glaring at Frederick, so he made one last attempt for his sake; he cleared his throat. "Mr. and Mrs. Darcy, it is true that none of this is my business, but I am going to say something quite forward and intrusive, and I will start off by apologizing for it in advance. When I am done, you may order me not to involve myself in your family affairs, and you would be correct to do so, for I do not have the right." He sighed. "I ask you to be lenient with your son concerning his conduct tonight, for he more than had cause. Yes, I know he had admitted starting the fight, but he was provoked beyond endurance, and so all this was damaged." He indicated the overturned tables and chairs, stained linens, and broken dishes and glasses. "He has already stated his intention to make reparation for the damage. Please do not be too severe with him."

Darcy and Elizabeth exchanged a glance, and he exhaled. "Thank you for your consideration to our son. I will consider what you have said." Then he looked away.

"You are most welcome, Mr. Darcy." Lord Ravenswood gave Frederick an encouraging look; he wanted to give him another physical gesture of support but restrained himself. Then he and a subdued Miss Calvert took their leave.

Darcy refocused his glare on Frederick. "To the carriage – immediately!"

Frederick nodded. "Yes, Sir." He walked out first, followed by his sisters and their parents. He could hear his father's angry breathing all the way to the carriage, and knew this long night was not yet over.

CHAPTER 14

The ride back to Cavendish Square took place in complete silence. Julia tried to pat Frederick's arm in encouragement, but he just shook his head at her and sat staring ahead, as if facing his own execution. He knew it was only a matter of time – a short one at that – before his father lashed out at him. Elizabeth kept shaking her head in disbelief, while Jane Elizabeth focused her eyes on the carriage floor, afraid to look up, and their father remained impassive, frowning as if fighting off a headache.

The hall clock was chiming only eleven when they entered the house. Frederick stopped in front of his father, who flung out his arm. "Into the drawing room *now*," he snapped. Frederick went.

Elizabeth's own anger crumbled. "Fitzwilliam, please! Remember Lord Ravenswood asked us to be gentle with him," she pleaded.

"Yes, Dearest, I remember." She could not recall a time he had ever spoken so coldly to her. "Let us all go in and join our son in the drawing room." He gestured for them to proceed.

They entered, where Frederick stood in the middle of the floor in his torn, stained, disheveled clothes, his hands clasped behind his back. Elizabeth, Julia, and Jane all sat down. Darcy shut the door, then strode over to Frederick, whom he pulled around to face him. Frederick closed his eyes; Elizabeth gasped, and Julia and Jane winced.

"What did you think you were doing?" Darcy shouted. "Do you not care how your actions affect others, including your own family? And what about all the glasses, plates, and furniture that were damaged? I am very displeased and, yes, ashamed of what you have done tonight! Well, what more do you have to say in your defense?" Frederick didn't answer, so

Darcy grabbed his arm. "Answer me! Your little escapade will be all over London tomorrow, and I even expect to read about it in the newspapers!" Darcy shook his arm, and Frederick surprised him by flinging it away.

"Do not strike me, Father," he said hotly.

"Frederick!" his mother cried, as Jane and Julia hugged each other.

"I demand an answer from you," Darcy thundered, and grabbed Frederick's arm again, pulling him close.

Frederick had never seen him so angry before, nor had any of the others. He calmed his voice and met his father's gaze as he was held fast. "All right, Father, go ahead and strike me then, for I can see that you want to." He closed his eyes again, expecting his father's hand to rake across his face, something he had never done before. Jane's makeshift repair became undone and his shirt fell open, baring his chest.

"Frederick!" Elizabeth cried out again. Darcy made a choking sound and pushed him away. Rubbing his face and neck, he walked a few steps away, muttering.

"No, Mother," Frederick exclaimed, "I know that fighting is wrong and ungentlemanly, and that you both disapprove of it for good reason. But this time, tonight, I feel justified in having done so."

"Justified?" his father retorted. He took a couple of steps towards him, but stopped when he saw the others flinch. He exhaled some anger, with effort. "*This* time you are justified, you say? Frederick, this is not the first time you have fought Richard Grantley! Is this to become a hobby of yours? Pray tell us when your next bout with him shall occur, and where!"

"I fought him tonight because I had to!" Frederick snapped. "Would you like me to repeat all the insults he gave us, if you haven't heard them enough times already? If you would, in *that* I would obey you." Darcy made another angry sound and turned away. "Father, Richard *insulted* Julia, then his sister insulted *Jane*! Now Isabelle Grantley I could do nothing about right then, but Richard I could – and did!"

"Haven't your mother and I told you how we expect you to behave as a gentleman, without cruelty, bullying, or violence? Your conduct tonight was atrocious!"

"I was defending Julia's honor and paying them back for their attacks on Jane! Did you not know that they were spreading rumors about Julia being loose and wanton? Was I supposed to ignore that? Do *you* care about that?" Darcy and Elizabeth exchanged a horrified glance. "Well, that is exactly what they were doing! And, as the future Master of Pemberley, unless you disown me, I acted to defend my sisters from such vicious lies! I must, if I am worth anything at all! I demanded an apology for Julia's sake, and when Richard refused and went on to slander me again, then Jane, Henry, and little Henry David –," Frederick stopped to catch his breath, "that is when I hit him the first time, and we kept on fighting."

For the first time he felt what it would be like to be the Master of Pemberley, the power and responsibility that came with the role, and how he had used some of that power. He stepped in front of his father. "I know fighting is wrong and undesirable, but sometimes it is necessary! I will apologize to the Ventnors and anyone else you desire me to, and for as long as you wish, but I will not apologize for knocking Richard down!"

"Frederick." Darcy shook his fist at him.

"Fitzwilliam! Frederick! Stop this at once," Elizabeth cried out. "I cannot believe how you are speaking to each other, and you are frightening the girls!"

Father and son stood breathing hard and staring at each other. Now Julia disentangled herself from Jane's arms and went over to their father. She looked at her sister, who nodded.

"Father," Julia said, determined, "Jane Elizabeth and I are most grateful to Frederick for standing up and defending us both. I do not like fighting either, but all that Mr. Grantley and Miss Isabelle said was unforgiveable, cruel, and slanderous, and I do not believe anyone could withstand such provocation. Frederick was justified. I am glad he fought Grantley and knocked out some of his teeth, for he more than deserved it." She nodded to her shocked father. "And now you and Mother can strike or punish me however you see fit for saying so." She waited.

Elizabeth's shock and horror could not be any greater. "*Julia!*"

"I am sorry to willfully defy you, Mother, but I approve of what Frederick did."

"As do I," Jane Elizabeth declared.

"Julia, Jane!" their father thundered, but his expression was one of disbelief. "How can you approve of such behavior, even if it is your own brother's? I am sorry to remind you that true gentlemen do not go brawling about at balls, destroying property in other people's houses! Let me tell you what Frederick has done – since he has done so while defending you, he will now appear as ill-mannered and be censured as much as Grantley for his conduct! Does that not matter to you as well? It matters to your mother and me! I ask you, then, what kind of way is that to settle differences, especially in public?"

Julia lowered her eyes, but neither she nor Jane Elizabeth flinched at experiencing their father's rare anger. "Again, I am sorry, Father and Mother, but I cannot – and will not – reprove Frederick for what he has done. Punish me as you wish; I will gladly share Frederick's." She shrugged, and Jane Elizabeth nodded again. Their mother made a furious sound, but their father was stunned into silence. Julia went over to Frederick and kissed his swollen cheek. Then Jane did the same, saying, "We are grateful that Frederick defended us." Then all three stared at their parents, to their consternation. Never had any of their children defied their wishes and advice or refused to acknowledge one's fault – and now three of them were doing so together.

"Children!" Elizabeth cried, helpless. "Fitzwilliam, can you not make them understand?"

He paced back and forth in front of all three set faces. No, he had never known such defiance. He stared at each one of them, son, daughter, and daughter alike, but they did not flinch, not even Jane Elizabeth. He had never known such anger and determination directed at him and Elizabeth; no, this was something completely new and he could not understand or defeat it. He paced for several more moments, drawing in angry breaths, but each time he looked at his children they met him with the same stony eyes. His head was throbbing and he suddenly covered his eyes. He was too old for this – he realized a stalemate was the best he could hope for, and he longed for their family to be harmonious again. He could not bear the thought of them being angry at each other – such a thing hadn't occurred since he and Elizabeth joyfully welcomed their first child into the world. How could they let it come to this, to jeopardize all their happiness only to affirm that he and Elizabeth were right as parents? No, he was defeated, and he knew it. Good God, he had been sorely tried, and was just plain worn out by the whole thing. What a terrible evening it had been!

He stopped pacing and took three deliberate breaths. His face relaxed into the urbane expression he usually wore. He went over, took Elizabeth's hand, and kissed it; then he embraced each of their children, Frederick being the last, though he resisted him.

"My dear children," Darcy said at last, "I regret berating you all, especially Frederick, and frightening you with my anger – and my treatment of him."

"Father?" they all said at once, and, for the first time that night, Elizabeth looked hopeful.

"You all have quite persuaded me to the correctness of your opinions. I shall appreciate Frederick's spirited – and physical – defense of you both, Julia and Jane. I now agree that he was justifiably provoked and, like Lord Ravenswood said, I am not sure I could have checked my own impulses in the face of such provocation, for example, if terrible insults were leveled at your dear mother." He went back over to his son, whose eyes were filling. "Frederick, I should not have been so furiously angry with you. You were correct that I – I wanted to strike you for your misconduct, as hard as I could; thank God I did not, for I probably would have hurt you very much, to my shame. I am afraid, however, that I lost my composure and self-control anyway. I have never beaten you, not even when you were a small child, and I mustn't start now."

"Oh, Father!" They hugged each other.

"Frederick." Elizabeth stood, firm and reproachful; he and Darcy started as she advanced upon them. "My dear young man, I make clear my disapproval of your brawling in public, striking another person repeatedly, and destroying others' personal property, no matter how unintentional it was, as well as your own finery and decency – if I have not already!" She glared at Frederick for what seemed like a full minute, then let her face relax. "But, like your father, I find I cannot do so any longer." She pulled him to her, ruined suit, bare chest, and all. "From now on, just try to keep your head and your temper in check, please, my dear future Master of Pemberley."

His eyes spilled over. "Yes, Mother," he barely answered.

Another minute passed. Darcy still felt somewhat shaky, but his face cleared. "Well, let us all take advantage of this early evening and get some well-deserved rest, shall we? We can all use it and find ways to relax tomorrow."

"The next ball is not for three days, is it not, Fitzwilliam?"

"That is correct." Darcy thought much of their tension was ebbing as fatigue overtook them.

"Is there anything else we should do, Father, before we retire for the night?" Jane Elizabeth asked.

He thought for a moment and glanced at Frederick, weary and weaving in his ruined clothes. Darcy thanked her. "I think it is time for your brother to take a well-deserved late bath and wash off his battle stripes." He paused. "I would also like our valet to check your bruises and find something decent with which to cover yourself. All the London *ton* must have seen your torso tonight, Son."

"Yes, Father." Frederick blushed, trying to pull his shirt closed again, but failing.

"What about me, Father, for I defied both you and Mother?" Julia asked.

"And I as well?" Jane Elizabeth added.

Darcy looked at Elizabeth, who drew both daughters to her. "I do not see that any measures need to be taken, do you, Fitzwilliam?"

"No, Lizzie, I quite agree."

"Then you should both go off to bed."

"Yes, Mother," Julia and Jane chorused. However, before they could leave, Frederick spoke up, rubbing his eyes. "What about me, Father? What should I do tomorrow? Surely I cannot be given over to my leisure after tonight's events, can I?"

Darcy nodded. "No, I suppose we cannot allow that." He thought for a few moments. "All right, Son, I am ready to pronounce your punishments."

The others stiffened, but Frederick straightened and held his father's gaze. "I am ready."

Darcy looked at him. "There are three parts to your discipline. First, you shall write a full apology to Sir Romanus, Lady Margery, and Miss Dorothea Ventnor for tonight's mayhem that ruined their ball." Frederick nodded. "Second, I am confining you to your room for the next three entire days, except for mealtimes and supervised recreation, say, a few hours each day. However, I am most certainly not disowning you." Frederick nodded again, but his sisters protested.

"Father, please don't!" Julia cried. "Forgive me, but that is too harsh!"

Before he could reply, Frederick exclaimed, "No, Julia and

Jane! Do not oppose Father on these strictures, for I shall obey them!"

"Thank you, Frederick," his father said, as his sisters subsided doubtfully, "but there is still one more part to your punishment." Frederick swallowed. "This is the third part, for now, and into the future." Darcy's expression grew stern again, and Frederick braced himself. "If you *ever* fight anyone else again – even Richard Grantley – I swear that I will send you back to Pemberley bound and under armed escort! Do you understand?"

Frederick gulped. "Yes, Father, I do."

"Please promise me, Son, that you will do not anything that would result in you being sent back to Pemberley tied up and guarded."

"I – I promise I will try very hard."

"Good, Frederick. I trust that you will be successful."

"*Fitzwilliam*," Elizabeth scolded.

"It is all right, Mother," Frederick said. "I accept these punishments, for I must atone somehow for my misconduct and defiance." More tension disappeared from the room as they all began moving toward the doorway.

"Tell me something," his father wanted to know. "How do you propose to pay for all the damage at Dutton Ampner? I remember you made a definite, public promise on that point."

"I have already given it some thought," he replied. "When I return to Cambridge after the season is over, I will hang out my card, declaring my services as a competent tutor in Latin and composition; and, with the reasonable rates I shall charge, I will collect what I earn and send it to the Ventnors – with your approval, of course." After all, he was the son of a gentleman who would be working for hire.

"Of course I approve, Frederick."

"I am quite impressed with your plan," Elizabeth remarked, smiling. "I know you will be busy, for Sir Romanus will present you with a full accounting of all that is owed."

"Er, yes." Frederick thanked his parents. "It may take me a while until I graduate from Cambridge as a result, but I will do so."

The clock chimed twelve and Darcy started. "I shall tell Forrester to draw you a bath and dress your wounds." He gestured to the door. "Your temporary confinement, Frederick, begins now."

"Yes, Sir." He wished them all a good night and obediently left the room, his head and body aching all over.

The hot bath relaxed and refreshed him some, but as the valet handed him his nightshirt and began examining all the damaged finery, he felt some of his muscles tightening. As he tried to get comfortable under the covers, Frederick felt both satisfaction and doubt over his actions during the ball.

Could he have handled the situation differently? Frederick could not see how. Richard and his sister had been too insulting and never would have apologized for anything they said. Trying to discuss and resolve the situation using gentlemanly words and phrases would not have satisfied anyone, the offenders or the offended. He didn't think he could have borne the shame of not standing up for his sisters after they had been slandered and disparaged.

In the end, his father accepted his defending Julia and Jane, but he still might not have approved of his use of power in fighting to defend them; perhaps the next time Frederick exercised his judgment in some different circumstances he might.

And when would the next opportunity for him to make such a decision present itself? Would he be as ready to act as he did this time, or would he hesitate and try to protect his position and prestige, especially if it occurred in front of others? It also seemed like he reacted more than he simply acted, because Richard had provoked him beyond endurance. His final thought, before his mind was ready to start wishing for sleep, was, whatever he did, would it be the right decision?

He decided he could think a lot about these questions during his three-day confinement, as he drifted off to sleep.

CHAPTER 15

In contrast to his defiant attitude the previous night, Frederick meekly accepted his confinement. Either Jordan or Peter summoned him so he could bathe and dress, and he was escorted to and from each meal with his family. He continued to behave in a subdued manner, keeping his eyes downcast and veiled, and said nothing unless he was directly addressed. Nicholas and Anne were allowed to visit him for half an hour each morning and afternoon, but not a moment longer. Frederick sat down to write his apology to the Ventnors: he informed Jordan when it was completed, and the footman relayed the news to his father. In the middle of the afternoon, Sir Romanus and his family arrived at Cavendish Square, and Frederick was escorted to the drawing room, where he found them with all his family.

After greetings were exchanged, Frederick presented his letter to Sir Romanus and apologized to all of them, including Miss Ventnor, who still looked miffed. His gaze focused downward, he stepped back as his father stated how he was being punished for his transgressions. Miss Dorothea's face softened as her parents exchanged glances. Now Sir Romanus in turn presented Frederick with an itemized account of all the items – fine china, glassware, and furniture – that had been broken or ruined as a result of the fight. Frederick nodded and looked at the total: sixty-three pounds, four shillings, and a sixpence; he sighed inwardly, but he had promised to make repayment and knew he would be tutoring for a very long time. He placed the paper in his inner coat pocket.

Sir Romanus transfixed him with a firm but not unfriendly glance. "I am relieved that Mr. Darcy, your father, is not disowning you," he addressed Frederick.

"Thank you, Sir Romanus. Despite my punishments, my

parents are being very fair and understanding of my regrettable conduct last night in your fine house." He sighed. "No, Sir, I am not disowned, but if I ever fight someone again," here he glanced at his stern father, "I very well might be. I promise you all I do not intend to try my father's patience any further."

"Good, young sir, and well said!" Sir Romanus nodded, while Darcy and Elizabeth gave Frederick warning glances not to say anything that even hinted of levity, though the Ventnors and his sisters did not seem to mind. Frederick hurried to add, "Again, I am most abject in my apologies for what I have done, especially ruining such a special occasion for Miss Ventnor."

That young lady now gave a small smile and, with a nod from her mother, said, "I accept your apology, Master Darcy."

"As do Sir Romanus and I," Lady Margery said. She sensed her husband stiffening beside her, but she lightly placed a few fingers on the back of his hand, and he remained silent. She could not help herself; she really liked Frederick, even though he had helped wreck a corner of her grand ballroom. And the Darcys' request for them to visit turned out to occur before receiving one from the Grantleys. Sounding relieved, Frederick thanked all the Ventnors; then Sir Romanus stirred and transfixed him with another glance.

"If you would indulge me, Master Darcy," he began, "I should like to ask you something."

"Of course, Sir Romanus." Frederick swallowed, as Lady Margery looked at her husband. Frederick felt like quailing but dared not.

"I am still bothered by the fact that young Mr. Urquhart boldly claimed that you expected Richard Grantley to dance with your sister, and you took offense when he would not comply, and demanded he apologize, which he also refused to do. You, on the other hand, stated that you demanded he apologize because he insulted your sister and other family members." He exhaled. "I would like to know which is the real reason you fought Grantley."

Frederick paled; he thought the visit had been going well, but now...He cleared his throat to answer. "Richard did insult my sister, Sir, along with the rest of us, and that is why I demanded he apologize to Julia." Julia wanted to speak up to defend him, but a quick glance from their mother checked her.

Darcy spoke up. "Sir Romanus, the fight erupted in the way my son has described it, and our daughters Julia and Jane, as well as other friends and guests at the ball, have corroborated it."

"Then I am satisfied, and I thank you. It is quite frustrating when people gossip, and different versions of events circulate at the same time." Sir Romanus gave a thin smile, then returned his gaze to Frederick. "Since you have apologized to us at least three times and they all have been accepted," he added, "there is no need to do so again. We understand what provoked you, so let us not speak of it anymore." He changed the subject. "Mr. Darcy, your father, has told us you are proficient in Latin and composition skills, as well as oratory."

Frederick brightened as the tightness in his chest eased. "Yes, Sir, I believe I am, and I will be offering my services as a tutor when I return to Cambridge once the season is over." He swallowed. "That is how I intend to earn the funds to replace everything that was damaged in your house."

Sir Romanus harrumphed, and his wife and daughter both smiled thinly. "We will be quite appreciative of your efforts. What an enterprising young man you are – very fitting, I think, for the next Master of Pemberley." Frederick blushed and mumbled his thanks, as his siblings exchanged glances.

It was time for the Ventnors to leave. Frederick remained in the drawing room with Peter, ready to return to his room. However, as they were leaving, Miss Ventnor turned to Frederick and said, "I really do accept your apology, Master Darcy. I admit that I was quite sad and upset over what happened last night, and angry with you and young Mr. Grantley." She smiled. "However, no other debutante this season will have such an exciting evening or memorable a ball!" Blushing darker, he mumbled some more.

"Now, Dorothea," Lady Margery said.

Elizabeth took the young lady's hand. "How sweet and understanding of you to say so, Miss Ventnor! As Frederick's mother, however, I beg you not to encourage him, much as I appreciate your sentiments."

Smothering a giggle, Miss Ventnor nodded, curtsied, and left.

Still red in the face, Frederick turned to his parents and shrugged. "I do not know what to say. I never expected –"

"Then do not say anything at all," his father interrupted. He went over to the bookcase, selected a large volume, and handed it to him. "Here you go."

Frederick reached for the book and found it to be the thickest volume of Gibbon's *Decline and Fall of the Roman Empire*. Seeing his son's eyes fill with misery, Darcy said, "You are beginning to like learning history, are you not? Then you can read that for the rest of the day." Frederick nodded and looked down. "If you are wondering why I am doing this, it is because your mother and I have just experienced the extraordinary novelty of hearing a young lady say she is pleased with the idea that a vicious fight prematurely ended the dancing at her debutante ball, and that she finds it all exciting and memorable, even to be admired." He gave him a curt nod. "That is all. What the world is coming to, I cannot imagine! Now, Son, please return to your room."

"Yes, Father." Clutching the book and clenching his jaw, he left with Peter. Well, at least his father hadn't given him something like Fordyce's *Sermons*.

Once they were sure he was safely upstairs, Darcy and Elizabeth shared a laugh. "Dearest," she said, "that was inspired!"

"Heaven help him if he gets any more such twisted encouragement, for I will not." He laughed again and took her in his arms.

Frederick continued to serve out his confinement in silence. He read, napped, paced, wrote to Alex, Eric, Staunton, and his cousins, and tried to focus on remembering what he had learned in his classes. He also thought about what it would be like to be Master of Pemberley, and what he would do in certain situations. The second day, accompanied by Peter, he took a long walk through the park not far from the house. While the rest of his family was out paying calls, he was also given time to sit in the small, walled garden behind the townhouse, where he could enjoy more of the fresh air in solitude. It was at times like these he missed Rex, Regina, and their litter the most; he hoped they would remember him when he returned to Pemberley.

On the second afternoon after the Ventnors' ball, Peter knocked on Frederick's door and stepped inside the room. Frederick had been dozing, slumped in his chair, the Gibbon volume resting open against his waistcoat. "Master Darcy, sir," Peter said, "your father requests your presence downstairs in the drawing room. Lord and Lady Hartford are paying a visit, and he wishes that you attend with the rest of the family."

Swallowing, Frederick blinked several times. He got up, placing his book on the table, which was strewn with various papers, inkwells, and other books. He checked his hair in the mirror, then smoothed down his coat and waistcoat. He looked slightly rumpled, but it would have to do. He cleared his expression and nodded to the strapping young footman. "I am ready, Peter."

He entered the drawing room, where he saw Richard's parents present as well as his own; everyone looked quite serious, though the Grantleys appeared more severe and stiff than his own parents. He bowed properly to Lord and Lady Hartford. No one said anything for a moment, then Darcy and Frederick began speaking at the same time, to make apologies;

they looked at each other and stopped talking.

Lord Hartford held up a hand. "Gentlemen, and Mrs. Darcy, thank you for receiving Lady Hartford and me today." He turned to Frederick. "I requested your presence, young sir, for there is something I would like to say to all of you."

"My lord?"

"Please do not be uneasy that we are calling upon you today," he cautioned them. "I am not here to argue my son's side or remind you of the loathsome things he said about all of you." He paused. "I am here to apologize for his unspeakable conduct."

Lady Ursula quickly added, "And I am here to apologize for upbraiding your daughter, Miss Julia Darcy, when she spoke the truth at the ball. That she did, but I would not hear a word against my son." She looked away. "However, I am now well informed as to his despicable behavior and habits. I am most ashamed, and truly sorry." Julia now blushed, sinking into a deep curtsey, as Jane Elizabeth and Mrs. Winston held each other.

Elizabeth's smile could not be more gracious. "Thank you, Lady Hartford! I appreciate your understanding and sentiments, and I know Julia does as well." Julia gave firm nods and added her thanks. "We want to protect our children, do we not?" All four parents seemed to agree, but Darcy and Frederick struggled to contain their surprise at what they'd heard.

"Lord Hartford," Frederick spoke up, "I am very much to blame for what happened. I did throw the first punch, and I hit your son many times, intending to hurt him – and I did."

"Yes, you did, but we also know that Richard provoked you beyond endurance, as he apparently has done before." Lord Hartford shook his leonine head. "You responded by defending your sisters, your family, and yourself. Why, any man, regardless of his age, would do the same."

Still surprised, Frederick was humbled. "Thank you very

much, my lord, for your understanding and consideration." He was sincere, but also hoped this unexpected apology would not earn him another volume of Gibbon, or worse. He dared not bet in which direction his father's temperament leaned.

Finally, Darcy spoke up with his thanks. "You must believe that Mrs. Darcy and I do not intend Frederick to solve all his problems by fighting, but we also realize that this was an extraordinary situation. We have plenty of apologies of our own to make, both Frederick's and ours, which began with the Ventnors for the ruination of their ball."

Lord Hartford gave a hollow laugh. "I do not know about that, Mr. Darcy. Some people, no matter who or how old they are, crave excitement in many forms." Darcy and Elizabeth exchanged a glance, and Frederick looked away. Now Lord Hartford smiled at him. "Young man, I hear it is a princely sum you have promised to repay, on Richard's behalf, as well as your own."

"Yes, my lord, that is true. I feel it is my responsibility to make restitution since I started the fight."

"How much is this sum, may I ask?"

Frederick told him, which raised the eyebrows of Richard's parents. Lord Hartford's eyes flickered away for a moment, then returned to him. "Our son was responsible for the damage too. You hardly knocked over those tables and broke everything yourself." He cleared his throat. "That is why I would be happy to offer to –"

Again, Darcy and Frederick began talking at once, interrupting Lord Hartford. Despite this lapse, Frederick won and apologized. "Thank you for offering, my lord, but I must insist. My father would not – and should not – be responsible for paying for all the damage we caused. If that is so, then why should you?" He shrugged. "Our fight was neither your fault, nor my parents'. I am only a very young man, but I believe it is my responsibility to make amends, despite your generous offer."

That earned Frederick a smile from Lady Ursula. "Well said, young man," Lord Hartford acknowledged. "Very well then. Allow me to say once again how much Lady Ursula and I appreciate all your apologies. However, there is more I would like to say."

"Yes, my lord," Darcy said, indicating that they should all sit down, while Elizabeth rang for refreshments. Once they were all served, Lord Hartford resumed with a heavy air.

"We came not only to apologize for Richard's conduct, but also to discuss his shortcomings." Frederick and his parents could not help exchanging glances. "Please do not protest, for this must be said, as difficult as this is for Lady Hartford and me. Please also let me admit to all of you that, though I am quite proud of our four children overall, our son Richard possesses several undesirable qualities." He sighed. "And he displayed all of them the other night in public, at Dutton Ampner."

"Really, Lord Hartford –"

Richard's father held up his hand again. "No, Mr. Darcy, let me have my say. I love my son as I do all our children, but Richard can be too proud, boastful, and condescending, which he demonstrated when he criticized your family." He sighed again. "Now it seems I must add the facts that he is a seducer, which I suspected, and a card cheat, which I did not, to that ignoble list. That is why he did not accompany us here, because I would not tolerate the slightest deviation from perfect behavior. Ah, he is only twenty years of age, a very young man! Thank God our older son, Rupert, is solid, dependable, and free of vice." Lord Hartford looked out the window. "I have been told that you were sent down from Cambridge," he remarked, his gaze returning to Frederick, "but I think that whatever you are supposed to have done pales in comparison to Richard's sins." Frederick swallowed and looked at the carpet.

"It is the same with our daughters," Lady Ursula confessed to Elizabeth. "Susannah, the elder, is kinder and responsible, but I fear we have spoiled Isabelle completely." Elizabeth could not speak, but took her hand in sympathy.

After a pause, Frederick looked at his father, who nodded, and spoke up. "Lord and Lady Hartford, I am truly sorry for losing my self-control and beating up your son – in public. I grew very angry at his words, and my anger fueled my fists. I hope he is not seriously injured."

Lord Hartford gave him a crooked smile. "No, Richard is not badly injured; he is only bruised as you are, and less two teeth, as you know." He shot Darcy a look. "This may sound strange to all of you, but I am glad that someone stood up to Richard, as your son did. Richard needs to learn self-restraint and better manners. Lady Ursula and I have tried, but I think it is clear we have failed. I do not know if his behavior can be improved upon now, or Isabelle's for that matter."

Darcy nodded. Frederick caught his eye again and started to rise; he thanked their guests, then excused himself so Peter could take him back to his room. There was much he would like to think about. Julia and Jane also left, escorted by Mrs. Winston. Elizabeth offered to give Lady Ursula a tour of the house including the garden, an offer she accepted gladly, leaving the two fathers alone over the glasses Darcy poured out for them.

After a couple of sips, he remarked, "Thank you, Lord Hartford, for your comments just now. It will mean a great deal to Frederick and ease his mind about all that occurred the other night, as well as to Mrs. Darcy and me. However, I still fear that it comes at a great price, for I am not excusing my own son's behavior, and I am reluctant to hear you criticize your own son in this matter. Both young men are at fault here."

"Agreed, Mr. Darcy, and I understand your reluctance. But I feel Richard's punishments – and the lack of regard he is going to experience from now on – are well deserved. Richard can be brutal and cruel, and I am aware of how he has wounded your son, and why." Lord Hartford's face twisted with distaste and

Darcy nodded, his eyes looking down. "Mr. Darcy, I admire your son's character and fortitude in all of this; truthfully, I wish Richard was much more like him."

"My lord, that is great praise indeed!" Darcy exclaimed. "I thank you for such sentiments, but again I hesitate to accept and relay them to Frederick, for I do not wish to flatter him and turn his head. Overall, he is maturing quite well, but he has not left his boyhood completely behind for true manhood. He still bears watching and guidance, for which Mrs. Darcy and I are quite prepared."

"I see. Thank you for your honesty regarding your son, but my compliments to him still stand."

Darcy thanked him. "I shall be happy to relay your compliments to Mrs. Darcy." They sipped their drinks in silence. Darcy cleared his throat, and said carefully, "I think there is one more subject we should discuss, that is, what do we do about my Frederick and your Richard from now on? Frederick's 'confinement' ends tomorrow, and it will be a month or two before he starts repaying the Ventnors, but what happens the next time they meet, for they surely will? And what can we do about it ahead of time?"

Lord Hartford considered all he had said. "Well, Mr. Darcy, that is the question. It seems our sons do not like each other."

"They hate each other, my lord."

"Ahem! Well, yes, that is so; 'hate' is not too strong a word in their case," sighed Richard's father, nodding. "Cambridge should be a big enough city to keep them apart, except for the fact that they attend the same university, King's College. And, like yourself, I do not want any further incidents to occur between them."

"I most certainly do agree."

Lord Hartford nodded again. "Therefore, I am considering removing Richard from Cambridge. I would like him to depart for Jamaica to work as a secretary on the voyage to the overseer of our family plantation there, and to continue in that capacity once he arrives, for some time."

Darcy's eyebrows rose. "Are you not concerned about your son being so far away from you and the university for such a long time?"

Lord Hartford smiled. "Well, Mr. Darcy, I think it will do Richard much good. To Jamaica he shall go, and I hope he will learn responsibility and some composure, if not a more pleasing personality and outlook on life. As his father, I am only too ready to concede his defects of character and his mistakes."

"My own son makes mistakes, and we all have defects of character, I myself as well as he."

"As do I, which includes having too much pride in my own family to check their behavior." Lord Hartford shrugged. "Again, I feel Richard has much more to improve in his character than young Frederick." He smiled. "As we spoke of earlier, like you and Mrs. Darcy I am fortunate to have more than one son. Lady Ursula agrees with me that Rupert, my heir, is a fine son, ethical and proper, if not the most outgoing or quick-witted. Other than our daughter, Susannah, Rupert has turned out the best of all our children, thank God."

Darcy swallowed. "I see. Then I must wish all your children health and happiness." He refilled their glasses.

"Thank you, Mr. Darcy."

After a couple of comfortable sips, Darcy resumed. "So, there will be two more balls before the height of this season is over." He looked at Lord Hartford, who was regarding him with a level stare.

"Yes, two more opportunities for them to meet, or more."

Darcy set his jaw. "Which they probably will. The first of the two balls is not for another two days. I assure you, Mrs. Darcy and I will be speaking often with Frederick, Julia, and Jane about everything that is expected of them and how they are to behave at all times, in any situation." He took another sip. "I will personally instruct Frederick. He has been given many stern warnings, which I shall repeat – that he is not to fight with your son or anyone else *no matter what*. However, if he forgets himself, the consequences will be dire: I will send him back to Pemberley under a form of house arrest – bound, with an armed escort. If so, he shall not return to Cambridge for some time, and will spend his days performing hard labor around the estate."

Lord Hartford was equally grim. "I have warned Richard quite strongly as well. If he misbehaves or is careless with his speech, whether to your children or to anyone else for that matter, not only shall I pull him out of university and send him later to Jamaica, but I will also cancel his allowance, have him charged with theft from all his cheating at cards, and clap him in a debtor's prison for an unspecified length of time."

"Excellent," Darcy said.

"Thank you, Mr. Darcy." Lord Hartford nodded. "May I say that I find the arrangements for your young man to be perfect and most appropriate?"

"You may."

The two fathers exchanged determined, baleful looks, then a moment later threw back their heads and roared with laughter.

"Thank you, Lord Hartford!"

"My pleasure, Mr. Darcy!" The master of the house refilled their glasses again.

That night after dinner, Frederick was struggling to stay awake reading a little longer and heard a soft knock on his bedroom door. He was surprised when his parents stepped into the room. They took in his tired but peaceful face, tousled hair, ink-stained fingers, and disheveled state; for Frederick had shed his waistcoat and cravat, and was sitting in his shirt-sleeves, with his shirt unbuttoned almost to his waist. He was rubbing his eyes as Elizabeth spoke.

"What is this I see, Frederick? Are you forgetting how to dress as a young gentleman, or is this something new, and you are now comfortable going about with your chest bared? I certainly hope you have not been looking out a window in such a shocking state of undress." Darcy hid a smile.

Yawning, Frederick buttoned up his shirt. "I am sorry, Mother. But it does get rather close in here after several hours – not that I am complaining!"

"I see." She stepped aside and nodded for Darcy to continue. "Thank you for covering up your nakedness for my sake, however."

"Er, yes, Mother. But why are you both here?" He began to look alarmed. "Have I not followed your strictures? Have I gotten myself into more trouble?" He noticed his father was not carrying any thick books.

"No, my dear." Elizabeth smiled and sat near him.

Darcy approached. "Frederick," he said kindly, "we wanted to tell you that your confinement is ended after tonight, and starting tomorrow at breakfast, you are free to move about the house again, and go out with us or on your own. You have followed all the rules I set down after the Ventnors' ball. That is all."

Frederick sagged in relief. "Thank you, Father."

Darcy smiled. "No new volumes of Gibbon for the time being."

"Again, I thank you!" However, his parents made no move to leave. He yawned again and looked at them. Now his father sat down next to him. Frederick immediately turned to face him, but also pushed his chair back a couple of inches. His father noticed and sighed.

"There is more I would like to say, Son." He paused. "First, I sincerely regret having appeared so threatening to you after the ball. I have always prided myself on my self-control, and I came very close to striking you and causing you physical pain because I was so angry, and I felt justified in being angry with you. Can you not be afraid of me now?" His eyes pleaded, and Frederick's opened wide.

"Of course, Father!" They embraced while Elizabeth dabbed her eyes.

Darcy thanked him, and they separated after a moment. "There is just one more thing I would like to say." Frederick waited. "I still do not approve of your fighting in public, but I do admire you for your courage and determination in standing up for Julia and Jane, and for all of us. I could not say it that night, but I say it now, as I have come to realize that I was placing a higher value on perfect, gentlemanly behavior than protecting one's family and personal honor. I shall try not to make that mistake again."

They shook hands as Frederick thanked him and emitted another huge yawn.

"We had better let you get some rest, dear," Elizabeth said, rising. Darcy did likewise, and turned back to Frederick, who was itching to pull his shirt open again. "So, you really knocked out two of Richard Grantley's teeth?"

"I did, Father. And if I had not been restrained by Mr. Foxborough and Mr. Tunney, I probably would have given him more blows, and he to me." Frederick shrugged. "I wanted to lay him out flat."

Darcy reached over and patted his shoulder. "Good."

"Fitzwilliam!" Elizabeth nearly shrieked.

"What troubles you, Dearest?"

"How can you approve of fighting?" she attacked. "And what about all the things they broke, flailing about? In addition, do you realize how many fine suits of clothes our son has managed to ruin in just one year? Pemberley may now have to have its own textile mill to meet the demands for his wardrobe!" She lapsed into outraged silence.

"I have said I do not approve of fighting," he replied, trying not to smile, "and I have not forgotten about the rest. I assure you, I remember all the tailors' bills I have been receiving for some time! However, I have come to agree that in a rare, extraordinary situation, fighting may be necessary, and that Frederick was justified in fighting Richard Grantley because of his insults." Frederick blushed and sagged in his chair, while his mother shrugged helplessly. "I trust that Frederick knows he cannot go through life using his fists to settle everything, and that this event was truly one of a kind." He looked at Frederick, who gave them both a firm nod.

"*Ohhhh,*" Elizabeth moaned, "I am done with both of you tonight! I will never understand men and their inclinations to beat each other to pulp! Good night, Frederick, and sleep well." And out of his room she sailed.

Frederick wanted to laugh, but gave yet another yawn instead. Darcy patted his shoulder again, rising to leave. "Is Mother upset because you changed your mind?"

Darcy paused at the door. "Well, perhaps she is, for I am about to find out! However, one of the wonderful things about your mother is that she speaks her mind, and therefore does not stay angry or upset for very long – usually."

"I see," Frederick said, staggering around to prepare for bed, "but what will you do if Mother remains angry?"

Darcy smiled. "As a secret between you and me, maybe I will let her beat me with a pillow or sofa cushion." With that, he nodded and left the room, leaving Frederick doubled over with laughter until he cried.

CHAPTER 16

The next two days passed as Darcy and Elizabeth intended, filled with discussions and warnings to their children. This allowed some of Frederick's bruises to fade, even though he seemed to forget about them. Now, this evening, he was leading Julia and Jane out to the carriage for the fifth debutante ball of the season. He was exquisitely dressed in an outfit he had already worn but had not yet ruined for any reason. It seemed their parents' warnings were going to continue until the precise moment they entered the main door and started smiling and greeting everyone.

"Now remember, you three," Elizabeth pointed a gloved hand at them, "not a cross word or snide remark, or physical movement toward anyone's person, or even in anyone's direction, no matter what the provocation is! Do you understand? Not even if you are like the Christians being led out to face the lions of the Colosseum! Julia! Jane! Frederick! Are we clear on all that?"

"Yes, Mother," his sisters answered in a dutiful but slightly weary tone. Then they both looked at Frederick.

"Yes, Mother. Yes, Sir," he said grudgingly. He was tired of all the warnings he had been given, for he had heard nothing else for three entire days, but quickly straightened up and made his expression and tone pleasing, when he saw his parents glare at him. "I will not do anything a gentleman would not do," he promised.

Julia gave her sweetest smile. "Do not worry, Mother, for I shall make sure Frederick behaves himself." He wanted to be cross with her, but she smiled again and kissed his cheek, which made him blush.

"Excellent," their father replied crisply, exchanging a glance with their mother. As Frederick helped settle his sisters within the closed carriage, Darcy spoke in a low voice to Elizabeth before they climbed in themselves. "It is just as we feared, Lizzie," he remarked. "It is the talk of London – all about the fighting Darcy heir who flattened young Grantley, the lord's son, a boor and a cheat." He grimaced. "There is also some gossip floating around that Frederick fought Grantley because he expected him to dance with Julia. Apparently, some people still do not believe that Grantley insulted her and us, so Lord Lennox and the Wainrights told me yesterday during their visits."

"Oh," moaned Elizabeth, "I feel a very bad headache is starting, Dearest, but I will not stay home to nurse it! Do you think Frederick will keep his head tonight, and in the future? For the Grantleys are sure to attend! A meeting between them is unavoidable."

"Let us hope he does," he said grimly. "Their fight coming upon the heels of Henry's scandal, the first, late Darcy heir leaving behind an illegitimate child, and his poor, unwed Christina expiring in our care – then Jane Elizabeth's imprudent actions..." He shook his head. "All this, and any additional confrontations could permanently link our family with scandal and rumors of unacceptable behavior of all kinds! It is our children I am worried about, not the two of us."

Elizabeth shook her head also. "I am worried, too." She hugged him tight. "I will be praying for an uneventful evening." Nodding, he helped her into the carriage.

This evening's ball was being given at New Hampton Court, a modest palace in the heart of London not far from several royal residences, and the home of James Fitzrobert, the Earl of Sheffield. Julia and Jane looked like princesses themselves in their full gowns with capes and modest trains, and it was rumored that royal visitors, perhaps even Princess Victoria, the Heir Presumptive herself, might make an appearance. Frederick was excited enough and regretted the one visible bruise remaining on the left side of his face. Julia had offered to cover it with some cosmetics, but of course he had given a manly refusal; now he was reconsidering, but it was too late for that.

The evening started off well. They were not long inside the palace when they met up with Lord Ravenswood and Miss Calvert, the Eastons, the Stoddards, and all the Foxboroughs; so, for quite some time they enjoyed the agreeable company of their friends. Twenty minutes later, while their parents chatted up the Foxboroughs, Frederick and his sisters excused themselves to get some refreshments. No sooner had they reached a station than they heard a familiar loud, disagreeable voice – Richard Grantley's.

"What are they doing here?" Jane Elizabeth asked angrily. Frederick and Julia had not seen her look so sullen in a very long time.

Frederick touched her gloved hand. "The same thing we are, Jane. Please try to stay calm! Our invitations to this ball were not rescinded after the Ventnors' so I imagine that, in all fairness, the Grantleys' were not either."

"Your magnanimity amazes me."

"*Jane!*" Julia chided.

"It is all right, Julia," he said, smiling. "I think we are a bit on edge after all the warnings Mother and Father have given us! I know I am." He shrugged and smiled wider. "Well, we know Richard and his family are present, so we don't have to dread whether they are or not. Besides, we all have been through so much. Why do we not just try to enjoy ourselves a little tonight?"

His mood was infectious, and even Jane Elizabeth managed a smile. "That's better," he said happily. "I know I am looking forward to dancing with Angelina Molyneux, Pamela Easton, Cecilia Calvert, and Sophia Stoddard, if I can manage it."

"You'd better hurry to secure those dances," Julia advised good-naturedly, as her social compass reasserted itself. "Oh,

Frederick, before I forget, do try to save one dance for someone I would really like you to meet – a lovely young lady named Rosamund Woodleigh." He assented, and Julia promised to make the introductions later.

The evening progressed quite successfully. Frederick, Julia, and Jane, as well as their parents, found themselves welcomed, popular, and sought after, much to their surprise. None of them had much time for a moment of relaxation, or even refreshments, when they spent so much time making introductions and conversation; but other guests seemed to be seeing to their needs nonetheless. The three siblings' dance cards filled up quickly, and Julia was happy they all had dances with their desired partners – including Frederick with Angelina Molyneux and Rosamund Woodleigh, Julia for two dances with Sir Timothy Carlisle, and Jane Elizabeth with Simon Easton, Ben Ruth-Davis, a young man named Justin Longford, and one also with Sir Timothy! The Darcy siblings began to realize they were being favored with polite, but constant attention and interest, although they still occasionally received a glare; friends of the Grantleys, no doubt.

What the Darcys did not know was that the Grantleys were being snubbed. Darcy's assessment to Elizabeth was correct – the news of the fight was circulating all through the *ton* and the rest of London society. And so popular opinion, fueled by facts, history, and even less than facts – had decided against the Grantleys. The Grantley siblings found themselves given polite but cold shoulders at best, and sometimes clear hostility. Susannah Grantley had never looked so pitiful in public, and even her sister, Isabelle, was sobered by the lack of regard they had previously expected and enjoyed; she tried to remember her manners, with mixed results. Frederick gave in to his newfound, manly, popular status by successfully evading the looks of Lucy Robinson, Honoria Watson, and Alexandra Vinson; but otherwise he and his sisters remained on their guard.

Julia hadn't forgotten the Grantleys were present somewhere within the palace, but she tried to remember how high her spirits had been during the first two balls. Starry-eyed, she began to enjoy herself and sparkle again. A brief encounter threatened to darken that sparkle, however.

Julian Tunney's white teeth shone in his tanned face and wide smile. "Miss Darcy, how lovely to see you again! May I dance with you this evening?"

She felt her cheeks drooping along with her mouth but managed to keep her lips in a prim line. "I am afraid my dance card is full, Sir."

Undeterred, he kept smiling, which annoyed her. "Then let us chat before your partner claims you for the next dance."

"I think not, Mr. Tunney." She was angry he was attempting to speak with her, after she thought she had made it clear she did not welcome his company or attentions. "Would you dance with me if I were of the same faith as the Stoddards?" she almost snapped, then remembered her mother's warning about making untoward remarks.

Surprise spoiled his handsomeness, and anger hardened his eyes. "Well," he began, then almost spluttered. "What difference does that make? Perhaps you misunderstood what I said." He tried to smile again and ended up only looking crafty. "Perhaps I am not as particular as you think! Pleasure and spending one's time with the right person outweigh any judgments as to character and upbringing, though they can be important."

She glared at him. "I did not misunderstand you, for you made yourself quite clear. Please excuse me." She made a deliberate turn away from him and took a couple of steps.

He tried to grab her arm. "I would like to keep chatting with you, Miss Darcy."

"I cannot say the same." She gave a great shake to free

herself, then gave him another glare, and began to stride off when she heard someone call her name; thankfully, it was a different male voice trying to catch up with her, and not Julian Tunney's.

She was extremely grateful when a very cheerful, smiling Gregory Lawson stepped up, completely halting Tunney behind him, to reach for her hand. "I have been looking forward to dancing with you," he told her gallantly, and her smile was as wide as his.

She enjoyed the pleasure of dancing with him; he didn't mention whether he had heard any rumors about the fight between Frederick and Grantley, or even make references to the evening at Dutton Ampner. The evening became even more pleasant when Sir Timothy appeared in yet another elegant outfit to claim his first dance with her; and Frederick was only too happy dancing with Miss Carlisle.

"I am extremely glad Miss Carlisle is recovered from her illness!" Julia remarked to Sir Timothy as they danced.

"Thank you, Miss Darcy." He gave her a wide smile. "Poor Catharina felt very low for three entire days and I was quite concerned about her, although the doctor assured us that she had a very common cold that would not keep her down for long. As you can see, she is quite well again, for which I am most grateful – as I am for your consideration for her health and well-being."

"Not at all, Sir Timothy." She blushed. Trying to change the subject, she remarked, "I hope Miss Carlisle was not too disappointed at missing the ball at Dutton Ampner, though she was ill."

Sir Timothy considered that. "Well, Catharina was disappointed, I admit," he said carefully, "but I also had insisted she refuse all social engagements and remain at home to recuperate. She really would have liked to attend the ball, but I am afraid she would not have been able to last through the long evening, and, though I am no physician myself, she seemed rather dizzy, so all that dancing and whirling about could not have been advisable in her condition. Besides," he smiled at her again, "there were to be more balls, like this one."

"That is true," she assented, "though it may have been a good one to miss after all."

He looked at her, and she looked away, smiling. "Ah, yes," he finally said, "I believe I heard about some rather extraordinary events that occurred during it." A smile played at the corners of his mouth, but he said nothing else.

She laughed. "I apologize, for that was an impolite remark I made. Yes, the ball was extraordinary for obvious reasons, and I do hope that, if Miss Carlisle had been well enough to attend, she would have not been shocked and distressed by what did occur."

He caught that. "Not at all, Miss Darcy, there is no need to apologize, for I quite understand." He cleared his throat. "However, it is now my turn to make a less than perfect remark." He continued as her face registered surprise. "I must admit to you that, even had Catharina been well, my sister and I would not have attended the Ventnors' ball. You see, we could not – and would not – have attended in any case, for we were not given an invitation to it."

She could not have been more surprised. "Not invited? Whyever not, for is not your sister making her debut this season?"

He looked apologetic. "She is. However, I am sorry to inform you, Miss Darcy, that Sir Romanus Ventnor, unlike the Earl of Sheffield, is close friends with the Earl of Chester – and the entire Ravenswood family."

"I cannot believe it," she exclaimed, though in a very low voice not to be overheard. "Are you saying that you and your sister were deliberately not invited to the last ball?" She forgot the Carlisles had been present at the Calverts' ball at Woodside.

"That is precisely what I am saying. I am sorry to distress you, but it is true that the elder Lord Ravenswood, the Earl, does not hold my family or me personally in very high regard."

"I do not know what to say," she said finally, "though I am most sorry to hear it." True, the younger Lord Ravenswood had expressed his lack of admiration for the splendid young man with whom she was dancing. But for his distinguished family to resort to such petty snubs, that widened her eyes. She was determined to continue enjoying the evening, but by now she was heartily sick of the prejudices and slights traded among the London *ton*. Did she really hope to marry among such people?

He thanked her and swallowed. "I hesitated to tell you this, but I know how much an accomplished and ethical young lady such as yourself appreciates truth and fairness." She thanked him in return and changed the subject to a safer topic as they danced.

She was all set to act distantly with young Lord Ravenswood when he came to claim her for the first of their two dances. However, his well-timed compliments and remarks kept her distracted from her resentment, and she found herself enjoying their time together. She only remembered to be indignant after he left. Julia wasn't one to hold a grudge, so she shrugged inwardly and promised to think about it later; maybe Frederick could help her sort it all out. Still, her thoughts kept returning to memories of the Calverts' ball; it appeared that young Lord Ravenswood had successfully harangued his father to let the Carlisles attend their ball at Woodside. It also appeared that the Earl had had his revenge with Sir Romanus' help at Dutton Ampner.

However, it was another high point during the evening when a short time later, between dances with Lord Ravenswood, Julia was finally able to introduce Frederick to Rosamund Woodleigh. She was sure her brother would like her, which certainly seemed to be the case when he beheld the young lady. Miss Woodleigh was wearing an elegant but simple gown of lavender silk, with a white lace wrap around her shoulders, white gloves, beautiful long garnet earrings, and a simple string of pearls around her neck; usually given to wearing her hair in a tasteful bun, tonight she wore her hair in a pleasing Grecian style, with curled tendrils hanging down to caress the sides of her face and neck. Julia saw Frederick's smile reach to his eyes, despite his bruise, and he gave Miss Woodleigh a deep bow and a fine greeting. Later, Julia would notice him leading his partner to a refreshment table and seemingly at ease chatting with her. Julia felt certain Miss Woodleigh would not find Richard Grantley nearly as pleasant, and congratulated herself on having found a young lady Frederick really seemed to like, and not fear.

During the next break in the dancing, about two-thirds of the way through the ball, the musicians suddenly struck up "God Save the King." As rumored and expected, Princess Victoria made her appearance, accompanied by her mother, the Duchess of Kent, and three other female attendants!

The young princess wore a perfectly domed white silk dress, with pastel blue gauzy sashes gracefully looping around her skirts and fastened with equally light silk rosettes. Her simple braids formed a coiled bun at her neck, and a glittering tiara crowned her short front curls; long white gloves covered her arms and hands. The Earl and Countess Sheffield made their formal greetings and invited Her Highness to enjoy the pleasures their home had to offer. The princess replied in a clear and gracious voice her thanks for her wonderful reception at New Hampton Court, as well as her desire to meet the season's debutantes who were present.

The young ladies and their escorts eagerly and properly lined up to be presented to the Princess and Heir Presumptive. However nervous he might be, Frederick's natural reserve took over, but Julia was thrilled; they had not yet been presented at Court, but this would make a wonderful rehearsal for that event. Julia wanted to look around for their parents and Jane Elizabeth, but forced herself to keep her behavior perfect.

As did Frederick, especially when their turn came. Curtsey and bow were executed deeply and flawlessly. After the formal greetings were exchanged, Princess Victoria favored Julia with an unexpected remark.

"How pleased we are to meet you tonight, Miss Darcy," Her Highness said, "for your father, the Master of Pemberley, is well known to us, and we have heard much about how you are one of the stars in this season's firmament."

Julia sank to the ground again, expressing her thanks. As she did so, Frederick noticed the Duchess of Kent looking at his face and realized she must have seen the bruise. That damned bruise, he wanted to curse; he should have let Julia paint his face like she had offered to, but he used every scrap of willpower to maintain his formal, correct, and nonchalant demeanor. Again, he bowed deeply to the Princess.

Julia had risen, getting ready to move on for the next couple behind them to make their presentation, when it appeared Princess Victoria was about to speak again. She had turned to one of her ladies to relinquish her flowery fan when, for some strange reason, the lady did not hold on to it, and it clattered to the floor, opening wide.

It was as if there had been the sound of a gunshot. Frederick immediately bent down, retrieved the fan, carefully closed it shut, and handed it to Her Highness as he inclined his head.

"Thank you, Mr. Darcy." Her Highness smiled at him as she took it from his gloved hand, and the Duchess turned a look on the mortified lady-in-waiting. Princess Victoria favored them with a glance and wished them a good evening as the Duchess smiled. They replied in turn and moved away.

As they walked slowly away, their hearts still pounding, Julia said softly, "Frederick, if we did not have to behave ourselves right now, and hadn't been warned to do so many times, I swear I would throw my arms around you and give you a big kiss."

She heard him chuckle as they kept their eyes forward and

contained. "Thank you, Julia," he said, "but it is not all that important, is it? It just – happened."

"Not important you say? You only retrieved Her Highness' fan and returned it to her, behaving like a perfect gentleman! How many people manage to do that? I would say you were magnificent, dear Brother."

"Thank you, Julia," he mumbled. "After the Ventnors' ball my behavior could use some rehabilitation." Now it was her turn to chuckle.

"I am so excited and so parched. Let us go find you a well-deserved glass of wine, and some punch for myself."

"Agreed." They drifted away as the long series of presentations continued.

They both relaxed with their full glasses in the large meeting room next to the ballroom, but their contentment was not to last. A surly Richard Grantley pushed his way through some indignant gentlemen right toward them.

"Darcy," he growled, "and Miss Darcy. Greetings."

He lurched over to the refreshment table and demanded some wine, which the footman served him with distaste.

Julia's eyes were wide with fright and she clutched his arm. "Oh, Fred! What shall we do now?"

He smiled. "Courage, my dear sister! You will keep your promise to make me behave, and I – I will behave."

"No matter what?"

"No matter what."

Richard gulped down his wine and demanded more. The footman did not want to give it to him, but an older manservant did and told him to go away to a place where he would not embarrass anyone.

"Never thought the Earl of Sheffield would employ such ill-mannered, disrespectful people," Richard snapped. "Well, if

I have your approval to do so, *Sir*, I am going to talk to these people over here." He lurched back towards Frederick and Julia, as the two footmen glared at him and turned away.

"*Frederick!*" she screamed in a whisper.

"Steady," he whispered back.

Richard leered at them both as he weaved on his legs. He was dressed in a suit whose material was as elegant and rich as Sir Timothy's. However, due to his disposition, lack of sobriety, and perspiring, he didn't make a very fine appearance. His hair was lank and his jaw stubbled and swollen, although no bruises were visible on his face. Richard saw their hesitation and waved a hand in the air. "I know, I know," he said, "no hostilities, Papa told me. Let peace reign." He laughed, but still approached Frederick and gave him a push in the shoulder. Julia gasped and covered her eyes.

Frederick blinked. "Hello, Richard. Enjoying yourself tonight? And have you presented Miss Grantley to Her Highness?" None of them noticed the noise around them was picking up, and that a large group of people seemed to be coming into this room from the ballroom.

"Aren't you the clever one?" Richard sneered. "No, I haven't, since my father, Lord Hartford, decided to do it in my place." He grimaced. "But aren't you the opportunist as well? Presenting your sister here and picking up the royal fan?" He hiccupped. "Everything is going just fine for you Darcys, is it not?"

Frederick rolled his eyes. "It wasn't like that at all, Richard, it just happened." Grantley gave a snort. "You would have done the same thing, if it had happened to you."

"And done it better than you, I daresay! But I didn't get the chance!" Richard almost shouted, displeasing not a few people around them. "Sneaky, little –" he began to snarl, but stopped; he remembered his father's threats of debtor prison. "Sorry, Darcy, I forgot – peace it is." As Richard reached over to clutch his hand, the dampness of his palm matted Frederick's glove and he wavered a little more on his legs. His fine suit was losing its shine and press, and he kept mopping his face with a limp handkerchief. Frederick wanted to wipe his hand on his trousers but dared not make any movement.

"Come on, Frederick," Julia urged, "I see Sophia and Samuel Stoddard over there with no one to talk to." She tried to lead him away when Richard turned too quickly back to the table and almost lost his balance. Frederick, who recognized the stages of progressive drunkenness from his own experiences, hurried to support him. "Richard, you look a little tired. Let's go sit down somewhere for a few minutes, shall we, maybe outside?" He looked at Julia, who instantly understood, and off she went to get any sympathetic young man she could find nearby.

"Leave me alone," Richard complained, looking bilious. "I just need something more to drink." His eyes fell on someone's newly-poured full goblet of wine on the table and he snatched it up, sloshing some wine over his French cuff before the footman could object.

"No, Richard, you don't need that," Frederick said quickly, trying to take it from him. "Let's just go outside and get some fresh air." He looked around and saw the welcome sight of his sister hurrying back with Samuel and Daniel Stoddard, Justin Longford, and Simon Easton, along with Ben Ruth-Davis.

"I said, leave me alone!" Richard snapped, coming away with the glass without spilling any more of it. He took a large swig, and when Frederick tried to take it again he flung its full contents into his face.

Momentarily blinded, Frederick heard several gasps, including his own, and Richard's guffaws. Frederick clutched the corner of the refreshment table and managed not to imbalance it so it would fall over, but two glasses did wobble, one of which finally lost its battle to stay upright, and fell, shattering on the floor. Frederick's stinging eyes closed; another glass he'd broken! More notoriety he'd receive, and perhaps Lloyd's of London would have to offer a new type of insurance policy that covered unforeseen damage at social events such as debutante balls.

Everyone braced for an explosion of violence, but he stumbled forward a couple of steps, unfortunately in Richard's direction, causing a couple of onlookers to flinch. One of the two footmen rushed from behind the table to help wipe his dripping face, then blot and brush his sodden cravat, waistcoat, and lapels, while making regretful sounds. "Hold still, young sir. Almost done. Steady now." Having widened his arms from his sides so the footman could dry him off, Frederick emitted a frustrated grunt while worry creased the faces of more onlookers.

Once the footman had snatched the wet towels and retreated behind the table again, Frederick could see the extent of the stains; oh well, he sighed, another suit ruined. Thank goodness it hadn't been a burgundy. No one made a move to clean up the broken glass.

Richard was still laughing, but Frederick gave him a reproachful glance. "That was a very stupid thing to do, wasting all that perfectly good wine. Now we are all going to go outside for some fresh air."

"What? No!" Richard protested, as he found himself grabbed on both sides by a Stoddard, with Simon in front of him, and Ben and Justin behind him; he was trapped. "I don't want to!" The hubbub was quite near them now, and Frederick's heart sank – it was the royal party, coming through on their way to the dining rooms!

"Hurry, fellows," he urged them, as Richard cried out in protest again. *"Be quiet!"* Frederick hissed at him. He thought they would make it out of the room into the grand hallway and be on their way to the garden before the royal party reached them. But they had waited just a little bit too long to make their escape, albeit a staggering one, thanks to Richard.

Richard was still struggling and complaining when everyone fell silent around them and snapped to attention. People were bowing and curtseying as Her Highness approached, and now she and the rest of her party stood only about ten feet away from their sorry group, with curious, displeased expressions. Frederick now wished he held a sword he could fall upon. All the young men let go of Richard and made their bows. Richard stumbled forward several feet, glad to be free of them, and smiled, then blanched. "Your Highness," he said in a composed voice, and went into his formal bow – which he could not complete, because he lost his balance and stumbled forward, towards the Princess herself!

Frederick saw fear in Princess Victoria's face, as it looked like Richard would fall or roll right into her. Frederick dashed forward between them and managed to push Richard forcefully off to one side. He stumbled over him, but managed not to bump into anyone else, knock them over, or damage anything – except their own composure. He lost his own balance and sank down over a damp and stunned Richard, who cried out.

Frederick heard gasps and screams. He got up slowly and approached Her Highness, who was fanning herself furiously, but was otherwise composed. He bowed to her again and spoke. "If I may be so bold, Your Highness, may I ask if you have been harmed or inconvenienced in any way?" He thought he sounded incredibly stupid.

Her eyes fluttered. "Thank you, Sir, we are quite unharmed." She looked more closely at him. "Mr. Darcy, is it?" Her expression cleared, though she noticed his damp, stained finery. "How nice to meet you again so soon, even under such circumstances." She smiled. "Thank you for your most timely assistance; we are most grateful, are we not, Mama?" She turned to the Duchess, who gave only the slightest of smiles.

Inwardly, Princess Victoria sighed; this was why she didn't like impromptu, unscripted public appearances – anything could happen. She was beginning to regret her rather sudden decision to come to New Hampton Court, though she had known about the opportunity for almost a week. She also had to admit she eagerly looked forward to meeting this season's debutantes, and vaguely hoped Sheffield or one of his sons might ask her to dance. She much preferred dancing with them than with her uncle, the King. Here she could enjoy a rare evening outside her own controlled palace apartments, even with her mother, the Duchess, in attendance. Well, now it seemed that all she was to gain was the evening spent outside in the capital and meeting all the glittering young ladies. She would make certain to enjoy herself in whatever she did the following day.

There was an angry sound as the Earl of Sheffield and his oldest son John rushed forward. "Your Highness!" the Earl sputtered with indignation. "I am most sorry for this disgraceful display in our home that has marred your most gracious visit! This young hellion will be thrown out immediately, and I will only tell his father afterwards!"

The Stoddards, Ben, Simon, and Justin surrounded Richard, who was lolling around and moaning. "Oh, dear," Frederick said aloud. He turned toward the Princess and the Earl, speaking quickly. "Please excuse him, Your Highness, for his behavior, because it is obvious that he is rather – unwell at the moment; I believe some fresh air and some cold water to drink will help restore him." Richard gave a moan that made several people wince. "Please, my lord," Frederick pleaded to the Earl, "we need to get him outside – *immediately.*" The Earl understood and gestured for them to continue.

Princess Victoria nodded. "Thank you for seeing to the welfare of that young man," she said, exchanging a glance with the Duchess. "We are sorry it must be curtailing your enjoyment of such a splendid ball," her gaze flickered ever so slightly, "but we are most grateful for your assistance, are we not, Fitzrobert?" The Earl nodded.

"Thank you, Your Highness." Frederick inclined his head, then hurried over to help the others raise Richard to his feet.

"I feel dizzy," the unkempt lout cried, stumbling, but they prevented him from falling.

"Come on, Richard," Frederick said soothingly, not caring who heard him, "let's go sit down outside." They hustled him out and made it to the garden in only a few minutes, while he struggled and complained the entire way. Frederick did not care either about the icy glares and indignant murmurs of the crowd as they passed by; he only worried about getting Richard into the garden in time, and what his parents would do to him when they found out about this – if they hadn't already witnessed it.

Once outside in the garden, they released Richard and let him stumble around. The surly brute was still belligerent enough to try to punch them, and clipped Justin Longford on the jaw. Frederick wanted to throw him bodily into the fountain to cool him off, but restrained himself.

They quickly procured a large pitcher of cold water, and Ben Ruth-Davis tried to get Richard to drink some of it from a glass, but Richard flung that all over him. Then they tried to wipe his face with a wet towel, but he pushed them all away. Finally, Daniel Stoddard nodded to his brother, who took the pitcher and emptied it over Richard's head. Soaking wet, Richard choked, howled, and cursed, but was suddenly overcome with retching. It went on for ten horrible minutes, but Richard eventually managed to empty his stomach into a bushy spot with their help. He somehow remained clean himself, though he was still very wet; with a light moan, he fell back and curled up on the manicured lawn, insensible.

The other young men took deep breaths to calm down, as the servants, along with the wrath of God personified in Lord Hartford, came out to take charge of Richard.

"Bloody idiot," Simon Easton said, not caring who heard him. They were all wiping dirt, grass, and regurgitations from their fine clothes.

Justin Longford looked at all of them. "Well, what a fine

appearance we all make! Shall any one of us be granted another dance this evening? And who would want to sit next to any of us at dinner, assuming they would seat us in the first place?"

They looked at each other, listless, befouled, and disgusted. "I agree with you that the chances are slim, Longford," Frederick replied, "so we will just have to console ourselves with the memory of Richard Grantley's debut into London society." The others roared with laughter, and slapping him on the back, went back inside to find some wine and continue cleaning themselves off.

The Earl of Sheffield and John Fitzrobert were furious over what had occurred, after the graciousness of Her Highness to appear at the ball. They were grateful, however, to all the young men for getting Richard Grantley out of the house before he became violently ill. The Earl ranted and raved at his peer, Lord Hartford, for a full ten minutes in his private study before his anger and indignation were exhausted. The stony-faced father promised the Earl that, once sober enough to understand them, his son's punishments would be lasting and severe, imposed without mercy.

The six young men made quite a sight when the Earl and his son got a good look at them in one of the drawing rooms; all that finery stained or as good as ruined. The Earl shook his head; well, so was Grantley's, and he recalled with satisfaction seeing the soaked, unconscious young lout being carried upstairs. He consulted with John and his younger brothers George and Edward. They generously agreed to provide their guests with whatever cravats, waistcoats, and coats that would fit them and not look mismatched from their own wardrobes. Luckily, they all did manage to find something to wear, as the servants began trying to clean their soiled clothing. Newly outfitted, and with doses of cologne for good measure, they could now return to the young ladies, dance with them, and forget about Richard. The banquet had been delayed because of the royal visit and its aftermath, but Frederick looked forward to the sumptuous dinner. Princess Victoria was pleased to have places cleared for her and the Duchess, and enjoyed at least three courses of a private banquet served them in a quickly-prepared drawing room before their dignified exit from New Hampton Court.

All was going well when he met up again with his parents and sisters. Only Julia knew the reason for the change in his appearance but kept her peace. They exchanged glances, and Frederick saw the stone set in his own father's eyes. "Ulp!" he let out, as he felt his father's grip tighten on his arm.

"Frederick," his father said evenly and slowly, "I am certain you will enlighten your mother and me as to why you are wearing a different coat, waistcoat, and cravat than the ones you wore when you arrived here this evening, will you not?"

"Of course I will, Father." Frederick closed his eyes as Darcy held him fast.

Darcy barely thanked him, but did not lessen his grip, and Elizabeth touched his arm in a mute appeal. "I also trust the reason will not get you sent back to Pemberley bound and under arrest?"

Frederick brightened. "No, Father! That is, I – well – don't think it will." His parents exchanged another, more resigned glance.

"I see. I suppose I am glad to hear it." His father exhaled and frowned. "Then I expect you will discuss this turn of events with us after we return home after the ball, no matter how early in the morning it is."

"Yes, of course!" Frederick agreed. "And Father?"

"What is it, Frederick?"

"Could you please lighten your grip on this coat sleeve? For it belongs to George Fitzrobert, the Earl's son, and –"

A storm rose in his father's eyes, and Frederick fell silent.

"Please, Son," Darcy said, passing a hand over his face, "not now. Do not say another word about it until we discuss it all later." He sighed. "I cannot bear thinking what this is all about." He shook his head. "I am getting much too old for this."

"Fitzwilliam," Elizabeth scolded, almost rolling her eyes, and they all relaxed after Frederick promised to spare his father.

Frederick, Julia, and Jane resumed dancing with their partners as their parents shared a couple of dances with each other. Somehow, Frederick contrived to have a second dance with Rosamund Woodleigh, who complimented him on his appearance. She remarked that she rarely enjoyed the opportunity to dance with the same partner, who sported different attire each time, on the same evening. Frederick laughed for what seemed a full minute, regardless of propriety. Two dances later came the final dance of the evening with Julia, and then it was time to queue up and go into the huge banquet.

Astonishment. Disbelief. Pride, horror, disgust, anger, relief, and even amusement. All these registered in their parents' faces as Frederick told them everything that had occurred at New Hampton Court during the evening. They remained silent for several moments after he finished, as the mantel clock chimed two.

"You retrieved the Princess's fan," Elizabeth said, wide-eyed despite the hour.

"Richard Grantley drank himself into distress," his father said in a flat voice.

"You prevented an accident to Her Highness."

"And there was no fight."

Frederick cleared his throat. "No, Sir, not that Richard didn't try to start one with all of us, not just me. However, he was so drunk after he almost fell into Princess Victoria, he was rather harmless – except for his getting sick." Now Elizabeth and his sisters' expressions registered something distasteful; revulsion was not something they usually displayed. "I'm sorry, Mother, Julia, and Jane, but that is what happened – and that is how we all became dressed in the fine clothes of the Earl's sons." He hoped to receive his own the next day, after the Earl's servants attempted to clean them. "I am most appreciative of the gratitude and generosity of the Earl and his sons, for I would not have been able to dance or dine in such a state; it was the same for Samuel and Daniel Stoddard, Justin Longford, Ben Ruth-Davis, and Simon Easton."

"What a boon for London tailors," his father deprecated. "Well, Dearest," he remarked to Elizabeth, "have you anything to say about yet another evening of extraordinary events?"

She blinked. "I am rather speechless, Dearest." Then she smiled. "I am so proud of you both! Frederick, you kept your promise, and you both earned the recognition of Her Highness!"

Darcy finally smiled himself. "Yes, that is wonderful! Both of you acquitted yourselves in the best manner." Frederick and Julia blushed. Darcy's gaze turned serious, though still kind. "Your mother and I are most impressed, Frederick, with your fortitude in such an awkward and trying situation, as well as keeping your promise to behave at all costs, which you did most successfully."

Frederick sighed, lowering his gaze, and thanked them. "So, you will not have me clapped in chains and dragged off to a dungeon somewhere?"

"Frederick," reproved Elizabeth, but Darcy laughed. "No, Frederick, I shall not. Though I think Master Grantley might be."

The levity drained from Frederick's face, and his parents exchanged a glance. "I know it is all his own fault," he said, "but I feel badly for him. As hateful as Richard can be, I am sure he did not intend to behave the way he did tonight or cause all that trouble." He looked away. "He was so drunk, as I have been, at Cambridge. That is why I knew he would get sick everywhere! Oh, again I am sorry, Mother, Julia, and Jane," he hurried to add, as they recoiled a second time. "But I cannot censure him too much, for I saw the look on Lord Hartford's face." He turned to his parents. "I would rather die than face such wrath from both of you!"

"As we know Richard Grantley will face," his father commented in a soft tone, also serious again.

Frederick nodded and, looking at the fire in the grate, added, "I also feel very badly for Lord Hartford. I do not know how he will face the consequences of what Richard has done, for he did it publicly, in front of so many witnesses." He sighed. "I could not bear it, if I had behaved so. I would have exposed you all to ignominy and derision, and Pemberley as well." Misuse of his power and prestige could be costly.

"You need not worry, for you have behaved incredibly well," Elizabeth said. "And your compassion for Lord Hartford, and even for poor, misguided, ill-mannered Richard Grantley, is most admirable, my dear son."

"Thank you, Mother." He looked down, then back into the fire.

"Well," Darcy stirred, "I think we can consider this to have been a relatively, if not completely, fine evening! I am happy to tell you, Julia and Frederick, that your mother, Jane Elizabeth, and I were also presented to Her Highness tonight. And, from some of your comments, it seems that all three of you enjoyed the ball!" He suddenly moved his cheek closer to Elizabeth's. "As did your mother and I." Elizabeth gave a murmur of pleasure, and Jane Elizabeth smiled.

"A happy, successful evening for all of us," Darcy repeated, "despite the cost to your clothes, eh, Frederick?" Silence reigned. "Son?" Frederick was too embarrassed to answer, which intrigued his parents.

Julia smiled. "Did you not enjoy meeting and dancing with Rosamund Woodleigh?"

"Yes, I did very much," he managed to say, and blushed to the roots of his hair.

CHAPTER 17

They all went upstairs soon afterwards to get some well-deserved rest, but Frederick found himself pacing in his room while shedding only some of his clothes, certainly not his trousers or boots, despite the late hour and his tired feet. He felt too warm and excited to sleep, so he took the still unfinished volume of Gibbon and his candles and went down the hall to one of the small sitting rooms on this floor. There, in his shirtsleeves and unbuttoned shirt, he sat, intending to read until the Roman history dulled his mind, which he hoped would occur sooner rather than later.

He dutifully read for at least fifteen minutes. He did not feel any closer to sleep, but his neck began to throb. He kept rubbing it – along with his face – when he heard a sound; he looked up. Julia wandered in and sat down next to him, carrying some needlework. Frederick could not remember the last time he had ever seen his sister in her nightgown, with her dark hair streaming down over her shoulders.

"Couldn't sleep either, could you, Fred?" she asked. She was getting used to seeing her brother's bare chest, after seeing him recently in various stages of undress.

"No," he replied in a voice as low as hers. The clock chimed three. "I was hoping this would put me to sleep, but it hasn't yet."

She wrinkled her nose when she saw the title. "I can't imagine why." She brightened as she worked her needle. "Well, this coming day is going to be completely open, so I think none of us will need to rise very early for any reason."

"Thank goodness for that." He gave up trying to read; he just wanted to sit and wait for sleepiness to come, and listen to whatever his sister might say. After a few minutes, Julia spoke again.

"I do not mean to complain, but I will be glad when this season is over."

"Why, Julia? What do you mean?"

She sighed. "Well, there is everything you, Jane Elizabeth, and I have experienced. I did not know what London society was truly like but, despite all the pleasant and interesting people we have been fortunate enough to meet, there are plenty of others who are rude, unpleasant, and undesirable!"

"Like the Grantley siblings; I agree with you," he said lightly, hoping to make her smile, but she kept her eyes on her sewing.

"Yes, they probably head the list," she kept stitching, "but there are others."

"I see." He thought of the three predatory young ladies, though he did not mention them. "Were you thinking of someone else in particular?"

"I was." She jabbed her needle into the cloth. "Julian Tunney, for one."

"Tunney?" Frederick was surprised. The young gentleman was well liked and sought after, though he hadn't spoken all that much to him. He knew and liked the Eastons and the Foxboroughs a lot better.

"The very same." Julia made a face. "He criticized the Stoddards and complimented me on my condescension in associating with them because they are Jews."

Frederick was aghast. "But that – that is –" He choked and looked about him.

She pursed her lips. "Precisely. At Dutton Ampner he went on for several minutes about how low they were, and how they should not be welcome in 'our' society. I was quite angry, and I defended them, as they are our friends. I hope his half-sister Miss Duncan does not feel the same way as he, but based on her behavior, I think she might."

He was quite upset himself, for he liked the Stoddards too. "That is quite understandable, Julia, and I am glad you told me this! So, what did you do?"

She finally smiled. "I gave Mr. Tunney a piece of my mind and left him in the middle of the dance floor. I will never dance with him again."

"Good for you!" he approved. "If Tunney had said that to me, I would have –" Then he saw Julia's expression. "Well, I would have wanted to, anyway."

Her face relaxed into another smile. "I would not blame you if you had."

He looked grim. "Has Tunney tried to speak to you since?"

"He has, but I have only given him the minimum of politeness, not one more second than is necessary." She didn't want to tell Frederick more but thought she had better anyway. "He tried to ask me to dance with him tonight at New Hampton Court."

Frederick sat straighter. "What happened?"

Her lips formed another line. "Even though Mother told us all to be careful what we said, I asked Mr. Tunney if he'd ask me to dance if I were a Jew like the Stoddards." He gaped at her. "First, he tried to claim I misunderstood what he had said at the previous ball, then pretended that such considerations didn't matter anyway. He wanted to keep chatting, but I abandoned him a second time." She shrugged. "I find him extremely disagreeable, even contemptible, and trust he now understands how I regard him."

"Good," he repeated. A moment later he asked, "Has anyone else's behavior upset you?"

She didn't answer right away. She stopped sewing and finally said, "I think you are right that Lord Ravenswood and Sir Timothy Carlisle don't like each other." She told him what each one had said about the other, and when.

Frederick was starting to feel tired. Widening his eyes, he rubbed his neck and exhaled. "I am sorry to say, that doesn't sound good, does it? Lord Ravenswood admits that he doesn't like or respect Sir Timothy much, and Sir Timothy claims the Ravenswoods used their influence to bar him and Miss Carlisle from the Ventnor's ball, though not their own." He shook his head. "I thought that only the Grantleys – oh, never mind."

"No, that's quite all right." The corners of her mouth turned down as she sewed some tight stitches. "I know exactly what you mean. Much as I love the balls and my fabulous gowns and meeting everyone – and appreciating everything Father and Mother are doing for me and my future," she dropped her work into her lap, "I will say it! I am just *disgusted* with some of these people!" She shook her head, not noticing his surprise. "Our neighbors back home, whether highborn or not, are not so petty and vicious as some of these people here." She sagged. "Oh, Fred! I thought we would be moving amongst the highest society here in London! The highest, most desirable, and the most interesting!"

He felt rather dull. "Well, haven't we been doing that?"

She gave him a pitying look. "Yes, we have on the most obvious level, just face to face. However, these people are *not* our betters, as they are held up to be! Look at how some of them have treated us, and what is more important, look at how they treat each other." She bit her lip and picked up her sewing again.

After a moment, Frederick shook his head and sighed. "I am sorry for being so dense right now because I am very tired. I know that you are right; some of these people are ill-mannered, vicious, and more." He reached over and patted her arm.

She sewed less forcefully. "Thank you, and you need not apologize for being so tired." He thanked her in return.

A couple of minutes passed as she concentrated on handiwork, and he just sat. Finally, she bit off the thread and turned to him. "I don't know what to do. What should I do?"

As tired as he was, he was taken aback. "What do you mean?"

She closed her eyes. "Fred, I like them both. I like Sir Timothy – his manners, his voice, his looks, his intelligence, his clothes, and his kindness to his sister. I also like Lord Ravenswood – his manners, his voice, his looks, and all the attention he has paid me, as well as his kindnesses and regard. Of course, both of them have done so, and I haven't forgotten about Gregory Lawson either! Returning to the other two young gentlemen, I like their sisters, Miss Cecilia and Miss Catharina!" She saw alarm growing in Frederick's face. "Now please do not be concerned, you or Father, for neither one – I should say, none of the three – has declared his intentions to me, if he has any." Frederick sighed in relief. "But if they do – I am not being vain now, only mentioning the possibilities – I swear to you, dear Brother, I would not know what to do if they did." She paused. "And the fact that two of them do not like each other, one whose family apparently snubbed the other, who is only too happy to tell me so – I am quite confused."

He swallowed. "Cannot your own feelings help guide you, as well as your firm principles and spotless behavior, to make a choice if need be?"

She looked down. "Not when I like all of them, regardless."

That floored him. "I see." He was exhausted, and his head hurt trying to think, but he wanted to help her. "Er, Julia? Please forgive my question, but have you ever imagined – uh – what it might be like to be married to any of these gentlemen? I mean, have you ever dreamed about what would your life be like spending it with each one of them – being together with him day after day, and not just dancing or talking with him?"

She looked at him for a full minute. "No, I have not," she said at last. "What good questions you have posed! I am embarrassed to say that I have not begun thinking about such things, especially with all these amusements, distractions, and whatnot going on!" She kissed his cheek. "But I shall begin doing so." She gave a self-deprecating smile. "Ah, I am too concerned with appearances and shallow manners, and whatever happens in the moment! You are right, I should think more about what kind of man would please me as a husband, and whether any of them possess the qualities I desire and admire. I do not mean to sound selfish, for I would hope that I possess qualities a man would desire for his wife."

Frederick smiled and kissed her hand. "I think you have many fine qualities a man would desire in his wife."

"Oh, Fred, how sweet! Thank you!"

He grinned and looked down. "I was only stating the obvious." He felt himself growing more tired. He looked up when he heard her giggle.

"Fred," she said, blushing, "are you really going to go around everywhere you can with your shirt open? It is not gentlemanly, you know, and Mother will get wild about it if she catches you."

He struggled to sit up, which pulled his shirt open wider. "Does my chest bother you, Julia? It is very comfortable this way when it gets warm or close." Come to think if it, he had never seen his father's or Henry's shirts unbuttoned and open like this.

She laughed. "No, I suppose it does not, because I am getting rather used to seeing your bared body, from the results of your adventures." She gathered her needlework, rose, and turned to smile at him. "It also makes me think about other gentlemen of my acquaintance." Indeed, she wondered what Louis Calvert's and Timothy Carlisle's chests looked like; and did that matter?

She left the room, giggling and bidding him a good night, as Frederick shook his head again. No, he shouldn't be influencing his sister towards certain kinds of thoughts, because of his own lax behavior! On the other hand, was he not himself attracted to the physical charms of his dance partners? He rose, smiling, as he buttoned his shirt, enough to cover himself in case he happened to encounter a servant or parent, though he couldn't imagine who would still be up at such a late hour.

He loped off to go to bed, but back inside his room more

thoughts crowded their way into his consciousness so that he could not sleep. He sat down on the edge of the comforter and pulled his shirt back open.

He had to admit that he hadn't thought a great deal about what this season would mean for Julia when she started receiving marriage proposals. He expected that she would, and that she would eventually accept some young gentleman's proposal. There would be an engagement which would last a certain amount of time, during which she would divide her time between her fiancé's family and her own, but it ultimately meant that she would no longer be living with them at Pemberley.

Now he realized he had given almost no thought at all to Jane Elizabeth's future, for she was facing the same considerations as Julia. Frederick exhaled. He couldn't imagine losing two of his sisters in a short time. Pemberley would be a lot quieter, even with little Henry David to raise, and Frederick would miss them in a way different from him being away at university; it was always understood he would return to Pemberley, even if he wasn't the master. Perhaps he hadn't thought much about Jane Elizabeth's prospects, but it was likely she would receive at least one proposal as a result of the season. It was also likely she might not desire a match yet because she was only sixteen, or she hadn't met anyone she was likely to fall in love with, or she was still recovering from the mistreatment she'd received as a result of her behavior with Ned Crowley.

Well, hopefully she would find someone with whom she shared a mutual love and want to receive his proposal of marriage. Then another thought occurred to him: how would he use his status and power as Master of Pemberley to help her? Would he have to step into her personal relationships, and what if he didn't approve of her choice for her spouse? Would he have to use his power to dash her hopes, and suggest she wait for someone else to enter her life, someone he thought would make a better husband for her?

These thoughts gave him pause. It was fairly likely that Jane Elizabeth would resent his interference and perhaps be so infuriated she would defy him and do as she pleased. And how could he ask her to wait for someone else to come along? What if no one did? He did not think he could ever face her again if that occurred.

He didn't want to interfere in any of his siblings' lives, but he also knew their welfare, and Henry David's too, would become his responsibility once he was master. His father would have definite ideas about how long Julia's engagement should last, once she had formed one, and he would not hesitate to state his opposition to her match if he felt the young gentleman was unworthy or unsuitable in any way. With a sigh, Frederick realized he might have to do so, but tried to calm himself with the thought it was unlikely that either Julia or Jane would choose someone who wouldn't be suitable or worthy of them.

He suddenly wavered on his feet; it was time. He pulled off his boots and trousers, then struggled into his nightshirt. He stood briefly by his bed, but then collapsed into it and slept for hours.

As Emma again helped Jane Elizabeth out of her finery that late evening, Frances Winston decided to discuss a particular subject with her young charge. Mrs. Winston enjoyed Jane's chattering on about New Hampton Court, the young ladies she had met, the variety of delicious dishes, the music, and the dancing, but there was one topic she said nothing about.

Mrs. Winston resolved to ask Jane about it during their walk the next day, a longer, leisurely one to Hyde Park, which interested them both. The lady companion was relieved that this day Julia was visiting her Aunt and Uncle Gardiner in Cheapside with her mother. Mrs. Winston enjoyed the

Gardiners' society very much; she was grateful Edward's health was steadily improving, but she was also pleased that their exclusive outing would grant her free rein in directing their conversation to the desired subject.

They wandered along the gentle pathways for quite some time, admiring the stately trees, motley groups of flowers, and the park's other pleasing features from under their parasols. They finally took a respite on a carved stone bench overlooking a placid pond.

Mrs. Winston relished the breezes that caressed their faces. As they diminished, she spoke. "It seems you enjoyed the ball at New Hampton Court."

Jane stirred with a smile. "I certainly did."

"You have told me at length about it."

Jane's smile dimmed. "I did savor it! I hope I didn't go on about it too much!"

Mrs. Winston patted her hand. "Do not worry, my dear. I enjoyed hearing every detail." Jane looked relieved, and Mrs. Winston waited a moment before continuing. "Have you also enjoyed meeting so many people in such a short time?"

Jane nodded. "I have, though I cannot remember them all."

Mrs. Winston glanced at her. "Does your enjoyment include meeting some of the young gentlemen?"

Jane looked surprised. "Well, yes, I think so."

"Any gentlemen in particular?"

"Mrs. Winston!"

She took Jane's hand. "I apologize for my forward question. But surely you understand why I ask." Jane looked down. "This is your debut as much as it is Julia's. You are coming out into society; yes, that is part of it, but there is another – and that is meeting potential mates." Now Jane looked away. "If that is one's intent, or goal."

"If."

"Jane, please look at me." When she complied, Mrs. Winston

apologized again. "Correct me if I am wrong, but such reflections seem to cause you some disquiet."

Jane gave a helpless shrug. "Yes, they do, well, because of…" she quivered, "you know…"

"I do." A long pause ensued as they looked about them. "I am sorry to press you, but it is something to consider. Have you really no thoughts about any of them? Or do you rather disregard them if you do?"

Jane was about to reply when a strolling couple stopped in front of them.

"Miss Darcy, what a pleasant surprise!"

Jane rose so she could make a proper curtsey. "Sir Timothy and Miss Carlisle! This is truly a pleasure!" Rising, she indicated Frances. "Please allow me to introduce my companion and friend, Mrs. Frances Winston."

After greetings were exchanged all around, Sir Timothy smiled at them, then his dimpling sister. "Now that we are all met, shall we take a stroll through these lovely gardens?" When the others eagerly agreed, he extended his arm to Jane. "Would you do me the honor, Miss Darcy?" She gladly acquiesced, while Mrs. Winston and Catharina began an animated conversation behind them.

Neither Jane nor Mrs. Winston was certain how far or long they had ambled along, but the light on this pleasant middle of the day began to change as towering, puffy clouds assembled and spread above them. Jane sighed contentedly, having forgotten where she was.

"How beautiful," she breathed. "I feel as if I am viewing a masterpiece by Mr. Constable or Mr. Turner."

Sir Timothy had been listening intently to her words. "I find that quite perceptive and appreciative, Miss Darcy." As she pinked, he added, "I consider myself so fortunate – no, we are so fortunate, I mean, Catharina as well – to have met your sister, Miss Julia Darcy, as well as yourself!"

"Thank you, Sir Timothy!" Jane would have dithered or

worse, but she was conscious of his gentle touch on her gloved hand. Of course, he would mention Julia; hadn't he been paying her much attention? Still, her thoughts and Frances' questions weighed upon her. "We are so fortunate to have made your acquaintance and that of your lovely sister," she managed.

He preened. "I am so grateful for Catharina, and her welfare is paramount to me."

"That is most obvious, Sir Timothy, for which you are to be commended!" She blushed at her own forward remarks, but he only thanked her with a wide smile.

Jane regretted feeling no additional touch from his hand. "We – that is, my family and I – look forward to socializing more with you and Miss Carlisle." She kept her gaze on the wide path in front of her.

"As do we, Miss Darcy."

Smiling, she clasped his friendly arm. They continued their stroll until Sir Timothy recalled they would be visiting and sharing tea with other friends. She and Mrs. Winston took a gentle leave of them, and the two pairs moved in opposite directions.

Mrs. Winston reflected that she and Jane would arrive home at Cavendish Square in time for their own tea as they set off in that direction. She relished the faint blush in Jane's cheeks the rest of that day and well into the next.

CHAPTER 18

The next evening at Kensington Palace, some distance from Cavendish Square, Princess Victoria reclined with her mother, the Duchess of Kent, after dinner. She sat on a luxurious sofa, while her mother stretched in the most comfortable chair in their shared chambers. Victoria was grateful to be back home, as rigid and familiar as it was, away from London proper and its tumult, even though she had enjoyed attending the ball and small, private banquet at New Hampton Court.

Unfortunately, her uncle, King William the Fourth, and Queen Adelaide had decided to pay a state visit to her mother and herself. Victoria sighed and rolled her eyes at this unwelcome situation. Her mother had limited contact with her uncle, and neither King nor royal niece shared close familial relations. Still, he and all his retinue were here at Kensington for at least two weeks, so Victoria would have to bear the summons and appearances demanded of her as the Heir Presumptive, not something she wished to do. After several moments, she smiled and thought about something she wished to ask the King. She wasn't always at ease in his presence but was determined to visit his chambers and make her request.

Victoria waited until her mother was well settled in her chair, then stood up and announced she needed to speak to her uncle, the King, on a matter of national importance; but no, she did not require her mother to accompany her. Leaving the Duchess nonplussed yet curious, Victoria made her way, attended, to the King's suite.

His Majesty looked up from his papers when she walked in and curtsied. "Good evening, Uncle, Your Majesty." She approached his desk. "There is an important matter I wish to discuss with you, for I would like to ask you for something."

The King's eyebrows lifted slightly. "It must be important,

since the Duchess, your mother, does not accompany you." He smiled, but she did not react. "Very well, my dear, what do you wish to discuss with me, and what are you requesting?" He indicated that she sit, and she complied.

Victoria told him. The King regarded her, his eyes piercing from beneath his thick brows, but not unkind or severe. "That is quite an extraordinary request! Are you certain of what you desire, and that this young man is worth it? I have heard of this young fellow's family, so I know he comes from a fine one and, as you say, he did manage to save you from injury at the hands of that other young brute." King William wiped his brow. "Yes, it could have been a national calamity if he had knocked you down."

"Yes, Uncle. Then that is reason all the more to honor young Mr. Darcy. He saved me, the future sovereign, from injury."

The King cleared his throat. "My dear niece, I know this young man has done you a great service – which he should, may I remind you – and he sounds like a gentleman, but to award him..." he trailed off. "Would not some other type of award be appropriate, like pinning a medal to his manly chest? Or giving him a letter I have signed thanking him for his service? Or even –"

"You mean some kind of monetary gift."

The King almost rolled his eyes. "Well, the idea had crossed my mind."

"No, Uncle," Victoria said carefully, "a monetary award will not do. His father, Fitzwilliam Darcy, the Master of Pemberley estate in Derbyshire, has more than ten thousand pounds a year, so their family is not lacking in prestige or financial standing. Since the Darcys do not lack for money, what I am most humbly asking of you is more appropriate, I think."

"Is it now?" King William kept his expression firm. "Is this not the same Darcy family that suffered a recent scandal? Did not one of Fitzwilliam Darcy's sons father a child out of wed-lock, unbeknownst to anyone, and then manage to go off and get himself killed?" Victoria looked down. "Much as I do not wish to condemn the entire family because of this kind of trag-edy, I fail to see the justification for elevating such a young man, no matter how fine he seems, and making it hereditary."

Victoria counted to ten. "Your Majesty – Dear Uncle – it is true that Mr. Frederick Darcy's older brother did all that you mentioned. However, the Darcys demonstrate fine principles of integrity, service, loyalty, and bravery! For they have for-mally adopted this love child as their own. Young Mr. Darcy not only prevented me from harm, but he also helped save three small children from a deadly fire over this past year, and was injured in the process! He is not only a gentleman, but also a hero."

King William harrumphed. "So the young fellow who saved you is a younger brother of the one who died?"

"Yes, Uncle."

"He has not gotten himself into any trouble, has he?"

"Well," Princess Victoria said slowly, "no, not really, though I have been informed he and that uncouth young Grantley heartily dislike each other, and that they came to blows at Lord and Lady Ventnor's ball last week." She thought it better not to mention that Frederick had been sent down from Cambridge.

"Did they now?" The King sat up.

"Yes, Uncle. Apparently, according to witnesses, this Grantley did nothing but insult his sister, then his family, and," she could not help blushing, "his worth as a man."

"What an arrogant cad this Grantley sounds like! And they fought in public?"

"They did. By all accounts, young Mr. Darcy knocked him down so hard that Grantley, who had provoked the fight, was almost senseless and lost two teeth." She grimaced.

"How vulgar!" The King clapped his hands together. "I regret that I missed such a spectacle." He paused when he saw her expression. "It has been a long time since the navy, my dear, and even longer since I have seen a good bout between two hotheaded men." He cleared his throat. "So, what became of the loser?"

"He is to be sent to Jamaica by the end of the month for an extended stay."

"Ah, exiled by his own family, I presume." The King regarded her with an even stare. "So, my dear niece, what were you saying about the Darcy family? Since the young man became involved in a fight at a debutante ball, does this not make him as rough and ill-mannered as the one who provoked him?"

Victoria had expected this reaction. "I mentioned that the Darcys are a long-established family with a fine lineage, and have been well regarded by all, except for the recent scandal. Regarding the illegitimate child, I repeat that they have acknowledged him and are doing all they should to raise him as their own." She paused, then carefully added, "Please also remember, Uncle, that three years ago, Mr. Fitzwilliam Darcy went on record to support your Reform Bill." The King's eyebrows formed a line, and she paused again. "Therefore, I cannot think of better reasons to honor the son of such a fine family and help restore their prestige at the same time."

"I see." It was the King's turn to pause. "But because of the scandal, not the fight – I am afraid that I do not –"

"Your Majesty." Victoria's voice had become firm. "I am asking you most earnestly for this as a personal favor to me. Yes, there has been a scandal, but do we not have similar incidents within our own illustrious family, and are we not the House of Darcy, but the House of Hanover? I refer to our aunt, the late Queen Caroline, and the behavior of some of my uncles..." She deliberately trailed off.

"Victoria! My dear royal niece, you go too far!"

"I am most sorry, Uncle." Her tone implied anything but. "Please forgive me for speaking of such indelicate subjects, but my point remains that our family has not been entirely free of scandal, although we are the ruling House in England, so how can we condemn the Darcys for theirs?"

King William grunted. "Point taken, my dear." He sighed and shifted in his chair. "What is this young man's sister like, that is, the one making her debut, whom Grantley insulted?"

Her tone lightened. "I have met Miss Julia Darcy this past week at New Hampton Court, and I would say all positive accounts of her are confirmed. She is a delightful creature, vivacious, pleasing, unspoiled, and quite stunning – one of the standouts this season. It is widely expressed that potential beaux, some very highborn, will be lining up for her hand."

The King considered that. "This is truly your desire?"

Victoria set her gaze and Hanoverian chin. "Yes, Uncle."

He gave her another look. "You are certain that this young Mr. Darcy is no wastrel, libertine, or scoundrel? I do not wish to elevate him, only to find out that he is a Don Juan, a profiteer, a brute, or a traitor, and no better than the one he fought."

"I am certain, Your Majesty! He is not now, nor will he become any of those kinds of undesirable people!" She took a moment to calm herself.

He watched her. "You would like it to be a hereditary title?"

"Yes, Uncle."

He thought for another moment. "Well, my dear Victoria, young Frederick Darcy has done you – and all of us – a great service and seems to have behaved himself much better than his adversary." He sighed. "Very well, then, I shall reward this young man quite handsomely – since you seem to think so highly of him! Mind you, my dear royal niece, I will impress upon him the responsibility that comes with his reward and elevation – and that you may call upon him personally to serve you in any capacity, at any time, during your reign as Queen." He gave her another look and she bowed her head.

"As you say, Uncle," she said, "we may have need of stalwart subjects like the Darcys in the days ahead, for one never knows. I believe we can count on their aid and service to the

Crown if we ever need it, such as they, father and son, have demonstrated to us so far."

King William gave a hearty laugh. "Well said, my dear! You have been thinking like the Queen you shall be! You have considered well in thinking about the future." Still smiling, he slapped the arms of his chair. "I suppose I can refuse you nothing, Victoria, or so it seems."

She gave a small laugh. "Of course you can refuse me, Uncle, my Sovereign, but please do not!"

"I shall not refuse you, nor reverse my decision," he replied graciously. "You shall have your young Mr. Darcy elevated."

She smiled. "I am certain he will be quite humbled by this honor, and that he will be loyal and dependable if I ever have need of his assistance." She knelt, took her uncle's hand, and kissed it.

"There, there, that's a good child," the King said, smiling and patting her arm.

Victoria rose and gave him her deepest curtsey. "Thank you, Your Majesty."

"You are welcome, my dear." He rose from his chair and kissed her on the forehead. "I will see to it immediately tomorrow morning. Now be a good young lady – and Princess – and let this old man – and King – get some decent rest. Good night, Victoria."

"Good night, Uncle, to you and Her Majesty, Queen Adelaide." She took her leave and returned, accompanied as usual by a trusted servant, to her own quarters. Her mother stepped out to greet her.

"You have been in discussion with His Majesty all this time?" Only the Duchess' eyes betrayed her curiosity.

"Yes, Mama, but I am much too fatigued to talk about it now. Please forgive me, but I would like to get some rest."

If her mother was disappointed or upset, she did not show it. "Of course, my dear," the Duchess said. "Let us go in, and I hope you sleep well."

Victoria wished her mother the same, then went inside

their shared chambers. She was too old and too royal to skip, but she felt like doing so. She could not laugh with delight, for news of that would be all over Kensington tomorrow; maybe she could while she played with her beloved spaniel, Dash. Instead, now she only smiled, and let feelings of satisfaction surge through her.

CHAPTER 19

A few days after the Earl of Sheffield's ball, it was time for yet another. This evening's event was being hosted by Sir Ambrose Roylston, his wife Lady Judith, and his sister Lady Maura, at their rambling manor house called Bethulia on the south side of London. Still to come were the formal presentations at Court, as well as a grand picnic outing at Sausville Gardens along the Thames and other events, but the Roylston ball was the last of the initial heights of the season.

Julia felt buoyed by their success at the Earl's ball despite the tumult Richard Grantley had caused, so she had positive expectations for this evening. Frederick's feelings were more tempered; he remembered how much he had enjoyed most of the ball and did not see any reason why he should not enjoy this one. Still, he was hoping for a pleasurable but very uneventful evening, one that would not result in damage to his finery or give him a reputation.

They found they retained their popularity from the previous ball, and there was barely time to meet and chat with everyone they wished to, but Julia found all the guests most congenial. To the Darcy siblings' great relief, none of the Grantleys were present at Bethulia, and Rachel Urquhart was escorted by her father instead of her brother; Julia thought she looked pensive, but happier. Julia also saw Julian Tunney and Mary Duncan, and Frederick spotted the three predatory young ladies, but even they did not present any problems. Julia gave Mr. Tunney and his sister a proper but short greeting, only for propriety's sake, and moved over to the Stoddards and the Eastons, while Frederick greeted the three laughing young ladies and promptly started telling them about how fascinating it was to read Gibbon and Adam Smith. As expected, their eyes glazed over, and they abandoned him *en masse* when a group of laughing, energetic young men strolled by. Frederick gave a silent sigh of satisfaction and went over to sit with Jane Elizabeth; he would later send both his sisters into gales of laughter when he told them how he had bored this trio of young ladies on purpose.

Julia was gratified the most by the regard they were being shown. None of them experienced any snubs, and when she made eye contact with people from a distance they would acknowledge her, usually with a smile and none of the hostile glances they had received many times before. Even Mrs. Porter-Douglas and Mrs. Ruth-Davis made it a point to come over with their children and speak with Julia and Frederick. Mrs. Ruth-Davis even went so far as to compliment Julia on her gown. Julia was quite pleased, satisfied, and relieved all the same.

Now she was facing a group of determined but very pleasant young gentlemen – for Lord Ravenswood, Sir Timothy Carlisle, and Gregory Lawson had converged upon her within seconds of each other. Luckily her dance card could accommodate all three of them, as popular as she was again. She realized she was also silently being granted the power to choose her partners, as opposed to her potential partners choosing her.

"Miss Darcy." Gregory Lawson bowed low. "It is my great pleasure to see you again. May I prevail upon you for two dances this evening?"

She sank to the floor, curtseying to all three of them. "Of course, Mr. Lawson," she smiled, rising to her feet. She turned to the other two gentlemen, giving them her most dazzling smile. "Good evening, Lord Ravenswood and Sir Timothy! How wonderful it is to see you both again." The gentlemen bowed deeply, and had barely given their greetings when Gregory Lawson spoke again.

"I thank you, Miss Darcy, for allowing me to dance with

you, after the first dance when your brother leads you to the ballroom floor."

Julia remained pleasant and polite in her replies but noticed a drooping of Lord Ravenswood's expression. That gentleman looked rather unhappy, then she noticed Sir Timothy's good-natured, casual enjoyment of the situation. Oh dear, she thought, please don't let any of the young men come to blows or even verbal jousts! After all they had experienced, she just wanted to enjoy the ball.

"Then I must ask for two dances as well, begging Mr. Lawson's pardon." Sir Timothy smiled, and the two young men inclined their heads to each other.

"Of course, Sir Timothy," she said rather quickly, "I look forward to dancing with you as well, after Mr. Lawson." Lord Ravenswood's handsome face darkened, but he kept his voice pleasant, charming, and polite.

"Then may I request to dance with you after Sir Timothy, or when you have an opening?" he asked with a strange smile. "And, surely, if you can grant Mr. Lawson and Sir Timothy two dances apiece, there is room on your dance card for one, or maybe two dances with me as well?" One corner of his mouth had drooped, and Julia saw a pleading flash in his eyes, which gave her heart a pang.

She felt herself starting to blush. "Of course I can, Lord Ravenswood, and I do." He returned her smile, but gave rather cold glances to the other young men, who just smiled back at him in a knowing way.

"Thank you, Miss Darcy."

"You are most welcome, my lord." The other young men thanked her as well, and all three took a respectful step backward when Frederick arrived to claim her hand for the first dance. He exchanged polite greetings with all of them, and then it was time for everyone to make their way to the dance floor. Gregory Lawson went off to dance with Rachel Urquhart, and Sir Timothy with Mary Duncan, while Lord Ravenswood first danced with his sister Cecilia, then with Sir Timothy's sister Catharina, and finally sat out the next few dances until he could dance with Julia for the first time.

Smiling, Julia was ready when Gregory Lawson claimed her from Frederick. She had just noticed Sir Timothy approaching Jane and their mother and engaging them – her? – in animated conversation.

Intrigued, Julia returned her gaze to Mr. Lawson, who took her left hand and kept slightly behind her as they made their way to another part of the ballroom floor. She appreciated his pains not to crush her full skirts, but she suddenly became aware of something brushing her dress just below her right hip. Surely, he had not tried to touch her like that, and in public! But she could not imagine what else it might have been and dared not acknowledge or call attention to it; instead, she hurried forward to make him catch up with her. He held her perfectly and they began to dance; with both his hands engaged, Julia did not experience any further, odd sensations of being touched, so she began to doubt herself. Maybe she had imagined the whole thing, after all; or it might have been a chance contact with another person who was too embarrassed to apologize. However, she promised herself, if something like it happened again, she would nip it in the bud, even if she had to reprimand him for it.

"How beautiful you look this evening," he was complimenting her. "Each time I see you, Miss Darcy, I think you are more beautiful than the time before."

She blushed deeply. "Why, thank you, Mr. Lawson, for your extraordinary compliments! I am afraid that I do not deserve them, for there are many beautiful young ladies present this evening, all very stylish, elegant, and at ease in the whirl of London society, whereas I am the daughter of a county squire, a simple girl from the country."

"Nonsense, Miss Darcy," he laughed. "You may come from the countryside, one as beautiful as Derbyshire, but you are much too accomplished to be merely 'simple.'"

"Thank you again, Mr. Lawson, but –"

He laughed again, and she subsided. "Your accomplishments outshine those of so many other young ladies present tonight," he said. "On that point I shall not waiver! However, I can describe you, if you allow me, as an extraordinary rose from the English countryside."

"Oh, Mr. Lawson, please no more!" She really could not keep accepting such effusive compliments. She remembered he had behaved this way before.

"There is no need to thank me," he said gallantly, "for I believe what I said, and I like to bestow compliments, especially when they are so well deserved."

She could only give nervous smiles, so he took pity on her and changed the subject. He still held her perfectly, but she felt him holding her a little closer. As he was taller, she found herself looking up into his eyes and seeing every feature of his face. She saw him smiling down at her and inclining his head ever so slightly.

Their waltz went on for several minutes, and he talked about the upcoming seasonal weather and how it affected his family's rice and sugar cane crops, as well as the dangers of crossing the Atlantic Ocean to the Caribbean during the summer storm season. He would continue these subjects during their second dance, as well as holding her just a little closer than propriety dictated. His gloved hold on her own covered hands was always light, but constant.

Julia tried to steer the conversation toward traveling to and living in the Caribbean islands, but he always seemed to revert to discussing more mundane business matters, which she did not find very interesting. She sighed inwardly and tried to look attentive and appreciative to what he was saying.

Luckily her dance card was nearly full, so she would only have the two dances with him. She looked forward to her dances with Sir Timothy and Lord Ravenswood much more; she did not look forward to Mr. Lawson holding, flattering, and boring her. Julia was not vain, so constant, exaggerated compliments made her uncomfortable; yes, less was definitely more when it came to that. She also did not allow young men to take liberties with any part of her person – her mother had seen to that. As to his discussing business matters and agriculture with her, she gave herself a rueful smile. She remembered that she wished a desirable man to be intelligent about something, but in Mr. Lawson's case she really didn't find it all that interesting.

Julia was scolding herself for being shallow and inconsistent, when Sir Timothy came to claim her for the next dance. She immediately brightened and enjoyed their dancing together. She was enjoying their light conversation, free of any dull, pedantic subjects or outrageous compliments, when he surprised her with a strange remark.

"I could not help noticing," he said with a smile, "that Lord Ravenswood seemed quite displeased not to have been the first man to ask for dances with you this evening."

"Oh, Sir Timothy, you cannot mean that!" She could not help smiling, though, despite his rather impertinent remark.

"But I do, Miss Darcy," he replied laughing. "Now I must beg your forgiveness for my impertinence! I could not help enjoying myself just now, but I do think Mr. Lawson was also enjoying Lord Ravenswood's discomfiture over the fact that we both anticipated his request."

"Lord Ravenswood should not have felt so," she answered with her own smile, "for this is a ball, and usually there is ample time in which to secure a young lady's hand for a dance or two, is there not?"

"How true that is," he agreed, "but I am also certain there was more to Lord Ravenswood's disappointment than not being the first one to ask you to dance tonight."

"What do you mean?" She thought she knew, but asked anyway.

"Forgive me, Miss Darcy, but I assure you I know how poorly Lord Ravenswood regards me and my interests!" He laughed. "How shocking and inappropriate it is for me to associate with talented artists and actors, though I think they are the cream of our society!" He shook his head, still smiling. "It was very gallant of him to dance with Catharina tonight. Honestly, though, I do not care how he and his family regard me; it does not bother me at all. I am a gentleman, a free man, and I shall do as I see fit, within reason, of course."

"Of course." What else could she say? But since he had introduced the subject, she spoke up. "Forgive me for asking, Sir Timothy, but when others disregard you so poorly and dismissively, does this lack of regard truly not bother you?"

He sobered. "No, Miss Darcy, I speak the truth about my own sentiments. Lord Ravenswood is free to dislike and disapprove of me if he wishes to, and I have enough pride that I will not try to change his opinion of me." If they weren't dancing, he would have shrugged. "I am not completely immune from being affected by such opinions, for I do not believe anyone really can be. However, I would only care if my actions – or the so-called reputation that has been inflicted upon me – affect poor Catharina and her chances for a fine match, and happiness in her own married life."

"I see." She thanked him for his candor.

"Thank you for being patient and excusing my impertinence."

"Not at all." She paused, then smiled. "If I may be so bold as to say so, I do not think you should worry about Miss Carlisle's chances. Everyone comments on how lovely she is, what fine manners and a pleasing personality she has, and how considerate and caring you are towards her in everything. I, of course, share these opinions of your sister, and even Lord Ravenswood expressed similar sentiments, without any prompting."

Sir Timothy looked surprised. "I am rather speechless," he managed. "I am sorry, for I did not expect a member of the Earl of Ravenswood's family to give my sister and me much credit, if any. Thank you very much for telling me so."

"You are most welcome." After a moment of silence, she gave him a small smile and kept her eyes downcast. "Perhaps you would be willing to concede then that Lord Ravenswood does not look upon you so unfavorably and that, in all fairness, he finds much to admire in you?" It was daring and impertinent on her part, but she wanted to try.

Now he looked pensive and less amiable. "Perhaps, since I am certain you are correct, but I will have to consider this before I can accept such a conclusion. For I know I do not inspire positive comments from the Ravenswoods." He looked away. "Catharina's future is another matter, much more important than my personal feelings. If I were callous and uncaring of her happiness, I might be tempted to encourage a match between her and one of the Calverts, for example, if Lord Ravenswood had a young brother close to her in age. But I could not treat my lovely, only sister in such a cavalier fashion, as if she were a commodity, without regard to her own wishes. And I would not recommend such a match to her."

Oh, dear, that was quite censorious of him. "Of course, Sir Timothy."

He looked down at her, let his expression become amiable again, and apologized. "Now let us talk of happier subjects," he said, as they kept dancing. Julia was very relieved as he discussed the prospects for the current theater season, and neither one mentioned Lord Ravenswood nor his family during their second dance.

Lord Ravenswood was much more gallant and pleasant, even giving Sir Timothy a gracious greeting when he stepped up to claim her hand for their dance. Julia had enjoyed dancing with Sir Timothy, despite their serious discussion, but realized she was just as happy to dance with Louis Calvert, Lord Ravenswood.

They chatted as they whirled about. She was enjoying his laughter and improved spirits, and could not take her eyes off him. Lord Ravenswood was always immaculately dressed, but she never noticed his finery as she did Sir Timothy's; no, she liked gazing upon Louis Calvert's face, especially when he gave her such warm glances. However, he finally gave a rueful smile, and brought up a subject she hoped she had heard the last of for the evening.

"Miss Darcy," he said earnestly, "I must apologize for my sullen, boorish behavior earlier this evening. I am a young man, not a mere boy, but I know how I should behave, and I was not behaving like a proper gentleman. To be honest, I was annoyed that two other gentlemen had asked you to dance with them before I did, and I did not like it. I was quite envious." He shook his head. "So the great lord is easily miffed by such things, it is true! It is a flaw in my character, and I ask you for your forgiveness! I also intend to be as polite and sociable to both gentlemen – as well as to any of your other dance partners tonight, for the rest of the evening!" He gave her a beseeching look. "Again, I am sorry for my ignoble behavior."

Julia blinked at such a remarkable speech, but quickly smiled. "You must not keep asking me for forgiveness, for you have done me no wrong, or shown me indifference, or a lack of respect." His regretful eyes still pleaded, and her heart melted. "All right, then, my lord, I cannot refuse you that – or anything, I think – when you look at me so." She gave him a wider smile. "I do forgive you then, Lord Ravenswood. Ah, that is what I wish to see! Your eyes and expression are light, and filled with happiness!" She laughed.

"Thank you, Miss Darcy," he managed.

"You are most welcome."

They kept on dancing in contented silence, through a second dance. They realized this waltz was nearing its end, so with his face and voice still bright, he spoke.

"Miss Darcy, have you any openings left on your dance card this evening?"

She gave him a coy glance. "In fact, my lord, I do. It is the second to last dance."

"Then may I request your hand as my partner for that dance?"

"It would be my pleasure." Her heart stirred. "The dance is yours."

He thanked her again. "I am looking most forward to the pleasure of your companionship."

"Thank you, Lord Ravenswood." He gave her a deep bow and a warm smile, then departed. She heard him give the Stoddards a hearty greeting.

Blushing with pleasure, she made her way to the side of the room during the brief break in the dancing. She had no sooner rejoined her mother, sitting and sipping lemonade, yet looking rather tired – when Jane Elizabeth hurried over, regardless of propriety.

"Jane!" Julia said, before their mother could. "Do not hurry so!" Then she smiled. "What is exciting you?"

Jane Elizabeth did not mind her sister's comment, and her expression and color were high. "Oh, Julia, Mother! You will never guess!" Rarely did she get so excited.

"What is it, Dear?" Tired though she was, Elizabeth seemed interested.

"Yes," Julia said, "please do not keep us in suspense any longer."

"All right, for I do not think you would have guessed correctly." She put her hands together. "Sir Timothy Carlisle has asked me to dance with him once again this evening!"

Julia's eyes widened. "Did he now?" How interesting, she thought. She was not jealous, so it did not cause her any disquiet because he had been paying attention to her. She was glad that a young man of his caliber was paying Jane Elizabeth some attention, which Julia thought would build up her confidence and help her in the future. It was Jane Elizabeth's debut as well as hers, and even as the eldest, Julia felt she should not receive all the attention between the two of them. "How wonderful for you, because Sir Timothy is a fine dancer! How you will enjoy yourself!" Elizabeth gave her daughters a wan smile.

"I thought he was only being kind at the Earl's ball, so this is quite wonderful of him." Jane Elizabeth giggled. "I may let him ask for a second one! I do hope he will."

"I'm sure he will assent, though you could ask discreetly if *he* has any openings on his card later on," Julia offered, while their mother smothered a chuckle.

"Do you really think so, Julia?"

"I do, Jane." She patted her sister's arm. "Do attempt it, and above all enjoy yourself! I think Sir Timothy is approaching to claim your hand."

Jane Elizabeth thanked her. "I know I shall! I will tell you how it turns out." She was still very excited but brought her expression and demeanor under some control by the time Sir Timothy greeted them, his eyes as bright as his finery. Jane Elizabeth took his offered arm, while Julia brought her mother another glass of lemonade and waited for her next partner, Justin Longford.

Meanwhile, Frederick felt quite happy when he secured not one, but two dances with Rosamund Woodleigh. After his first dance with Julia, then Pamela Easton, Sophia Stoddard, and Cecilia Calvert, he was glad to sit one out and chat over drinks with Lord Ravenswood, with whom he felt he was fast becoming friends. He appreciated the young nobleman's regard for Julia, as well as his attempts to help him curb some of his own behavior. They discussed experiences at their respective universities, and Frederick found himself grateful for Lord Ravenswood's advice. Still, he felt himself growing more anxious as the time approached when he would dance with Miss Woodleigh.

He sought her out to claim her for the dance and found her sitting with her mother, guarded by two young men. Frederick held his breath. Miss Woodleigh was stunning, like Julia. Her dark hair was curled into soft, elegant ringlets, and she wore a gown of pastel pink satin with tasteful long, white gloves, emerald earrings, and luminescent pearls to match. Her green eyes were lively and pleased when he bowed low to her.

"Miss Woodleigh, it is an honor and a pleasure!"

"Thank you, Mr. Darcy." She gave a low curtsey. "How wonderful it is to see you again. May I present my mother, Mrs. Woodleigh, and my older brothers Peter and Howard?"

Frederick made equally polite greetings to all of them, silently marveling at how attractive the entire family was. Mrs. Woodleigh was quite beautiful herself, matron though she was, and her daughter obviously took after her in many respects. She assured Frederick he would soon meet her husband, an importer of fine china and linens from the continent. Rosamund appeared to be his own age, and her brothers close to Lord Ravenswood in theirs. Both Peter and Howard Woodleigh were dark-haired, muscular, and handsome, Howard clean-shaven and Peter sporting a fine mustache; their simple finery emphasized their strong, athletic bodies. Her brothers had attended King's College in Cambridge, and Frederick looked forward to comparing notes over their experiences; he was also happy to learn that a younger brother, John, currently attended there.

Peter Woodleigh grinned at him. "So, you are the 'fighting' Mr. Darcy, the one who put young Richard Grantley in his place! Pray tell us, what does this evening hold?" His mother and sister scolded him, while Howard laughed without malice.

"Well, Mr. Woodleigh," Frederick answered, giving a chagrined laugh himself, "I must say that there is to be absolutely no ill behavior on anyone's part, especially my own! For my father, Fitzwilliam Darcy of Pemberley, has sworn that if I do, I shall be sent back home in chains, not to be seen by anyone for an unspecified amount of time, while I chop wood and do other types of hard labor around the estate."

Peter Woodleigh grasped his arm, though he was still smiling. "Please forgive me for my levity, for I meant no offense." When Frederick nodded, he sobered. "Thank you, Mr. Darcy! We are aware of what caused the fight with Lord Hartford's son." His family members exchanged glances and nods. "We find your defense of your family to be most admirable."

"Thank you, Mr. Woodleigh, and thank you all! However, I must behave properly myself, which I have promised to do." Smiling, Frederick looked at Miss Woodleigh. "I would not wish Miss Woodleigh or any of you to think ill of me. I must not give you any reason for lowering your regard for me and my family." The young lady smiled and inclined her head.

"I am certain we would not find any reason to do so," Mrs. Woodleigh answered with some warmth. "Now come and meet my excellent Mr. Woodleigh, the father of all these you see before you, for he will be quite pleased to make your acquaintance."

"Thank you, Mrs. Woodleigh." Frederick turned to find his hand shaken by a stocky, pleasant, avuncular-looking man with a firm, hairy grip, and large side-whiskers. After the introductions and resulting chatter, it was time for the next dance. Frederick tried not to look overeager as he turned to Miss Woodleigh, but the others could not help noticing his interest and pleasure at the prospect of dancing with her.

"Enjoy the waltz." Mrs. Woodleigh nodded to them, as Frederick took Rosamund's gloved hand in his own to lead her toward the dancers. They took their positions on the dance floor and began to waltz when the music started up.

"How well you dance, Mr. Darcy!" Miss Woodleigh was smiling. "Has anyone ever told you so?"

He gave a sheepish smile. "No, Miss Woodleigh, I must admit, for I am truly just a competent dancer, and nothing more. I have given my poor sister Julia many moments to regret my lack of dancing skills." Then his face and voice brightened. "But I do like to waltz. Do you not as well?"

"Absolutely, I do!" she answered, laughing. "And I am most grateful that you love the waltz, too."

He gave her a big smile. "Then I would venture to say that we are well matched this evening!" She laughed again in agreement.

As they whirled away, she asked him, "Now, Mr. Darcy, if you would oblige me, please tell me how you came to rescue Princess Victoria's fan. We are all dying to know the story first-hand!" Frederick's laughter could be heard over the music.

Later that evening, the second to the last dance before the banquet, Julia danced with Lord Ravenswood for the third time; a definite risk, but she felt no concern. She felt very comfortable as he held her perfectly, and wished they did not have to relinquish each other when the dance was over. She sighed with contentment and, though he smiled in return, he seemed rather distracted.

"The ball will soon be over, and it will be time for our late dinner," she finally remarked.

"Yes, Miss Darcy, it will." He collected his thoughts and gave her a wider smile. "Much as I must admit to being famished, I do wish we could go on dancing longer."

"As do I, my lord."

He was silent for several moments but kept smiling at her whenever she looked at him, which was often. What could be bothering the man? "Is not Bethulia a beautiful setting for a ball like this?" she asked.

"It is, absolutely!" But Lord Ravenswood lapsed into smiling, pleasant silence once again.

Julia felt like sagging, but she was a Darcy. Keeping her posture perfect, she enjoyed their waltz, even if Lord Ravenswood's thoughts seemed elsewhere. Finally, she heard him sigh.

"Miss Darcy."

"Yes, Lord Ravenswood?"

"I know that tonight is the last official ball of the season, though there are several other events to come within the next month." He paused. "Come tomorrow or the next day, I would like to call upon your father and mother in Cavendish Square – and ask their permission to let me call upon you." He gave her a serious look but began to smile immediately. "And more than once at that. Would that be acceptable to you, Miss Darcy? Would you welcome my calling upon you?"

She could not answer right away; she needed to get her soaring heart under control and maintain her poise. When she finally did answer, she felt confident. "Yes, that would be most acceptable, Lord Ravenswood. I would welcome your calls." She smiled widely. "I am most grateful, for your attentions to me are quite an honor, as well as a definite pleasure." She had not thought once of Sir Timothy or Gregory Lawson.

"Thank you very much, Miss Darcy!" He was smiling broadly now.

As they kept dancing, she suddenly had an idea. "Pardon me, my lord, but I do not think that this dance needs to be our last this evening, regardless of where we end up seated at the banquet."

"No?" He seemed surprised. "But the ball is nearly over, and there is only one dance left. Surely you cannot have an opening remaining. And a *fourth* dance with the same partner." He shook his head. "How could such a thing be managed, and would I not be subjecting you to needless idle gossip and speculation if we did?"

Julia laughed. "Perhaps that is what would occur, Lord Ravenswood, but I would not mind it." She gave him a warm smile. "I am sure my brother would relinquish the final dance together we have scheduled. That way we could dance together one more time tonight and, if anyone wishes to comment upon it, they must do so during the banquet, for the ball will be over. I am sure Frederick will be agreeable to this, for I know he likes and esteems you very much."

"I am honored," he said humbly. The feelings were mutual.

"So, Lord Ravenswood, I feel certain we shall have the next dance together, regardless of what anyone might say. I will speak to Frederick immediately about our *unprecedented* fourth dance tonight."

Even as they were dancing, he turned his handsome head to brush his lips against her gloved hand. "Thank you, Miss Darcy," he exclaimed. As the waltz music went into its final bars and their dancing slowed, he breathed, "Please call me Louis from now on, when we are together like this – please, no more 'Lord Ravenswood' or 'my lord,' I beg of you!" He was thinking Cecilia would be as delighted as he.

She gave him her widest smile yet. "How daring that is! I should not...but I would like to." She lowered her eyelashes. "I promise you I shall – right after you speak to Father and Mother about calling upon me, my lord!" Now, Lord Ravenswood's laughter could be heard far throughout the vast room.

Jane Elizabeth's spirits remained high as she danced not once, but twice with Sir Timothy. Like many other young ladies, she could not help appreciating the richness of his finery, or his handsome, pleasant face, so she kept her glances downward. The memory of their chance meeting at Hyde Park after the Earl's ball kept giving her warm pleasure. She found herself liking him very much; everything he said seemed interesting to her, and she was pleased to find he enjoyed reading poetry as much as she did. They even admired some of the same poets, like Wordsworth and Shelley. Now they were discussing the theater season. She hoped to discuss more painters with him as well.

"I have been living here in London these past few months," Jane Elizabeth told him, "and been fortunate to attend two plays at the Drury Lane and an opera at Covent Garden, thanks to my relatives, the Gardiners and the Staleys."

"Only two plays and an opera since you have been here in London?" Sir Timothy asked in mock surprise. "Surely that is not enough, for London has so much to offer!"

She smiled, liking the sound of his voice. "Thank you for your concern for my cultural welfare, Sir Timothy, but I cannot always be attending performances, as fine and enthralling as I have found them. I must attend my daily lessons! Still, I also enjoy visiting museums, and my brother, Frederick even escorted our youngest sister Anne and me to a lecture at the Royal Society."

That impressed him. "If I may ask, what was the subject of the lecture you attended, and what were your thoughts about the experience?"

"The lecture was given by a gentleman whose name I cannot remember, but a wealthy, successful man of business and industry, nonetheless. He was proposing that a canal be built from the Nile Delta at Cairo, in Egypt, due east to the Red Sea, so that shipping routes to and from India would be much shorter." She smiled again. "I did not understand all the technical engineering details the lecturer thought would be required, but it was amazing to hear how much would be needed to build such a canal – men, time, money, and materials. And it was also very interesting to learn about Egypt." She gave a small laugh. "Anne was quite stimulated by this lecture. She found it so interesting that she went straight to our father as soon as we returned home to Cavendish Square, and recommended that he invest in such a project, if a well-managed company were formed to undertake it."

Sir Timothy gave a great laugh. "Your sister, Miss Anne, sounds quite extraordinary, Miss Darcy. Pray tell me, how old is she?"

"She is eleven years old." He looked surprised. "Yes, our sister Anne is quite an amazing girl. She is very intelligent, the most studious of us all, and we think she should attend a college for women, even if it is abroad, for she cannot be satisfied, except with more knowledge, and the more practical it is, the better."

"How remarkable! It sounds as if she would be able to run an estate of her own someday," he marveled.

"Yes, I believe she will be capable of doing even that eventually. Mathematics, history, science, industry, languages, writing – all these interest her." She shook her head, smiling. "She is definitely *not* interested in painting, dancing, playing the piano or some other kind of instrument, and embroidering, the normal types of accomplishments acquired by genteel young ladies! However, Anne does well in her deportment, much better than I, due to her natural reserve."

"What an interesting family you have," he complimented, for which she thanked him. "Your older sister is very accomplished in all respects and has been dazzling London society these past weeks, even earning a grace from Princess Victoria herself. Your younger sister thirsts for knowledge, which is amazing itself, at her tender age. And, if I may say so, Miss Darcy," he paused, "you are very accomplished in your own right, with your extensive reading and love of the arts! I remember your appreciative and discerning comments about our talented landscape painters. I have been informed on excellent authority that you sing and play the piano extraordinarily well."

"Thank you, Sir Timothy!" She nodded to him while blushing. "Perhaps someday I will have the opportunity to do so for you and Miss Carlisle."

He gave a great smile. "That would be wonderful!" He thought for a moment. "Perhaps I – that is, we, Catharina and I – could call upon your parents in Cavendish Square."

"Oh, yes, please do! We would be most honored and gratified by your visit, and I would very much like Miss Carlisle to meet the rest of my family! We have a splendid library, though it is not as extensive as the one back home at Pemberley."

He nodded to her. "Then we shall we happy to do so. I will ask Mr. and Mrs. Darcy for permission to call on you – that is, all of you," he added quickly, "at your home."

"That would be wonderful!" she exclaimed. "How we will all look forward to that! I am sure that Miss Carlisle will enjoy the visit, for she is such a beautiful, pleasant, and accomplished young lady herself."

"Thank you for your compliments to my sister." He gave a warm smile. "Catharina is very dear to me, and I try to do the utmost to ensure her happiness, health, and comfort. It heartens me when you tell me of your wishes to have your sister Miss Anne formally educated! How wonderful that is! Women are intelligent creatures, not just attractive and accomplished, and deserve to be educated as much as we men are."

"Bravo, Sir Timothy!" Jane Elizabeth was truly excited, but kept her voice under control. "I most heartily agree! I wish for more formal education myself, as well. I am fortunate that both Father and Frederick are most supportive of this."

"How glad I am to hear that! You know, Miss Darcy," Sir Timothy lowered his voice, "Catharina also wishes to continue her education, although she is now officially out in society like you and your sister, and all the other debutantes this season. I wish to indulge her in this. I do this quietly, because I know it is not typical for young ladies of the *ton* – or young ladies in general – to attend university. There could be disapproval, but I am certain there are such institutions on the Continent that she could attend. I tell you this in confidence."

"Of course, Sir Timothy." She could not think of much else

to say at first. "Thank you for sharing such an ambitious and admirable undertaking with me. I am sure Miss Carlisle will be most grateful to you."

Smiling, he thanked her in return. "But we have left the subject of attending performances behind. Perhaps you will be attending more of them."

"I do hope to."

He cleared his throat. "Perhaps your family would be able to attend the opera with us, for we have a box at Covent Garden. I shall ask your parents about this as well."

"That would be wonderful! Oh, thank you so much for your generosity!"

His smile grew wider. "In addition, Miss Darcy, there will be other events worth attending in London in the weeks to come. I hear the Sausville Gardens are quite beautiful." He enjoyed seeing her face light up with anticipation.

"I dare not hope for so many amusements," she laughed, "but I would definitely look forward to them."

"Then let us see what your father and mother have to say on the subject."

"Absolutely, Sir Timothy!" As they kept dancing, Jane Elizabeth was thrilled at the prospect of remaining in London so she could attend more events with Mrs. Winston – and hopefully the Carlisles. What a great deal she had to tell Julia!

Long after the Roylstons' ball ended, Julia sat up sewing in the upstairs sitting room. She did not mind the lateness of the hour for, again, little was planned for the next day and she knew she could sleep and rise late. She was not ready to rest, for both Lord Ravenswood and Sir Timothy, and their behavior, had given her much to think about.

Much as she liked both young men, they were quite different in their manners, interests, and temperaments. Julia had to admit that Frederick had a point. Both gentlemen were high-born, wealthy, and well-mannered, especially around her; but how well did she know either man, outside of several dances and some short conversations? She decided she knew more about Lord Ravenswood – she would not even think of him as 'Louis' until he had spoken to her parents – because she had sat next to him at three banquets, whereas she had never sat next to Sir Timothy during dinner.

What did she know about him? She knew he doted on his sister Catharina and took good care of her. She could also appreciate his splendid appearance and the fabulous cut of his fine clothes. His conversations about the theater and the arts were most stimulating, for that was apparently how he liked to spend his time – and one of the reasons Lord Ravenswood did not like him. Sir Timothy seemed to have enlightened ideas on some subjects, like the education of young women and the value of their opinions.

Julia paused in her sewing. She really didn't have much of an idea what Sir Timothy thought about anything else, or if he even had any other interests. He never mentioned any kind of outdoor activities like so many young men did, nor discussed such serious subjects like politics. Sir Timothy would not be likely to do so with her, it was true, but she could not recall hearing him making comments to her father, Frederick, or any other gentleman about business, investments, estate matters, or sporting activities, as many did.

It was also interesting to discover something that could bother Sir Timothy and ruffle his usual pleasant demeanor. He seemed unhappy – perhaps even resentful – of the lack of regard he received from the Ravenswoods, and presumably whoever else agreed with them. She had thought Sir Timothy to be more self-confident and as assured as he appeared in his rich, eye-catching attire. However, she did not expect any kind of thawing to occur between the two suitors; that was certain.

That left Lord Ravenswood himself. At least that young

man was honest and more open about what he thought of Sir Timothy, and had the grace to know his behavior was less than sterling, even if it was because he held a low opinion of the other man. Julia liked how he and Frederick seemed to be becoming friends, and how much he had helped them both during their awful experiences at the balls given by the Ventnors and the Earl of Sheffield.

What intrigued Julia the most about the handsome young lord was how unhappy he became when other young men captured her attentions and her hand for dances. Dancing with many partners was expected as part of the London season, but he could barely conceal his jealousy and irritation when Gregory Lawson and his nemesis, Sir Timothy, made their requests before he could. She thought he must like her very much to account for that...and this thought made her feel warm and happy inside. He wanted to call upon her at Cavendish Square; how she looked forward to that! They had enjoyed their unprecedented fourth dance at Bethulia, which did provoke glances, but as it occurred at the end of the ball and just before dinner, Julia was not aware of any gossip circulating about them – not that she cared or tried to eavesdrop on those around her. This also warmed her. Giving her a warm gaze, Frederick had been happy to step aside so she could dance with Lord Ravenswood. And that noble young gentleman had kept his promise to behave friendly and gentlemanly with every one of her partners, and any other young man with whom she shared a conversation tonight.

Now her thoughts turned to Gregory Lawson. Her mouth tightened as she sewed. No, she did not care much for him after all, and was glad the last of the debutante balls was over. She would not have to worry about being asked to dance with him or Julian Tunney ever again. Julia thought young Mr. Tunney finally understood that his attentions to her were now unwelcome, but she did not relish the idea of meeting Mr. Lawson again either. She let her hands rest. Oh, he wasn't so very bad, not really, but she did not find him interesting, and there was that subtle business about the way he had held her, and perhaps touched her inappropriately, during the ball. What if he decided to call on them? She sighed. She hoped he would not, but she was not going to worry about it, for that was not in her nature.

She was starting to feel a little sleepy; good, she would be able to rest soon. But, as tired as she was, she realized that Jane Elizabeth had given her something to think about.

Her sister could barely contain her excitement from the moment they left Bethulia for Cavendish Square. Jane Elizabeth had plenty of time to talk about how she enjoyed the ball, for the ride home was a long one, considering Bethulia was situated on the southern side of the city; Julia and Frederick were content to let her chatter on. Their parents seemed interested and pleased, even amused, by Jane's enthusiasm, but she saved plenty of details to tell Julia once they went upstairs to retire for the rest of the night.

So Jane Elizabeth had enjoyed dancing with Sir Timothy, and twice at that! Julia could understand why her sister liked him. They shared interests in drama, the theater, and other arts like poetry, and had chatted a lot before they danced. Julia didn't mind – she was glad an important young man was showing some interest in her sister. Julia was receiving more than her fair share of attention from eligible young males and she was very happy for Jane Elizabeth. Besides, she seemed to be favoring Lord Ravenswood, so maybe a friendship or more, between Jane Elizabeth and Sir Timothy, would be beneficial for both of them. She wished her sister success. Her own thoughts tonight about Sir Timothy did not translate into any misgivings for her sister. Jane Elizabeth was ecstatic that he and Miss Carlisle wished to visit them at Cavendish Square.

Oh, dear, Julia suddenly thought. What if the Carlisles decided to call on the same day as Lord Ravenswood and Miss Calvert? Wouldn't that be interesting? This made her giggle softly. Then their mutual dislike could continue at close quarters, and their rivalry could take on a new form. Not that either gentleman would misbehave for, even if they did come calling on the same day, both would probably demonstrate fine manners. Still, the idea amused her.

The clock chimed three. Julia gathered up her sewing and quietly drifted off to her bedroom. It had been a very long day, but an extremely fine one.

Elizabeth and Darcy also sat up a while in their bedroom. They had enjoyed each other's company in the adjoining sitting room with their refreshments – weak, warm toddies with lemon slices. Now they relaxed in the bedroom, Darcy sitting on the edge of the bed and Elizabeth already sitting up under the covers.

"This must be the most extraordinary season London has ever seen," she remarked in a tired voice. "I do not think there is anything else that could happen and surprise me at the same time, and yet I am all amazement."

He chuckled, though he did not like the weariness in her tone. Elizabeth looked very tired, as she had appeared all evening. Trying to keep his tone light, he said, "Nonsense, Lizzie! Of course we are amazed at the way things are turning out, but especially because they are happening to Julia, Frederick, and now Jane Elizabeth." He chuckled again. "Certainly there must have been seasons in the past when remarkable events occurred, not just this year's!" He reached over and took her hand. "Yet I agree that quite a lot has happened already, and wonder what else is in store for us in the near future."

She gave him a wan smile. "I am certain we shall find out soon, if anything else does occur."

He raised her hand to his lips. "So, what wonderful, remarkable things occurred at this evening's ball? Let us count them." He held her hand with his left, while he held up his right to count on his fingers. "Lord Ravenswood requests our permission for him and his sister Miss Calvert to call upon us, especially Julia." He bent one finger down. "Sir Timothy Carlisle – wasn't he also paying attention to Julia? – intends to ask our permission for him and Miss Carlisle to call upon us – especially Jane Elizabeth." He bent forward another finger. "And Frederick seems quite taken with that incredibly beautiful young lady; what is her name? Ah, yes, Rosamund Woodleigh."

Elizabeth nodded. "It is all as you say. Many people noticed that Lord Ravenswood danced *four* times with Julia, not that she seemed to mind! That is almost a scandal itself! Thank goodness he is asking to call on us, for they are as good as engaged as we speak!" She shook her head. "Jane Elizabeth only danced twice with Sir Timothy, but we all heard how much she enjoyed them both, not that she had a dearth of other partners tonight, thank goodness! And yes, Dearest, I think you are correct that Sir Timothy had been paying his attentions to Julia for a time. Well," she shrugged. "It seems that Lord Ravenswood has beaten out all the other young men Julia has met – Simon Easton, the Stoddard brothers, and even the Foxborough brothers! According to Jane Elizabeth, she and Sir Timothy seem to have interests in common, which may lead to something. We shall see." He nodded at that, and she smiled before her next remark. "I agree with you, too, Dearest, that Frederick seems to like Miss Woodleigh very much."

"How many times did they dance together? Two or three, or do you know?'

Her eyes closed briefly. "Only twice, I am certain. But I do not think our son or Miss Woodleigh would have minded another turn on the dance floor together. Frederick was actually cheerful and laughing with her."

"May it all turn out for the best, for all three of our children," he sighed, smiled, and kissed her hand.

She smiled, but her eyes closed again. She yawned, and her exhausted look when she opened her eyes wrung his heart.

"Dearest," he said softly, "are you feeling well? For you seem so very tired tonight. I do not remember seeing you this tired before, or in recent memory."

"I do feel tired," she replied, her head drooping a little. "In fact, I feel very tired," she complained, then tried to smile. "I am very sorry for that, Dearest! But I have not been feeling as well as I usually do these past few days."

"Dearest," he said tenderly, "I had noticed, but I thought perhaps it was due to all the appointments, calls, events, and amusements we've been making and experiencing." He stroked her hand, which made her quiver. "How are you feeling this late night?" He moved into the bed so he could sit up next to her. She laid her head on his shoulder.

"Oh, Fitzwilliam," she sighed, and kissed his cheek. "I have been out of sorts frequently, and these last two days I have felt aches in every place imaginable, and, well, rather strung out overall." She rubbed her temples. "I feel tired, like a headache is always threatening, and it is hard to concentrate. And my appetite!" She gave a short laugh. "As tired as I am, I find myself thirsty and always ready to eat something! I must have eaten two loaves of bread, a seed cake, and countless other treats between meals in the last few days; if this continues, I will have to ask Edith or Mathilda to let some of my dresses out." She looked into his concerned eyes. "Yet, my stomach feels upset some of the time! I suppose it should be no surprise, considering how much I have eaten this past week, but I am at quite a loss to understand why." She shook her head. "I have been blessed with good health all my life, so I find it puzzling that I am experiencing all these things now."

"Thank you for telling me, Dearest, but please let me call for the doctor tomorrow," he pleaded. "I – I just wish to know that you are fine. Perhaps it is all the worry and excitement over our daughters' debuts, and everything else that has happened..." he trailed off and kissed her.

"Mmmm, yes," she managed to say. "I quite agree, I think maybe I should consult a doctor, not that I think anything is wrong," she smiled at him, "but to make sure all is as it should be. I think you are right, Dearest; I am sure it is because of the extraordinary things that have been happening to all of us, but especially our children!" When he did not smile, she asked, "Why are you worrying so much? In the end, it only comes down to some aches and pains, thirstiness, and indigestion."

Darcy pressed his advantage. "You rarely feel ill, just as I do. That is what makes all this rather extraordinary, and not something to ignore or dismiss."

She nodded. "Is there anything else that concerns you?"

He took her hand and squeezed it. "It is just that I have never seen you look this weary." The pleasing rosiness that usually tinged her cheeks seemed more faint, even dull, over the past week, but he did not tell her this.

She giggled. "Well, all these balls, banquets, and late evenings must certainly contribute to that! I will simply try not to stay up into the wee hours so much and get plenty of rest."

"All right, Lizzie, but please do!"

She squeezed his hand in return. "How I love you, Fitzwilliam, for your concern over my health!" She smiled, then sighed. "Yet you are not the only one who is, for I admit I am as well." He gave her another deep kiss and waited for her to continue.

"I am surprised as you are that I have been feeling ill," she said. "I cannot afford to be sick, especially now. How can I help Julia and Jane through the rest of their debut season if I am? I must be ready to offer whatever guidance and support I can to them, as they both are about to begin receiving gentlemen callers, and whatever may result from their visits!" He nodded. "That applies to Frederick as well, and any young lady he may fancy calling upon, perhaps Miss Woodleigh, or another. They will all need me, that is, both of us." She paused.

"Even if Julia and Jane don't receive a single proposal, and no changes occur in our family in the near future, I am sure all our children would be concerned if I fell ill." She leaned over to give him another kiss as deep as his. "I do not want you, or anyone, to worry about me. Much as I do not care for doctors, I will be sensible." She smiled, more brightly this time. "Above all, please do not remain so concerned. I am sure everything will be fine, Fitzwilliam, you'll see!"

His smile was shakier. "Of course you are right, Dearest. Later this morning, I will arrange for the doctor to visit you here as soon as possible."

"Thank you, Dearest, for your loving concern."

"Thank you, Lizzie – for everything."

He blew out the candles, and they gently reclined together in each other's arms.

CHAPTER 20

Not long after the Roylstons' ball, it turned out to be a fine, warm day in London. Julia was quite at her leisure, but felt tired from all her amusements, and on this day she found the Cavendish Square house stuffy and uncomfortable. She longed to walk about in the fresh air; not even the quiet serenity of the house's little garden, where Frederick had taken some relaxation during his confinement, could satisfy her. She should tell someone where she was going, but her mother was busy, Jane Elizabeth and Mrs. Winston were out shopping, and Frederick had gone with their father to meet some people. Even Nicholas and Anne were occupied with their lessons. Lord Ravenswood had visited and promised to call again in a few days. Well, she did tell Mrs. Jordan that she was just going to step outside to walk up and down the square. Mrs. Jordan agreed but advised her to stay close to the house; if she decided she wanted to take a longer walk, she should come back and have Peter or her son Jordan, the other footman, accompany her. Julia agreed, took her wrap and parasol, and set out.

At first, she did as she had promised; she walked up and down their block along the square, first on their side of the street, and then on another. She looked over at their lovely modest house, and hated the idea of going inside to its tasteful paneling and furnishings on such a beautiful day. Julia decided she was going to return and ask Peter to accompany her when she saw Mrs. Jordan sending him off in haste, probably to go purchase something in Oxford Street. She saw Julia and waved to her, then went back inside after Julia returned the wave and smile; but Julia remained where she was.

Bother! Now she decided she wanted to enjoy more of the sunshine, so she suddenly turned and walked in the direction of Regent's Park. She knew she should not be walking unaccompanied through London, even in their own fine neighborhood; but today she longed to be free and on her own and suddenly felt like pleasing herself, something she rarely did. So off she went to go walking in the park.

Some passersby did glance in her direction, but she kept her eyes lowered and her expression demure. Would someone try to prevent her? Would Mrs. Jordan send her son or Peter after her? She felt exhilarated when she turned into the gate of Regent's Park, no one having stopped her. As she kept walking, she thought she heard someone call her name; she turned around a couple of times, but no one she knew appeared.

Julia walked on in quiet contentment throughout the park for some time. Finally, she felt like sitting down for a while, and relished the gentle breeze that took the edge off the warm afternoon. She sat down on a stone bench partially sheltered by some trees, in an area where she saw almost no other people, and relaxed. Imagining she was somewhere on the grounds of Pemberley, she savored the fine day for several moments.

"Miss Darcy! What a pleasure this is to meet you so soon again, and so unexpectedly!"

Julia looked up at the smiling Gregory Lawson. "The pleasure is all mine, Sir."

"Is it not a fine afternoon?"

"It is," she agreed, smiling. "I simply could not remain inside the house a moment longer! My mother keeps saying that I will ruin my complexion this way, but I do enjoy walking, as I have done many times over all the grounds at home in Pemberley."

"I hope I am not intruding –"

"No, Mr. Lawson, not at all. I am quite at my leisure, as you can see."

He looked around. "Are you not accompanied by someone, then?"

She felt it best to tell the truth, since it was obvious she was alone, even if she would end up being scolded for it later. "Well, I really am not, you see," she smiled again. "I slipped out of the house, and no one was available to escort me."

"I see. What a shame." His tone did not dim, however. "Forgive me for saying so, Miss Darcy, but it is not advisable for young ladies to be out by themselves, even in the better parts of London, such as this."

"You are correct, Mr. Lawson, and it is quite all right," she sighed, "for I expect to be reprimanded for my behavior when I return home. I just could not help myself."

He sat down next to her without asking, and his face had an odd expression. She moved over on the bench to give him more space, which he took up. "I expect that you will be," he agreed, and then looked at her. "Are there other things that you cannot help doing, Miss Darcy?"

He was making her nervous, and his question could not be considered polite or appropriate. Julia began thinking she should not be here in this place, sitting on a bench with a young man, without any kind of chaperone nearby. She tried to think of something to say, but could not; he just smiled, asked her to forgive him, then again asked how she liked the weather.

"It is quite wonderful today," she said quickly, and rose. "Oh, I am very late and will be missed at home! Please forgive me, Mr. Lawson, but I really must be going."

"Then I shall accompany you – at least to the gate, shall I?" he replied, just as quickly. He had risen and taken her arm in a movement lacking grace or patience. They started walking toward a gated entrance, as Julia's eyes searched all around her, but no one was close enough to help her.

"Really, Mr. Lawson, there is no need!"

"I must insist, Miss Darcy. You have no chaperone, a role I shall be happy to fulfill for as long as I am needed." He held her arm fast.

"I do not require it, but thank you all the same." Yet he did not release her. She felt a horrible, sinking feeling. "Please, Sir, I beg of you to release my arm and let me pass."

He gave her a pleasant smile, but his eyes were dark. "I am sorry, Miss Darcy, but I do not see any good reason for doing so."

She swallowed. "You forget yourself, Mr. Lawson."

"Do I?" he replied. He grabbed her and dragged her inside a shady area surrounded by trees.

"Mr. Lawson, no!"

He pushed her back against a tree and kissed her – hard. She opened her mouth to scream when he kissed her again, mashing his mouth onto hers. He was crushing her to him with his left arm, while she felt his free hand groping up and down her dress, all over her body. "No!" she cried again. She struggled against him and tried to slap him, without success.

His entire face was suffused with passion. "I want you, Miss Darcy, and I shall have you!" he breathed close to her quivering mouth and kissed her hard again. "I hope you are as free with your favors as the rumors I have heard say you are, for you are a most delicious creature!" He groped her again, and she gave a final, desperate scream.

Gregory Lawson's eyes widened in alarm, and he released her so he could flee. He had wanted another deep, mashing kiss, but there wasn't time. Julia had fallen to her knees, sobbing. Before he could run, however, fists crashed into his face and chest. Gasping, he tried to swing at his assailant, but the other man punched him in the midsection again. Lawson collapsed and stayed down, writhing and moaning in pain.

Louis Calvert, Lord Ravenswood, was breathing hard. Lawson recognized and cursed him; Calvert restrained himself from kicking him. Instead, he drove his bloodied fist into Lawson's upper chest, then his abdomen as Lawson cried out. Calvert went over and knelt near Julia, who was still sobbing. He offered a handkerchief, but did not touch her. "Miss Darcy, it is I, Lord Ravenswood. Are you all right? Did Lawson hurt you in any way?" She shook her head, but her sobs were still violent, and she was trembling so much that he carefully put an arm around her – keeping his contact very light and loose.

"No," she sobbed, "he didn't hurt me! But he kissed me several times – forcing himself on me, and his hands were –" She gave him a watery look of horror. "He dragged me off into these trees! I tried to resist him, but he was too strong! I don't know what would have happened if you hadn't stopped him!" She clutched him and buried her head on his shoulder. "Oh, thank you for saving me, my lord! This is all my fault!"

"Shhh," he said tenderly as he held her and let her cry. After a while she stopped trembling and asked him to let her repair her appearance, her clothes, and her face. He nodded and stood up. He turned away to leave her to own ministrations, and walked over to where Lawson still lay, moaning and unable to get to his feet. The fallen man opened his eyes and saw him looking down at him with contempt. "Cur!" he gasped out.

Lord Ravenswood thought of Lawson forcing himself on Julia Darcy with his mouth and hands, and his handsome face twisted. She was still fixing her appearance, with her back to them. "You vile, disgusting, filthy *blackguard*," he breathed, and gave Lawson a forceful kick upward between his legs. Too hurt to scream, Lawson gave a great gasp, shuddered, and lay still.

"Lord Ravenswood?"

He composed his face and turned. There stood Julia, her cheeks puffy and her eyes dull, but the rest of her appearance seemed normal and presentable. "Come, Miss Darcy," he said kindly, "let me take you to my carriage, and I will see you home safely to Cavendish Square."

She nodded. "What about him?" Her eyes flickered over to the prone man with the bloody mouth.

He did not prevaricate. "I will have two of my men hold him, and I will send someone to inform the authorities. Please do not concern yourself further about him or let him frighten you. Gregory Lawson will be brought up on several charges, to all of which I shall swear to testify."

She sagged in relief. "Thank you, Lord Ravenswood! I would have been lost – completely lost – without your help." She clutched his arm and they walked away from the dim, secretive trees. Onlookers had arrived after hearing her screams, and Lord Ravenswood quickly informed them of what had occurred to forestall questions and get her away from the park. At his urgent request, two gentlemen hurried off to call in the authorities.

"I must ask you," she managed. "How did you find me here?"

"Did you not hear my calling your name?" he replied. "I saw you on Regent Street about to enter the park. I was going to hurry over to meet you, but then I met some other acquaintances who delayed me..."

"I see." Her voice became unsteady as she trudged along. "I really must apologize," she said, "because I have caused you all this worry and trouble – and it is my fault for my stupid, careless, willful act! I just wanted to get out of the house and enjoy this fine day! However, no one was available to accompany me, and I did not wait or tell anyone where I was going. I am to blame for my own ravishing!" She shook her head and burst into new tears. "I will have to agree with my father and mother when they accuse me that I should have had better sense! I should have. Oh, I am so very sorry!"

He spoke soothing words. "If you will forgive me, Miss Darcy, yes, you should not go out unaccompanied, even in this part of London. However, you are not to blame for the actions of a callous, rapacious brute trying to force himself upon you! Such men, no matter who they are, should be in prison!" He felt great satisfaction in being the one who saved her and was with her now – and had flattened the odious villain. His final, crushing kick also gave him satisfaction and great shame, since Lawson had already been down. When he thought of Lawson's hands groping Julia Darcy's exquisite person, though, he wanted to kick him again.

Julia tried to lighten her expression. "Will you defend me so firmly when it is my turn to face my parents for my conduct? For most of the fault is mine; my own carelessness almost caused my downfall."

"I would gladly do so," he declared.

"Thank you, Lord Ravenswood." She could not expect him to.

His conscience plagued him. "Er, Miss Darcy?"

"Yes?"

"Forgive me, especially at this moment, but I must ask you this." She waited. "After such a horrible experience, are you truly comfortable in *my* presence? Lawson is a man, and he forced himself on you when you were alone and defenseless." He swallowed hard. "And I am a man as well, and you are alone with me now..."

"Please stop, I beg of you," she said, weary. "We are almost near the entrance to the park, and there are several people around us, unlike how it was back there." She sighed, and he almost had to hold her up. "I thank you for your consideration but, respectfully, I do not think you are going to drag me off somewhere into the trees and ravage me – like *he* did! I do not think it is within your character to do such a thing."

"Thank you, Miss Darcy! But...I used physical force... like your brother did, even though he had to...defend you." His thoughts were becoming disordered. "Young ladies, and women in general, rightly condemn such violence that we men sometimes commit." He cleared his throat, thinking how feckless he sounded. "Do my actions repel you, or make you fearful that I am capable of such violent and rapacious behavior?"

"You saved me," she said. "Need I say it again? Well, I have been fought over twice, once by my older brother and now by you." She paused. "And as a man being 'capable' of violence, as you put it...forgive me, for this is not the type of subject young ladies discuss, or even ask about, but –”

“Yes, Miss Darcy?”

“Were you referring to that last kick you gave Mr. Lawson?”

He halted and flushed, completely exposed and ashamed. “So you did see me do it.”

“I did.”

“A gentleman, a highborn man, does not do what I did!” he burst out. “What must you think of me now?”

She didn’t answer right away, and he suffered. Finally, she remarked, “It is all so very strange, for I used to like Mr. Lawson.”

“He is an *animal*,” Lord Ravenswood replied with venom. And so am I, he added, in silent misery. Aloud he exclaimed, “You caught me; yes, you did! So, am I such a fine, noble lord? Do you not think me now a violent and brutal man like Lawson and Grantley? For I have behaved so.” He could not look at her.

She clutched his hand. “No, Lord Ravenswood, I do not.” She paused. “Rather, I wish you had done even more than you did.” Surprised, he turned to her, and her eyes met his. “You see, it will take me a long time to forget him forcing his mouth onto mine, and his hands touching me all over.” She shuddered. “I want to go home so I can take a long, hot bath, even on a day like this, and burn this dress, for I do not ever wish to wear it again.” She looked at his astonished face. “I think you are a fine gentleman, and my savior this day. Will you please take me home now?” Her lower lip trembled.

“Of course, Miss Darcy,” he swallowed, and led her to his carriage.

CHAPTER 21

The carriage ride was short and uneventful, but Julia grew sad and fearful again the closer they got to her home. Regardless of propriety, she held Lord Ravenswood's hand the entire way, and he made no effort to change that. He gently helped her down from the carriage and into the house. A very concerned Mrs. Jordan was first relieved to see Julia, then outraged when Lord Ravenswood told her what had happened, and what Julia had said she intended to do.

"I will inform Mrs. Darcy immediately, Lord Ravenswood, if you will please excuse me, and I will have Emma wait on Miss Darcy." She swept off.

Elizabeth sailed in and received the awful news from Lord Ravenswood. She barely had time to thank him before Julia cried "Mother!" and buried herself in her arms. Julia became quite inconsolable for a while, and alternated between the arms of her mother and sister. "My poor darling," Elizabeth kept saying over and over, but they finally got her upstairs for her bath and some quiet rest afterwards. Jane Elizabeth insisted that Mrs. Winston stay with her for as much time as she could spare, because she knew she would have a calming effect on Julia.

Elizabeth informed Darcy and Frederick what had happened when they arrived home before dinner. Aghast, both blanched, but she managed to calm them down enough when she insisted that Julia was safe, physically unharmed, and quietly resting. Lord Ravenswood had long departed from the house, saying he needed to be home at Woodside to look after Miss Calvert's comforts; Darcy swore he would go at the earliest possible time to Woodside and personally thank him for all he did for Julia, and Frederick begged to accompany him. Then they all gathered for a late, somber dinner, while Julia remained upstairs in her room with Mrs. Winston.

Once dinner was over, Darcy and Elizabeth had a long talk about what they would discuss with Julia when she awakened the next day. They would always be grateful for her deliverance but would impress upon her the needs for propriety and safety, as well as remind her of the mistakes she had made, even if it distressed her. Julia was an obedient girl, usually sensible, and therefore unlikely to repeat them; her parents only worried that she might lose some of her confidence and bright personality because she had been attacked by a man she met during her debut who was considered a gentleman, and trustworthy. To them, Gregory Lawson had always seemed pleasant and well-mannered, if rather bland, but none of them would have ever thought him to be the callous animal he had revealed himself to be. Now Darcy and Elizabeth were comforting each other over the day's sad circumstances – and the threat to yet another one of their children's happiness.

"You know, Fitzwilliam," Elizabeth finally said, drying her eyes, "sometimes I wish we'd never decided to have Julia and Jane's debuts here in London. Look at everything that has happened, although I know it is not all our fault! Our family has been changed forever; how I wish we had kept them safe, unexposed, and out of sight at Pemberley!" She spoke again when she saw how he tried to protest. "Do me a favor now, Dearest. Please go and see how Frederick is doing, for he looked terribly upset about what happened to Julia. I think it would be better if you do, rather than I, tonight." She rubbed her neck.

"Yes, Lizzie, of course I shall." He cleared his throat and wiped his own eyes. It would never do to let Frederick see him like this. "Are you sure you are feeling all right, Dearest?"

"I am; it is only that I have been feeling rather tired again, even lightheaded." She smiled at him. "I will be fine, Dearest. Now please go and put Frederick's mind at ease about his sister, if that is possible." He nodded and left her.

As late as it was, Darcy found Frederick pacing in the drawing room downstairs. He was glad to see that Frederick had not helped himself to any spirits, though he looked upset enough to have considered it. "Frederick?"

"Good evening, Father."

Twinges of pride and concern made him hesitate. "Are you feeling all right?"

"Yes, Father, I think I am." He shook his head. "I am only concerned about Julia! I wanted to go and look in on her earlier, but I didn't want to wake or disturb her, or upset her with my presence – well, because of what Lawson did…" He trailed off, looking away.

"That was very considerate of you, Son, but I am sure she is concerned about you as well, for your mother said she kept asking about you all through the evening. Julia, I am happy to say, is unharmed and calm, and you will be able to see her tomorrow, whenever you wish."

Nodding, Frederick flopped down onto the couch. He put his head in his hands, then ran them through his hair. Darcy sat down next to him and waited. A few minutes later, Frederick spoke.

"I am very grateful to Lord Ravenswood for coming to Julia's assistance, preventing Lawson from…harming her." Grimacing, he shook his head. "But, Father, how can I be Master of Pemberley if I fail to protect one of my sisters, or even Nick?"

Darcy put an arm around his hunched shoulders. "Please listen to me, Frederick, for you are taking far too much upon yourself."

"Father!"

"No, Son," he said in a gentle voice. "How can you blame yourself for what happened to Julia? Your sister is a beautiful young lady making her mark in society, and neither you, nor I, nor your mother can be there every moment to watch over her. We do the best we can, but we cannot protect her from *everything.* Besides, someday soon, she will resent our watchfulness, for she is growing up rapidly, and quite well."

"I wasn't able to help her." Frederick looked miserable.

Darcy gave him a reassuring pull on his shoulders. "Neither was I. I did not know what had occurred until we both came home again, long after it had happened. So, if I did not know, and you were with me, how could you have known and done something to prevent it?"

Frederick's eyes filled. "Thank you for saying so, Father. I understand, but I still feel awful for thinking Julia was safe, and yet she was not!"

Darcy hesitated. "Did any of us suspect what a vile, brutal man Lawson really is?"

"N—no, Father."

"You did not, and I did not. Neither did Julia or your mother, and probably not many other people here in London, either."

Frederick swallowed hard. "This is so difficult to accept, but I do see your point."

Darcy gave him another pull on his shoulders. "Frederick, you cannot control everything, no matter how hard you try," he said kindly. "Not now, and not even when you are Master of Pemberley, with all that entails! Trust me, your father, for it has taken me many years to learn that lesson – and so it will be for you." He gestured to the decanter, but Frederick shook his head, which pleased him, and he continued. "I cannot control the sun, the moon, or the weather to favor our crops, can I?" Frederick reluctantly shook his head. "Could I stop you from fighting Richard Grantley after all his insults to Julia, Jane Elizabeth, and even yourself?" Frederick hung his head, and Darcy pulled him close. "I tell you this: as master, you do the very best you can, day after day, for so many people – family, friends, servants, tenants, and neighbors alike. All of them are your responsibility. Even so, you cannot protect everyone from everything, or even loved ones from the consequences of the decisions that they make, no matter how hard you try. Master of a grand estate, yes; but God, no."

Frederick groaned. "Then what does it mean to be a powerful man like you?"

Darcy swallowed. "Being a powerful man means that you accept your responsibility over others, with all that requires – but know your limits, and seek help when you need it, which I guarantee will occur often."

Frederick clutched him for a few moments, then they separated. He took a couple of deep breaths and set his jaw. "Thank you, Father. I will never forget your words of advice tonight." He swallowed again. "If I may ask, though, what do you and Mother have in mind for Julia? I certainly do not blame her for what happened," he paused, "but what about her personal judgment?"

Darcy sighed. "I will be honest with you; your mother and I discussed all this earlier tonight." He got up and paced. "You must understand that I am not blaming her for what happened today, nor does your mother." Frederick nodded. "However, to answer your question, Julia did an innocent thing – she simply wanted to go outside on a beautiful day, unfortunately without a chaperone. She could have tried harder to find someone to accompany her, or waited a little longer, but she didn't – which she has freely admitted. Yes, her personal judgment was clouded today by her desire to indulge in a simple pleasure –" Here he paused when he saw Frederick's tortured expression. "Son! Neither your mother nor I feel Julia *deserved* what happened to her, because of her willful desire to go out in the fresh air alone! But she did not think her decision through; someone should have accompanied her, or she should have waited until Peter returned from the shops on Oxford Street – no more than that." He shrugged. "As we have said before, we did not know such a meeting would take place, nor that Julia would meet someone like Gregory Lawson, nor that we thought he was capable of such depravity." Frederick nodded again. "Now, as to what your mother and I have decided, Julia will remain inside this house for three full days, as you did, under supervision, no matter how fine the weather or how many invitations we receive. Julia will not dine with Sir Adam and Lady Rose Wainwright tomorrow evening, nor with the Gardiners and the Staleys the evening after that. Julia will remain here at Cavendish Square with Mrs. Winston, and Jane Elizabeth will attend in her place."

"I see. Thank you for telling me." Frederick took a deep breath and mastered his expression. "I agree with all that you have said about what happened today." He gave a lop-sided smile. "It also gives me much to think about in the days ahead." He raised his eyebrows. "I look forward to seeing Julia well rested tomorrow. Father, are you not tired yourself now?"

Darcy smiled. "Oh, I am extremely tired, and I am sure you are as well." He rose, and Frederick followed suit. "Come, Son, let us get some well-deserved rest."

"Yes, Father." Frederick followed him upstairs, loosening his clothes on the way.

It was almost noon the next day when Frederick presented himself at the door of Julia's bedroom. He knocked on the door and stepped inside; she was sitting in a chair near the window and concentrating on her needlework. "Julia?"

"Frederick!" He kissed her cheek. She was pale, but composed, and weary.

"You look well today," he said sincerely. "How are you feeling?"

She gave a small smile. "I am feeling as well as I can be, I suppose, dear Brother," she answered. "In short, I am most grateful for my rescue. I admit I made a very bad decision to go to Regent's Park on my own, with no one to chaperone me."

She sighed. "I am most guilty of that! I also realize I could have hardly expected someone like Gregory Lawson to assault me! And at first I liked him." She shook her head.

Frederick took her hands. "I am so very glad that you are safe and unharmed! I am also most grateful that Lord Ravenswood was close by to help you! I only hope that you are not seriously affected by such an event," he finished lamely. "Oh, what am I saying? How can I expect you to be all right, when a young man, only a little older than I, threatened you so?"

Julia's eyes were wide, but she tried to blink back tears that were starting. "Frederick," she tried, "I am most distressed by all that has happened – my decision to go walking alone, and the revelation of his brutality." She closed her eyes. "However, Lord Ravenswood prevented anything terrible from happening to me, thank God." She was not going to discuss any details about it with Frederick, not after all her parents' questions earlier this morning. She didn't want to repeat them; she wasn't sure he'd be able to hear such things, and hoped he would not ask her about them – which he did not.

He still looked miserable, despite his father's words the night before. "Julia, I am so sorry you were attacked and suffered such mistreatment!"

She rose, came over to him, and kissed him. "You, Mother, and Father have all been so solicitous toward my well-being," she said with a smile. "I am safe – and untouched – more than I deserve; but I have learned my lesson. I am also serving out my well-deserved punishment for my carelessness, which gives me plenty of time to think about things." She paused. "Thank God Lord Ravenswood stopped him before he," she swallowed, "really hurt me." She looked away. "Before I was completely lost."

"Please do not say such things!" Frederick cried. "True men do not take advantage of young women as he tried to do with you! I hope I would never forget myself and try to do the same! I could never forgive myself for such despicable actions!"

"You would never do that." She hugged him. "And I agree with you that no true, decent man behaves so. But now it seems I must guard my own behavior so that another licentious, lascivious man does not attack me! I thought I was safe from such brutality."

"Julia, my wonderful, beautiful sister!" He hugged her. "Please just promise me, your poor brother, that you will be very careful from now on!"

She looked up into his worried brown eyes and soberly answered, "I promise you, Frederick." They continued to hold each other for several minutes.

CHAPTER 22

The next day a courier arrived at Cavendish Square, and the interest the man in court dress generated among the neighbors was nothing compared to the effects he caused within the Darcy household.

"You are to be elevated to the baronetcy?" Elizabeth cried out as she read the letter. "You will become Sir Frederick Darcy?"

Darcy looked dazed. "Yes, by the order of the King himself...it is all here in this letter."

Elizabeth's hands fell limply to her sides. "I cannot believe it...you may have to call Mrs. Jordan, for I feel rather faint." Darcy quickly guided her to a chair so she could sit down. Her glance traveled over to Frederick. "A baronet..."

"No, Mother," he exclaimed, "please do not faint!" Mrs. Jordan had appeared with a warm toddy, which she gave to Elizabeth. "It really is nothing to be anxious or concerned about!" He didn't sound very convincing, for he was just as shocked as the rest of them. He actually looked terrified, and Elizabeth could see his hands were shaking, so she took pity on him.

She put her mug down, rose, and drew him to her. "Just think, to be given such an honor, and you are not yet twenty years of age!" Her eyes spilled over, and Darcy joined them; Frederick tried to smile as he accepted everyone's congratulations. "It is also hereditary, is it not?" Elizabeth said to Darcy.

"That is what the letter says. It means that all your children, Frederick, will be ennobled in this way, but especially your firstborn son, and then his."

Julia had been summoned from her room, and now spoke up. "How wonderful, Frederick! You're to be a baronet of the realm!" She looked positively starry-eyed; the importance of her debut paled in comparison.

Both Jane Elizabeth and Nicholas were impressed. Jane Elizabeth's congratulations were warm and heartfelt, but she could not help teasing him a little. "Princess Victoria must be very grateful to you for returning her fan!"

Frederick blushed, but laughed. "Oh, Jane! I believe this honor is probably my reward because I prevented Richard Grantley from falling into her when he was so drunk at the Earl's ball." He shrugged. "I can think of no other reason, nothing else I could have done to be given such an honor, much less be considered for it!"

Jane Elizabeth was pleased for him all the same. "Yes, Brother, I am sure you are right that His Majesty is rewarding you for protecting Her Royal Highness, the Heir Presumptive!"

"And a fine job he did of it, too!" Anne spoke up stoutly, but very happy as well. "Didn't you, Freddie?"

"Er, I guess I did it all right, as you say, based on this outcome!"

"You are too modest, Freddie. You really did save the Princess from harm!" She reached for his arm, and he bent down to receive her kiss. "I am so glad that you did, and that you are." He thanked her.

"It is a wonderful honor and reward, Master Frederick," Mrs. Winston said, congratulating him. "It is most befitting for the next Master of Pemberley."

"Thank you, Mrs. Winston. I will always remember what an honor it is, and try never to take it for granted, and lead people to think it was bestowed in error or was somehow undeserved."

"No one will think so," she replied, "for your sentiments and behavior are exemplary, if I may say so." He thanked her again. "You are most welcome, Master Frederick, though I know I will not be addressing you that way much longer."

"That reminds me," Darcy spoke up. "Shall I address you from now on as 'Sir Frederick'?"

His shoulders sagged. "Oh, no, Father, please don't!"

Darcy stared at him. "Do you mean to tell me – and all of us gathered here – that you do not appreciate what a great honor His Majesty the King has bestowed upon you? That you regret such an honor?"

Frederick knew his father was teasing him, but gave him a helpless look, the kind that children give their parents when they know they are being teased deliberately, but still must suffer through it. Elizabeth stifled a giggle, enjoying her husband teasing their son in a manner that reminded her of her own father. "Of course not!" Frederick almost spluttered. "I assure you I am most amazed and humbled by such an honor as this –" His chest was expanding as he worked himself up even more, trying to appear as noble as he would when he was addressed.

Laughing, Darcy took pity on him and said, "I am sorry, Son, for teasing you, for I could not resist. I know you are grateful and appreciative." He spread his hands. "Parents like to tease their children at times, though it is done out of love, not cruelty, that is all. I am certainly guilty of this."

"As am I," Elizabeth laughed, and their daughters exchanged glances.

Frederick visibly relaxed. "As you teased Henry at times, Father?" He was happy to see none of them seemed saddened at the mention of his name.

Darcy even laughed again. "Exactly like then."

The clock chimed, for it was now half past eleven. "Goodness!" Elizabeth exclaimed. "It is almost time for luncheon! How the time has flown this morning, though it is easy to understand why." She shook herself. "I shall go speak with Mrs. Jordan, for we must have a celebration at dinner to mark this incredible announcement!"

As they queued to leave the drawing room, Nicholas clapped Frederick on the shoulder. "I cannot believe it – my own older brother will be a baronet! That is truly amazing, and wonderful."

"Thank you, Nick."

"You're welcome, Frederick. You'll be addressed as 'Sir' – that is like being a knight, is that correct?"

"Yes, it is, but I am receiving a baronetcy, not a knighthood."

"Well, even if it is not the same thing, and you are to be addressed as 'Sir,' as a baronet will you need a page, like a knight has? For if you need one..." He shrugged.

"I do not know that I will be going on any quests in the near future," Frederick replied, laughing, "and I think you have grown so much that you are almost as tall as I...I thought that pages were rather small in stature, or smaller than the knights they served, anyway. So I really do not know." A sudden thought made him smile more. "However, if it turns out that I do need a page, I know whom I shall consider first."

Grinning, his brother thanked him. "Now I propose that you and I, and maybe Peter if he can be spared, go over to Lord's Cricket Ground for some long-delayed practice." Frederick seemed interested, so Nicholas continued. "I promise I will carry everything if you want me to, but I will show the newest baronet of the realm how to bat effectively."

"Fie, Master Nicholas Darcy!" Frederick cried, as they all laughed. "How dare you provoke me this way! Why, I can bat as well as you, and more! Who was it that prevented Cousin Charles from scoring all those runs the last time we played together at Pemberley?"

"That's bowling, not batting, and you know it," Nicholas said good-naturedly, "but that does not matter. I will help you sharpen your skills all the same, as befits a baronet of the realm. That way, Charles and Vincent will not be able to defeat us." They went on arguing, as Frederick tried to remain indignant but was failing. The others followed them out, enjoying their rivalry, leaving Darcy and Elizabeth alone momentarily. She smiled at him and turned to leave when she almost stumbled and rubbed her temples.

Darcy sprang to her side. "Dearest, are you feeling all right?"

She closed her eyes and tried to smile again. "I am well enough, Fitzwilliam, but I do feel tired again today – and this incredible news has just set me all aflutter." She gave him a peck on the cheek. "Do not look so dark, Dearest, for I will be fine! A little luncheon and some lemon tea will do wonders for me, so please do not worry."

"All right, then, I shall not – at least, I will try not to." He followed her into the hallway. "Yet you are feeling hungry?" He had noticed the ample breakfasts she had been having for at least a week.

She seemed a little surprised at his question, but considered it. "Why, yes, I do feel famished – as I said, that amazing letter arriving today, right on the heels of Julia's troubles yesterday...I feel I need to be keeping up my strength right now." She smiled at him over her shoulder.

"As you should be," he agreed.

Another thought made her smile. "I do hope Cook makes another seed cake for tea today, for I do love it! And I am going to have her make that wonderful little chocolate *gateau* for dessert this evening, to celebrate!"

Darcy did not have a sweet tooth, but even he enjoyed that special cake, if he had room for a piece of it. "That sounds wonderful," he said. "Better leave some room for it – and the seed cake, too."

"And those delightful little finger sandwiches," Elizabeth giggled, as her hand tried to sneak a smoothing of her bodice. However, Darcy caught the movement, and looked at her. "Oh, dear," she said, "I have been indulging myself a little too much lately, haven't I?" She sounded rueful. "I was afraid you had noticed, Dearest."

He kept his voice low and tender. "Yes, I had, just as you noticed how much of the spirits I was drinking a while back." She smiled, but he looked away. "Lizzie, how are you feeling now, at this moment? Please answer me, for I am still concerned that something is ailing you. Forgive me for saying so, but you haven't seemed to be yourself this past week or so."

She caught the concern in his eyes and swallowed. "I am sorry to keep causing you concern, Dearest, but to answer your question, I feel tired now as I have felt a fair amount of the time. For the last few days, I still have felt as if a headache was starting, only it never quite does." She shrugged. "My appetite remains increased, especially for the sweets, and I still seem quite thirsty." She looked at him. "Well, that is all of it. Now tell me what you think, Dearest, for I do not want you concerned about my health."

He nodded. "Well, I would ask you to rest as much as you can this afternoon, and I intend to call in Doctor Shelbourne, our family physician here in London, to come examine you tomorrow morning – if you will allow him! Just to make sure you are as fit as you always are, and put your poor husband's mind at ease."

She laughed and gave him a kiss. "Of course, I should be happy to have Doctor Shelbourne examine me – and prevent you from worrying about me anymore! I shall keep the entire morning open so that he may call if he is able."

He kissed her in return. "Thank you, Dearest! I shall let you know when he intends to call. I shall send Jordan over to his rooms on Baker Street to set the time."

She nodded and went off to meet with Mrs. Jordan. He gave a half smile and went outside to ponder things in the small, enclosed garden until it was time for luncheon.

CHAPTER 23

Two days after receiving the royal announcement of Frederick's elevation, on the morning of Julia's final day of being restricted to the house, Doctor Shelbourne arrived to examine Elizabeth. He regretted not being able to call the day before; as it was, the doctor's arrival this morning could not have been timelier, as Elizabeth had spent the entire previous day ill – dizzy and unable to keep much of anything down. The Cook's ministrations seemed to calm her stomach, but Darcy was plainly worried and cursed having to wait an extra day for the doctor's visit. Frederick and his siblings were quite concerned too, because their mother was rarely ill.

Doctor Shelbourne was a highly recommended London physician who liked to take his time. Darcy paced restlessly in the drawing room and finally distracted Frederick so much that he suggested they go off and play some billiards. Darcy had apologized, left Frederick to his thick volume, and retreated to his study; that is where Doctor Shelbourne found him when he finally completed his examination.

Darcy sprang from his chair. "Doctor Shelbourne, thank God! I have been driven to distraction...please sit down." He indicated the other chair. "May I get you something?"

"Well, no, Mr. Darcy, I don't think –," the doctor began, then reconsidered. "Perhaps I will, at that. Yes, for it will be appropriate under the circumstances when I discuss Mrs. Darcy's health." He smiled. "Just a tot, please, Mr. Darcy, thank you! That is excellent!" Then he saw Darcy's anxious face.

"Doctor Shelbourne, please...for God's sake, tell me..."

"I am so very sorry, Mr. Darcy, to cause you any anxiety, for there is no need for any. Many people will tell you that I am a very deliberate, methodical man, and never rush a diagnosis!" He harrumphed and smiled. "Please be assured, Mr.

Darcy, that your wife is fine, in perfect health, and there is no cause for worry."

Darcy gave him a helpless look. "But my wife – Mrs. Darcy – has been ill for twenty-four hours at least, which is most unlike her, and she has been feeling tired and rather run down for a couple of weeks." He did not mention her appetite. "We just thought it was because of all the late nights and excitements connected with our daughters' debuts – and the news of our son's elevation; have you heard about it?"

"Yes, I have!" Doctor Shelbourne said heartily. "Congratulations to you and Mrs. Darcy, and to the young gentleman himself! Master Frederick is a fine young man, a son I am sure of which you are very proud; I met him when I arrived earlier." That made Darcy nod and smile, so the doctor resumed, encouraged by his host's improved demeanor. "We were talking about Mrs. Darcy's health a moment ago. Yes, she described to me the same symptoms you just mentioned, including her increased appetite and fondness for certain types of foods – sweets of all kinds, in fact. However, I repeat to you, Mr. Darcy, that despite all these things, and the fact that Mrs. Darcy has been ill for a day with an upset stomach, she is in fine health. She is a very strong, healthy woman, I am most glad to say."

Relief flooded Darcy's face. "Thank God, Doctor, and thank you!" Then his smile faded. "But surely there is some explanation for her discomforts and her illness."

"Well, yes, there is." Doctor Shelbourne was smiling. "I usually inform patients and their families in a softer way, but I feel I cannot in Mrs. Darcy's case." He kept smiling at Darcy's confused expression. "Mr. Darcy, Sir, Mrs. Darcy has been experiencing these discomforts and has been ill for a day *because she is with child.*"

Astonishment spread over his face. "But..." He rubbed his face with a hand. "She is? I mean no offense, Doctor, but are you certain?"

The doctor laughed. "None taken, Mr. Darcy. However, yes,

I am quite certain. Mrs. Darcy is about two months along, and her confinement will probably end sometime in December."

"But how...?"

The doctor laughed again. "Oh, quite in the usual way, I am sure." He shook Darcy's hand. "Congratulations, Sir, for you shall be a father yet one more time!"

A series of smiles began flickering across his face, but he could not hold onto them as he tried to comprehend the doctor's news. "Well," he finally said, put down his glass, and paced a few times. "Forgive me, Doctor, but this is such wonderful, momentous, and unexpected news! I have been very concerned about Elizabeth's health, but now you tell me she is fine and with child!"

"Yes, it is all quite true. Mrs. Darcy, as I said, is a fine, healthy woman. I should be very surprised if she has any complications, as you have several healthy children already."

"We have," he mused. He started and grinned at him. "We do, and now we will have another! It is just that it is so unexpected – our youngest, our daughter Anne, is now eleven years old – and I thought that we were too old to have any more children...that is, I was thinking of myself much more so than Mrs. Darcy."

Doctor Shelbourne nodded. "Yes, in general, most childbearing occurs before a woman reaches a certain age, but in a case such as your wife's it is quite possible – and successful, I daresay." He cleared his throat. "Mrs. Darcy, if I may say so, also remarked about her age, which she admitted to; but I told her that did not preclude or prevent her from carrying another child to term. Since she does possess fine health and has no unhealthy habits, and if she is careful as I am sure she will be during her confinement, then everything should come to a very happy result." He patted Darcy on the shoulder. "If I am worth anything as a physician," he added with a smile, "based on Mrs. Darcy's answers about her condition, and my own examination, I am willing to say I think you may have yet another son."

Darcy gasped, and joy finally surged through him. "A son!" He threw back his head and laughed. "Of course, I would be happy with a healthy child, daughter or son, and I know Elizabeth would agree with me...but you also know that our oldest son died last year, do you not?" The doctor nodded. "So, to have another son! This is such incredible news!"

Doctor Shelbourne returned his smile. "Do not be concerned about Mrs. Darcy's appetite either, especially her fondness for the sweets, or anything else she may end up fancying. It is all quite natural."

Darcy grinned. "Then I will arrange to have a wagonload of seed cake at the ready, if need be."

The doctor laughed yet again. "That's the spirit, Mr. Darcy, for it is truly wonderful! I know you are eager to be with Mrs. Darcy, for she is awaiting you upstairs. Now, let us give a toast to Mrs. Darcy and yourself, the expectant parents! And let us even toast your son who is soon to be elevated." Darcy agreed and refilled their glasses, over the doctor's objections. "Not too much, Mr. Darcy, please, excellent though it is, for I have more patients to visit today!"

"Of course," Darcy was still grinning, "but you must have enough in your glass to make all these important toasts."

They shared a laugh and chatted for several minutes. When they had finished their libations, and Doctor Shelbourne left Cavendish Square to visit his next patient, Darcy could not contain himself any longer. His first duty, his first words, belonged to Elizabeth; he would break the news to Frederick later, and the rest of the family when she thought it prudent. He surprised everyone now by bounding up the stairs, pausing only at the top to collect himself, and carefully knocking on her bedroom door.

CHAPTER 24

After discussing it with Elizabeth, Darcy shared the wonderful new first with Frederick, then the rest of the family, including Mrs. Winston. The Darcy household was once again in an uproar, the third time in a single week, but it was another happy one. Frederick was overcome, joyful yet mindful of the responsibility of having a new, younger sibling to watch over when he became Master of Pemberley. He enthusiastically agreed with Julia that now little Henry David, who was not quite a year old, would have someone, almost a sibling his own age to share while growing up. Julia, Jane Elizabeth, and Nicholas were thrilled, the sisters hoping for another sister, while he wished for a brother. Anne took the longest to express her opinion; her parents feared she would not be pleased at being supplanted as the youngest in the family, first by Henry David, and now another sibling. However, Anne carefully thought it over, hugged her parents, and said she'd like to go forward with her plans to study abroad, since Pemberley would be well staffed with capable hands. Elizabeth shook her head at that, while Darcy and Frederick could not help laughing.

However, the surprises did not end with this announcement. Over the next two days, Julia received callers – first Mr. Seth Foxborough, then Mr. Samuel Stoddard. Visibly nervous and dressed in their finest, both young gentlemen asked to speak with Darcy in his study. Both stated their desire to ask for Julia's hand in marriage after a suitable engagement. Darcy was surprised at how quickly Julia had earned not one, but two marriage proposals. Knowing of Julia's regard for them, as well as some of each family's background, he allowed them to speak with her. However, he made it clear that, while he certainly did not object to either one of them as a potential son-in-law, it would be Julia's decision first and foremost. He would not try to influence her, and cautioned them that she might receive additional proposals, so she would have to be certain of her choice. Swallowing and nodding, while maintaining their pleasant and respectful demeanor, both Mr. Foxborough and Mr. Stoddard applied to Julia with their respective proposals in the drawing room.

Julia was surprised, pleased, and taken aback by them, all the same. She really did like and respect them, unlike the odious Julian Tunney and the vile Gregory Lawson. In fact, she more than liked the young gentlemen, but she had grown to like many young men she had met during the season, many with whom she wished to remain friends. Accepting one of their hands in marriage, though, was quite something else. Yet the time of decision had now arrived, the goal of making her debut in London. She had come, she had dazzled, and she had garnered proposals; now she had to decide if she loved any of these young men enough to marry and spend her life together with one of them. Julia wanted to be happy and marry for love, so she had much serious thinking to do. She would be haranguing her mother, even in her condition, and Mrs. Winston for advice.

However, she was not as overcome or paralyzed by the seriousness of the moment as she thought she would be; for she did have an idea from whom she would welcome a proposal of marriage without reservation. That young man had not yet done so, though he seemed to care very deeply for her, and she felt herself wanting to respond in kind. As propriety dictated, however, she must give anyone who applied for her hand an answer, and the sooner the better. Julia could not – and would not – play one suitor off another, or stall them until she obtained the proposal she desired, if it ever came at all; for it wasn't certain that she would, no matter how much it seemed right to her, as well as the young man's feelings for her.

She knew what she had to do. It wasn't easy, but as kindly

as she could, she told Seth Foxborough and Samuel Stoddard the same thing: that she was most honored and amazed to receive their proposals of marriage; that she wished to retain their good opinion of her and their friendship if possible; but that truthfully she loved someone else. She admitted that she had not received a proposal from this man, but she had to remain steadfast in her feelings. Finally, with tears in her eyes, she told them she was very sorry to disappoint them, for she could not accept their fine proposals.

Both young gentlemen were not so overconfident that they expected to be accepted with immediate certainty, but their hopes were still dashed. Seth Foxborough looked more dejected than Samuel Stoddard, but both thanked her for her sensitivity and consideration, as well as praised her for her constancy. Hats in hand, they left, sobered and diminished, and wished her the happiness and love from the one she truly desired.

Sighing, Julia wiped her eyes for several minutes, then asked Jordan to summon her parents, along with Frederick. They entered the room cautiously, as they examined her countenance for a hint of what she intended to tell them; they appeared concerned when she seemed tearful and downcast, but she shook her head and declared she felt fine. They all sat down, and Julia told them what she had decided.

"I sent them both away with thanks and regret," she concluded. "I like them both, but I do not love either one of them, or desire one as my prospective husband. I only hope I have not crushed them completely, for I would like to remain friends with them and their families, if possible. I cannot expect them to be happy with my decision, however, because I rejected their proposals."

"No, dear," Elizabeth said, stroking her hand, "but you have acted properly and perfectly, with true honesty and consideration. Surely they will be grateful for that, even if they are unhappy not to have won your hand."

"Thank you, Mother." Julia dabbed her eyes.

"I agree, Julia," Darcy said. "I would not have had an objection to either one of them, but I did make it clear to them that the decision was yours. I appreciate your concern for the young men's feelings, but all you have done is fine and admirable, and cannot be faulted." Julia thanked him in turn, and he leaned forward. "I would like to ask you something that may be difficult to answer." She nodded. "You told Mr. Foxborough and Mr. Stoddard that you love someone else; my question is, are you confident of receiving a proposal from this person you regard so highly?"

Julia considered before replying. "I should be confident, Father, for I believe the young man's feelings for me are as strong or stronger than my feelings for him. I just cannot expect – with certainty – that he will ask for my hand." She sighed. "I do wish he would, for I would have no hesitation in saying yes, and I am sure you would both find him acceptable as a son-in-law, even more so than the two young gentlemen who called today! However, I cannot feel it is a certainty, unless he actually proposes to me."

"Then we will all hope that you receive the proposal you desire," Elizabeth said softly, and Frederick nodded. He felt a lump in his throat at the thought of his sister going off to live as a married woman relatively soon, after a time for an engagement. Still, he wanted Julia to be happy, which she deserved to be.

Darcy and Frederick rose, and Elizabeth came over to sit by her. Julia gave her a small smile and rested her head on her mother's shoulder, but her eyes remained dry.

However, all was not completely calm inside her, as it turned out. That afternoon, Julian Tunney paid a call, but as planned, Julia did not receive him. The broad-shouldered Jordan, filling the doorway, stated that she was unable to have visitors and bid him good day without even letting him step inside the front door. Julian Tunney left slowly, abashed and dispirited. Julia had barely swallowed her indignation at his nerve in calling upon her after she'd made it clear she did not desire his attentions, when she was caught off guard.

Looking out a window, she saw Simon Easton strolling on this side of the square with his sister Pamela. It almost looked as if they would stop to call, but in the end they kept walking up the street. Still, it was enough to rattle Julia. Her confidence deserting her, she ran to her mother, who was discussing something with Mrs. Winston.

Elizabeth rose when she saw Julia's expression. "Julia! Whatever is the matter?"

"Mother," she begged wildly, "lock me up, please, I beg of you! I cannot take any more young gentlemen right now, even if they visit with their sisters accompanying them or not!" She sounded petulant, which she rarely was. "Today I have reached the end of my patience, for I cannot stand to see another young man, save one. Please lock me in my room and tell everyone I am indisposed. Please, Mother!" she pleaded.

Elizabeth hugged her, stroking her hair, and trying to calm her down. Over Julia's curls, she exchanged an amused but understanding look with Mrs. Winston. "There, there, Julia, I admit so much has happened in such a short time that it is no wonder you might feel overwrought; but no matter." She kissed her daughter's forehead and released her. "By all means, do go upstairs and rest for a while, and I promise to keep callers – gentlemen or otherwise – at bay all afternoon." Julia nodded and tried to smile. "Yet, if a certain gentleman should call, and I believe I know his identity, I will send Emma up to you to see if you wish to receive him." Elizabeth smiled. "Now, please go off to rest or do whatever pleases you, and everything will be fine, I know it."

"Yes, Mother. Thank you." Julia curtsied to them both and went upstairs. She slipped out of her dress and lay down to sleep on her bed. She fell asleep as she prayed for her desire to come true. She would awake refreshed later, in time for dinner.

Two more days passed, in which Jane Elizabeth received a call each day from Sir Timothy and Catharina Carlisle. Jane Elizabeth was delighted with their attentions, and she was granted permission to attend a concert of Berlioz at the Academy of Music with Mrs. Winston and the Carlisles later in the week. As Jane Elizabeth, Miss Carlisle, and Mrs. Winston chatted over refreshments, Sir Timothy requested to speak with Darcy in his study about the possibility of a formal court-ship of Jane Elizabeth. Sir Timothy was honest, telling him he had originally favored Julia, but realized that young lady's interests seemed centered on another man. Though a little younger, Jane Elizabeth and he shared many interests, and he had become quite enamored and protective of her in a very short time. He also remarked upon the difference in their ages – he was twenty-five years of age, while Jane Elizabeth was a tender sixteen – but he was not in any hurry, assuming Jane Elizabeth would accept his attentions and want them to con-tinue. Clearing his throat, Sir Timothy went on to point out that Julia was almost eighteen, and the man thought to be interested in asking for her hand was twenty-six.

Darcy told him he appreciated his comments but would not speculate on the success of either his suit, or Julia's prob-able one. Again, Darcy told him the success of his proposal lay with Jane Elizabeth, based upon her own feelings and wishes. If she welcomed Sir Timothy's courting, Darcy would pre-fer a longer engagement to a shorter one, perhaps two years in length, instead of just one year, due to her tender age. Sir Timothy nodded in agreement with a smile, and Darcy wished him success.

Meanwhile, Julia was still waiting for word of one desired

visitor. She wasn't impatient by nature, and seemed lively and untroubled enough, but Elizabeth did notice hints of uncertainty in the corners of her eyes as the second day dragged into a third.

She was reading in her room upstairs when Emma knocked and entered. "Miss Julia!" The maid could not keep the excitement out of her voice. "There is a gentleman caller downstairs asking for you. Miss, it is Lord Ravenswood!"

Julia jumped up. "Oh, how wonderful!" she exclaimed, as her heart sang. "I will be ready in one minute! No, two – just let me see." She ran over to her vanity table and fussed over her appearance, which was perfect as usual. With a smile reaching to her eyes, she followed Emma downstairs to the drawing room. Before she reached the bottom step, however, a sudden thought gave her a quiver of delight. She thought she would give him whatever he asked of her, but first she was going to tease him for making her wait so long for this visit! She neutralized her expression and, composed, entered the drawing room and drew the door closed behind her.

Lord Ravenswood rose and bowed deeply to her. She noted the rich blue velvet of his coat, his fine lawn trousers and gleaming black boots, and the colorful elegance of his cravat and immaculate waistcoat. She sank to the floor in her curtsey, and the color in her cheeks rose as she did to her feet. Yet her features remained impassive.

"Miss Darcy."

"Lord Ravenswood."

They traded inquiries after their health and that of their families. Julia sat down and gestured for him to do so. He did and immediately leaned forward; but she spoke before he could.

"Your call brings me great pleasure," she said, "though I seem to remember that you expressed your intention to visit before today." She put her hands in her lap and looked at him.

Lord Ravenswood's eyes registered consternation, his brows knitting, while his face drooped ever so slightly; he had not expected this reaction from her. Clearing his throat, he managed, "I am glad you welcome my call, and I apologize that I have not over the last few days." He fingered the baby red rose in his boutonnière and looked down. "I still thank you for receiving me today." He made a half-effort to rise from his chair. "However, if I have called at an inopportune time –"

Julia's playful teasing gave way to regret as she saw the wounded look in his eyes; they appeared as tragic as she had seen Frederick's. "Please stay, my lord," she said, touching his elegant sleeve, and finally gave him a smile. "I apologize if I seemed indifferent or insensitive to you," she said. "Is there something you wanted to tell me?"

He seemed to relax and almost smiled. "Well, yes, there is." He fingered the flower again as he collected his thoughts, then returned his gaze to her, one now steady and sincere, neither hurt nor desperate.

"Miss Darcy," he said, quiet but earnest, "I have taken the liberty to ask to speak to you alone first in this room. I hope it does not cause you any concern."

She had noticed, but it did not. "No, I am quite at ease this moment." She cleared her throat. "Before you do, shall I ring for some refreshments?"

"No thank you, Miss Darcy, for I came to discuss something with you." She nodded and waited for him to continue. "First, I would sincerely like to apologize for not having called upon you as I intended – and promised – for several days now." He shook his head. "I was detained by some estate business in Hampshire and had to travel there and back over the last few days. I am glad to say that everything that unfortunately claimed my attention from you has been successfully concluded, but I am most abjectly sorry for not sending word to you, and appearing to be inconstant in my attentions."

She smiled sweetly. "There is no need to apologize, Lord Ravenswood. But I am very happy to receive you today in such fine health and circumstances." She swore to herself that she would hear him out, and not tease him about anything more.

He smiled, but at first could not continue. He looked down, but when he looked up and at her again, her heart thudded inside. For young Louis Calvert, Lord Ravenswood, looked passionate.

"I had asked you not to call me 'Lord Ravenswood,' or address me as 'my lord,' when we are alone together, do you remember?" he asked in a soft, caressing voice. "And I believe you agreed you would not, after I obtained permission from your father to call upon you...which I have." His eyes gently blinking, he leaned forward. "Today, I have come to declare my love for you, Miss Darcy – Julia – and ask for your hand." He quickly dropped to his knees, while her heart soared. "Miss Darcy, I love you more than life itself. Will you make me the happiest of men and accept my hand in marriage?"

At first she could not answer, but then rose, smiling, and lifted him to his feet. "I ask you for your love, your regard, and your protection." She took his hand and kissed it. He shuddered with joy, as a huge smile lit up his face. "For I love *you* more than life itself, and I would like to live the rest of my life with you. So, yes, Lord Ravenswood, I do accept your hand in marriage most gladly and firmly, without any reservations!"

He gasped out his joy and thanks, fell to his knees again, and kissed both her hands. She knelt with him, and his lips gently brushed hers. He heard her give a warm, satisfied sound, and felt flushed and giddy all over. They held each other in happy silence for several moments. Finally she spoke, tingling all over.

"Will you then be going to speak with my father?"

He gave a happy sound. "Yes, I will, after this time together. I think – I hope – that he is expecting me."

She smiled up at him. "I think he and Mother are. Frederick will be so pleased too, for has very high regard for you."

He thanked her. "Frederick will be my dearest brother, and Cecilia will be ecstatic, for she has nothing but the highest regard for you."

She smiled and they gently kissed, longer this time. He held her, but did not move his hands around. He was careful not to, but that helped bring up one of the two points he needed to mention to her, before he talked to her father.

"Julia?"

"Yes, Louis?"

She felt warmth of pleasure ripple through his beautiful clothes. "I would like to ask you something."

"Please do so."

He hesitated only a moment. "I asked for your hand, and you have accepted me. But do you truly have no hesitation? I only ask, my dearest Julia, my dear fiancée – because you saw what I did to Lawson after he tried to force himself on you."

Her eyes half-closed, but her voice remained steady. "Oh, please, Louis, let us not mar our beautiful moments on such a wonderful day as this by mentioning him." She gave him a steady, firm, but not displeased, glance. "As I told you that day, you rescued and saved me, and I do not blame you, fear you, or criticize you for what you did." She put her finger under his chin and pressed her lips on his. He almost moaned, but stroked her hand. "So my dearest Louis, dearest fiancé," she said, "let us forget about him forever, and I repeat that I accept you and your love without hesitation."

"Oh, Julia," he burst out, "thank you for your understanding! How I love you and your sweetness!" He dared not kiss her lips again, so he kissed her hands instead. "I have been so envious and resentful of all the other young gentlemen who paid you attention! I know it is weak and ridiculous of me, but I wanted to push them all aside! I knew I could not, if I wanted your love, and I do most ardently. I wanted you to come to love me, not have me stride over, declare myself as if I were declaiming in public, and expect you to accept me!" Shaking his head, he laughed. "Yes, I, the great lord, was envious of the others – Sir Timothy, Lawson, even young Easton, to name three, even though this is part of holding debut seasons! I was frustrated because I always seemed to be anticipated by some other man, for dances or even a chance to chat with you. I felt I had to hold back, behave myself, and be patient. I did not want to." He looked at her in such a way that her heart melted; she longed to touch him all over and make him moan, music to her ears. "After what Lawson did to you – there I go mentioning his name again – I knew that I couldn't wait! A few visits a week were not going to be enough to satisfy me. I wanted you always and forever, and I had to know if you would accept me!"

"Well, now you will have me always and forever." They reached for each other and shared a long, passionate kiss, both making pleasing sounds. They held each other for several moments, but finally separated.

"It is now time for me to go speak with your father," he said in a shaky voice, and laughed. He mopped his face and neck, but he gave her the red rose from his boutonnière.

She gave him a radiant smile, kissed her finger, and touched it to his lips. "Then please do so, the sooner the better," she said, as he grinned. Her eyes shining, she kissed the rose and cradled it in her hands.

"I take my leave for now, Julia, my love!" He bowed to her. "How I love you!"

"I love you too, Louis." She gently guided him towards the door. "Now go speak with Father and come back to me as soon as you can."

In turn, Sir Timothy called on Jane Elizabeth, this time without Catharina, and offered his hand to her; she quickly, joyfully accepted him. They would have a two-year engagement but weren't concerned since the time would be filled with mutual joy and many embraces. Another wave of happiness surged through the townhouse.

The following afternoon, Frederick came up the front steps from the square and entered the front hall; he'd just returned from a lengthy lecture on crop rotation that his father recommend he attend at the Royal Society. He had been congratulating himself on taking so many notes over the last two hours, but immediately heard excited chatter coming from the main drawing room; so, handing Jordan his coat and bound journal, he went in to find Julia and Jane excitedly laying out plates, utensils, and edibles for tea.

"Your timing is perfect," Julia exclaimed, "for we are almost ready to ring for everyone to come and have their tea. Did you enjoy the lecture?"

He considered her question. "Well, it was rather long and tedious at times, but the subject was quite interesting, one that Father thinks will benefit Pemberley in the future; that is why he wanted me to attend, and I can show him all the notes I took." He looked at their cheerful faces. "It is good to be back home nonetheless!"

"I am certain you shall sleep well tonight after that long lecture," Jane Elizabeth observed, which made him grin.

"How was your afternoon?" His sisters exchanged a glance and started giggling. "I can't remember a single thing I did," Julia laughed. "I must have done something, but I don't seem to recall what it was."

Jane was still smiling. "I think I sat in the window seat and looked out over the square."

Frederick was amused. "All afternoon?" he asked, and she nodded rather sheepishly. "I think I can hazard a guess as to the reason for your forgetfulness, or distraction." He grinned wider.

It was Julia's turn to appear amused, as Jane's expression registered surprise. "And what might that be?"

"You both have been thinking only about your engagements!" He laughed, but not in a cruel manner.

"And what is wrong with that?" Jane countered.

"Nothing at all," he feigned surprise, "for I am sure it was a pleasurable way to pass the afternoon!" He was still smiling as Julia giggled and Jane looked a bit puzzled. "Especially since the subjects of your reverie are two excellent gentlemen, Lord Ravenswood and Sir Timothy!" Jane gasped as Julia covered her mouth to suppress a giggle. He tried to make his expression as pleasant as he could. "As the next Master of Pemberley, I cannot be more pleased and approving of your choices! Again, I say happiness and congratulations to you both!"

"Frederick!" Jane almost shrieked and threw a tea towel at him. "How dare you!"

"Don't you want my approval?" He couldn't help himself and started laughing. Julia had buried her face in a sofa cushion; she successfully muffled any sounds she might make, but her heaving shoulders betrayed her.

"Here is what I think of your approval!" Jane heaved two more towels at him, and then threw a sofa cushion that bounced off his waistcoat.

"Jane, don't!" Julia tried to protest, but she was laughing too hard, and her words were barely understandable. "You're making a mess of the tea all over the drawing room!"

"I do not care!" Jane glared at both of them, as Frederick tried to pick up all the items from the plush, dark carpet. Weak from laughing, he managed to pile the cushion and towels on the tea cart, then knelt down in front of Jane, spreading his hands, palms forward, in surrender.

"I – I was just teasing you, Jane," he gasped out. "I didn't mean it."

"You had better not have meant it." Holding another cushion, Jane was still glaring, but she watched him waving his hands, and Julia still giggling. Finally, Jane's expression lightened and relaxed, and she began to giggle herself.

Frederick gave a weak grin. "Peace?"

"Yes, Brother."

He rose and went over to take her hand. "I really can't be happier for both of you." She thanked him, then gave him a hug and a kiss.

Julia had almost regained her composure, but managed a shaky smile as she also thanked him. "Now let's ring for every-one to come in for tea." She had neatened all the tea items and listened for approaching footfalls as she suppressed a final giggle.

CHAPTER 25

The Darcy household remained in a happy uproar over both Julia's and Jane Elizabeth's engagements. Jane Elizabeth's with Sir Timothy would last a couple of years, until she turned eighteen, to which both parties were agreeable. Darcy was more flexible over Julia's because she was the eldest but, happy as she was loving Louis, Lord Ravenswood, and receiving his love in return, she was satisfied that her own would last at least a year. Neither gentleman appeared disappointed or impatient with these arrangements; both young men were content to cultivate their newfound love for their fiancées and would try to control their impulses to contrive ways to spend time alone with them.

The day soon arrived when Frederick, along with his entire family, was expected to appear at St. James' Palace for his elevation. As it approached, Frederick realized he was anxious – no, downright nervous – over the prospect. It was a great honor to be awarded a baronetcy, especially at his young age and with his father still living, in fine health. However, since Frederick had worried about acquitting himself well as Master of Pemberley from time to time, now he worried whether he would always behave as he should, considering his rank. He knew he did not deserve this honor, so would he be able to earn it during his years of manhood?

Frederick even worried about the ceremony itself, brief though it would be. He had confused the baronetcy with knighthood, and worried about the accolade to come, for he thought the King would rest a sword on one shoulder, then the other. For two nights in a row, vivid dreams disturbed him. He imagined the sword slipping and wounding him in the chest, as if he were unworthy and compromised. Logically Frederick did not think the Sovereign so clumsy or vicious as to run him through, but it still disturbed his sleep and extended into his waking hours. Darcy and Elizabeth could see his disquiet, so his father had a long talk with him in his study to discover what was troubling him. Frederick felt relieved when his father told him there would be no accolade, no swords, just the presentation of his badge of rank, and comments from His Majesty. Frederick's thoughts now swung in the positive direction; he hoped his new status would guide him and his descendants throughout their lives, and he admitted that he liked the sound of his title. Frederick also knew he must not become conceited or arrogant over it; so now he only worried that his behavior and responses would be perfect during the ceremony.

Now they were all standing at attention before the dais, shining in their finery, in a small reception room in the palace. Small? It was the size of Pemberley's main dining room, and there were many liveried guards about. Frederick steeled himself as the appointed moment arrived. His Majesty, King William the Fourth, entered, along with Queen Adelaide, Princess Victoria, the Heir Presumptive, the Duchess of Kent, her mother, and their ladies, and even more liveried servants. The members of the audience made their respective bows and curtsies.

The King looked at all of them. Formal introductions would be made after the brief ceremony, but he noticed the young gentleman, his parents, and all his siblings, including the oldest daughter, who as his niece had informed him was a stunningly beautiful creature. He also noted a pleasant, graceful woman who was the companion of one of the other daughters. He was amused by the actions – or lack of them – from the two youngest children. The boy looked nervous, though liveliness, maybe even mischief, showed in his eyes, and the little girl looked as self-possessed and regal as his royal niece.

Now the King focused on the young man. Frederick Darcy clearly resembled his father Fitzwilliam, the Master of Pemberley. The King felt pleased, because elevating the son would be like conferring an honor on the father, and the entire family by extension. Victoria's comment about how the elder Mr. Darcy had supported his Reform Bill had borne much fruit. Well, no matter, the King thought. He examined the younger Darcy, who kept his glance lowered but did not flinch. The King could see that the realm's newest baronet, Sir Frederick Darcy, would be a fine-looking man all his life, as his father appeared to be now.

The King decided he liked what he saw in the young man, for he appeared dependable. Intelligent. Capable. Conscientious. Able to handle responsibility, but not arrogant, callow, or immature like many other fellows of his age and class. Perhaps he did appear anxious and not entirely sure of himself. King William wasn't certain how well he would survive as a raw recruit on a naval ship, but he liked the earnestness and sensitivity he saw in his face. Well, the young fellow was not yet twenty years of age, so the King thought that he might develop more confidence in a short while.

It was time. King William set his gaze and cleared his throat. "Mr. Darcy, Sir, please approach the dais." Frederick complied, and bowed to him, Queen Adelaide, Princess Victoria, and the Duchess.

At the King's signal, a liveried, white-wigged servant approached. The man opened a large, flat case, and the King lifted a star-like badge from the velvet-lined interior with his gloved hands. He approached Frederick and placed the badge over his bowed head. King William barely got the blue, white, and red ribbon on which the badge hung around all the thick hair, but the ribbon turned out to be long enough. "I now pronounce you to be Sir Frederick Darcy," he said. Frederick made another deep bow, and then the King spoke again.

"It is traditional to say a few well-chosen words," His Majesty said, and Frederick straightened. "Ahem! Sir Frederick, you are now a baronet of the realm. We are very grateful for your recent assistance in preventing the Heir Presumptive, our royal niece, from coming to harm." Princess Victoria favored Frederick with a brief, direct gaze. "Much as we are grateful to you, we do not make this elevation lightly; it is not as if you are being awarded a prize in a competition." The King's eyes, firm but not unkind, bored into Frederick's. "With such an elevation comes responsibility, from you as well as your direct descendants, for this baronetcy is a hereditary one. A baronet must live up to his rank and act in ways that show the recipient's gratitude for, and merit of it." Frederick gave a firm nod. He wanted to lower his gaze, but the King kept a firm eye on him. "All this is expected of you, young sir. However, we charge you with one additional responsibility." Frederick did not dare to look about him, but he could detect a hint of interest rippling through the room. "Our charge is this – that you remain under personal obligation to the Sovereign, whether it is I, or the Heir Presumptive when she is Queen in her own right – have we need of your assistance. Do we have your understanding and acceptance of this responsibility?" Frederick nodded again and swallowed. "We largely feel that your responsibility in this regard, should you need to perform it, will come at our royal niece's request when she reigns as Queen." He paused. "Remember, Sir Frederick, as you now are, that the new Sovereign may call upon you at any point during your lifetime, and that you will fly to her and offer any and all assistance of which you are physically, financially, and intellectually capable to aid Her Majesty. Again, we ask you, do you accept this responsibility?"

Frederick nodded yet again and replied, "Yes, your Majesty, I do accept this responsibility. I thank you for this honor, this elevation, and your trust in my loyalty to the Crown, as well as my abilities. I promise to serve my Sovereign and my country faithfully, with my life, and every fiber of my being; I will not forget the promises I make today." He looked into the King's eyes and was relieved to see approval.

"Good man, Sir Frederick." King William smiled and briefly

touched him on his shoulder. Queen Adelaide gave a pleased smile, while the Duchess was looking down in a frozen stance. "Now let us have your family presented to us." The King and the royal party stepped down from the dais so the introductions could take place.

Though she maintained her perfect, proper demeanor, Princess Victoria could not be happier. Not only had her uncle the King made good on his promise to elevate young Mr. Darcy – now Sir Frederick – with alacrity, but she was also impressed with the young man's efficient speech. How fine, strong, and capable he sounded, far from the sorely tried, nervous young fellow who was trying to get rid of that bumbling, drunken oaf at the Earl of Sheffield's ball, even if the offender had turned out to be Lord Hartford's son.

Princess Victoria could not help smiling when Julia Darcy was presented to her. "How wonderful it is to see you again, Miss Darcy," she said, as Julia sank to the ground in front of her. "We trust that you have had an enjoyable and memorable season here in London."

"I have, your Royal Highness, most definitely so!"

Princess Victoria favored her with another comment. "May we also congratulate you and your sister on your engagements?" She turned to Miss Jane Darcy, who gave her as deep and perfect a curtsey as Julia had. "We understand that we have the pleasure of greeting the future Countess Ravenswood and Lady Carlisle. Congratulations and best wishes for your happiness!" The sisters could not be more gracious in their thanks.

The youngest boy and girl seemed awed into silence. Nicholas Darcy bowed carefully and barely got out his greeting to her, but Victoria did not mind in the least. She would later remember how he fared better with her uncle the King, when they traded remarks about cricket and other sports. She liked Miss Anne Darcy's reserve, but she also wished to put her at ease. "And what interests you, Miss Darcy?" she asked.

Anne thought a moment before replying to her future Queen. "I enjoy attending the Royal Society lectures, and I would like to attend university, even if it is abroad."

Exchanging a glance with her mother and her aunt, the Queen, Victoria blinked and said, "Well, that is a very fine goal, and we wish you all success in reaching it. We are confident your father and brother, Sir Frederick, will help you attain it. Perhaps we can also find members of Parliament who are sympathetic and interested in supporting education for young women." Anne nodded eagerly and curtsied perfectly.

As they moved away, Queen Adelaide remarked good-naturedly, "A worthy endeavor, my dear niece, even for that remarkable little girl. But do go patiently with your uncle the King if you do intend to broach the subject with him. Persuading him to elevate the young man is one thing; an Education Bill for young women, though more than admirable, is quite another."

"Yes, Aunt." Princess Victoria nodded, then moved on to greet Mr. and Mrs. Darcy.

<h1 style="text-align:center">CHAPTER 26</h1>

A few weeks later, Frederick had returned to Cambridge and was dining with his friends at their favorite eating house, Tudbury's. Having just finished a sumptuous feast, they were leaning back in their chairs, waistcoats expanded and cravats loose, and savoring the contentedness at being full, while they took pulls from their tankards.

"Ah, fellows," Frederick sighed happily, "how good it is to see you all again."

"A toast to the new baronet, Sir Frederick," Alex commanded, and Eric and Andrew Staunton followed suit.

Frederick was touched and grateful. "Here's a toast to friendship, and health and happiness for us!" He was glad they were all together; Frederick was eager for them to meet John Woodleigh, who might end up joining their close circle. His friends gave loud assents and drank some more ale, but kept their exuberance and volume in check, lest they attract the ire and disapproval of the proprietor and other patrons. Still, they were enjoying themselves, and had reached the stage where almost anything that was said would cause them to break out into laughter.

"You know, *Sir* Frederick," Eric grinned at him, "I still cannot believe all that has happened to you in such a short time! Who'd have thought so much would have occurred during a London season?"

"Well, it did," Frederick countered, "and didn't I tell you not to address me as 'Sir Frederick'? We are friends, after all!"

"Here he is, a baronet, and he's acting with all kinds of republican tendencies," groused Eric, but couldn't hold onto his scowl. "What is the matter? Still not used to it?"

"No, in fact," Frederick laughed, "I am not; and I really do fear that, if I strut around, all puffed up and insisting people address me as Sir Frederick, someone will end up chucking me into the muddiest part of the Cam." This caused another burst of laughter.

"Your concern is appropriate, Frederick, and well-founded," grinned Staunton, the oldest of them all. "Though I am certain that you will find ways of confounding and checking Master Haydock by using it in his presence."

"I intend to," he replied, and they all laughed again.

After a moment, they exchanged grins and Alex ordered another round. Frederick did not mind, for classes did not begin for another two days and he would be well-rested and sober by then.

"So, tell us again about this singular London season that has resulted in your elevation." Eric could not let it go. "I am still a little unclear on how it all unfolded."

"You are also a little unclear on a few other subjects after two full tankards," Alex remarked without heat. "Here's a third; now drink and listen up."

Eric thanked him with a murderous look as Frederick laughed. "It is as I told you. Richard's sisters Susannah and Isabelle were making their debuts. Unfortunately, from the moment we first met each other in public, he began taunting me, and escalated it to include both my sisters Julia and Jane Elizabeth; then his sister Isabelle and Ron Urquhart, our other former friend, joined in." Frederick shrugged. "It finally became so awful because they carried it too far; Richard insulted our entire family and spread false rumors about Julia, trying to give her a reputation."

"That blackguard!" snarled Alex. "So that is how the fight came about at the Ventnors' ball."

"Yes. Julia was extremely upset, and we were trying to get her and Jane Elizabeth away from Richard and Isabelle but, unfortunately, we walked right into them as we were trying to leave the ballroom." Shaking his head, Frederick closed his eyes. "Richard insulted Julia to her face and refused to apologize. Even Susannah Grantley and Ron's sister Rachel were upset by then. But that is how I lost my temper, started the fight, and helped wreck a corner of Lady Ventnor's ballroom." He stared hard into his ale. "To the extent of sixty-three pounds worth of damage."

"And knocked out two of Grantley's teeth, no less," Andrew approved, and patted his arm. "Frederick, I must say this – in all truth, Henry would have been very proud of all you did, protecting and defending your sisters, as well as fighting Grantley."

Eyes watery, Frederick clasped his hand. "Thank you, Andrew." He swallowed hard. "That means a great deal to me."

"I was most sincere, Sir Frederick," Andrew teased. Frederick groaned loudly and drank down a lot of ale, while the others laughed, the lightness of the evening restored. "In fact, you will be happy to know that with the masters' approval, I have already engaged three students to meet with you so you can begin tutoring this term in Latin and composition, most likely with more to follow."

Frederick groaned again, but this time he smiled. "Thank goodness, for I must begin paying off some of those sixty-odd pounds I owe the Ventnors!"

"Sixty-three pounds, four shillings, and a sixpence," Alex recited. "Will the Ventnors charge interest on this sum, Sir Frederick?" They roared with laughter as he dropped his head on his outstretched arms. "Good God, I hope not," they heard him mutter.

"Then please continue with the story, Frederick," Eric said cheerfully, and patted his arm. Frederick straightened up somewhat and took another swig of ale, wiping his mouth on the back of his hand. His head was starting to bother him, but he knew he would not be allowed to order any lemon water until he finished his tankard.

"Well, Father and Mother, and most of the *ton* – were furious with us – with *me* – for fighting in public, and we were both threatened with incarceration if we misbehaved again.

For three days I was confined to my room and lectured on how to behave as a gentleman, something not inevitable in their eyes. I am quite serious, Alex, so please stop laughing! As I was saying, I had been strictly ordered to behave myself no matter what. Then, three days later at the Earl of Sheffield's ball, everything turned upside down." Frederick drank some more ale. "Richard was there, of course. He was trying to behave himself, I will allow, but he was quite drunk early in the evening. Then Her Royal Highness and her party arrived, and there were presentations."

"That is when you retrieved her fan," Alex said.

"That is correct. Julia was quite giddy over it, though I didn't think all that much about it at the time. However, a little while later, Richard encountered us at a refreshment table. He started criticizing me for the whole thing and told us how he could have done it all better himself."

"Worthless bounder," Eric interjected.

"And rude as well," Frederick replied. "He splashed wine all over me, but he was so drunk by then that he looked quite ill. I was trying to get him outside with the help of others when who should approach, but the entire royal party! I could have cheerfully died at that moment – the look on Princess Victoria's face when she saw Richard's condition was indescribable, even priceless! Still, he tried to bow to her, but lost his balance."

"That's when you knocked him out of the way," Andrew said.

"Yes," Frederick grimaced. "We managed to get him outside, but it took six of us to do it, with him struggling all the way. And the mess he made!" Now Frederick was laughing. "All of us ended up dressed in the fine clothes of the Earl's sons!"

"I wish I could have seen Mr. Stoddard dump that pitcher of water all over Grantley," Eric said gleefully, and they all laughed.

"So where is Richard now?" Alex asked.

"I believe he is just about to arrive in Jamaica, at the family plantation to which he has been exiled."

"Do you think that will improve himself and his habits any?" Andrew asked.

Frederick shrugged. "I do not know, but I am willing to wager that he has probably 'fed the fishes' twice a night on his voyage over, since he left England." Another roar of laughter.

"So, out of gratitude for protecting the Heir Presumptive from bodily harm – even if it was a surly lout like Grantley – you are now Sir Frederick Darcy, young baronet," smiled Alex.

"Well, yes I am," Frederick laughed, "even though I still cannot believe it."

"You deserve it," Eric said. "You protected the Princess from harm and dealt with that oaf Richard at most difficult moments."

Andrew raised more toasts to Frederick, who blushed. "We should also toast the health and happiness of your sisters!" They did so, which pleased and gratified him. "This is quite a family you have, Frederick. There are you yourself, the newly minted Sir Frederick," he said in a serious tone, so his friend did not flinch, "along with the future Countess Ravenswood and Lady Carlisle. Pray tell us, what do you think the future has in store for young Nicholas and Anne?"

Frederick smiled. "I honestly cannot say. That also applies to little Henry David, and our new brother or sister who is expected to be born in December." More toasts followed, until they had finished all their ale but did not desire more.

It was now late in the evening and Tudbury's looked as if it would be closing for the night. They all stirred and tried to ensure their legs were steady beneath them, though Alex and Andrew seemed the steadiest.

"Come, fellows," Alex offered. "It is time for us to return to our dormitory rooms, and you, Staunton, to yours on St. George's Lane."

"You are correct, Alex, for it is time I got myself home." Andrew rose slowly from the table. He gently pulled Frederick's arm. "Frederick, let us go with Eric and the others. Remember that we are all supposed to pay a call on good friends of mine tomorrow afternoon."

"Yes," Frederick remembered, blinking. They all trailed out into the street after leaving a generous tip behind them.

"I will bring the carriage by Newnham at two o'clock," Andrew said.

"We will be ready," Eric promised, and with that, they exchanged farewells and split up for the night.

Somehow Eric and Alex had put on a slight burst of speed and were soon out of sight, as Frederick stumbled along to the door of Newnham in the silent, black night. He could hardly make out details of the street or the house. He had barely entered the front hall when a rustling figure appeared to block his advance.

Of course, it was Jeremiah Ridgeson; still fully attired, the dormitory master held a small candelabra that did little to dispel the interior's darkness. In his happy, relaxed, dulled state, Frederick couldn't help smiling; too numbed and calm to react further, Frederick simply wished him a good evening.

The master sniffed. "You are late in returning, Mr. Darcy."

Frederick grinned. "Forgive me, Mr. Ridgeson, but I am *Sir* Frederick Darcy."

The master's eyes bulged, and he did not reply for several moments. "Sir Frederick, you say?" he swallowed, with a nettled expression. "I do not accept such pretensions from my wards, young sir! I take my responsibilities very seriously."

"I see." Frederick paused. "However, you must accept my status as a baronet. Shall I show you my letter of elevation from His Majesty?"

Ridgeson struggled to speak through a coughing fit. "Er, no, *Sir* Frederick," he managed. "That will not be necessary." His beady eyes narrowed in the dim gleam from the candles. "You are still about quite late this night."

"So I am," Frederick observed, shrugging. "It is time I gained my chamber so that I can prepare to retire for the night. May I thus be permitted?"

The master jerked his head down and indicated Frederick step towards the staircase; he could see the master's face darken even in the house's lack of light. Frederick smiled and climbed to his welcome rest, satisfied to hear the door to the master's ground-floor chambers slam shut.

Andrew was as good as his word and, the following day, all four young gentlemen were being conveyed to a handsome brick house in a prosperous neighborhood. Frederick thought he had seen hints of a drooping nose and slack jaw peering from an upper window, but shrugged it away with pleasant musings. Though well rested from the previous night's pleasures, calm and composed, if not that energetic, suddenly Frederick recollected upon whom they were calling.

"Are we not paying a call upon the Woodleighs?"

"We certainly are, Frederick."

He smiled ruefully. "Well, here is my first real social test. I suppose I must be introduced as 'Sir Frederick Darcy.'"

"You suppose correctly!" Andrew grinned. "Now, do not be concerned about it, for you will soon be used to such social introductions."

"Right." Frederick half-smiled but lapsed into silence.

In the end, it lasted only a few moments. All four of them were received into the elegant, comfortable house, and welcomed by fellow student John Woodleigh, who was the same age as Frederick, Alex, and Eric. Young Mr. Woodleigh, in turn, introduced them to his mother, Mrs. Woodleigh, and his older brothers Peter and Howard, all of whom Frederick remembered from the recent London season. Proper greetings were exchanged all around, and then John Woodleigh spoke up, a bit eagerly.

"Sir Frederick," he addressed him, "please allow me to present our sister, Miss Rosamund." When the two of them caught sight of each other, they stopped, smiled, and broke their mutual glances for only a second; but it was enough for everyone in the room.

"Yes, Miss Woodleigh," Frederick said, smiling and bowing deeply to her. "What a great pleasure it is to meet you again so soon."

She curtsied deeply to him in return. "As I am to meet you again, Sir Frederick."

Andrew concealed a smile while Mrs. Woodleigh and John beamed; and Peter and Howard, and Alex and Eric, all exchanged glances.

CHAPTER 27

EPILOGUE

The day before his classes in the new term began, Frederick reported to the headmaster's stuffy, cluttered chambers to receive his instructions. Frederick still felt some trepidation about the meeting, but his spirits were high. He knocked on the stout door and entered. "Sir Frederick Darcy reporting to you as requested, Mr. Haydock."

The headmaster's head jerked up. "*What?*" he roared.

Frederick cleared his throat. "Respectfully, Mr. Haydock, I may now be addressed as Sir –"

"I heard you the first time!" snapped Julius Haydock. With a black look, he continued, "I do not believe you, nor did I think you capable of such silly dramatics! I warn you, young man, do not waste my valuable time with such fantastic tales!"

Frederick sighed. "I assure you, Sir, that it is true." He had expected this reaction. "My father directed me to give you this letter, and I believe it will address any doubts you may have on the matter."

Haydock snatched the letter from him and broke the seal, after he made a point of examining it. The headmaster read it all the way through, then let the pages fall from his hands to the desktop. He glared at Frederick. "Such presumption," he began, and choked. "The *insolence!*" he exclaimed, trying again. He leaned back in his chair to find Frederick looking at him with a calm, neutral gaze. He continued to fume for several moments, then suddenly leaned forward, transfixing him with a dire glare and an accusing finger. "All right, *Sir* Frederick, congratulations, very well done and all that!" he snapped. "That is more than enough, for I will not give you anything more. Let me remind you, my dear young baronet, that I am still Headmaster of this university! And baronet or not, *you* are still expected to master your studies and obey all the university's rules. Is that clear?" he bellowed, pounding the desk. "Sir Frederick," he added in a calmer tone.

"It is very clear, of course, Mr. Haydock."

"How glad I am to hear it," growled the headmaster. "What is more, I shall take this opportunity to remind you of your duties and responsibilities as a baronet, which your father summarized in his letter. You have not only been elevated to the baronetcy, but it is also a very great honor, a hereditary title, and not one to be sullied by you," he growled again, "or your descendants." He cleared his throat. "You also fall under a special obligation to the Crown, and you are compelled to go and report to His Majesty if summoned. Of course, we can adjust your classes and examination schedule to fit any such royal mandates. Ahem!" He glared at him again. "I trust you understand these grave and important responsibilities of yours. Manhood and the equivalent of knighthood go hand in hand! I remind you not only of these responsibilities, but also of your illustrious family – you must carry out your duties and not disappoint or shame them! I repeat, I hope you understand how permanent and binding this all is, Sir Frederick!"

Frederick's eyes had glazed over, but he replied evenly and carefully enough. "Thank you for reminding me as you have, Mr. Haydock, but His Majesty the King has already instructed me on all my responsibilities now and in the future, as well as to their importance." He looked over at the empurpled headmaster.

Still glaring, Mr. Haydock took several moments to calm himself and reclaim his booming voice. "Very well, Sir Frederick," he finally said in a steely, grudging tone, pulling some papers towards him. "Let us now discuss your classes this term."

Julia's debut was officially over, but she enjoyed staying on in London with Jane Elizabeth and Mrs. Winston at Cavendish Square. They continued to attend plays, operas, lectures, and exhibitions, which delighted them all and led to many stimulating discussions. Julia also cultivated the friendships she had begun with several young ladies she had met at the debutante balls. Jane Elizabeth grew to enjoy the company of Sophia Stoddard, Pamela Easton, Cecilia Calvert, Catharina Carlisle, Marcella Exley, Emma Darnley, and Lucinda Peterbrooke. Julia and Jane Elizabeth also socialized often with their Aunt and Uncle Gardiner, and their cousins, especially Clarissa and Henry Staley, and Sir Adam and Lady Wainwright. The sisters spent much time with their fiancés and their families.

About a year later, in June 1837, close to the time of King William's passing and Victoria's accession, at nineteen Julia married Louis, Lord Ravenswood, and became Countess. In the summer of the following year, eighteen-year-old Jane Elizabeth married Sir Timothy Carlisle. When he first started courting her sister, Julia had not been certain that Sir Timothy was the right man for Jane Elizabeth to marry, but over time their love, regard, and interests seemed mutual, so she ended up wishing them the best, and Jane seemed very happy to socialize in artistic, as well as society circles. The shadows of her past mistakes seemed to have faded away, but not before she informed her beloved fiancé of what she had done and all she had suffered. For Sir Timothy, none of it made any difference; it only made him cling more deeply to her and want to protect her as much as he could. His considerations to her were more beautiful than the pink and red roses he sent her almost daily. Mrs. Winston would remain with her as friend and companion into an indefinite future.

Julia basked in the love of her amorous husband and considerate brother, who quickly became close friends. Frederick was quite touched when Louis asked him to stand up with him at their wedding. Louis was happy to discover Julia's desire to travel, and he gladly took her on an extended grand tour of Europe, including Rome, Greece, Constantinople, and even St. Petersburg and Moscow. A couple of years later, they would sail across the Atlantic to tour America, including Boston, New York, Philadelphia, Washington City, Charleston, and as far south as New Orleans.

Back at Pemberley after the London season, Elizabeth continued to perform her duties as Mistress until the time of her confinement was near. Mrs. Reynolds first suggested, then agitated, and finally insisted that she give up her duties until the baby was born – or threatened she would leave Pemberley herself, forever. Shocked, Elizabeth had turned to Darcy, who simply shrugged, stating the housekeeper properly checked them; he could do nothing with her, for she had been like a surrogate mother to him. Before Elizabeth could object, he smiled and asked what they would do in the Great House without the indomitable Mrs. Reynolds. Outnumbered and outmaneuvered, Elizabeth surrendered as gracefully as she could, delegating her duties so she could rest. Truthfully, she would be grateful for her inaction, as she was growing big and uncomfortable with their seventh child. All the wonderful, traditional celebrations were put on hold or reduced, as Elizabeth's labor was expected to begin very close to Christmas.

In the early hours of December 21, 1836, Elizabeth gave birth to a big, healthy baby boy. She and Darcy were ecstatic and named him Thomas Anthony. This time, it took Elizabeth longer to get back on her feet, but as soon as she felt well enough – and Doctor Grantham concurred it was acceptable, with Darcy's stern agreement – she was taking back her duties, one by one, prying them back out from under Mrs. Reynold's more than capable fingers. Henry David, almost two years old, would grow to enjoy his new little playmate, though he was the younger boy's nephew.

Along with the joy of their new son, Darcy and Elizabeth experienced a wonderful reconciliation. Colonel Fitzwilliam missed them and their family and had come to deeply regret the rift he had created between them and his own family. Like Lady Catherine had long ago, the Colonel was suddenly moved to write to Darcy, apologizing profusely for his self-righteous behavior over Henry and Christina's headstone. Darcy, of course, forgave his cousin and encouraged their reconciliation. When the Colonel, Constance, and their sons arrived at Pemberley for the reduced Yuletide celebrations, just before Elizabeth's labor began, Darcy embraced Edmund in front of everyone, the Colonel almost wept, and that was that.

Frederick returned home to Pemberley twice that year after the season ended, first in the fall and then again in December before his mother's confinement. The first time he returned he was able to relax and enjoy being home again, the second time to help his father as much as he could before the birth of his new sibling. During his first visit, his father surprised him when he announced that he had commissioned portraits of all of them, even Jane Elizabeth, Nicholas, and Anne, which would then be displayed in the Portrait Gallery of the Great House. Darcy and Elizabeth especially wanted to capture Frederick's image for the first time in something larger than a miniature, because of his maturity and newly elevated status. His portrait was the first one commissioned and completed.

Not without some feelings of nervousness and unworthiness because of this honor, Frederick was surprised and pleased to look upon himself when the time came. The artist had painted him in his fine black suit, white shirt and cravat, and blue and gold patterned waistcoat, with his baronet's badge hanging from a multicolored ribbon around his neck. Frederick could not remember the man's instructions to him, but now he examined his own rendered expression.

The artist had captured it perfectly – his gaze was capable, thoughtful, and upright, but kind. Frederick felt the artist had probably taken liberties to make his unruly hair look tamed and much more attractive than it really was, but he still blushed at the finished canvas before him, as well as his family's joy over it.

"Why, Frederick," Julia exclaimed, "it is you, to the life! And what a fine look in your eyes!" He could only mumble a response, and blush darker.

"Yes, it is," Elizabeth agreed, and pulled him to her. He blushed harder still, then remembered to thank his parents for such an honor. Later, Darcy would have a brass plate attached to the frame that stated, "Sir Frederick Darcy, aged Nineteen Years [1836]."

When Frederick returned home after yet another completed term in December, the staff were still agog over the young gentleman – his elevation and progress at Cambridge, for they knew his team had won two more debates, and he had taken firsts in Latin and now mathematics. To them, their future young master seemed more confident, but no less fair or considerate for all his successes. Several of them, including Tom Nixley, agreed Frederick resembled his late brother Henry more than he ever had before, and continued to do so as he grew older. And, by the time of Thomas' birth, Frederick had made his first payment to Sir Romanus and Lady Margery Ventnor – nineteen shillings from his own tutoring, and two of the three double sovereigns his parents had given him as a reward for his achievements. He was very proud that, with some pocket change, he managed to reduce his indebtedness to an even fifty-seven pounds by year's end.

That did not stop Nicholas from organizing a surprise for his beloved older brother. One snowy morning, as Frederick strode out onto the terrace in his dark, heavy clothes and boots, Nicholas suddenly shouted, "All hail, Sir Frederick Darcy!"

Then he, Jane Elizabeth, and Anne pelted him with snowballs until he was half-buried in snow. Frederick finally managed to scramble up, snow in his mouth, his face murderous, but even his parents and Julia were laughing. So Frederick began laughing, too, as wet as he had become, striding back up to them in time to drop a fair amount of snow down his brother's back – and trousers, as Nicholas writhed and gasped. His youngest sisters pleaded for mercy, but their backs met the same fate.

Richard Grantley remained in Jamaica for three years following that eventful London season, before returning home to England. He arrived back at Cambridge when Frederick only had two terms left to complete his degree in mathematics and economics. Richard had managed to maintain his friendship with Rod Urquhart, but found that his parents, Lord and Lady Hartford, were still not welcome at Court. While Richard had learned to curb some of his surliness and excessive, licentious habits, he burned with a fierce hatred of Frederick and, indeed, all Darcy blood. Even the sight of his nemesis would fuel Richard's visceral hatred, and he wished Frederick every misfortune possible because of his new title. How could a cowardly, worthless fool like Frederick Darcy deserve to be elevated to the baronetcy? At the very least, Richard and all his family were truly highborn from the beginning! His implacable hatred of the Darcys made him forget that he could be addressed as *Lord* Richard because of his father, an Earl, but Lord Hartford and Richard's older brother Lord Rupert had never encouraged this no matter how much Richard had begged, complained, or sulked. That father and brother were afraid that this form of address, coupled with all of Richard's other regrettable behavior, would be the flashpoint that provoked revolution among the masses.

Richard's sisters fared better, despite the family's unofficial banishment from Court. Julian Tunney had tried to get

Susannah, then Isabelle, interested in him, but neither young lady was attracted to him or his respectable fortune. In the end, Susannah was happy to marry Sir Edward Chatterton, and Isabelle Justin Longford. Richard himself remained unmarried for a long time until he managed to entice a rich young debutante, Miss Henrietta Townsend, to accept him. The extremely unpopular Gregory Lawson emigrated to the West Indies, where he decided to live permanently on his family's plantation, which he populated with many children – some legitimate, some not.

As he matured, Nicholas Darcy grew tall and muscular, and his jaw lengthened so that he came to be considered handsome, with his deep voice, ginger hair and full whiskers, and cheerful demeanor. He never lost his fondness for fun and teasing, but he outgrew his delight at hearing whenever one of his siblings got into trouble, even Thomas, but especially Frederick. Nicholas' love and admiration for his brother continued to grow beyond all he had felt for poor Henry. Nicholas enjoyed being a big brother himself to Henry David and Thomas and taught them to love all kinds of outdoor activities, especially cricket. Nicholas maintained his fierce rivalry in that sport with his cousins Charles and Vincent.

Nicholas grew to enjoy participating in some of the physical labor around the estate, including training the horses, and learned the art of estate management from his father reasonably well, with his brother's help. The only thing he never really improved upon was his penmanship, which even Frederick and Anne still had difficulty deciphering. Everyone around Pemberley enjoyed his presence, for little bothered him, and his deep, hearty laugh could be heard all over the estate.

Anne Darcy grew into a tall, serious young woman, if not the perfect, true lady her mother, governess, and Julia had tried to train her to be, although her deportment and demeanor were flawless. Encouraged by her parents, Frederick, and elderly Mr. Bennet, Anne pursued knowledge of all kinds, and excelled at anything involving reading, writing, mathematics, or experiments. She gratefully studied under a series of tutors, not governesses. Anne even attended two terms at a fashionable finishing school for young ladies, which she hated; but in fairness, by that time her father and brother were finding tutors proficient in subjects that would interest her to be rare. Not all of them wanted to leave London for Derbyshire, either, even for the grandeur and comforts of Pemberley.

Luckily, in 1849, at the age of twenty-four, Anne attended the first classes of the Ladies' College in Bedford Square, Bloomsbury, London. A few years later she graduated with a degree in history and mathematics, and resolved to turn her energy towards furthering the education of young women, whether ladies or not. Anne did chafe at not being able to be elected to membership in the Royal Society at Burlington House, but she continued to attend many of its lectures.

As for Frederick and Rosamund Woodleigh, the story of their relationship must unfold at a later time. However, it's safe to state that Frederick completely forgot about the pleasant, pleasing Angelina Molyneux, and didn't remember Marianne Morton at all.

THE END OF DISTRESS & DETERMINATION, PART II

ABOUT ATMOSPHERE PRESS

Founded in 2015, Atmosphere Press was built on the principles of Honesty, Transparency, Professionalism, Kindness, and Making Your Book Awesome. As an ethical and author-friendly hybrid press, we stay true to that founding mission today.

If you're a reader, enter our giveaway for a free book here:

SCAN TO ENTER
BOOK GIVEAWAY

If you're a writer, submit your manuscript for consideration here:

SCAN TO SUBMIT
MANUSCRIPT

And always feel free to visit Atmosphere Press and our authors online at atmospherepress.com. See you there soon!

ABOUT THE AUTHOR

A lifelong devoté of Jane Austen and all her works, James Wollak is a recently retired financial data analyst and lives in San Francisco, California, a third generation San Franciscan. He is an avid reader, numismatist, and music lover, enjoying all kinds of music such as classical and opera, Motown and soul, ABBA, Celtic, blues, bluegrass, and zydeco. He also loves silent and classic Hollywood films, and the *Poldark*, *Downton Abbey*, and *Sanditon* series. He is a confirmed Anglophile, and *Pride and Prejudice* is his favorite novel of all time.